DISNEP

UNCLE SCROOGE

TREASURE ABOVE THE CLOUDS

Facebook: **facebook.com/idwpublishing**
Twitter: **@idwpublishing**
YouTube: **youtube.com/idwpublishing**
Tumblr: **tumblr.idwpublishing.com**
Instagram: **instagram.com/idwpublishing**

ISBN : 978-1-68405-424-4   22 21 20 19   1 2 3 4

For international rights, contact **licensing@idwpublishing.com**

COVER ART BY
JONATHAN GRAY
AND **ANDREA FRECCERO**

COVER COLORS BY
FABIO LO MONACO
FOR **FELM ART STUDIO**

ARCHIVAL EDITS BY
DAVID GERSTEIN

SERIES EDITS BY
CHRIS CERASI

COLLECTION EDITS BY
JUSTIN EISINGER
AND **ALONZO SIMON**

COLLECTION DESIGN BY
RICHARD SHEINAUS
FOR **GOTHAM DESIGN**

PUBLISHER:
CHRIS RYALL

Special thanks to: Stefano Ambrosio, Stefano Attardi, Julie Dorris, Julia Gabrick, Marco Ghiglione, Jodi Hammerwold, Behnoosh Khalili, Manny Mederos, Eugene Paraszczuk, Carlotta Quattrocolo, Roberto Santillo, Christopher Troise, and Camilla Vedove.

Originally published as UNCLE SCROOGE issues #35-37 (Legacy #439-441).

Chris Ryall, *President & Publisher/Chief Creative Officer*
John Barber, *Editor-in-Chief*
Robbie Robbins, *EVP/Sr. Art Director*
Cara Morrison, *Chief Financial Officer*
Matt Ruzicka, *Chief Accounting Officer*
Anita Frazier, *SVP of Sales and Marketing*
David Hedgecock, *Associate Publisher*
Jerry Bennington, *VP of New Product Development*
Lorelei Bunjes, *VP of Digital Services*
Justin Eisinger, *Editorial Director, Graphic Novels & Collections*
Eric Moss, *Senior Director, Licensing and Business Development*

Ted Adams, *IDW Founder*

Disney UNCLE SCROOGE

TREASURE ABOVE THE CLOUDS

TREASURE ABOVE THE CLOUDS 1
From Italian *Almanacco Topolino* #233, 1976
  WRITER: Carl Fallberg
  ARTIST: Marco Rota
  COLORISTS: Disney Italia and Digikore Studios
  LETTERERS: Nicole and Travis Seitler
  TRANSLATION AND DIALOGUE:
    Thad Komorowski

A TALE OF TWO BIDDIES 33
From Italian *Topolino* #3194, 2017
  WRITER: Giorgio Fontana
  ARTIST: Marco Mazzarello
  COLORISTS: Disney Italia and Digikore Studios
  LETTERERS: Nicole and Travis Seitler
  TRANSLATION AND DIALOGUE:
    Thad Komorowski

DONALD'S FIRST GET-RICH QUICK SCHEME ... 64
From Dutch *Donald Duck Weekblad* #6/2017
  WRITER: Evert Geradts
  ARTIST: Carmen Pérez
  INKER: Comicup Studio
  COLORISTS: Sanoma with
    Nicole and Travis Seitler
  LETTERERS: Nicole and Travis Seitler
  TRANSLATION AND DIALOGUE:
    David Gerstein

PERIL OF THE BLACK FOREST 19
From Czech *Kačer Donald* #10/2008
  WRITER: Carl Barks
  ARTIST: Daan Jippes
  COLORIST: Disney Italia
  LETTERERS: Nicole and Travis Seitler

THE LIFE AND TIMES OF SCROOGE MCFROG 63
From Dutch *Donald Duck Weekblad* #17/2016
  WRITER AND ARTIST: Carlo Gentina
    COLORISTS: Sanoma with Nicole and Travis Seitler
  LETTERERS: Nicole and Travis Seitler
  TRANSLATION AND DIALOGUE: David Gerstein

MONEY IS THE ROOT OF UPHEAVAL! ... 65
From Italian *Topolino* #911, 1973
  WRITER: Jerry Siegel
  ARTIST: Romano Scarpa
  INKER: Sandro Del Conte
  COLORIST: Disney Italia
  LETTERERS: Nicole and Travis Seitler
  TRANSLATION AND DIALOGUE: Joe Torcivia

COVER GALLERY 97

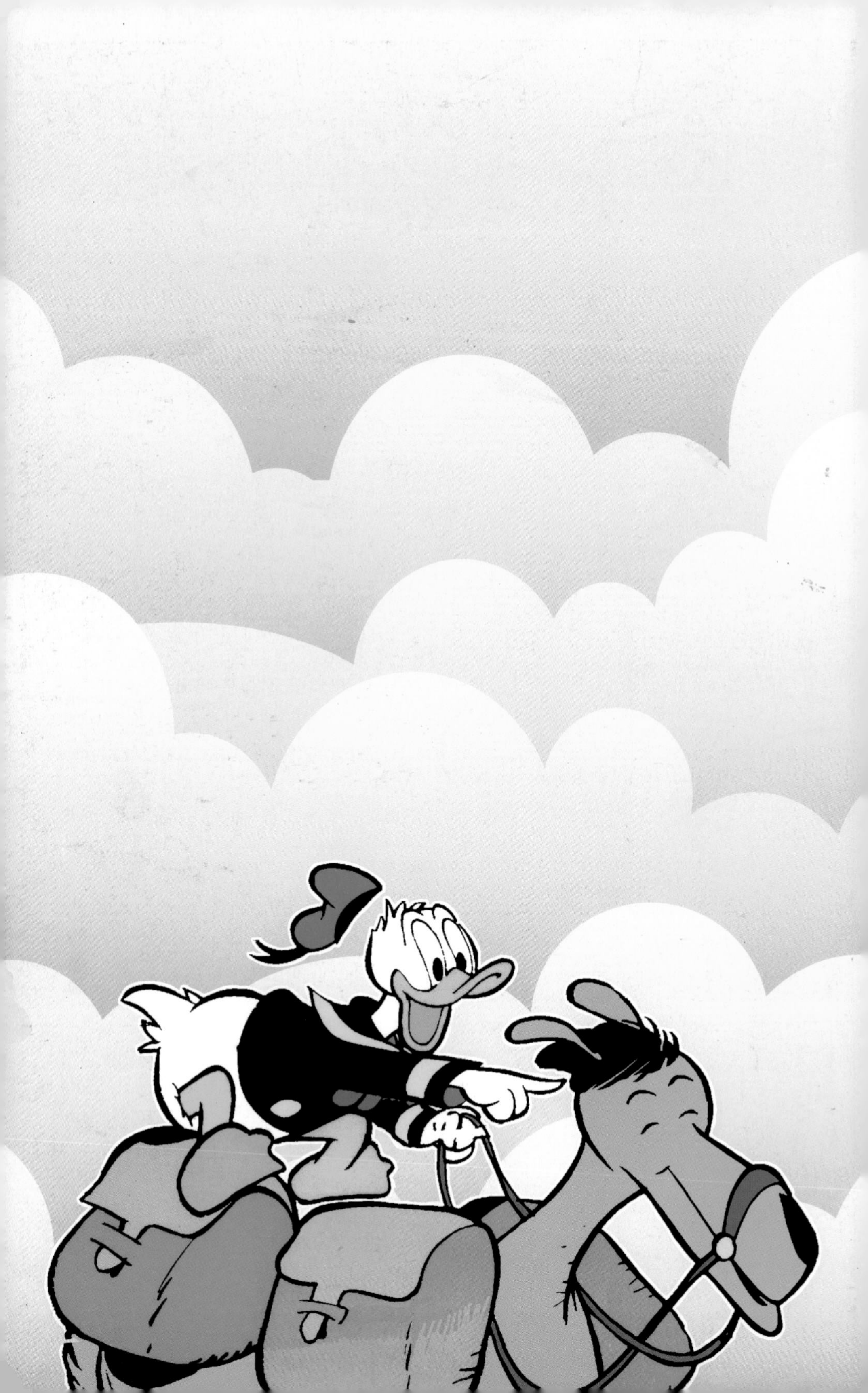

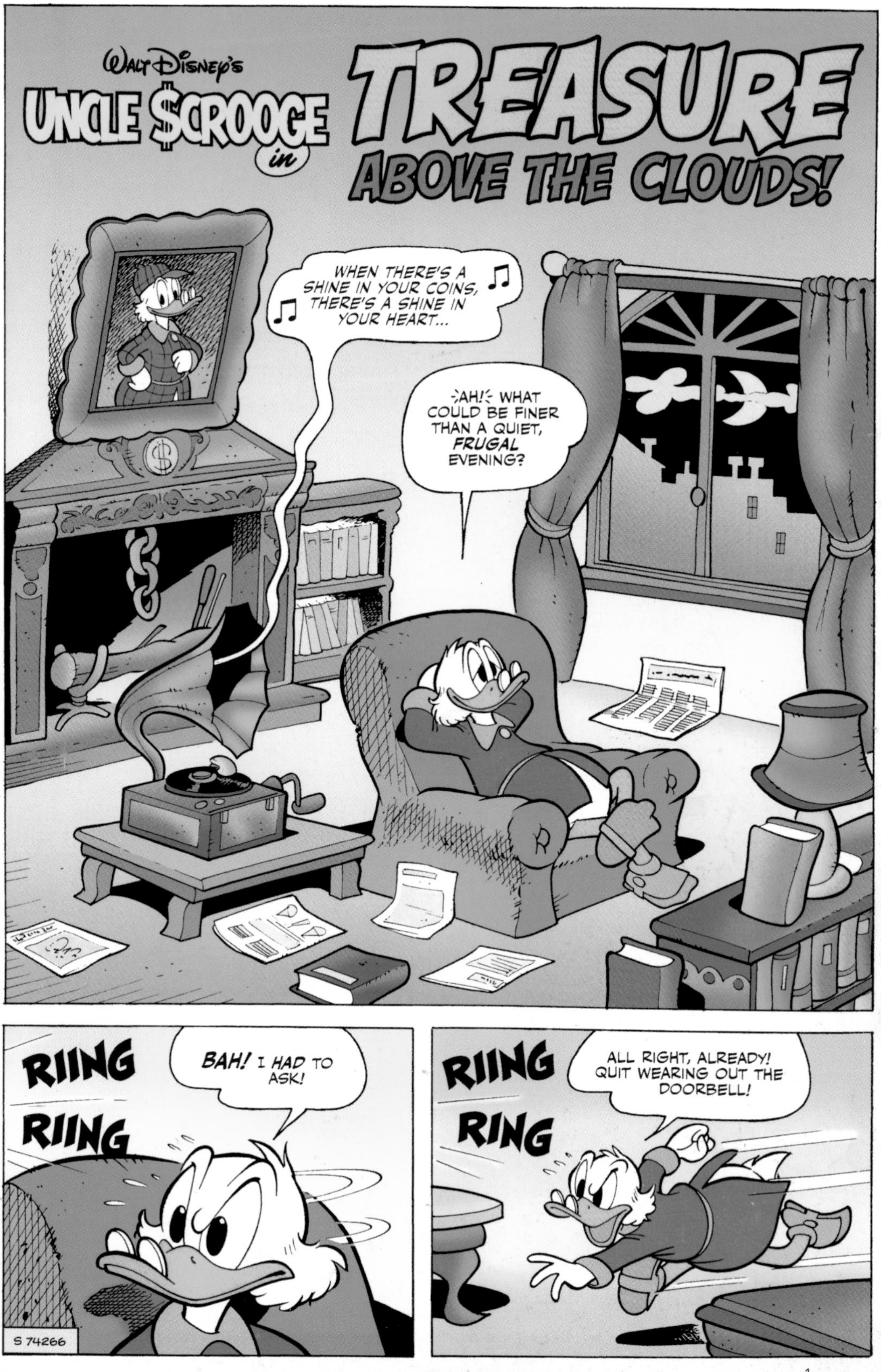
WALT DISNEY'S
UNCLE $CROOGE in
TREASURE ABOVE THE CLOUDS!
♫ WHEN THERE'S A SHINE IN YOUR COINS, THERE'S A SHINE IN YOUR HEART... ♫
AH! WHAT COULD BE FINER THAN A QUIET, FRUGAL EVENING?
RIING
RIING
BAH! I HAD TO ASK!
S 74266
RIING
RING
ALL RIGHT, ALREADY! QUIT WEARING OUT THE DOORBELL!

Originally published in *Almanacco Topolino* #233 (Italy, 1976)

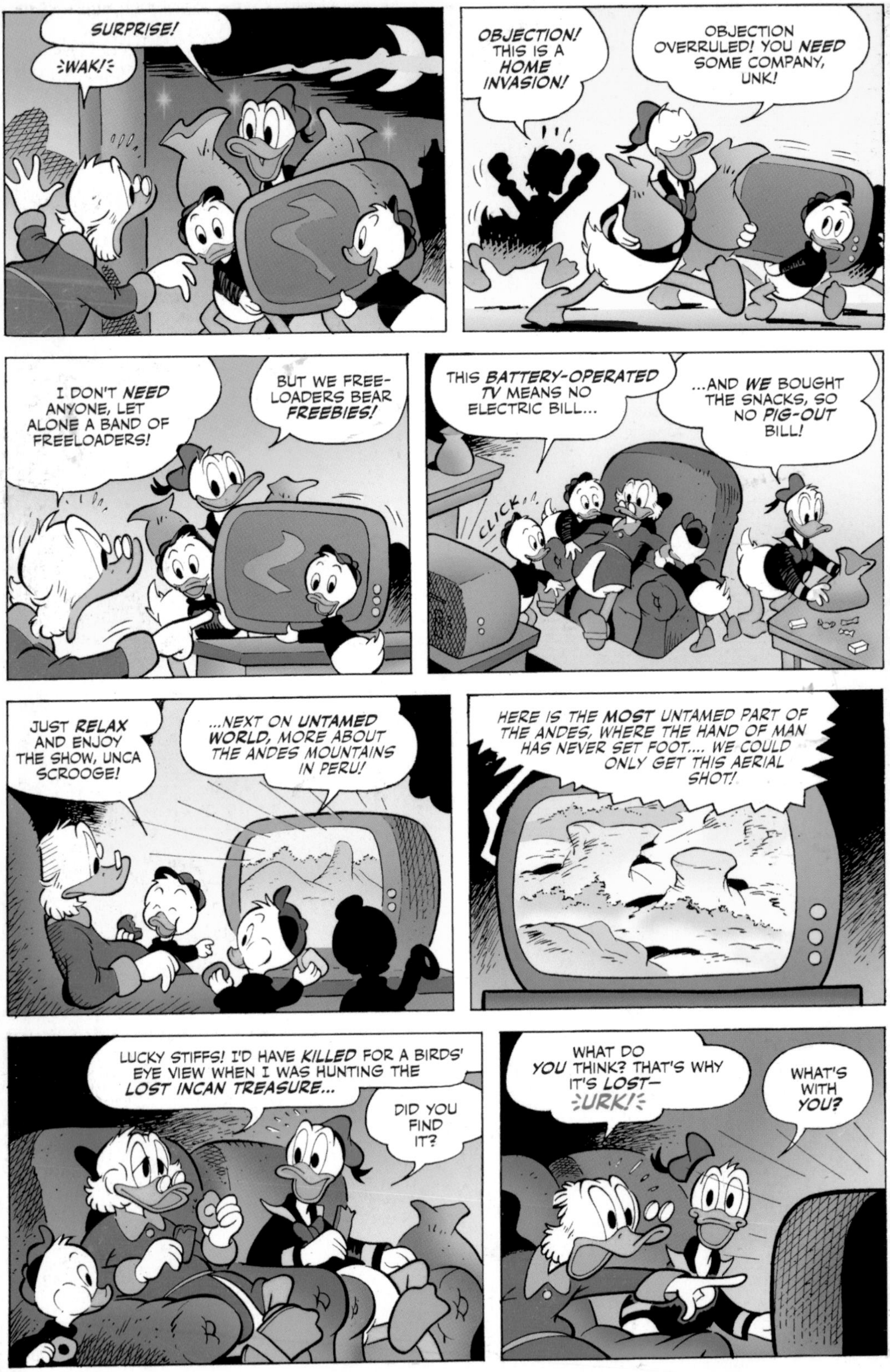

SURPRISE!
WAK!
OBJECTION! THIS IS A HOME INVASION!
OBJECTION OVERRULED! YOU NEED SOME COMPANY, UNK!
I DON'T NEED ANYONE, LET ALONE A BAND OF FREELOADERS!
BUT WE FREE-LOADERS BEAR FREEBIES!
THIS BATTERY-OPERATED TV MEANS NO ELECTRIC BILL...
...AND WE BOUGHT THE SNACKS, SO NO PIG-OUT BILL!
CLICK
JUST RELAX AND ENJOY THE SHOW, UNCA SCROOGE!
...NEXT ON UNTAMED WORLD, MORE ABOUT THE ANDES MOUNTAINS IN PERU!
HERE IS THE MOST UNTAMED PART OF THE ANDES, WHERE THE HAND OF MAN HAS NEVER SET FOOT.... WE COULD ONLY GET THIS AERIAL SHOT!
LUCKY STIFFS! I'D HAVE KILLED FOR A BIRDS' EYE VIEW WHEN I WAS HUNTING THE LOST INCAN TREASURE...
DID YOU FIND IT?
WHAT DO YOU THINK? THAT'S WHY IT'S LOST—
URK!
WHAT'S WITH YOU?

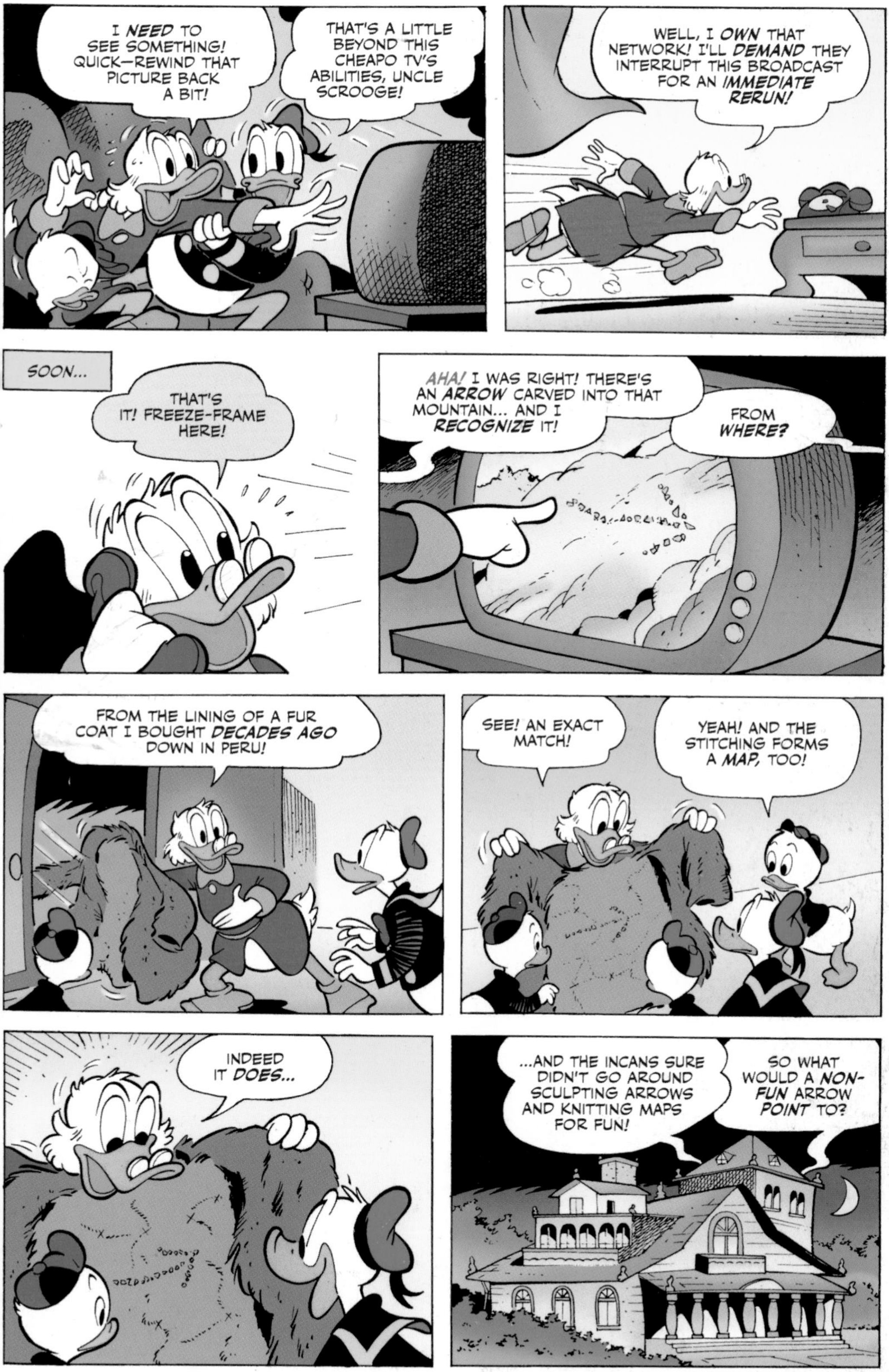
I NEED TO SEE SOMETHING! QUICK—REWIND THAT PICTURE BACK A BIT!
THAT'S A LITTLE BEYOND THIS CHEAPO TV'S ABILITIES, UNCLE SCROOGE!
WELL, I OWN THAT NETWORK! I'LL DEMAND THEY INTERRUPT THIS BROADCAST FOR AN IMMEDIATE RERUN!
SOON...
THAT'S IT! FREEZE-FRAME HERE!
AHA! I WAS RIGHT! THERE'S AN ARROW CARVED INTO THAT MOUNTAIN... AND I RECOGNIZE IT!
FROM WHERE?
FROM THE LINING OF A FUR COAT I BOUGHT DECADES AGO DOWN IN PERU!
SEE! AN EXACT MATCH!
YEAH! AND THE STITCHING FORMS A MAP, TOO!
INDEED IT DOES...
...AND THE INCANS SURE DIDN'T GO AROUND SCULPTING ARROWS AND KNITTING MAPS FOR FUN!
SO WHAT WOULD A NON-FUN ARROW POINT TO?

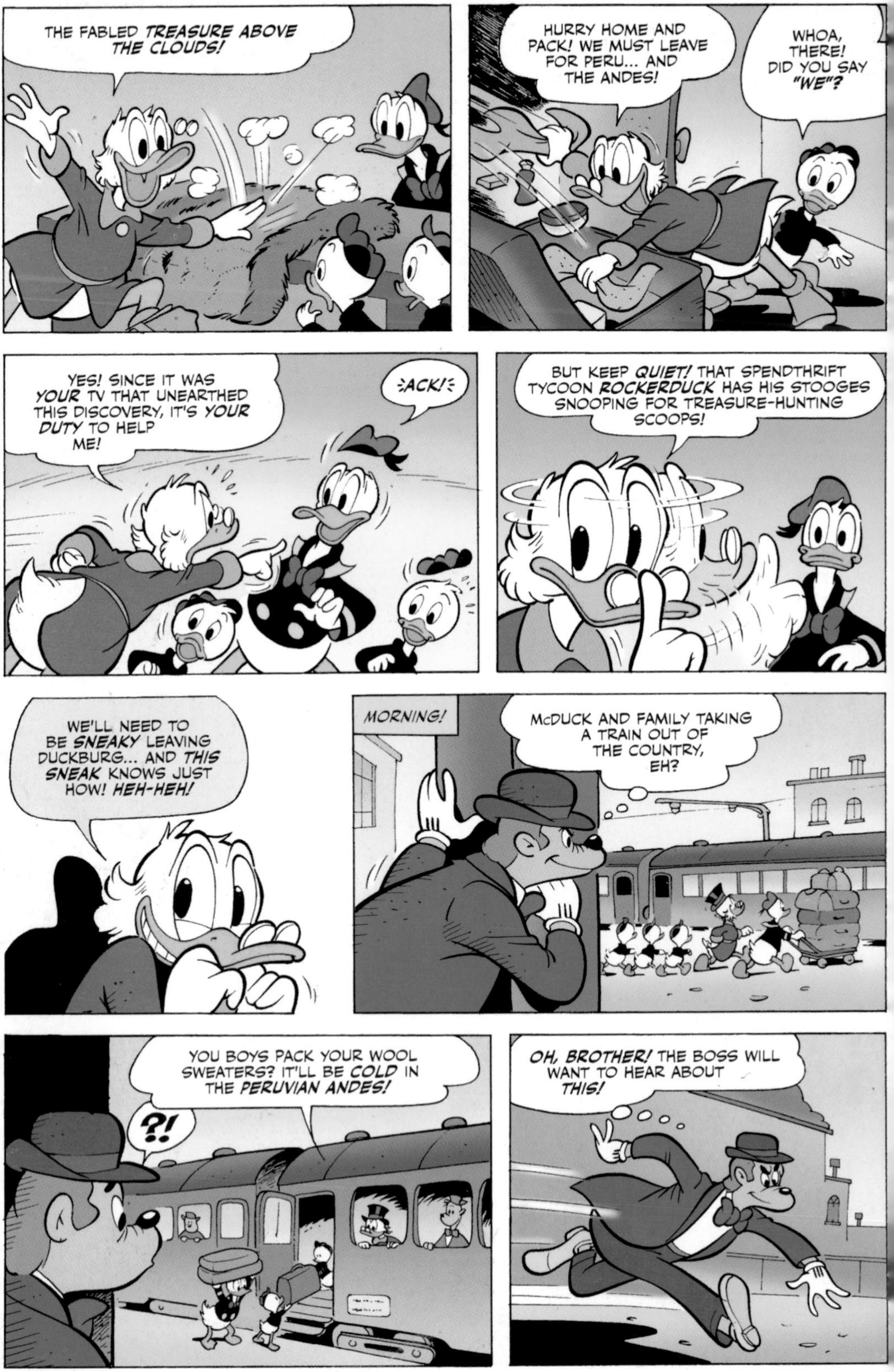
THE FABLED TREASURE ABOVE THE CLOUDS!
HURRY HOME AND PACK! WE MUST LEAVE FOR PERU... AND THE ANDES!
WHOA, THERE! DID YOU SAY "WE"?
YES! SINCE IT WAS YOUR TV THAT UNEARTHED THIS DISCOVERY, IT'S YOUR DUTY TO HELP ME!
ACK!
BUT KEEP QUIET! THAT SPENDTHRIFT TYCOON ROCKERDUCK HAS HIS STOOGES SNOOPING FOR TREASURE-HUNTING SCOOPS!
WE'LL NEED TO BE SNEAKY LEAVING DUCKBURG... AND THIS SNEAK KNOWS JUST HOW! HEH-HEH!
MORNING!
McDUCK AND FAMILY TAKING A TRAIN OUT OF THE COUNTRY, EH?
YOU BOYS PACK YOUR WOOL SWEATERS? IT'LL BE COLD IN THE PERUVIAN ANDES!
?!
OH, BROTHER! THE BOSS WILL WANT TO HEAR ABOUT THIS!

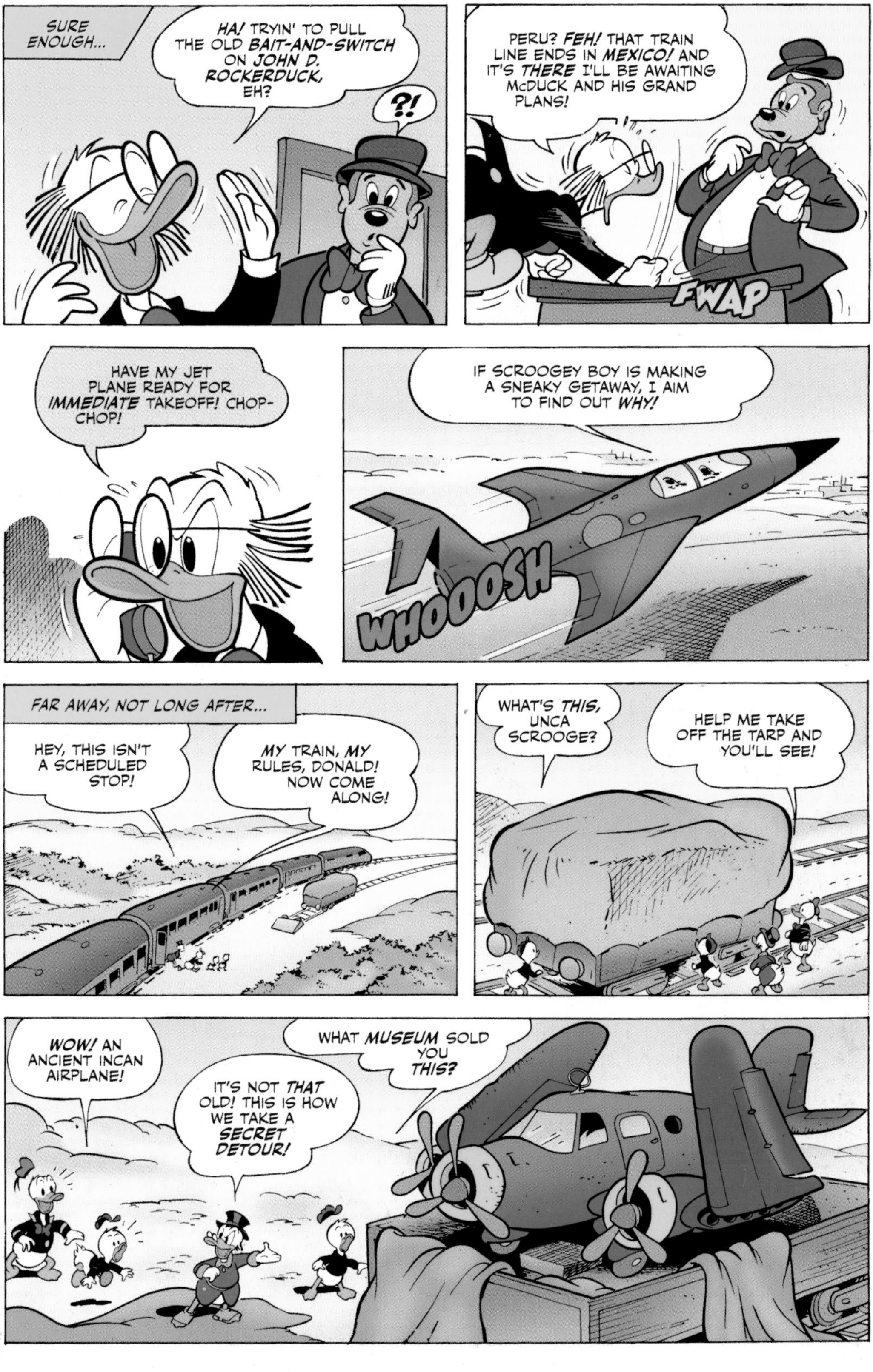
SURE ENOUGH...
HA! TRYIN' TO PULL THE OLD BAIT-AND-SWITCH ON JOHN D. ROCKERDUCK, EH?
?!
PERU? FEH! THAT TRAIN LINE ENDS IN MEXICO! AND IT'S THERE I'LL BE AWAITING McDUCK AND HIS GRAND PLANS!
FWAP
HAVE MY JET PLANE READY FOR IMMEDIATE TAKEOFF! CHOP-CHOP!
IF SCROOGEY BOY IS MAKING A SNEAKY GETAWAY, I AIM TO FIND OUT WHY!
WHOOOSH
FAR AWAY, NOT LONG AFTER...
HEY, THIS ISN'T A SCHEDULED STOP!
MY TRAIN, MY RULES, DONALD! NOW COME ALONG!
WHAT'S THIS, UNCA SCROOGE?
HELP ME TAKE OFF THE TARP AND YOU'LL SEE!
WOW! AN ANCIENT INCAN AIRPLANE!
WHAT MUSEUM SOLD YOU THIS?
IT'S NOT THAT OLD! THIS IS HOW WE TAKE A SECRET DETOUR!

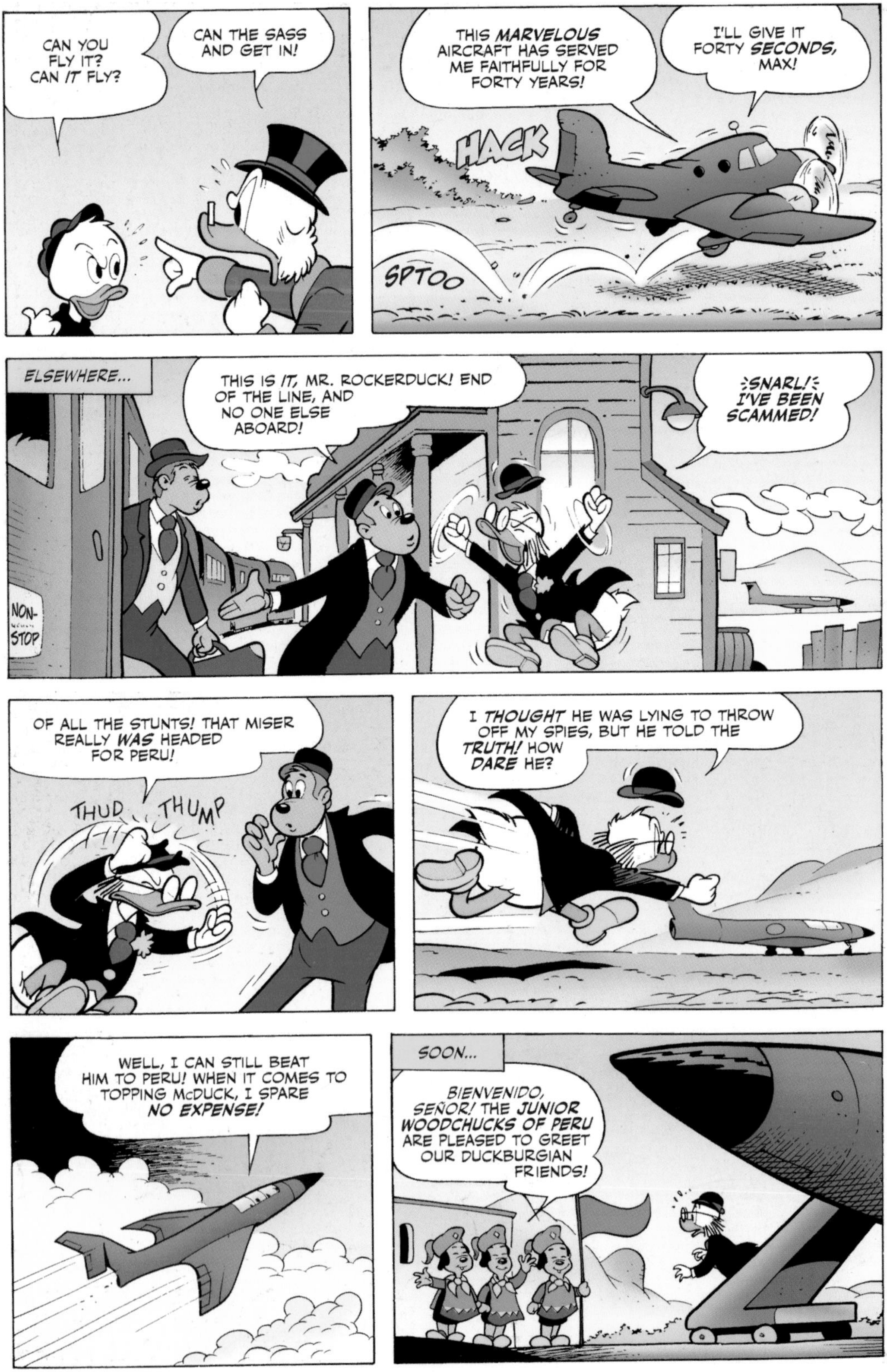
CAN YOU FLY IT? CAN IT FLY?
CAN THE SASS AND GET IN!
THIS MARVELOUS AIRCRAFT HAS SERVED ME FAITHFULLY FOR FORTY YEARS!
I'LL GIVE IT FORTY SECONDS, MAX!
HACK
SPTOO
ELSEWHERE...
THIS IS IT, MR. ROCKERDUCK! END OF THE LINE, AND NO ONE ELSE ABOARD!
SNARL! I'VE BEEN SCAMMED!
NON-STOP
OF ALL THE STUNTS! THAT MISER REALLY WAS HEADED FOR PERU!
THUD
THUMP
I THOUGHT HE WAS LYING TO THROW OFF MY SPIES, BUT HE TOLD THE TRUTH! HOW DARE HE?
WELL, I CAN STILL BEAT HIM TO PERU! WHEN IT COMES TO TOPPING McDUCK, I SPARE NO EXPENSE!
SOON...
BIENVENIDO, SEÑOR! THE JUNIOR WOODCHUCKS OF PERU ARE PLEASED TO GREET OUR DUCKBURGIAN FRIENDS!

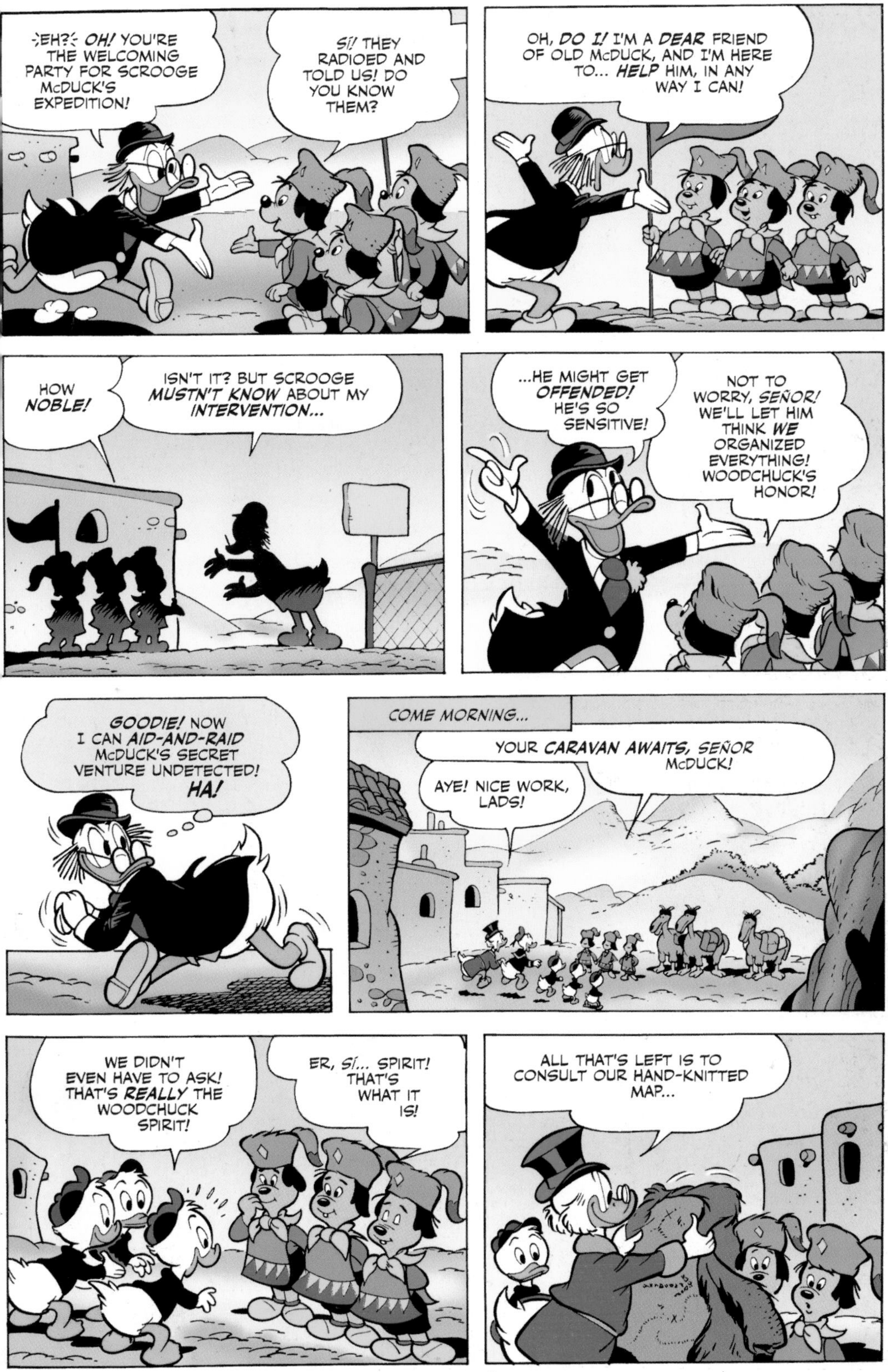
EH? OH! YOU'RE THE WELCOMING PARTY FOR SCROOGE McDUCK'S EXPEDITION!
SÍ! THEY RADIOED AND TOLD US! DO YOU KNOW THEM?
OH, DO I! I'M A DEAR FRIEND OF OLD McDUCK, AND I'M HERE TO... HELP HIM, IN ANY WAY I CAN!
HOW NOBLE!
ISN'T IT? BUT SCROOGE MUSTN'T KNOW ABOUT MY INTERVENTION...
...HE MIGHT GET OFFENDED! HE'S SO SENSITIVE!
NOT TO WORRY, SEÑOR! WE'LL LET HIM THINK WE ORGANIZED EVERYTHING! WOODCHUCK'S HONOR!
GOODIE! NOW I CAN AID-AND-RAID McDUCK'S SECRET VENTURE UNDETECTED! HA!
COME MORNING...
YOUR CARAVAN AWAITS, SEÑOR McDUCK!
AYE! NICE WORK, LADS!
WE DIDN'T EVEN HAVE TO ASK! THAT'S REALLY THE WOODCHUCK SPIRIT!
ER, SÍ... SPIRIT! THAT'S WHAT IT IS!
ALL THAT'S LEFT IS TO CONSULT OUR HAND-KNITTED MAP...

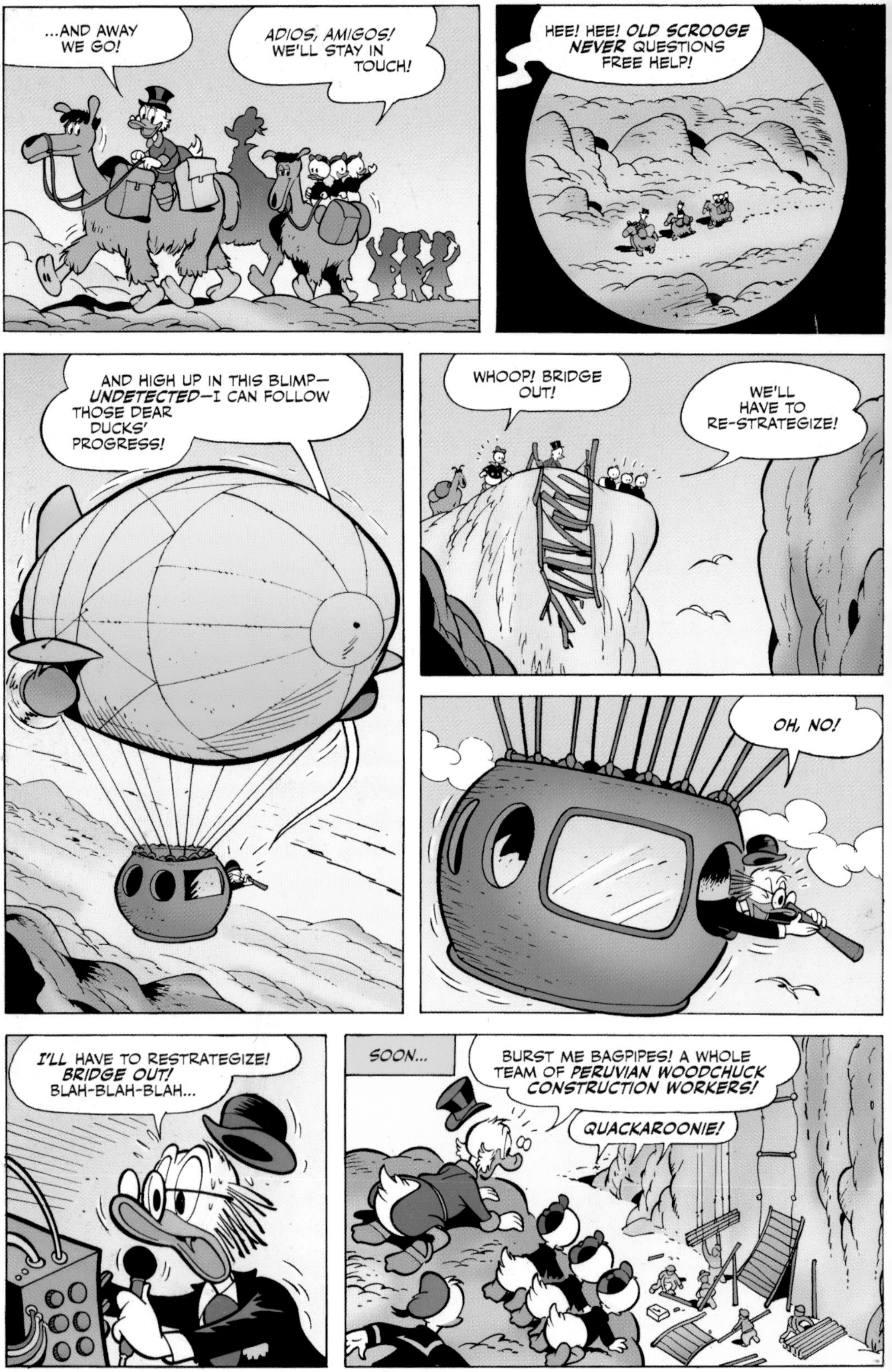
...AND AWAY WE GO!
ADIOS, AMIGOS! WE'LL STAY IN TOUCH!
HEE! HEE! OLD SCROOGE NEVER QUESTIONS FREE HELP!
AND HIGH UP IN THIS BLIMP—UNDETECTED—I CAN FOLLOW THOSE DEAR DUCKS' PROGRESS!
WHOOP! BRIDGE OUT!
WE'LL HAVE TO RE-STRATEGIZE!
OH, NO!
I'LL HAVE TO RESTRATEGIZE! BRIDGE OUT! BLAH-BLAH-BLAH...
SOON...
BURST ME BAGPIPES! A WHOLE TEAM OF PERUVIAN WOODCHUCK CONSTRUCTION WORKERS!
QUACKAROONIE!

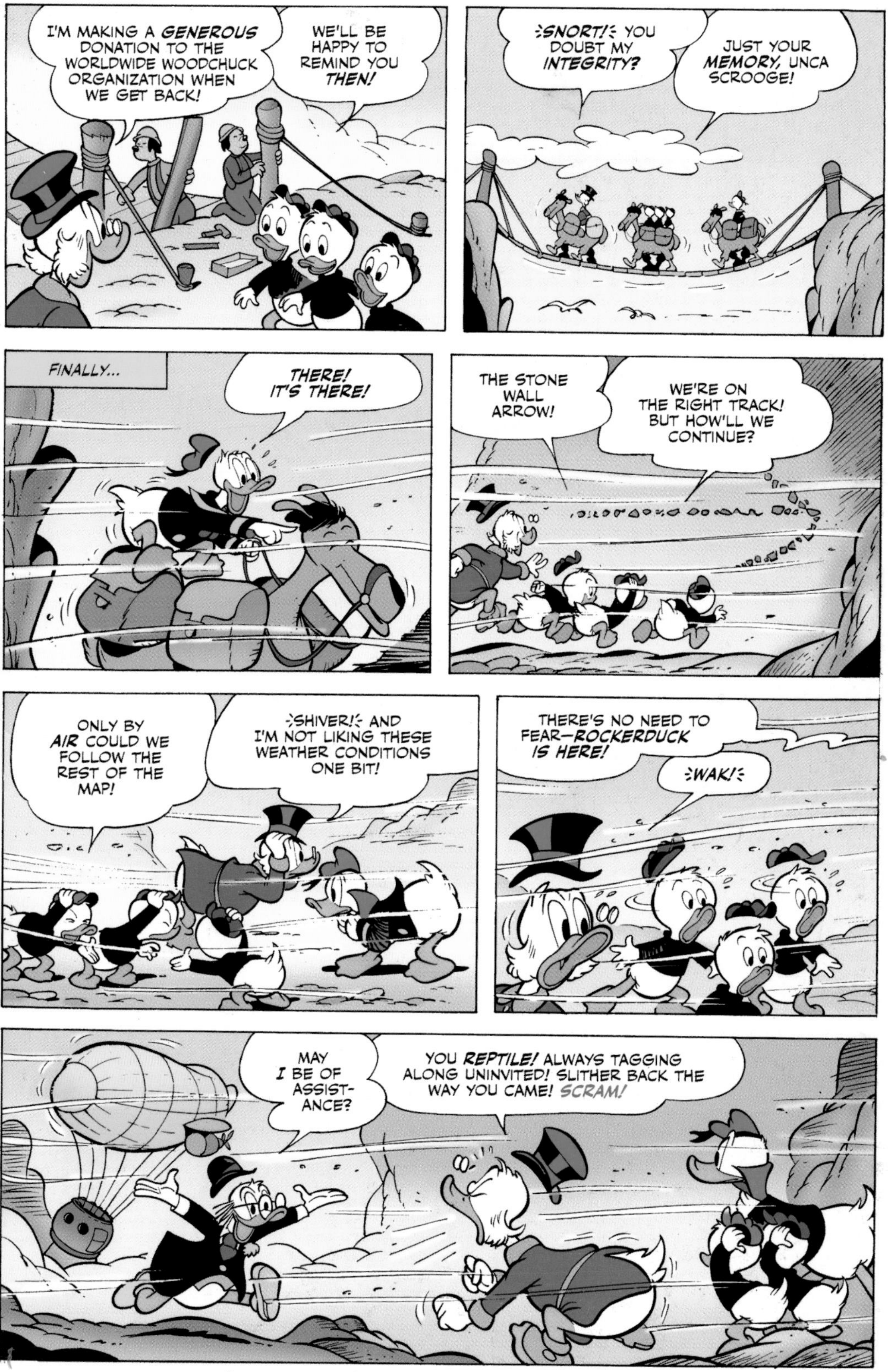
I'M MAKING A GENEROUS DONATION TO THE WORLDWIDE WOODCHUCK ORGANIZATION WHEN WE GET BACK!
WE'LL BE HAPPY TO REMIND YOU THEN!
SNORT! YOU DOUBT MY INTEGRITY?
JUST YOUR MEMORY, UNCA SCROOGE!
FINALLY...
THERE! IT'S THERE!
THE STONE WALL ARROW!
WE'RE ON THE RIGHT TRACK! BUT HOW'LL WE CONTINUE?
ONLY BY AIR COULD WE FOLLOW THE REST OF THE MAP!
SHIVER! AND I'M NOT LIKING THESE WEATHER CONDITIONS ONE BIT!
THERE'S NO NEED TO FEAR—ROCKERDUCK IS HERE!
WAK!
MAY I BE OF ASSIST-ANCE?
YOU REPTILE! ALWAYS TAGGING ALONG UNINVITED! SLITHER BACK THE WAY YOU CAME! SCRAM!

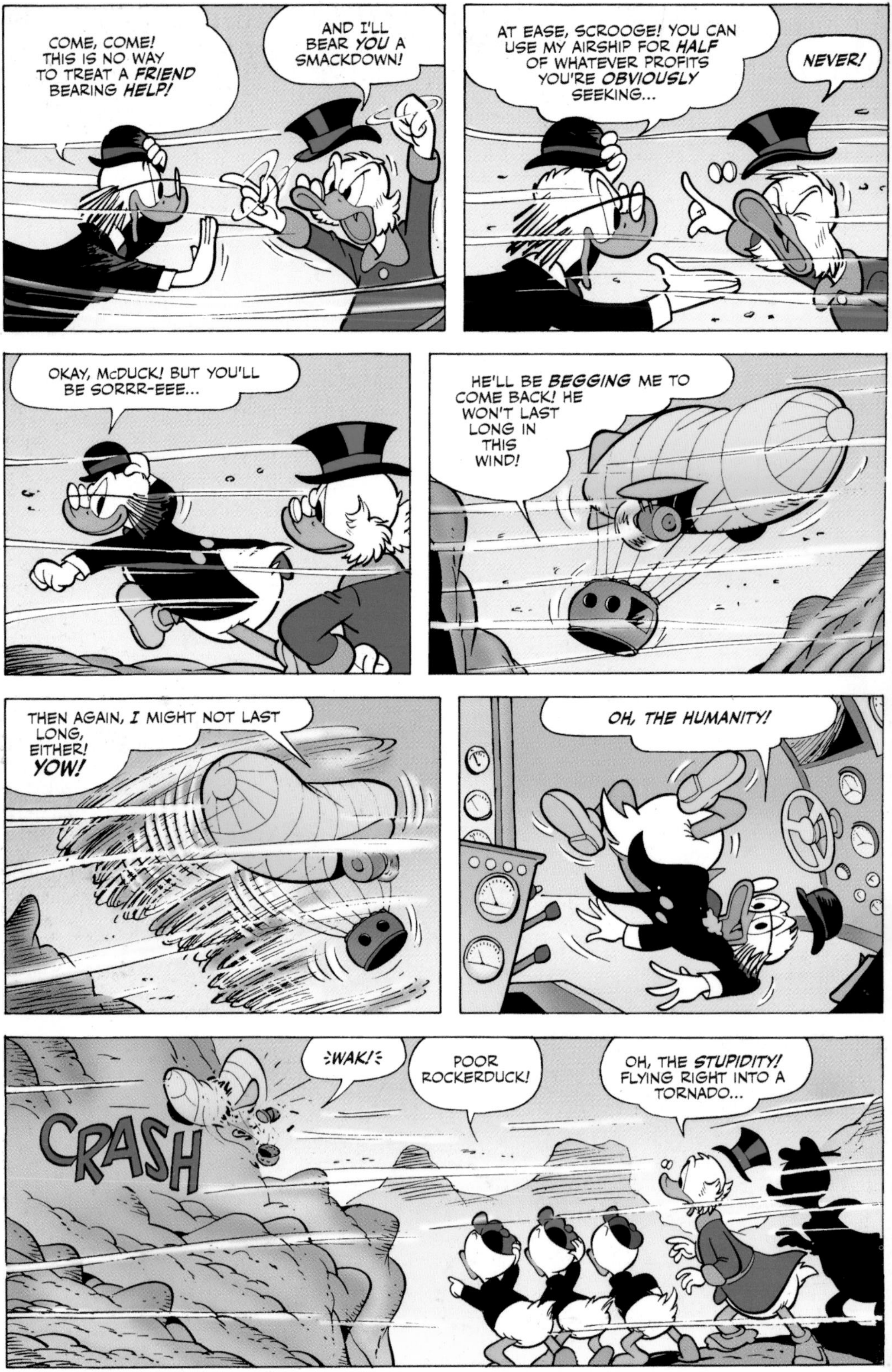
COME, COME! THIS IS NO WAY TO TREAT A FRIEND BEARING HELP!
AND I'LL BEAR YOU A SMACKDOWN!
AT EASE, SCROOGE! YOU CAN USE MY AIRSHIP FOR HALF OF WHATEVER PROFITS YOU'RE OBVIOUSLY SEEKING...
NEVER!
OKAY, McDUCK! BUT YOU'LL BE SORRR-EEE...
HE'LL BE BEGGING ME TO COME BACK! HE WON'T LAST LONG IN THIS WIND!
THEN AGAIN, I MIGHT NOT LAST LONG, EITHER! YOW!
OH, THE HUMANITY!
CRASH
WAK!
POOR ROCKERDUCK!
OH, THE STUPIDITY! FLYING RIGHT INTO A TORNADO...

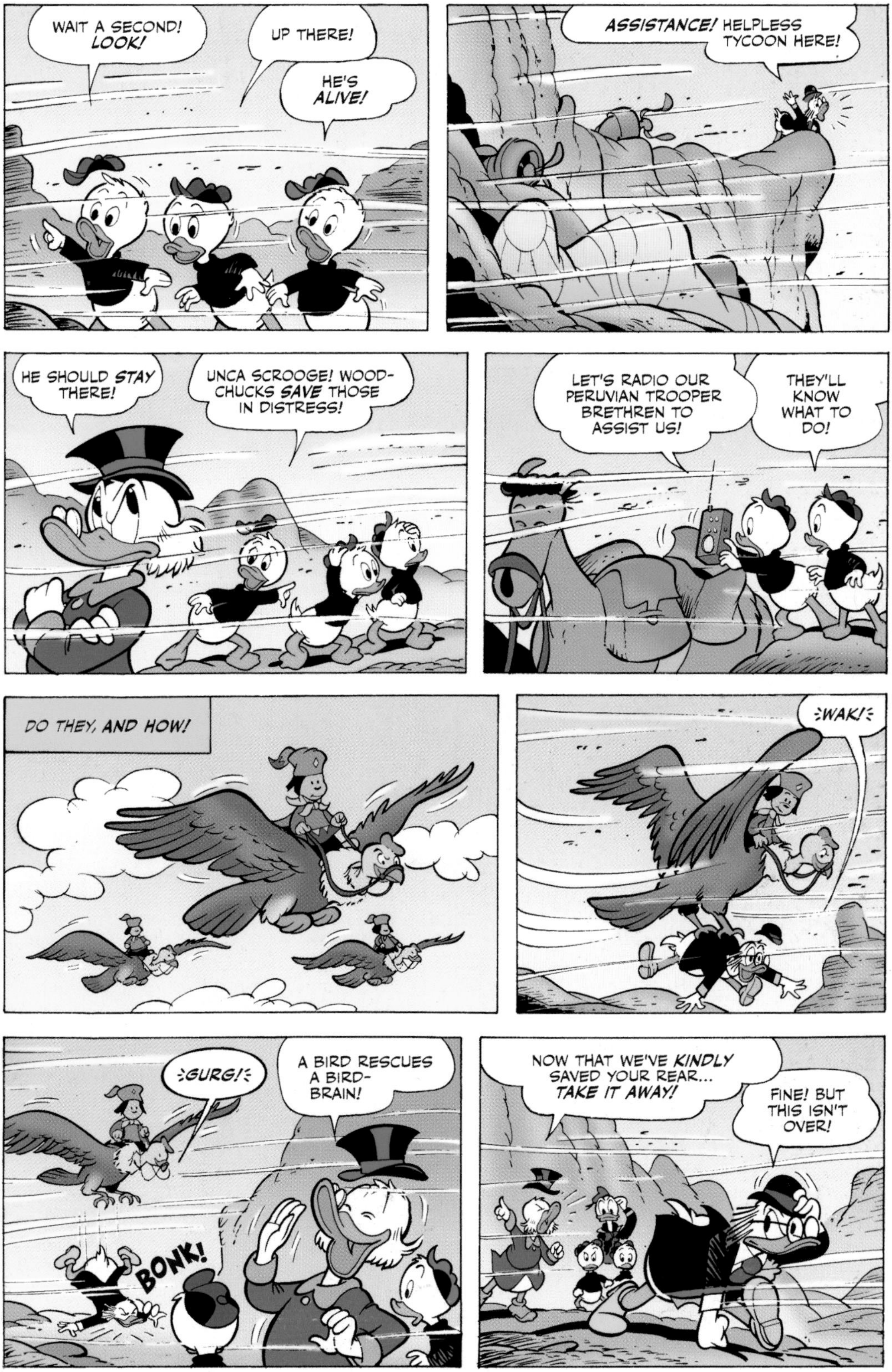

WAIT A SECOND! LOOK!
UP THERE!
HE'S ALIVE!
ASSISTANCE! HELPLESS TYCOON HERE!
HE SHOULD STAY THERE!
UNCA SCROOGE! WOOD-CHUCKS SAVE THOSE IN DISTRESS!
LET'S RADIO OUR PERUVIAN TROOPER BRETHREN TO ASSIST US!
THEY'LL KNOW WHAT TO DO!
DO THEY, AND HOW!
WAK!
GURG!
A BIRD RESCUES A BIRD-BRAIN!
BONK!
NOW THAT WE'VE KINDLY SAVED YOUR REAR... TAKE IT AWAY!
FINE! BUT THIS ISN'T OVER!

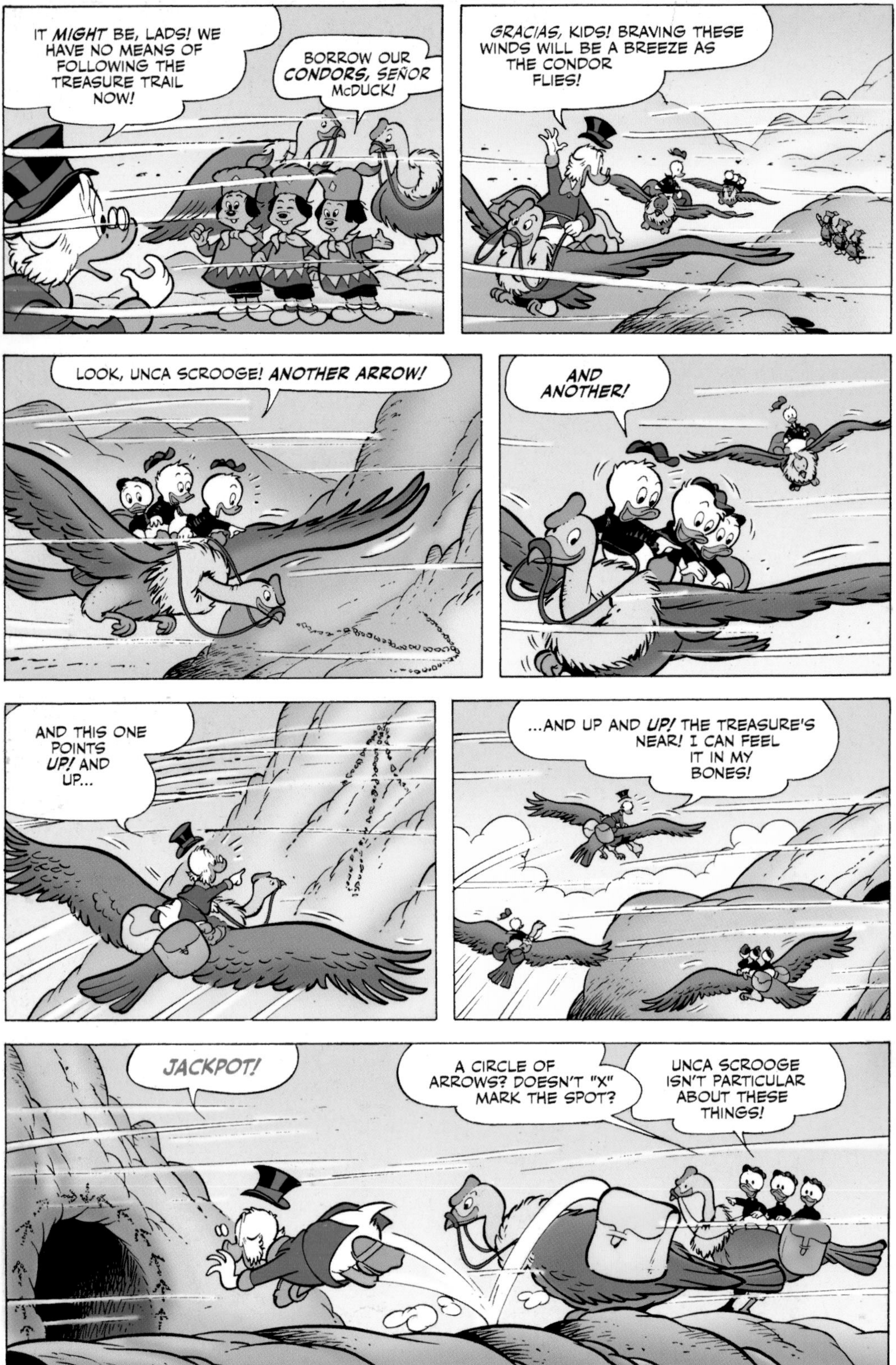
IT MIGHT BE, LADS! WE HAVE NO MEANS OF FOLLOWING THE TREASURE TRAIL NOW!
BORROW OUR CONDORS, SEÑOR McDUCK!
GRACIAS, KIDS! BRAVING THESE WINDS WILL BE A BREEZE AS THE CONDOR FLIES!
LOOK, UNCA SCROOGE! ANOTHER ARROW!
AND ANOTHER!
AND THIS ONE POINTS UP! AND UP...
...AND UP AND UP! THE TREASURE'S NEAR! I CAN FEEL IT IN MY BONES!
JACKPOT!
A CIRCLE OF ARROWS? DOESN'T "X" MARK THE SPOT?
UNCA SCROOGE ISN'T PARTICULAR ABOUT THESE THINGS!

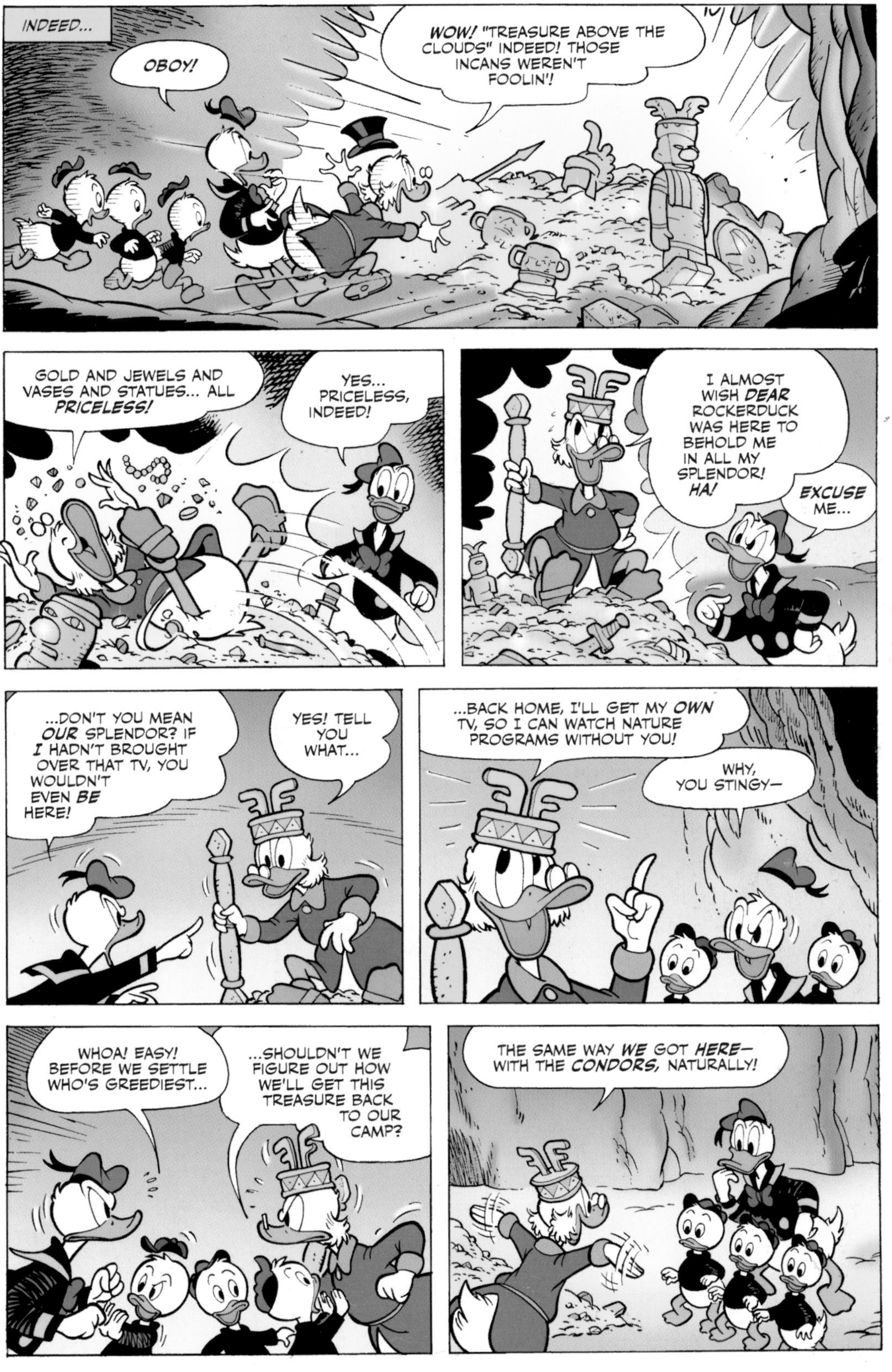
INDEED...
OBOY!
WOW! "TREASURE ABOVE THE CLOUDS" INDEED! THOSE INCANS WEREN'T FOOLIN'!
GOLD AND JEWELS AND VASES AND STATUES... ALL PRICELESS!
YES... PRICELESS, INDEED!
I ALMOST WISH DEAR ROCKERDUCK WAS HERE TO BEHOLD ME IN ALL MY SPLENDOR! HA!
EXCUSE ME...
...DON'T YOU MEAN OUR SPLENDOR? IF I HADN'T BROUGHT OVER THAT TV, YOU WOULDN'T EVEN BE HERE!
YES! TELL YOU WHAT...
...BACK HOME, I'LL GET MY OWN TV, SO I CAN WATCH NATURE PROGRAMS WITHOUT YOU!
WHY, YOU STINGY—
WHOA! EASY! BEFORE WE SETTLE WHO'S GREEDIEST...
...SHOULDN'T WE FIGURE OUT HOW WE'LL GET THIS TREASURE BACK TO OUR CAMP?
THE SAME WAY WE GOT HERE— WITH THE CONDORS, NATURALLY!

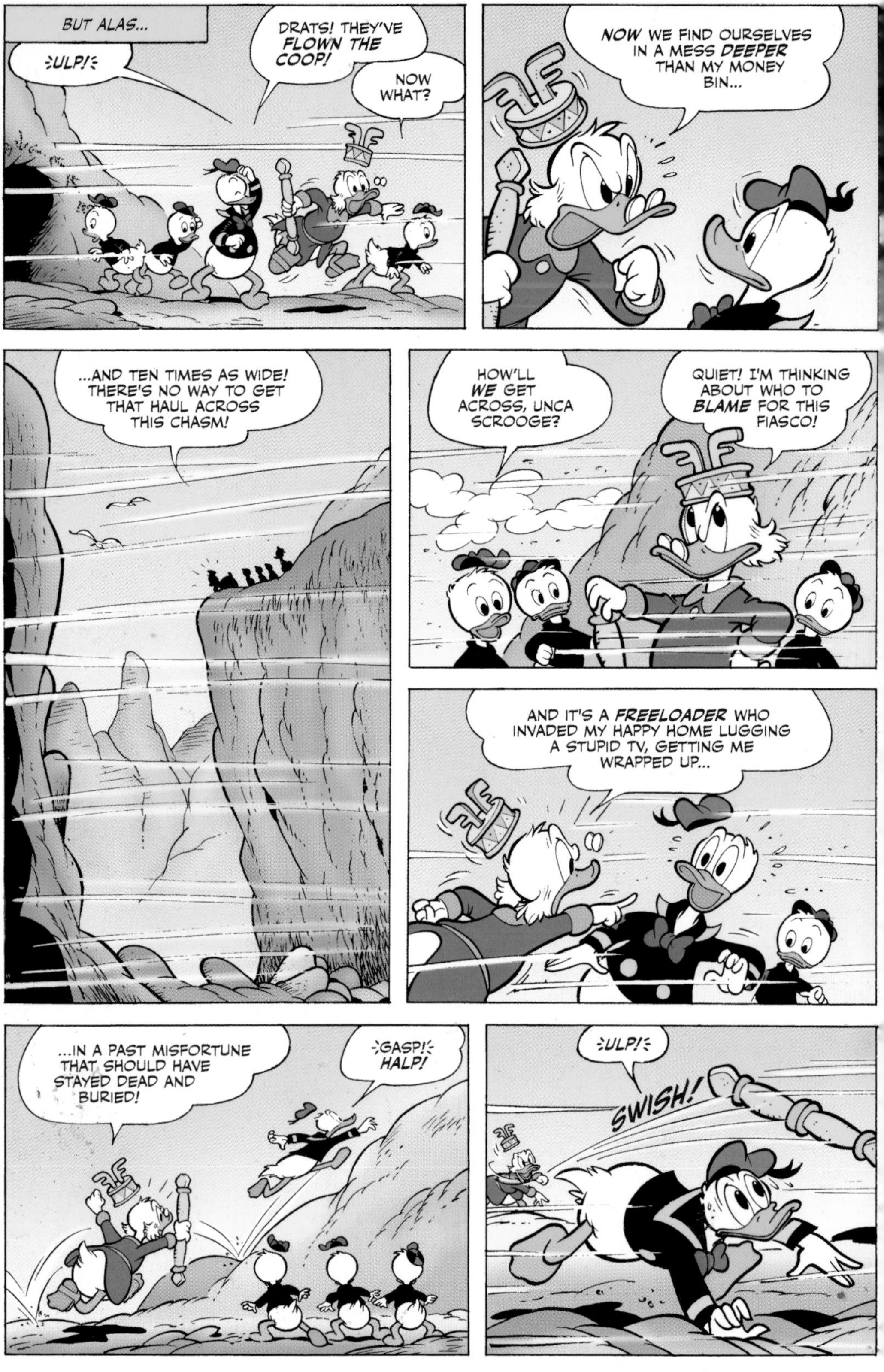
BUT ALAS...
ULP!
DRATS! THEY'VE FLOWN THE COOP!
NOW WHAT?
NOW WE FIND OURSELVES IN A MESS DEEPER THAN MY MONEY BIN...
...AND TEN TIMES AS WIDE! THERE'S NO WAY TO GET THAT HAUL ACROSS THIS CHASM!
HOW'LL WE GET ACROSS, UNCA SCROOGE?
QUIET! I'M THINKING ABOUT WHO TO BLAME FOR THIS FIASCO!
AND IT'S A FREELOADER WHO INVADED MY HAPPY HOME LUGGING A STUPID TV, GETTING ME WRAPPED UP...
...IN A PAST MISFORTUNE THAT SHOULD HAVE STAYED DEAD AND BURIED!
GASP! HALP!
ULP!
SWISH!

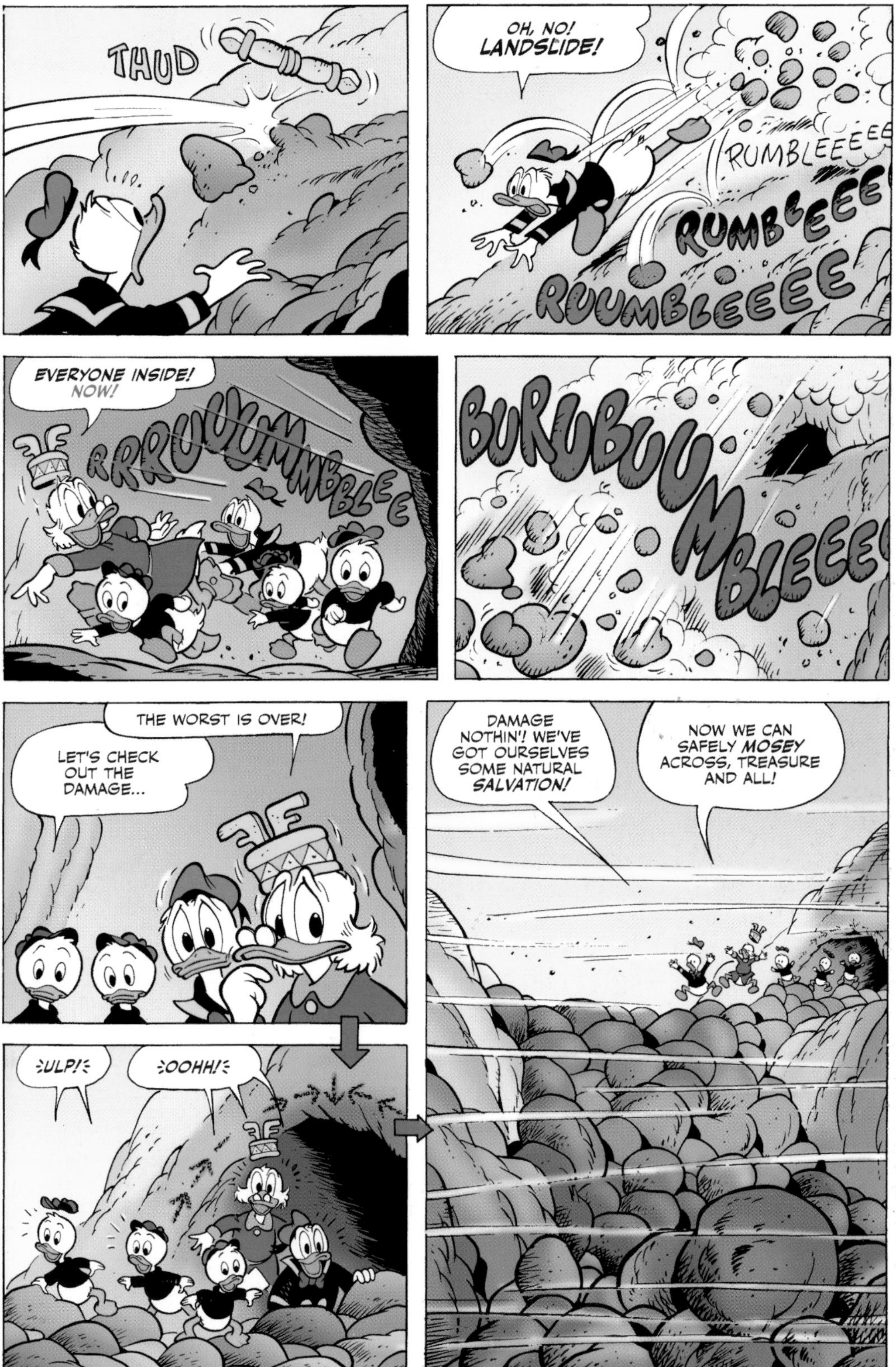
THUD
OH, NO! LANDSLIDE!
RUMBLEEEE
RUMBLEEE
RUUMBLEEEEE
EVERYONE INSIDE! NOW!
RRRUUUMMBBLEE
BURUBUUMBLEEE
THE WORST IS OVER!
LET'S CHECK OUT THE DAMAGE...
ULP!
OOHH!
DAMAGE NOTHIN'! WE'VE GOT OURSELVES SOME NATURAL SALVATION!
NOW WE CAN SAFELY MOSEY ACROSS, TREASURE AND ALL!

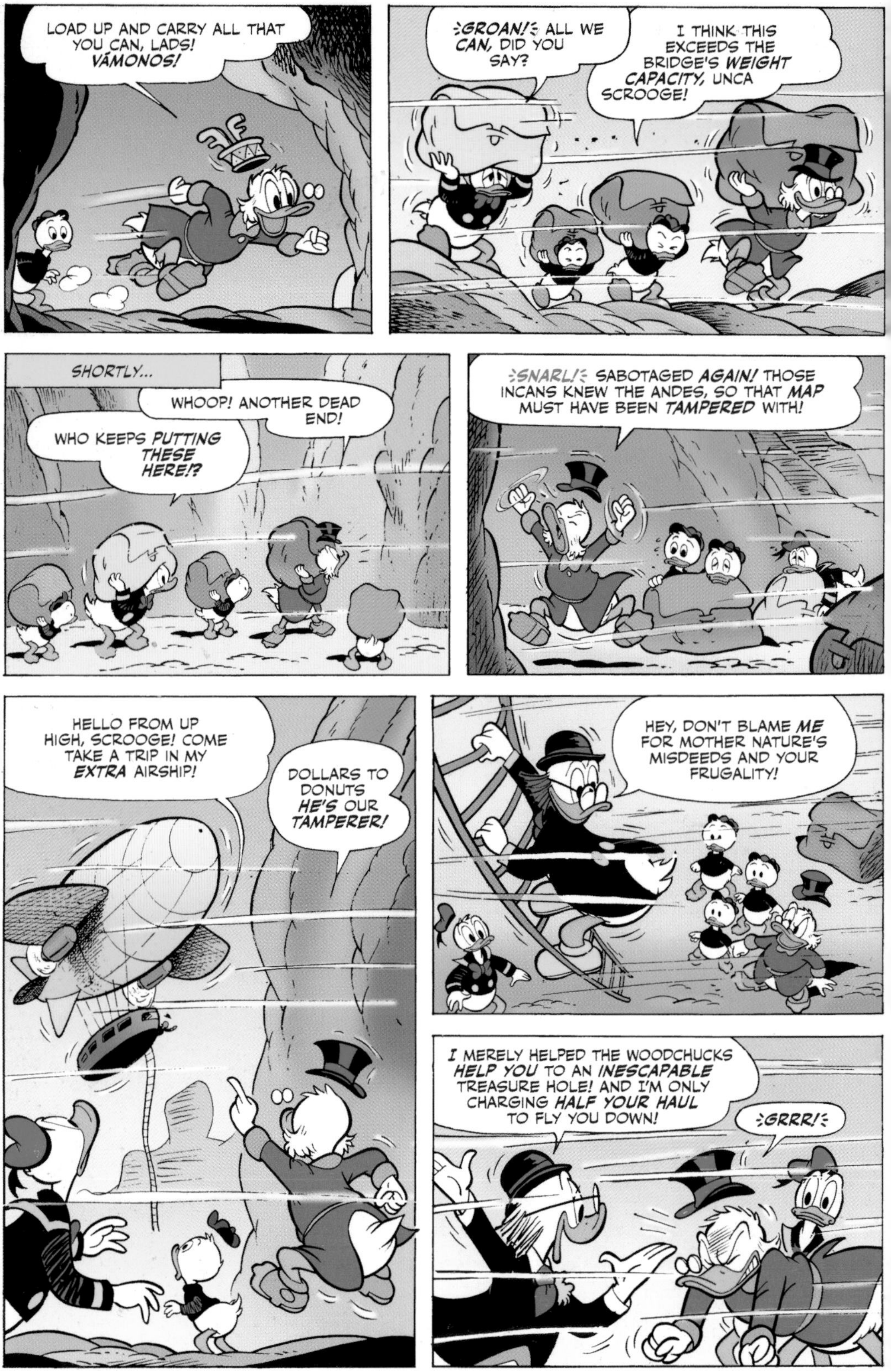
LOAD UP AND CARRY ALL THAT YOU CAN, LADS! VÁMONOS!
¡GROAN!¡ ALL WE CAN, DID YOU SAY?
I THINK THIS EXCEEDS THE BRIDGE'S WEIGHT CAPACITY, UNCA SCROOGE!
SHORTLY...
WHOOP! ANOTHER DEAD END!
WHO KEEPS PUTTING THESE HERE!?
¡SNARL!¡ SABOTAGED AGAIN! THOSE INCANS KNEW THE ANDES, SO THAT MAP MUST HAVE BEEN TAMPERED WITH!
HELLO FROM UP HIGH, SCROOGE! COME TAKE A TRIP IN MY EXTRA AIRSHIP!
DOLLARS TO DONUTS HE'S OUR TAMPERER!
HEY, DON'T BLAME ME FOR MOTHER NATURE'S MISDEEDS AND YOUR FRUGALITY!
I MERELY HELPED THE WOODCHUCKS HELP YOU TO AN INESCAPABLE TREASURE HOLE! AND I'M ONLY CHARGING HALF YOUR HAUL TO FLY YOU DOWN!
¡GRRR!¡

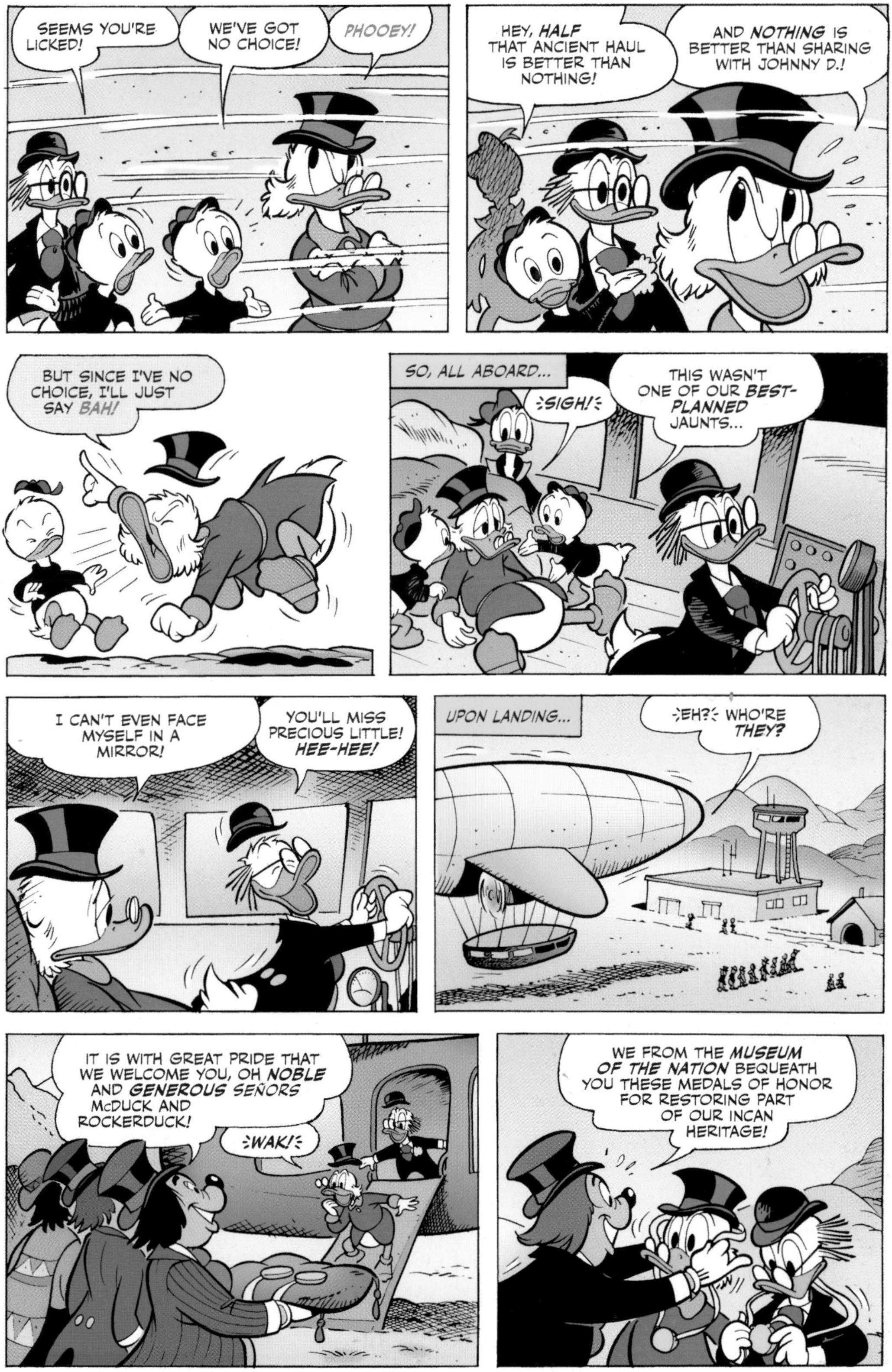

SEEMS YOU'RE LICKED!
WE'VE GOT NO CHOICE!
PHOOEY!
HEY, HALF THAT ANCIENT HAUL IS BETTER THAN NOTHING!
AND NOTHING IS BETTER THAN SHARING WITH JOHNNY D.!
BUT SINCE I'VE NO CHOICE, I'LL JUST SAY BAH!
SO, ALL ABOARD...
SIGH!
THIS WASN'T ONE OF OUR BEST-PLANNED JAUNTS...
I CAN'T EVEN FACE MYSELF IN A MIRROR!
YOU'LL MISS PRECIOUS LITTLE! HEE-HEE!
UPON LANDING...
EH? WHO'RE THEY?
IT IS WITH GREAT PRIDE THAT WE WELCOME YOU, OH NOBLE AND GENEROUS SEÑORS McDUCK AND ROCKERDUCK!
WAK!
WE FROM THE MUSEUM OF THE NATION BEQUEATH YOU THESE MEDALS OF HONOR FOR RESTORING PART OF OUR INCAN HERITAGE!

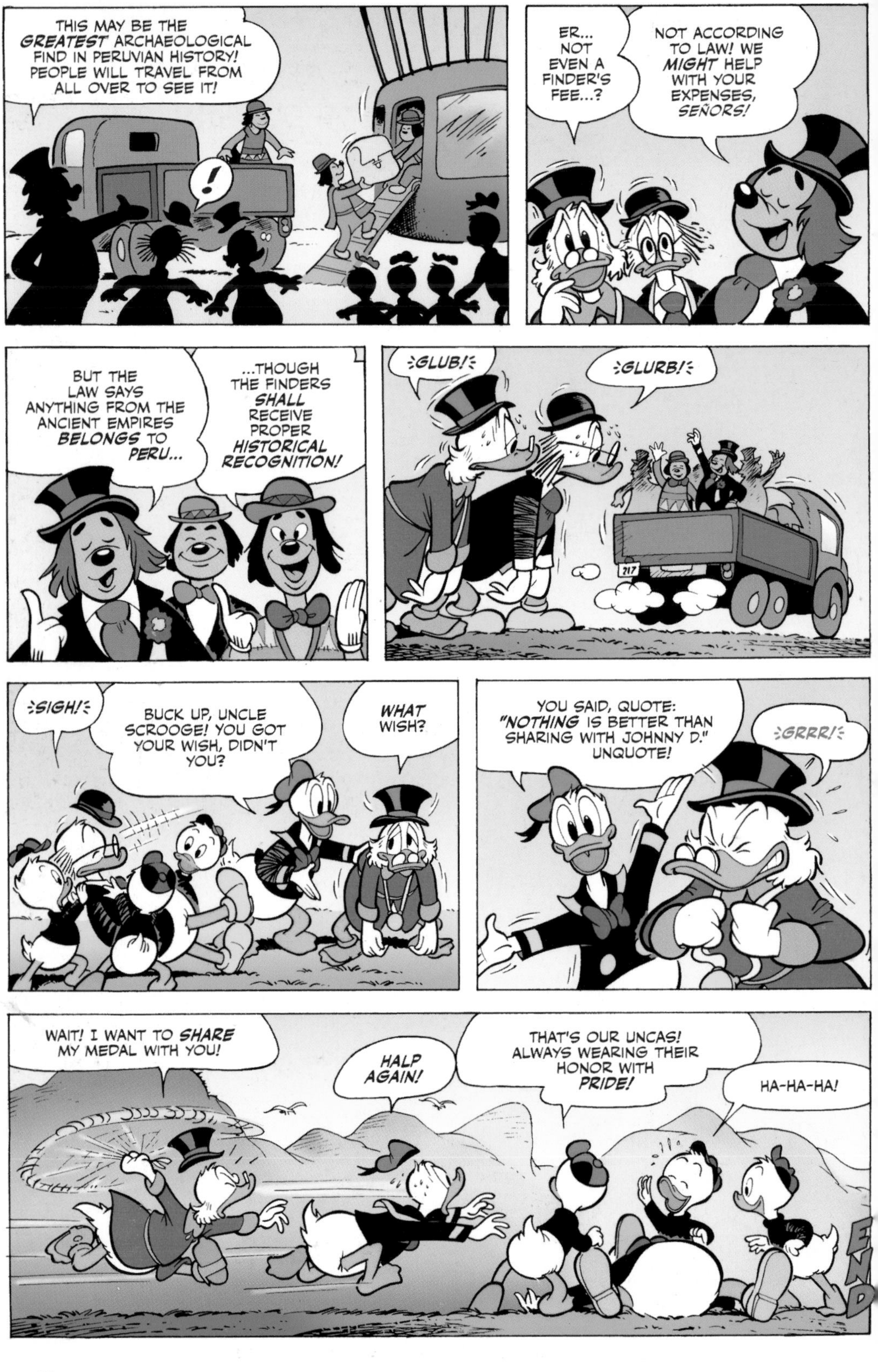
THIS MAY BE THE GREATEST ARCHAEOLOGICAL FIND IN PERUVIAN HISTORY! PEOPLE WILL TRAVEL FROM ALL OVER TO SEE IT!
!
ER... NOT EVEN A FINDER'S FEE...?
NOT ACCORDING TO LAW! WE MIGHT HELP WITH YOUR EXPENSES, SEÑORS!
BUT THE LAW SAYS ANYTHING FROM THE ANCIENT EMPIRES BELONGS TO PERU...
...THOUGH THE FINDERS SHALL RECEIVE PROPER HISTORICAL RECOGNITION!
GLUB!
GLURB!
SIGH!
BUCK UP, UNCLE SCROOGE! YOU GOT YOUR WISH, DIDN'T YOU?
WHAT WISH?
YOU SAID, QUOTE: "NOTHING IS BETTER THAN SHARING WITH JOHNNY D." UNQUOTE!
GRRR!
WAIT! I WANT TO SHARE MY MEDAL WITH YOU!
HALP AGAIN!
THAT'S OUR UNCAS! ALWAYS WEARING THEIR HONOR WITH PRIDE!
HA-HA-HA!
END

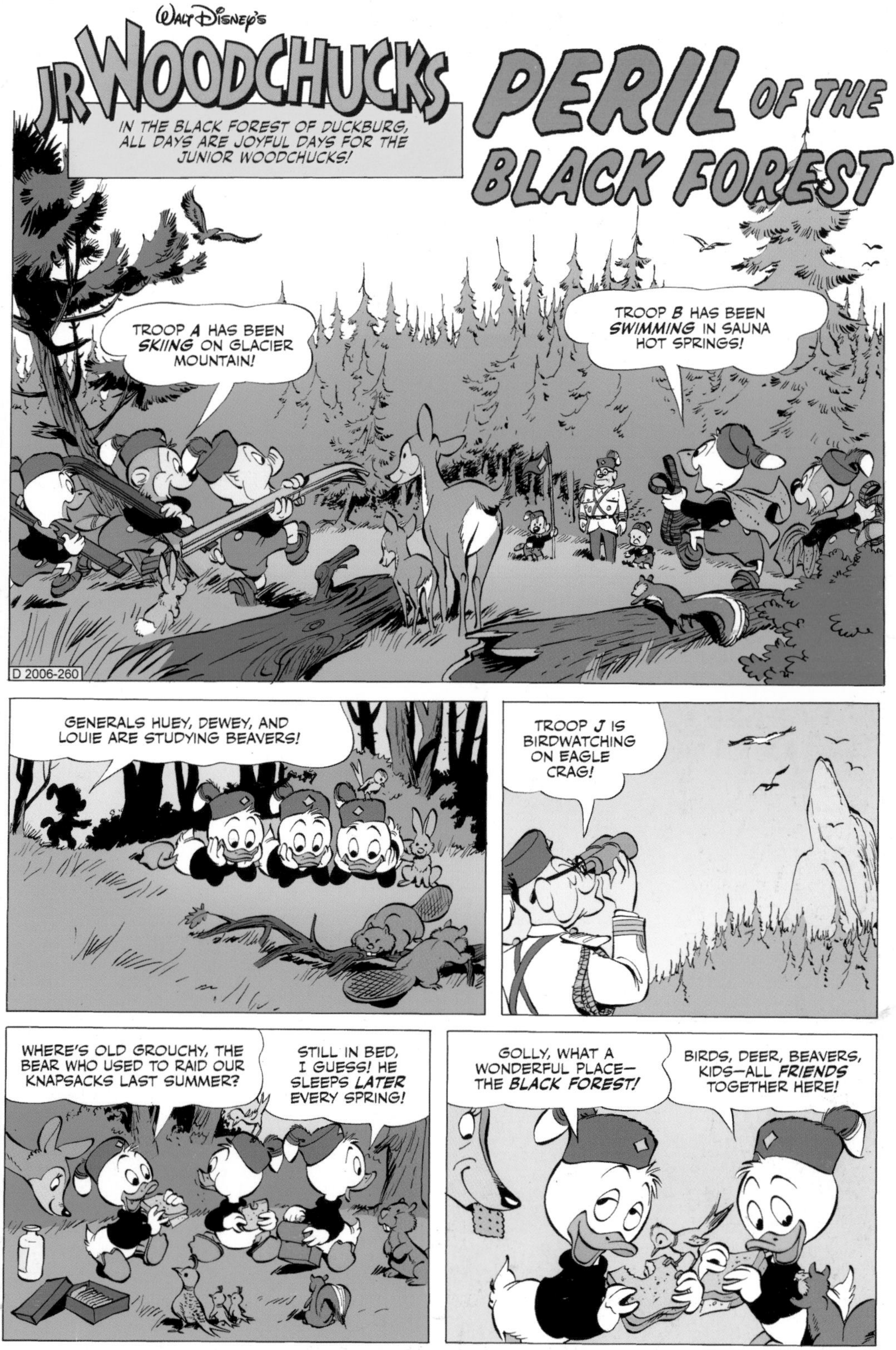
WALT DISNEY'S
JR WOODCHUCKS
PERIL OF THE BLACK FOREST
IN THE BLACK FOREST OF DUCKBURG, ALL DAYS ARE JOYFUL DAYS FOR THE JUNIOR WOODCHUCKS!
TROOP A HAS BEEN SKIING ON GLACIER MOUNTAIN!
TROOP B HAS BEEN SWIMMING IN SAUNA HOT SPRINGS!
D 2006-260
GENERALS HUEY, DEWEY, AND LOUIE ARE STUDYING BEAVERS!
TROOP J IS BIRDWATCHING ON EAGLE CRAG!
WHERE'S OLD GROUCHY, THE BEAR WHO USED TO RAID OUR KNAPSACKS LAST SUMMER?
STILL IN BED, I GUESS! HE SLEEPS LATER EVERY SPRING!
GOLLY, WHAT A WONDERFUL PLACE— THE BLACK FOREST!
BIRDS, DEER, BEAVERS, KIDS—ALL FRIENDS TOGETHER HERE!

Originally published in *Kačer Donald* #10/2008 (Czech Republic, 2008)

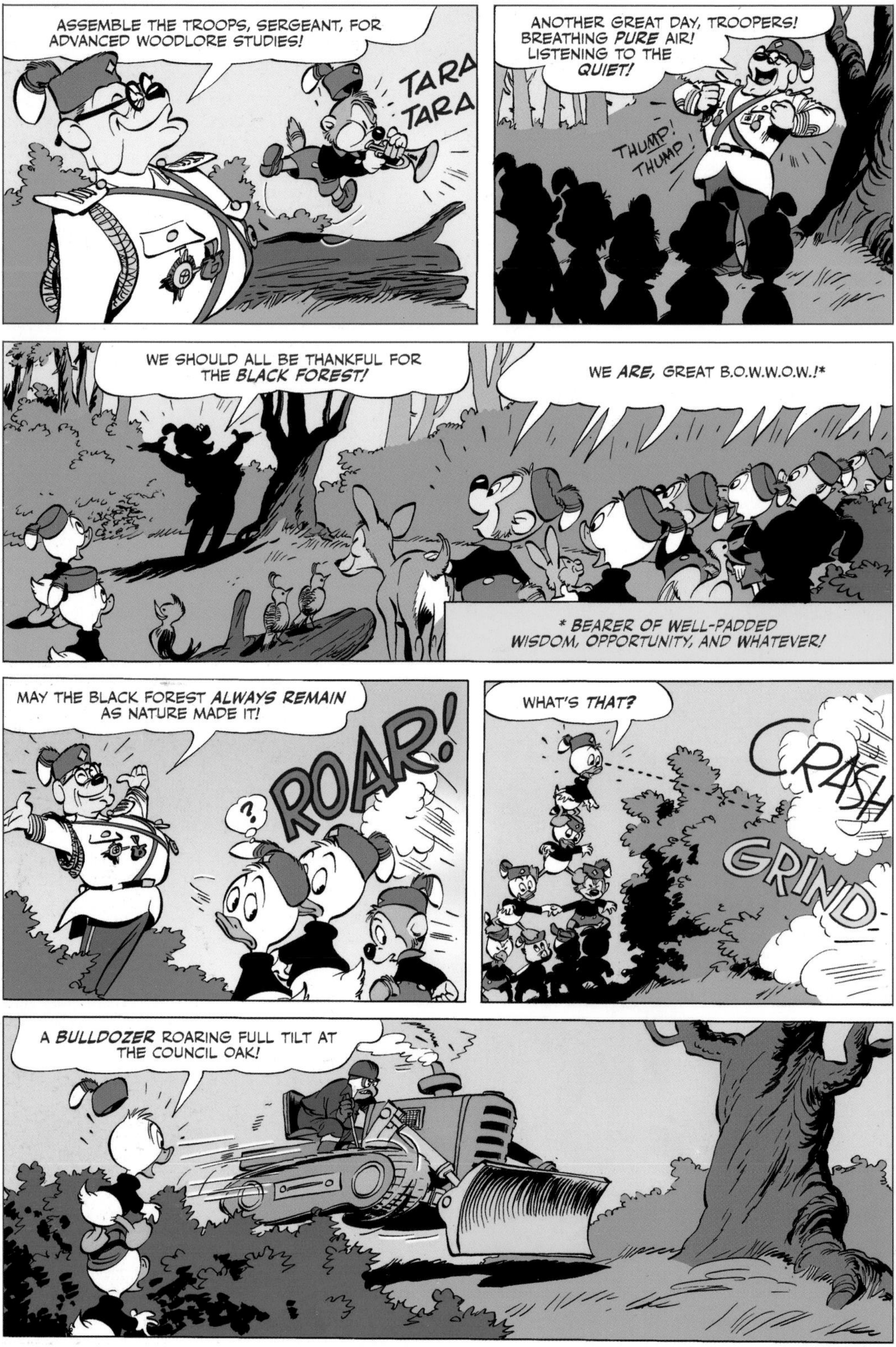

ASSEMBLE THE TROOPS, SERGEANT, FOR ADVANCED WOODLORE STUDIES!
TARA TARA
ANOTHER GREAT DAY, TROOPERS! BREATHING PURE AIR! LISTENING TO THE QUIET!
THUMP! THUMP!
WE SHOULD ALL BE THANKFUL FOR THE BLACK FOREST!
WE ARE, GREAT B.O.W.W.O.W.!*
* BEARER OF WELL-PADDED WISDOM, OPPORTUNITY, AND WHATEVER!
MAY THE BLACK FOREST ALWAYS REMAIN AS NATURE MADE IT!
ROAR!
?
WHAT'S THAT?
CRASH
GRIND
A BULLDOZER ROARING FULL TILT AT THE COUNCIL OAK!

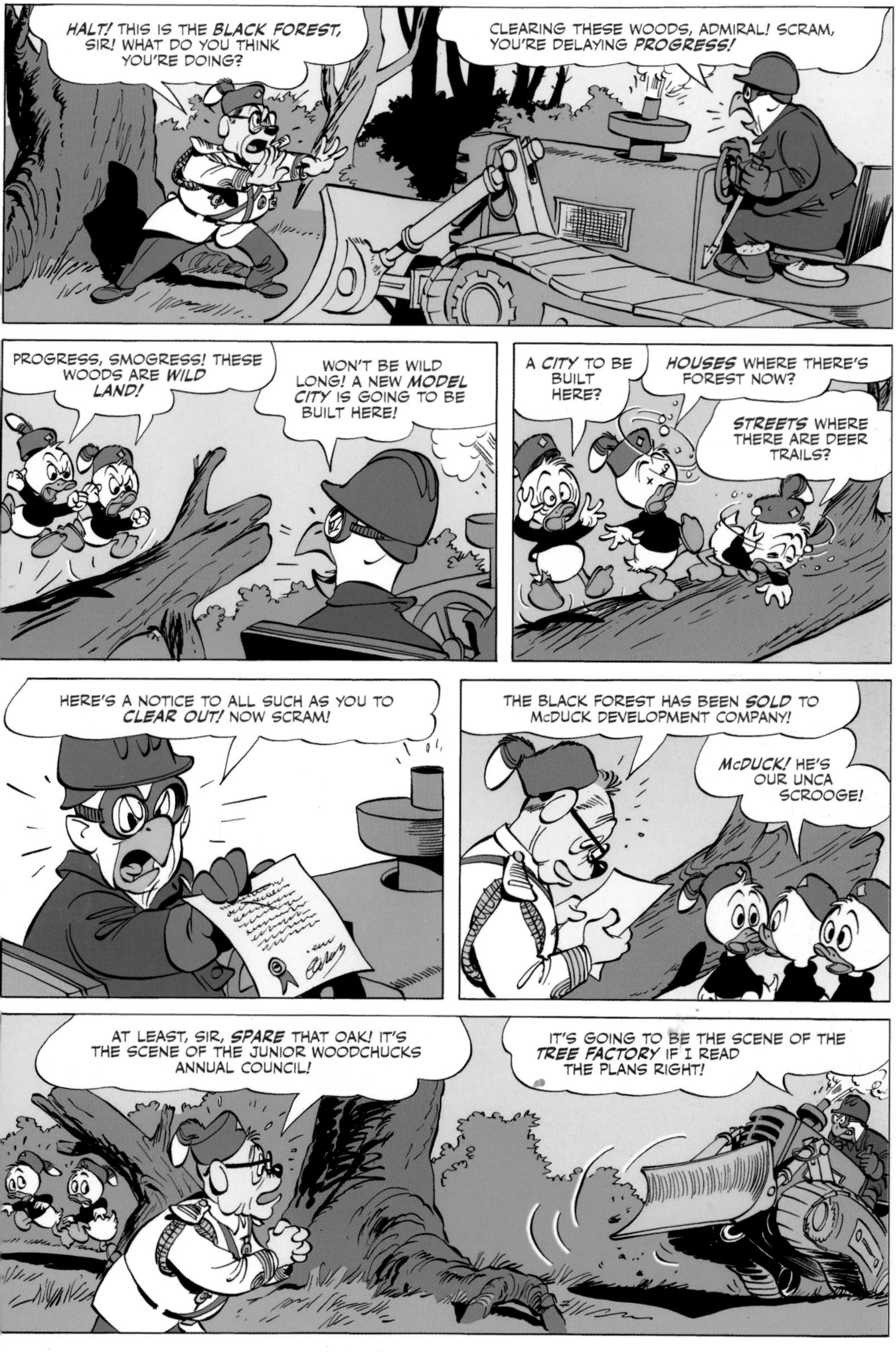
HALT! THIS IS THE BLACK FOREST, SIR! WHAT DO YOU THINK YOU'RE DOING?
CLEARING THESE WOODS, ADMIRAL! SCRAM, YOU'RE DELAYING PROGRESS!
PROGRESS, SMOGRESS! THESE WOODS ARE WILD LAND!
WON'T BE WILD LONG! A NEW MODEL CITY IS GOING TO BE BUILT HERE!
A CITY TO BE BUILT HERE?
HOUSES WHERE THERE'S FOREST NOW?
STREETS WHERE THERE ARE DEER TRAILS?
HERE'S A NOTICE TO ALL SUCH AS YOU TO CLEAR OUT! NOW SCRAM!
THE BLACK FOREST HAS BEEN SOLD TO McDUCK DEVELOPMENT COMPANY!
McDUCK! HE'S OUR UNCA SCROOGE!
AT LEAST, SIR, SPARE THAT OAK! IT'S THE SCENE OF THE JUNIOR WOODCHUCKS ANNUAL COUNCIL!
IT'S GOING TO BE THE SCENE OF THE TREE FACTORY IF I READ THE PLANS RIGHT!

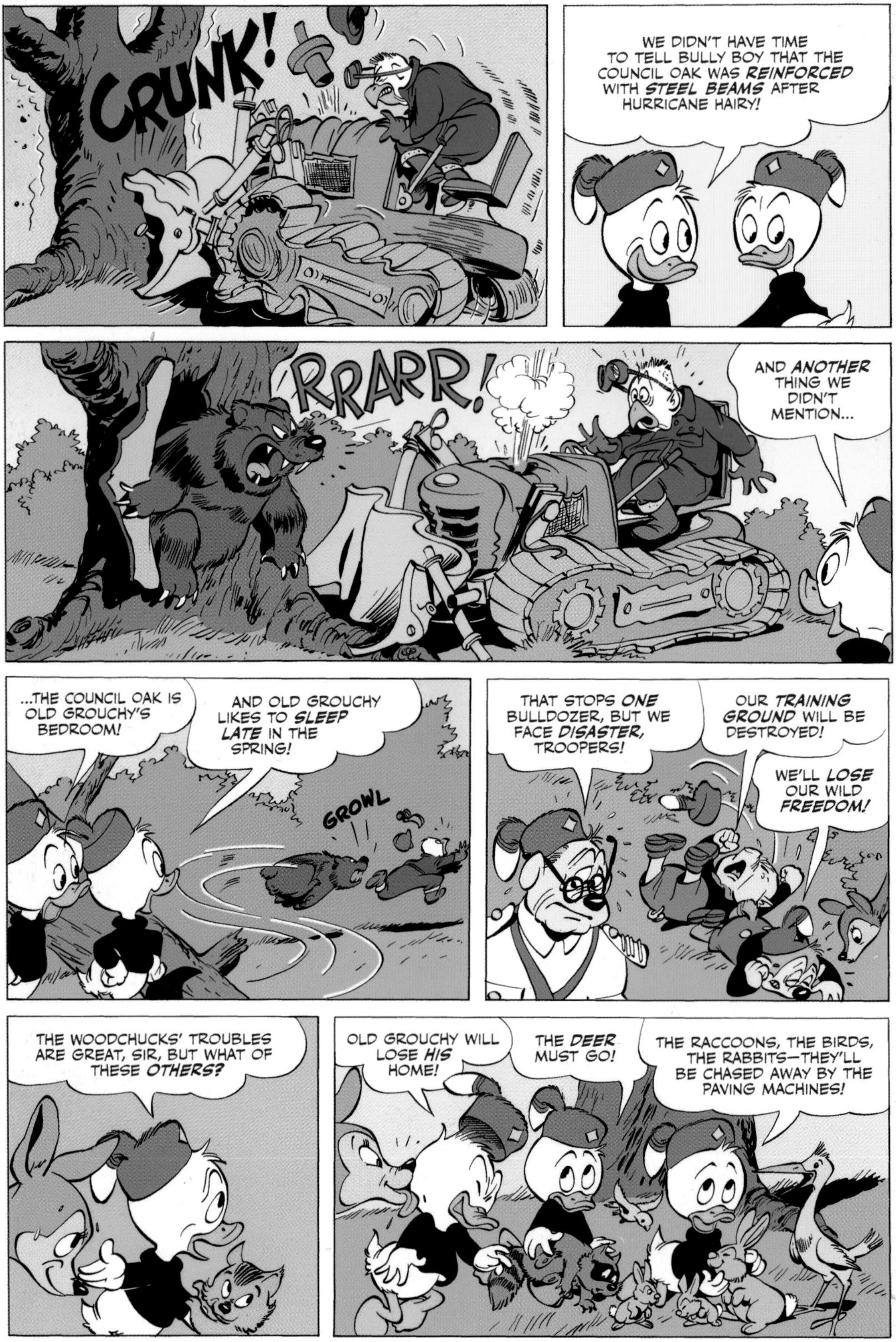
CRUNK!
WE DIDN'T HAVE TIME TO TELL BULLY BOY THAT THE COUNCIL OAK WAS REINFORCED WITH STEEL BEAMS AFTER HURRICANE HAIRY!
RRARR!
AND ANOTHER THING WE DIDN'T MENTION...
...THE COUNCIL OAK IS OLD GROUCHY'S BEDROOM!
AND OLD GROUCHY LIKES TO SLEEP LATE IN THE SPRING!
GROWL
THAT STOPS ONE BULLDOZER, BUT WE FACE DISASTER, TROOPERS!
OUR TRAINING GROUND WILL BE DESTROYED!
WE'LL LOSE OUR WILD FREEDOM!
THE WOODCHUCKS' TROUBLES ARE GREAT, SIR, BUT WHAT OF THESE OTHERS?
OLD GROUCHY WILL LOSE HIS HOME!
THE DEER MUST GO!
THE RACCOONS, THE BIRDS, THE RABBITS—THEY'LL BE CHASED AWAY BY THE PAVING MACHINES!

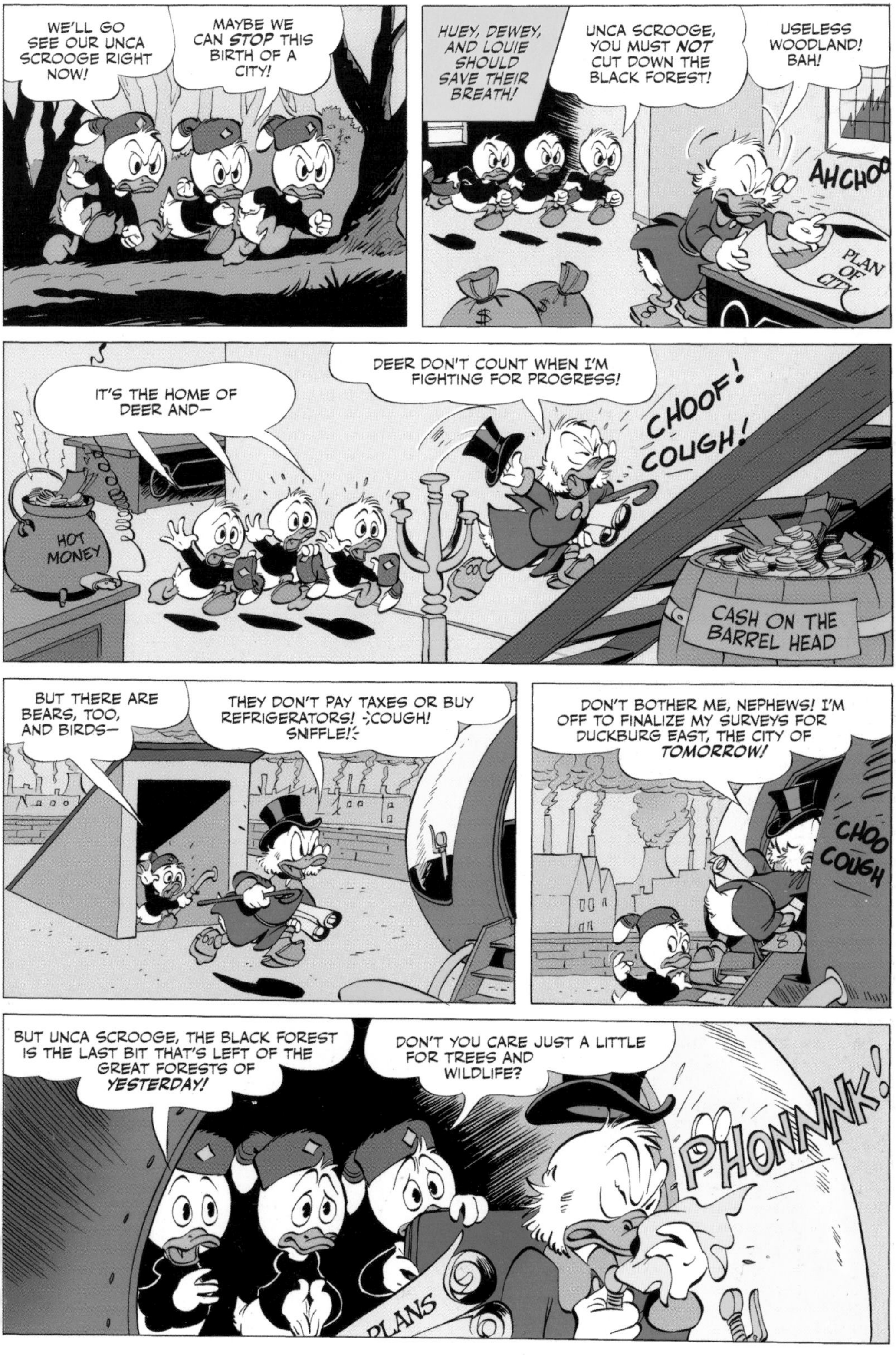
WE'LL GO SEE OUR UNCA SCROOGE RIGHT NOW!
MAYBE WE CAN STOP THIS BIRTH OF A CITY!
HUEY, DEWEY, AND LOUIE SHOULD SAVE THEIR BREATH!
UNCA SCROOGE, YOU MUST NOT CUT DOWN THE BLACK FOREST!
USELESS WOODLAND! BAH!
AHCHOO
PLAN OF CITY
IT'S THE HOME OF DEER AND—
DEER DON'T COUNT WHEN I'M FIGHTING FOR PROGRESS!
CHOOF! COUGH!
HOT MONEY
CASH ON THE BARREL HEAD
BUT THERE ARE BEARS, TOO, AND BIRDS—
THEY DON'T PAY TAXES OR BUY REFRIGERATORS! COUGH! SNIFFLE!
DON'T BOTHER ME, NEPHEWS! I'M OFF TO FINALIZE MY SURVEYS FOR DUCKBURG EAST, THE CITY OF TOMORROW!
CHOO COUGH
BUT UNCA SCROOGE, THE BLACK FOREST IS THE LAST BIT THAT'S LEFT OF THE GREAT FORESTS OF YESTERDAY!
DON'T YOU CARE JUST A LITTLE FOR TREES AND WILDLIFE?
PHONNNK!
PLANS

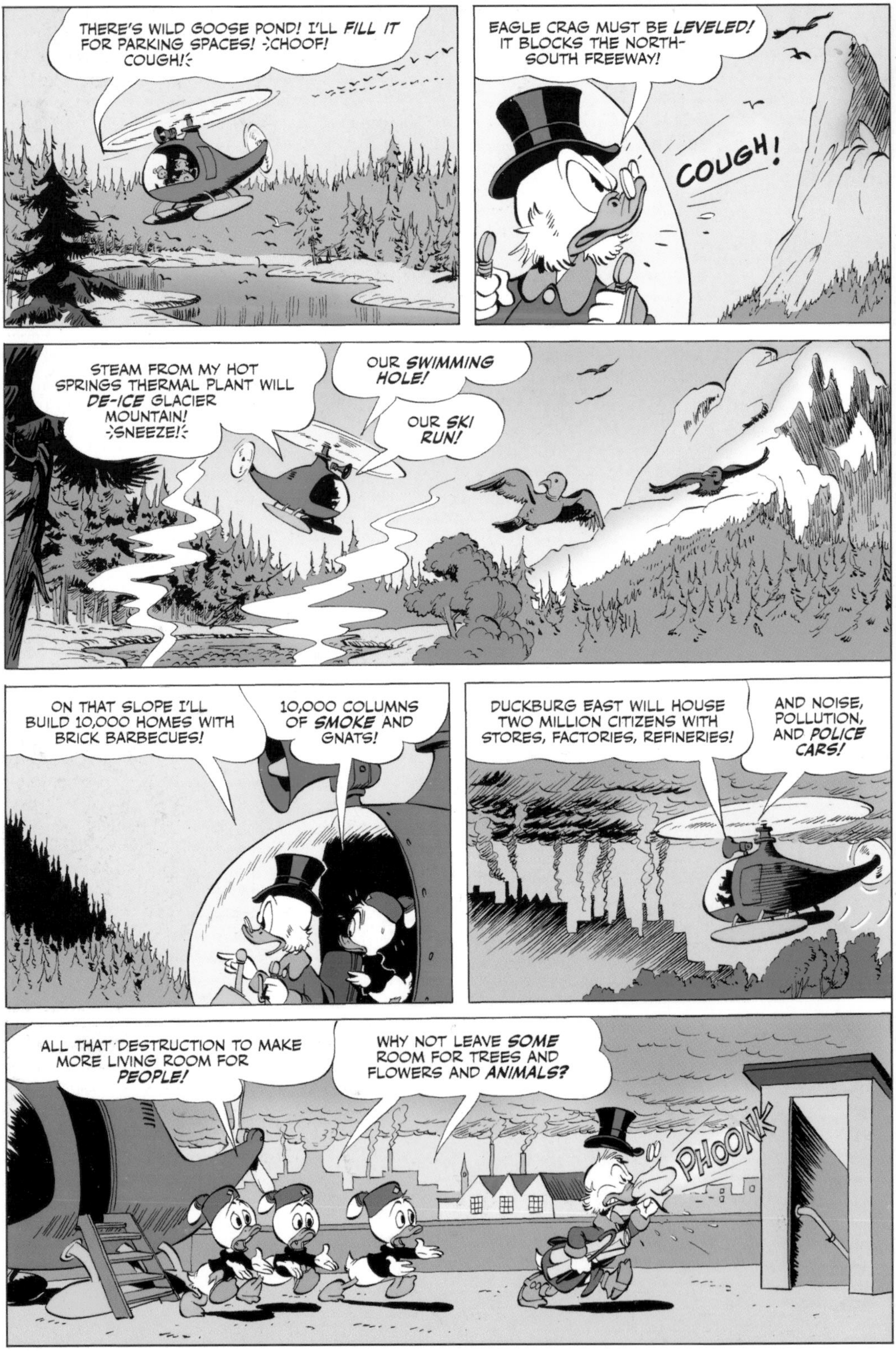
THERE'S WILD GOOSE POND! I'LL FILL IT FOR PARKING SPACES! CHOOF! COUGH!
EAGLE CRAG MUST BE LEVELED! IT BLOCKS THE NORTH-SOUTH FREEWAY!
COUGH!
STEAM FROM MY HOT SPRINGS THERMAL PLANT WILL DE-ICE GLACIER MOUNTAIN! SNEEZE!
OUR SWIMMING HOLE!
OUR SKI RUN!
ON THAT SLOPE I'LL BUILD 10,000 HOMES WITH BRICK BARBECUES!
10,000 COLUMNS OF SMOKE AND GNATS!
DUCKBURG EAST WILL HOUSE TWO MILLION CITIZENS WITH STORES, FACTORIES, REFINERIES!
AND NOISE, POLLUTION, AND POLICE CARS!
ALL THAT DESTRUCTION TO MAKE MORE LIVING ROOM FOR PEOPLE!
WHY NOT LEAVE SOME ROOM FOR TREES AND FLOWERS AND ANIMALS?
PHOONK

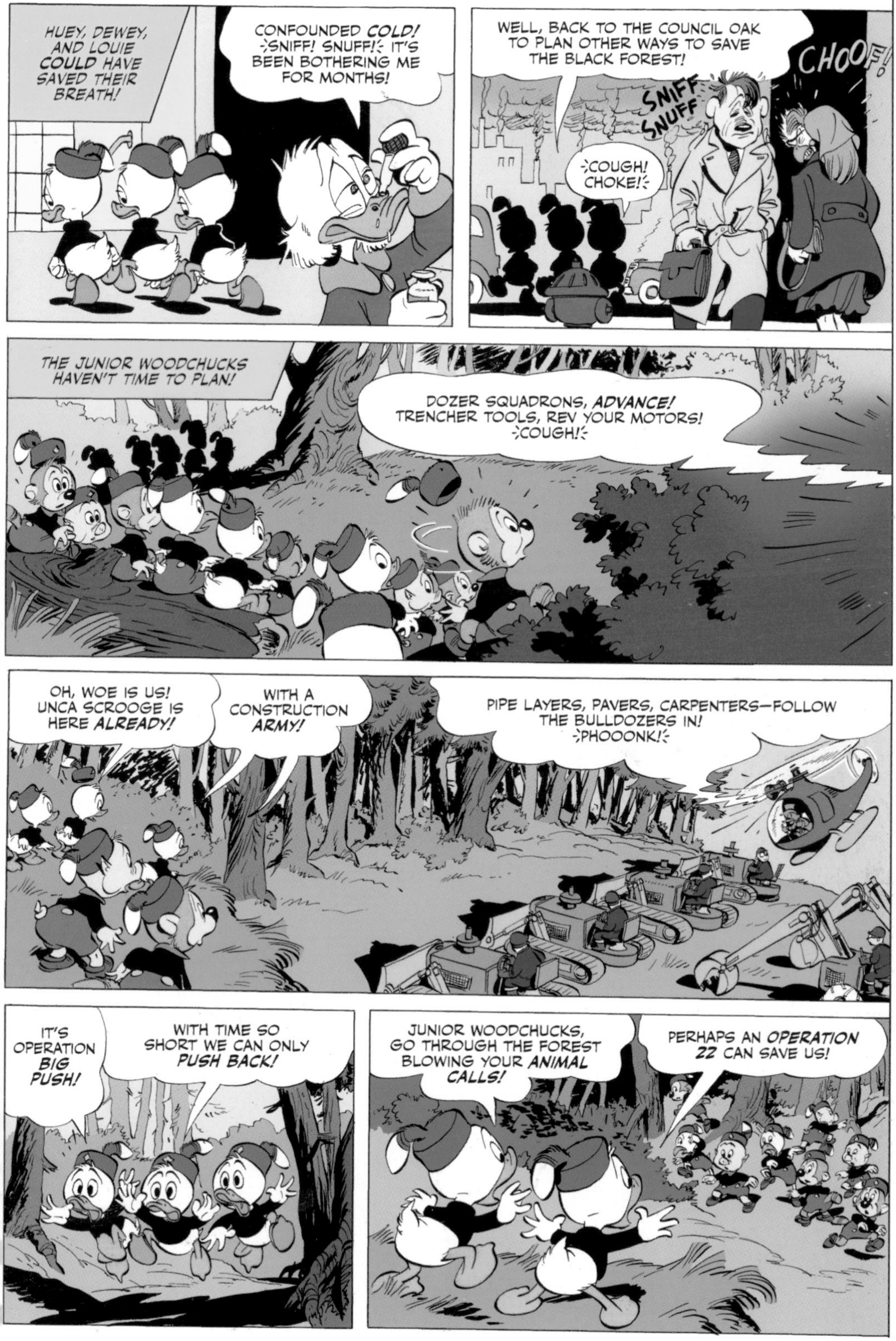
HUEY, DEWEY, AND LOUIE COULD HAVE SAVED THEIR BREATH!
CONFOUNDED COLD! -SNIFF! SNUFF!- IT'S BEEN BOTHERING ME FOR MONTHS!
WELL, BACK TO THE COUNCIL OAK TO PLAN OTHER WAYS TO SAVE THE BLACK FOREST!
SNIFF SNUFF
CHOOF!
-COUGH! CHOKE!-
THE JUNIOR WOODCHUCKS HAVEN'T TIME TO PLAN!
DOZER SQUADRONS, ADVANCE! TRENCHER TOOLS, REV YOUR MOTORS! -COUGH!-
OH, WOE IS US! UNCA SCROOGE IS HERE ALREADY!
WITH A CONSTRUCTION ARMY!
PIPE LAYERS, PAVERS, CARPENTERS—FOLLOW THE BULLDOZERS IN! -PHOOONK!-
IT'S OPERATION BIG PUSH!
WITH TIME SO SHORT WE CAN ONLY PUSH BACK!
JUNIOR WOODCHUCKS, GO THROUGH THE FOREST BLOWING YOUR ANIMAL CALLS!
PERHAPS AN OPERATION 22 CAN SAVE US!

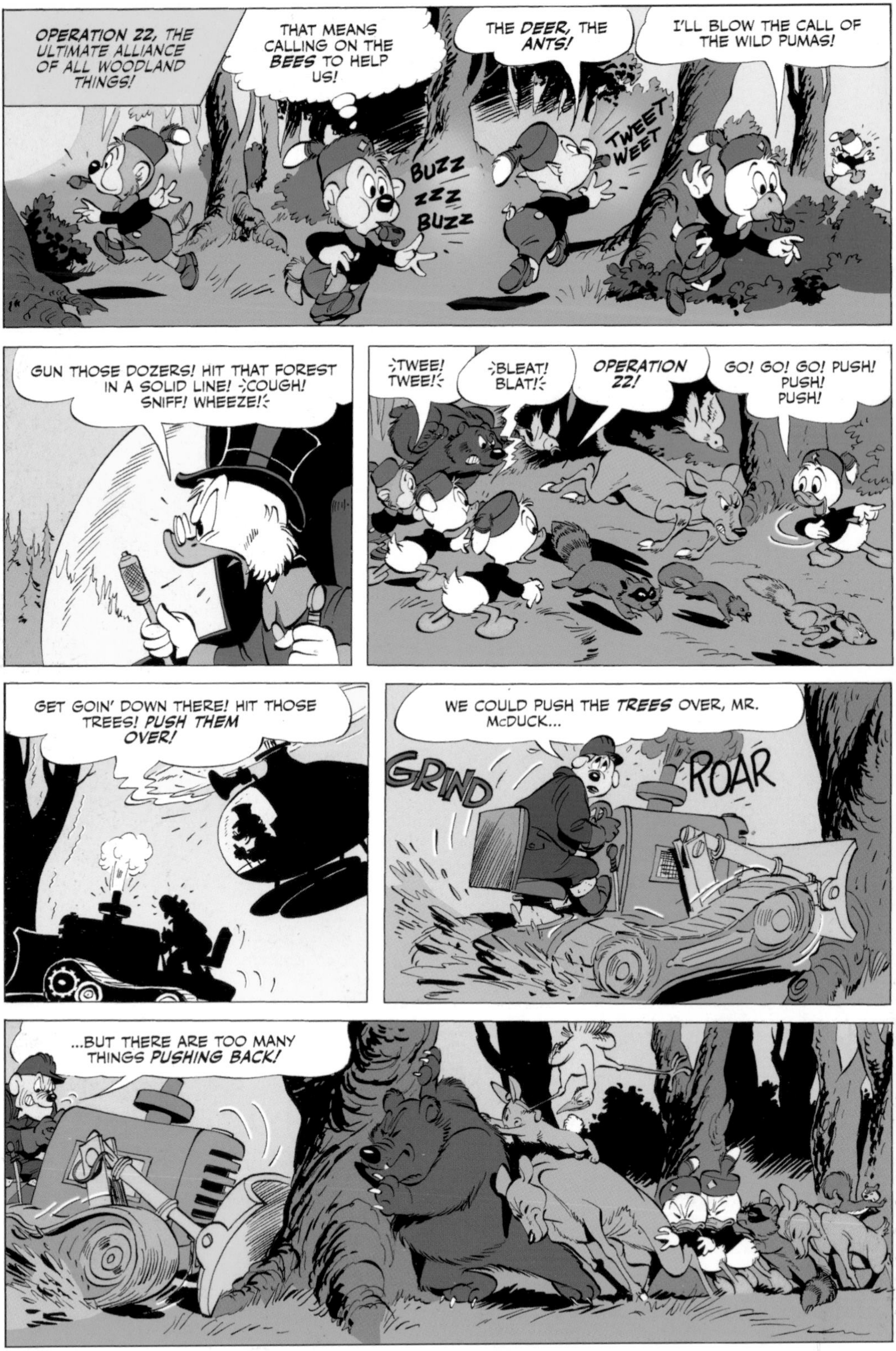
OPERATION 22, THE ULTIMATE ALLIANCE OF ALL WOODLAND THINGS!
THAT MEANS CALLING ON THE BEES TO HELP US!
BUZZ ZZZ BUZZ
THE DEER, THE ANTS!
TWEET WEET
I'LL BLOW THE CALL OF THE WILD PUMAS!
GUN THOSE DOZERS! HIT THAT FOREST IN A SOLID LINE! COUGH! SNIFF! WHEEZE!
TWEE! TWEE!
BLEAT! BLAT!
OPERATION 22!
GO! GO! GO! PUSH! PUSH! PUSH!
GET GOIN' DOWN THERE! HIT THOSE TREES! PUSH THEM OVER!
WE COULD PUSH THE TREES OVER, MR. McDUCK...
GRIND
ROAR
...BUT THERE ARE TOO MANY THINGS PUSHING BACK!

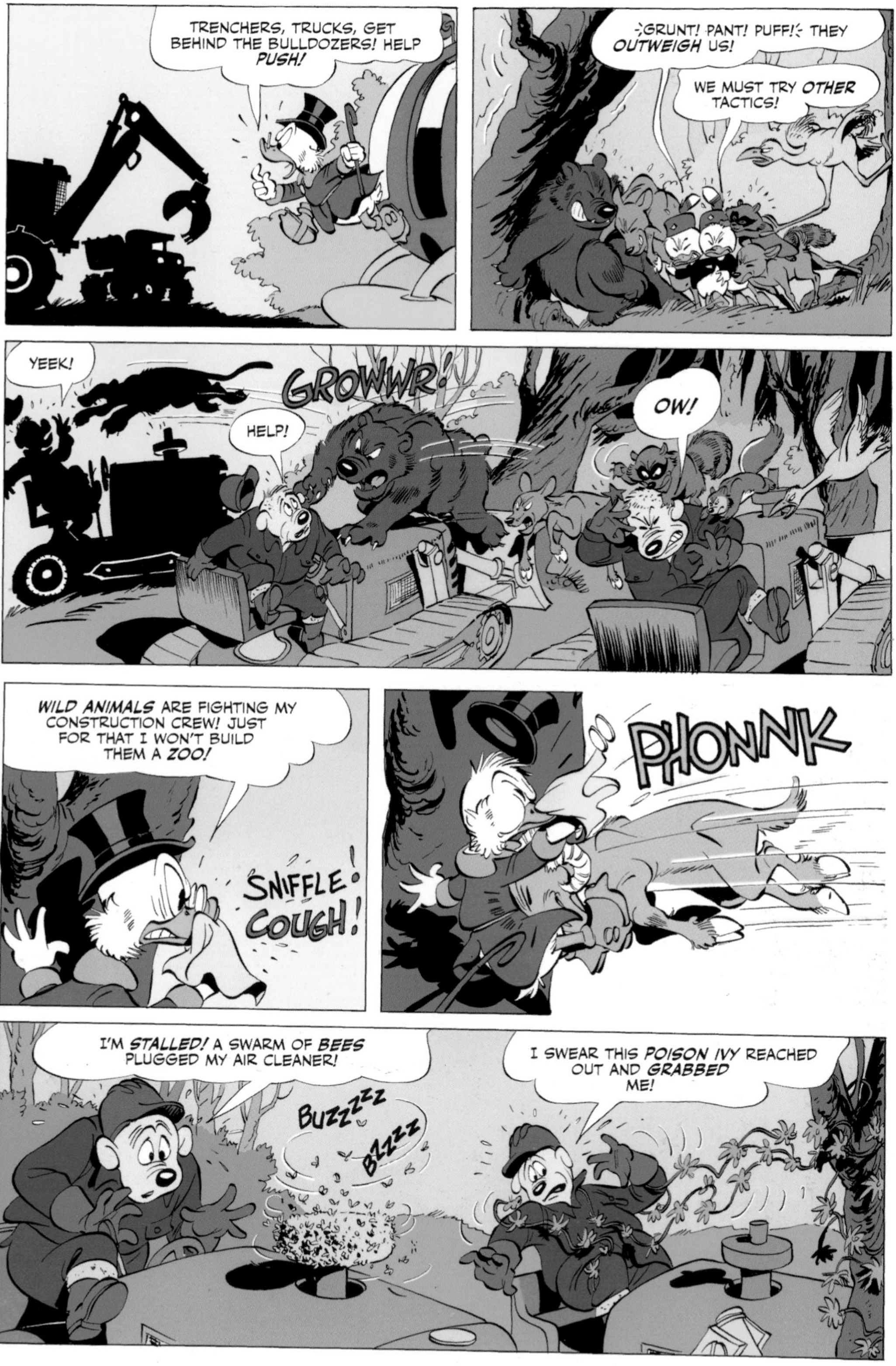

TRENCHERS, TRUCKS, GET BEHIND THE BULLDOZERS! HELP PUSH!
-GRUNT! PANT! PUFF!- THEY OUTWEIGH US!
WE MUST TRY OTHER TACTICS!
YEEK!
GROWWR!
HELP!
OW!
WILD ANIMALS ARE FIGHTING MY CONSTRUCTION CREW! JUST FOR THAT I WON'T BUILD THEM A ZOO!
SNIFFLE! COUGH!
PHONNK
I'M STALLED! A SWARM OF BEES PLUGGED MY AIR CLEANER!
BUZZZZZ
BZZZZ
I SWEAR THIS POISON IVY REACHED OUT AND GRABBED ME!

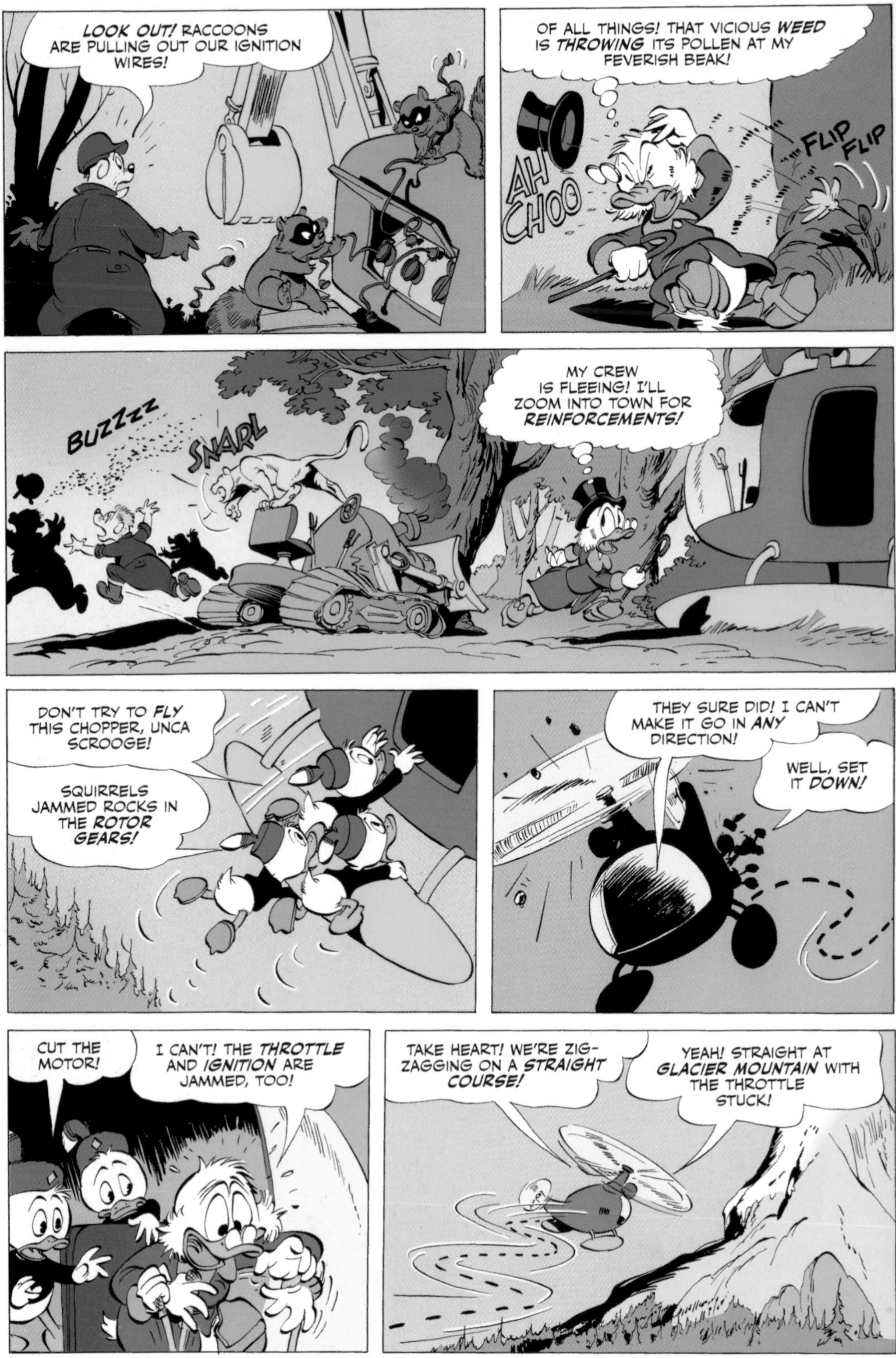
LOOK OUT! RACCOONS ARE PULLING OUT OUR IGNITION WIRES!
OF ALL THINGS! THAT VICIOUS WEED IS THROWING ITS POLLEN AT MY FEVERISH BEAK!
AH CHOO
FLIP FLIP
BUZZzz
SNARL
MY CREW IS FLEEING! I'LL ZOOM INTO TOWN FOR REINFORCEMENTS!
DON'T TRY TO FLY THIS CHOPPER, UNCA SCROOGE!
SQUIRRELS JAMMED ROCKS IN THE ROTOR GEARS!
THEY SURE DID! I CAN'T MAKE IT GO IN ANY DIRECTION!
WELL, SET IT DOWN!
CUT THE MOTOR!
I CAN'T! THE THROTTLE AND IGNITION ARE JAMMED, TOO!
TAKE HEART! WE'RE ZIG-ZAGGING ON A STRAIGHT COURSE!
YEAH! STRAIGHT AT GLACIER MOUNTAIN WITH THE THROTTLE STUCK!

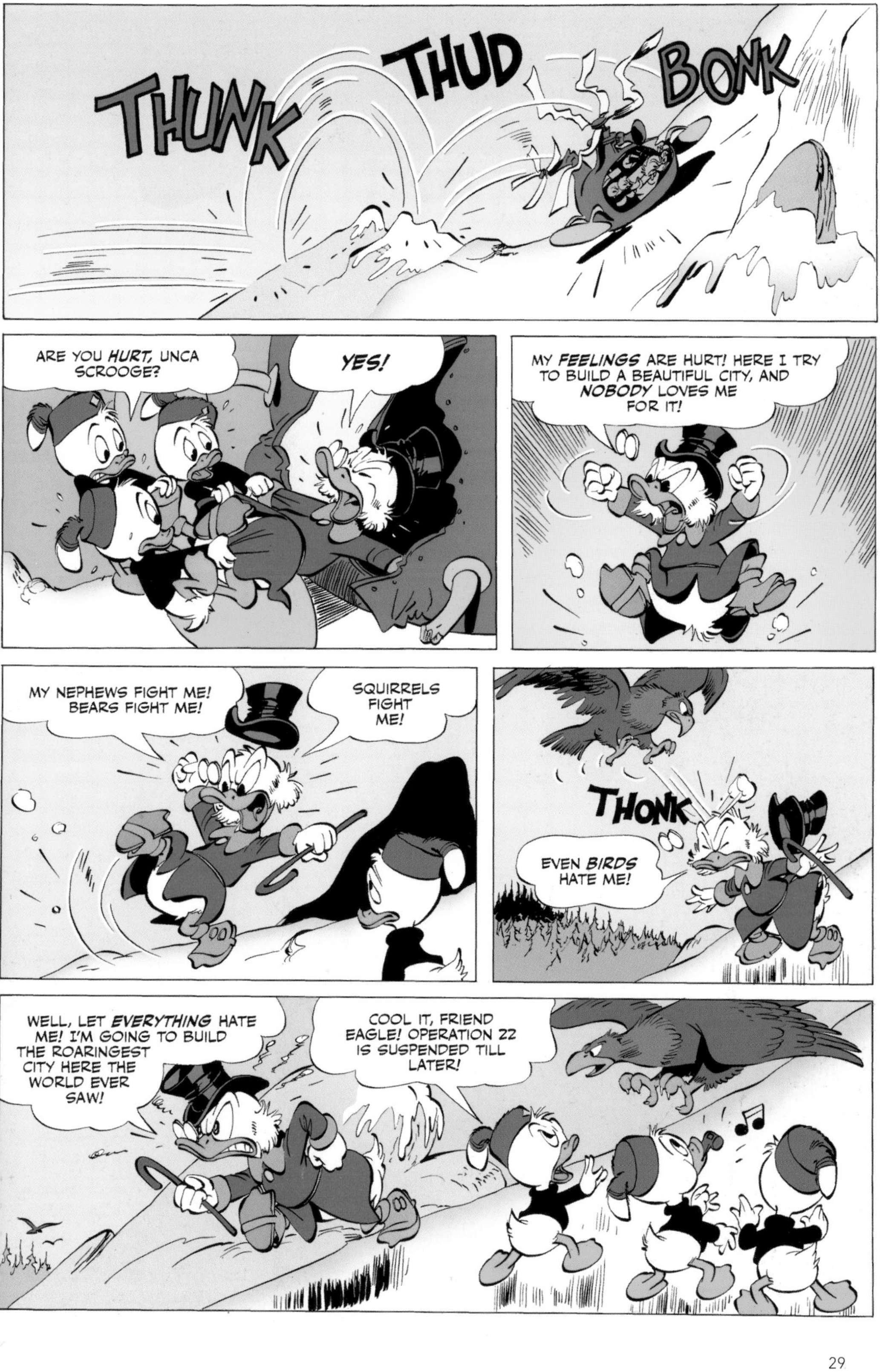
THUNK
THUD
BONK
ARE YOU HURT, UNCA SCROOGE?
YES!
MY FEELINGS ARE HURT! HERE I TRY TO BUILD A BEAUTIFUL CITY, AND NOBODY LOVES ME FOR IT!
MY NEPHEWS FIGHT ME! BEARS FIGHT ME!
SQUIRRELS FIGHT ME!
THONK
EVEN BIRDS HATE ME!
WELL, LET EVERYTHING HATE ME! I'M GOING TO BUILD THE ROARINGEST CITY HERE THE WORLD EVER SAW!
COOL IT, FRIEND EAGLE! OPERATION 22 IS SUSPENDED TILL LATER!

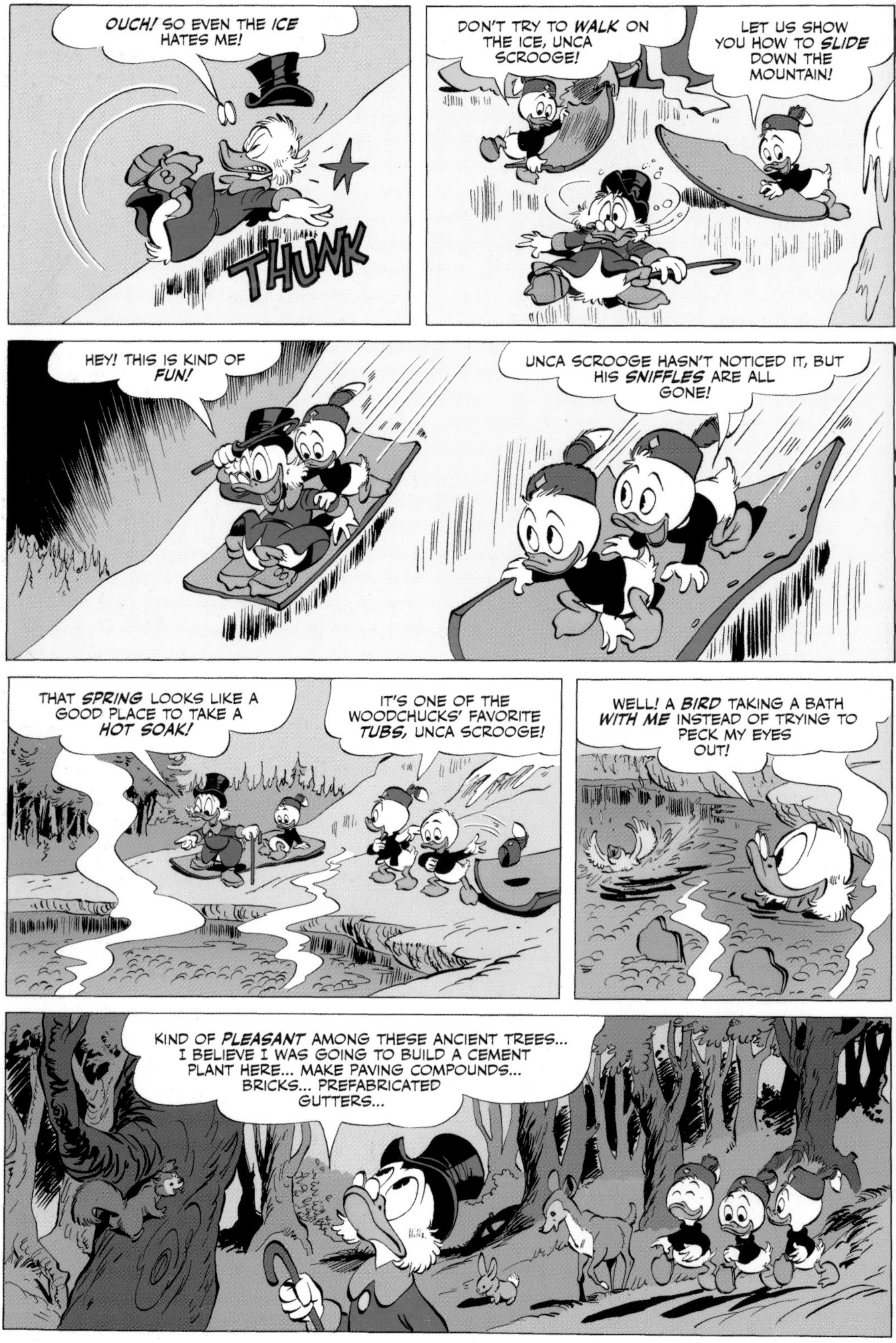
OUCH! SO EVEN THE ICE HATES ME!
THUNK
DON'T TRY TO WALK ON THE ICE, UNCA SCROOGE!
LET US SHOW YOU HOW TO SLIDE DOWN THE MOUNTAIN!
HEY! THIS IS KIND OF FUN!
UNCA SCROOGE HASN'T NOTICED IT, BUT HIS SNIFFLES ARE ALL GONE!
THAT SPRING LOOKS LIKE A GOOD PLACE TO TAKE A HOT SOAK!
IT'S ONE OF THE WOODCHUCKS' FAVORITE TUBS, UNCA SCROOGE!
WELL! A BIRD TAKING A BATH WITH ME INSTEAD OF TRYING TO PECK MY EYES OUT!
KIND OF PLEASANT AMONG THESE ANCIENT TREES... I BELIEVE I WAS GOING TO BUILD A CEMENT PLANT HERE... MAKE PAVING COMPOUNDS... BRICKS... PREFABRICATED GUTTERS...

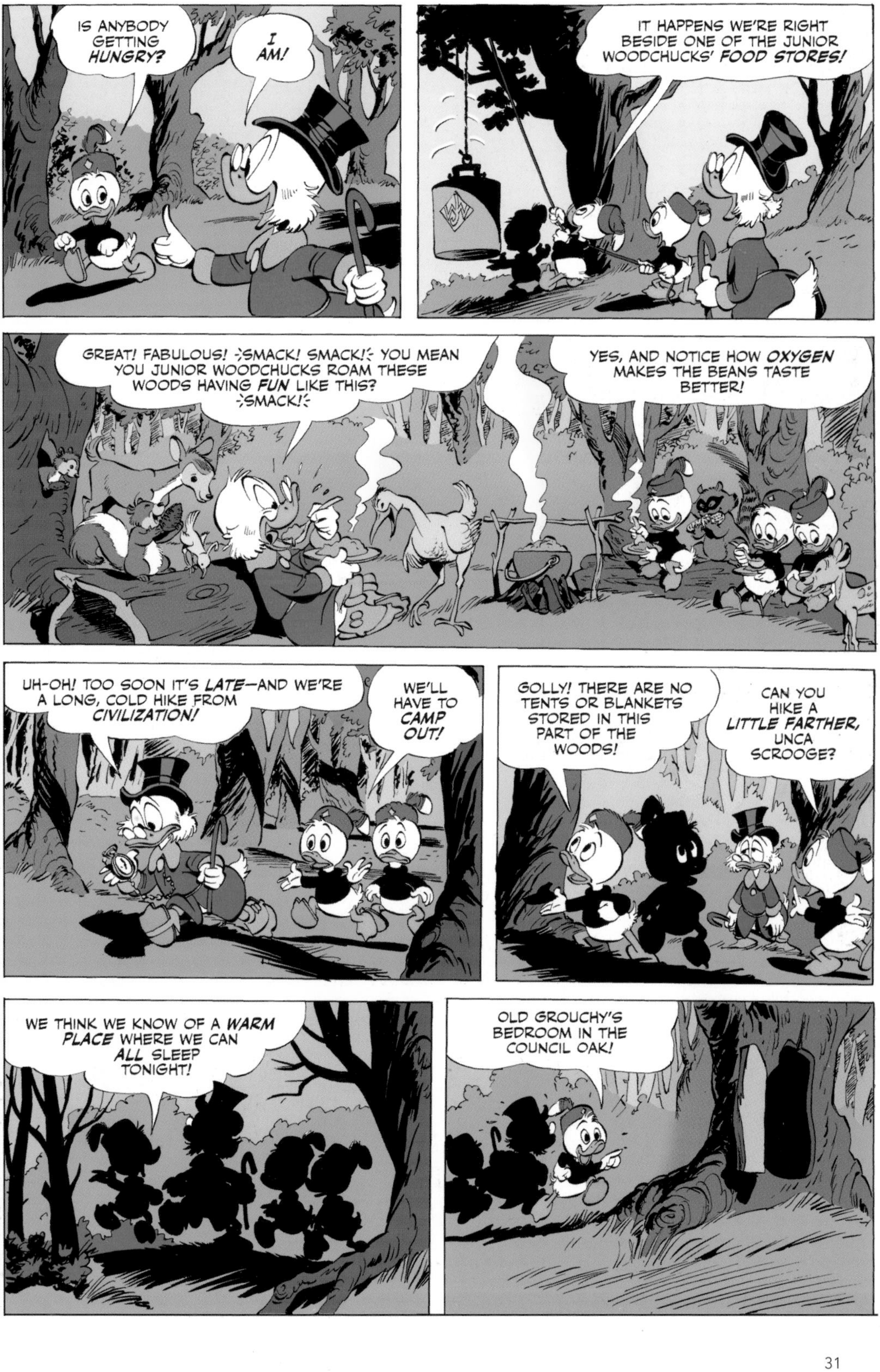
IS ANYBODY GETTING HUNGRY?
I AM!
IT HAPPENS WE'RE RIGHT BESIDE ONE OF THE JUNIOR WOODCHUCKS' FOOD STORES!
GREAT! FABULOUS! -SMACK! SMACK!- YOU MEAN YOU JUNIOR WOODCHUCKS ROAM THESE WOODS HAVING FUN LIKE THIS? -SMACK!-
YES, AND NOTICE HOW OXYGEN MAKES THE BEANS TASTE BETTER!
UH-OH! TOO SOON IT'S LATE—AND WE'RE A LONG, COLD HIKE FROM CIVILIZATION!
WE'LL HAVE TO CAMP OUT!
GOLLY! THERE ARE NO TENTS OR BLANKETS STORED IN THIS PART OF THE WOODS!
CAN YOU HIKE A LITTLE FARTHER, UNCA SCROOGE?
WE THINK WE KNOW OF A WARM PLACE WHERE WE CAN ALL SLEEP TONIGHT!
OLD GROUCHY'S BEDROOM IN THE COUNCIL OAK!

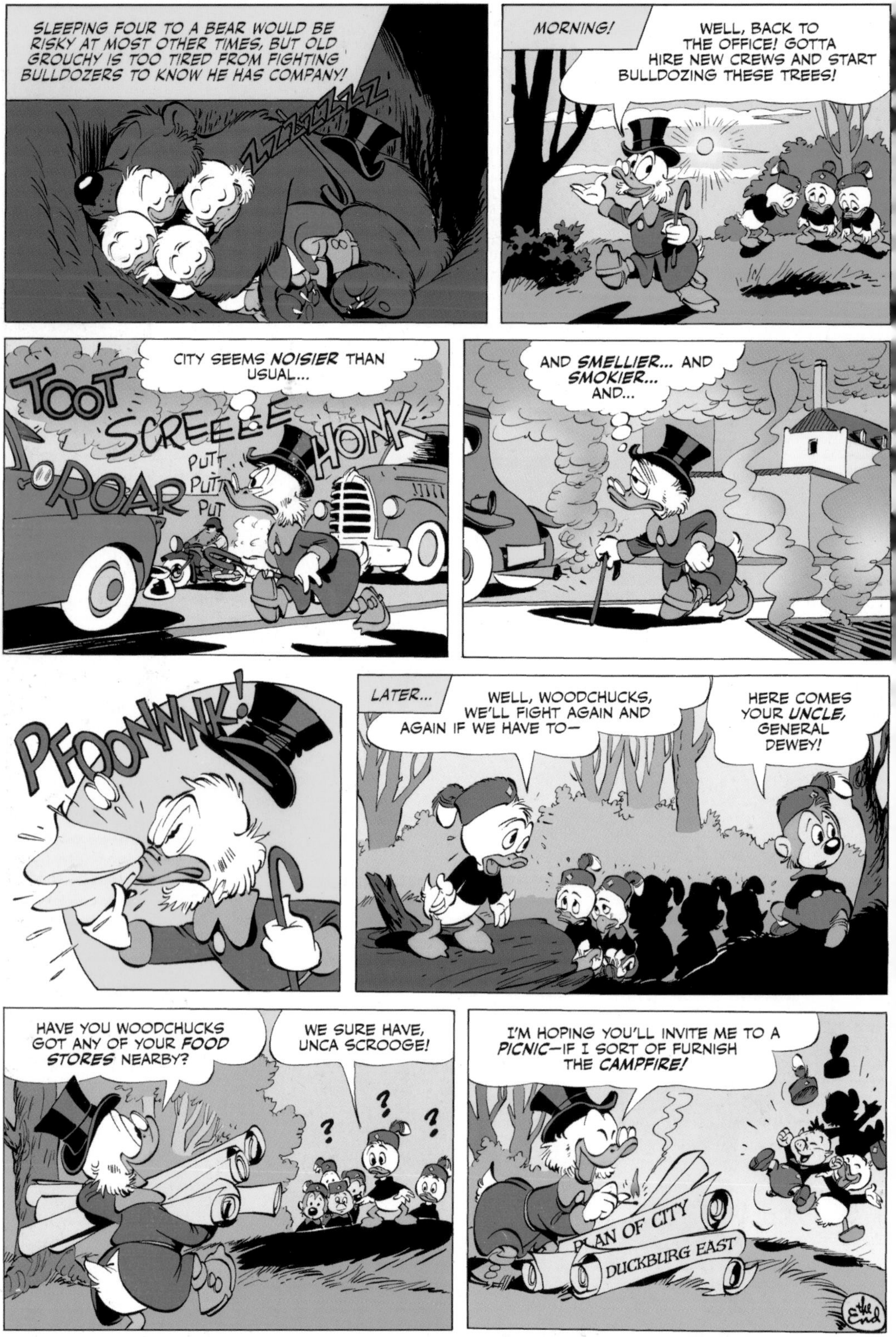
SLEEPING FOUR TO A BEAR WOULD BE RISKY AT MOST OTHER TIMES, BUT OLD GROUCHY IS TOO TIRED FROM FIGHTING BULLDOZERS TO KNOW HE HAS COMPANY!
ZZZZZZZZ
MORNING!
WELL, BACK TO THE OFFICE! GOTTA HIRE NEW CREWS AND START BULLDOZING THESE TREES!
CITY SEEMS NOISIER THAN USUAL...
TOOT
SCREEEEE
HONK
ROAR
PUTT PUTT PUT
AND SMELLIER... AND SMOKIER... AND...
PFOONNNK!
LATER...
WELL, WOODCHUCKS, WE'LL FIGHT AGAIN AND AGAIN IF WE HAVE TO—
HERE COMES YOUR UNCLE, GENERAL DEWEY!
HAVE YOU WOODCHUCKS GOT ANY OF YOUR FOOD STORES NEARBY?
WE SURE HAVE, UNCA SCROOGE!
? ? ?
I'M HOPING YOU'LL INVITE ME TO A PICNIC—IF I SORT OF FURNISH THE CAMPFIRE!
PLAN OF CITY
DUCKBURG EAST
the End

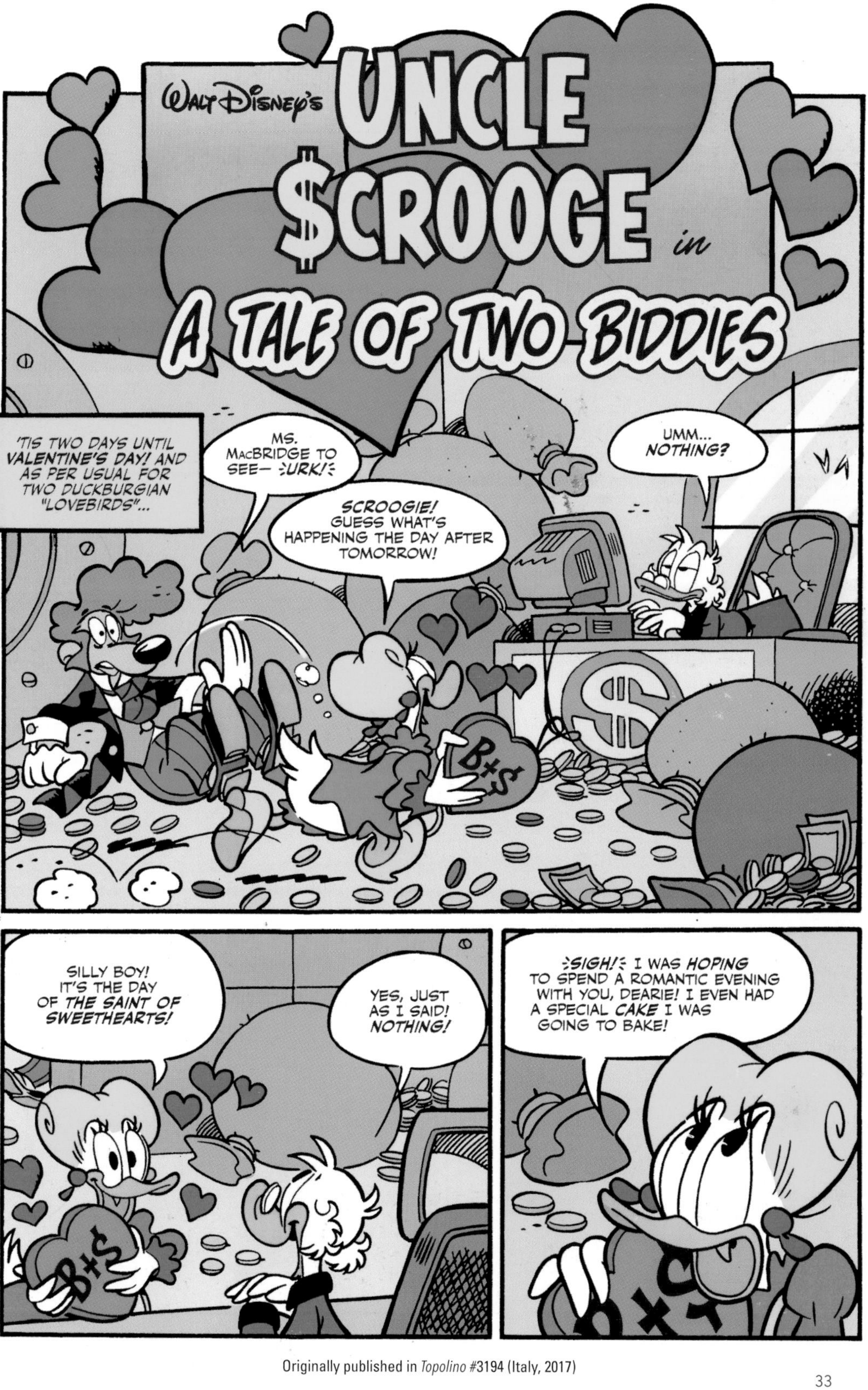
WALT DISNEY'S
UNCLE $CROOGE in
A TALE OF TWO BIDDIES
'TIS TWO DAYS UNTIL VALENTINE'S DAY! AND AS PER USUAL FOR TWO DUCKBURGIAN "LOVEBIRDS"...
MS. MACBRIDGE TO SEE— :URK!:
SCROOGIE! GUESS WHAT'S HAPPENING THE DAY AFTER TOMORROW!
UMM... NOTHING?
B+S
SILLY BOY! IT'S THE DAY OF THE SAINT OF SWEETHEARTS!
YES, JUST AS I SAID! NOTHING!
B+S
:SIGH!: I WAS HOPING TO SPEND A ROMANTIC EVENING WITH YOU, DEARIE! I EVEN HAD A SPECIAL CAKE I WAS GOING TO BAKE!

Originally published in *Topolino* #3194 (Italy, 2017)

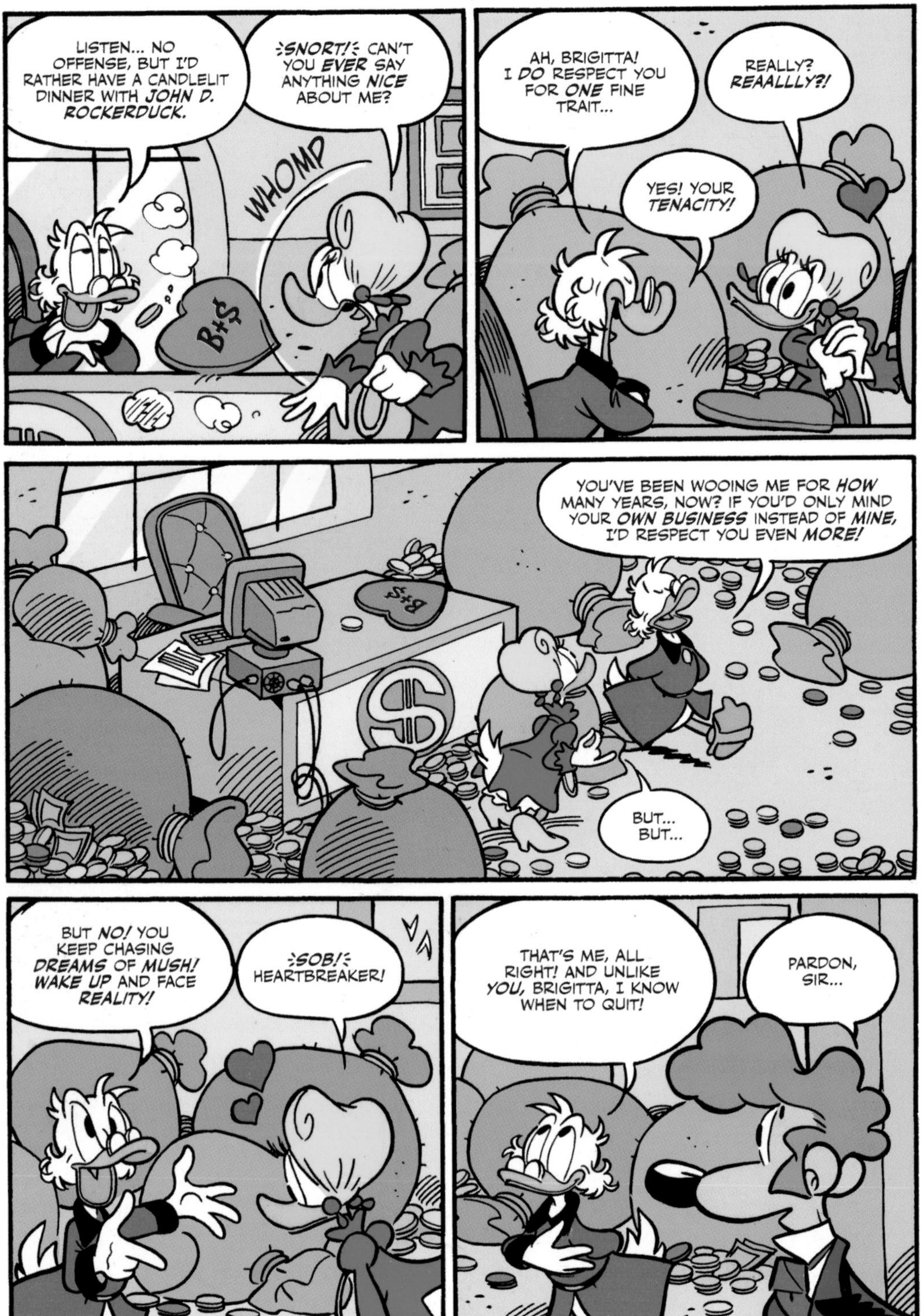
LISTEN... NO OFFENSE, BUT I'D RATHER HAVE A CANDLELIT DINNER WITH JOHN D. ROCKERDUCK.
SNORT! CAN'T YOU EVER SAY ANYTHING NICE ABOUT ME?
WHOMP
B+$
AH, BRIGITTA! I DO RESPECT YOU FOR ONE FINE TRAIT...
REALLY? REAALLLY?!
YES! YOUR TENACITY!
YOU'VE BEEN WOOING ME FOR HOW MANY YEARS, NOW? IF YOU'D ONLY MIND YOUR OWN BUSINESS INSTEAD OF MINE, I'D RESPECT YOU EVEN MORE!
B+$
BUT... BUT...
BUT NO! YOU KEEP CHASING DREAMS OF MUSH! WAKE UP AND FACE REALITY!
SOB! HEARTBREAKER!
THAT'S ME, ALL RIGHT! AND UNLIKE YOU, BRIGITTA, I KNOW WHEN TO QUIT!
PARDON, SIR...

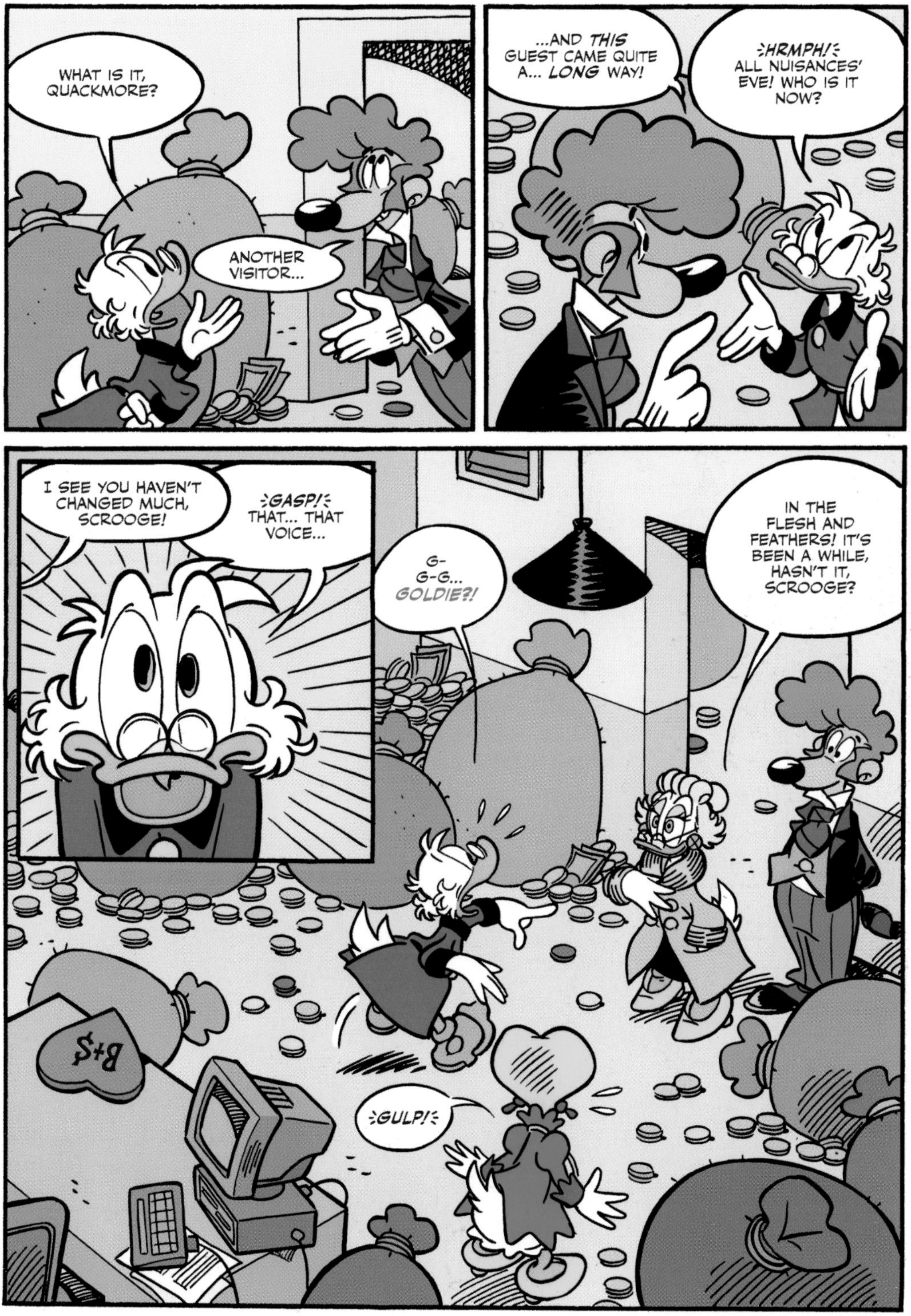

WHAT IS IT, QUACKMORE?
ANOTHER VISITOR...
...AND THIS GUEST CAME QUITE A... LONG WAY!
HRMPH! ALL NUISANCES' EVE! WHO IS IT NOW?
I SEE YOU HAVEN'T CHANGED MUCH, SCROOGE!
GASP! THAT... THAT VOICE...
G- G-G... GOLDIE?!
IN THE FLESH AND FEATHERS! IT'S BEEN A WHILE, HASN'T IT, SCROOGE?
B+$
GULP!

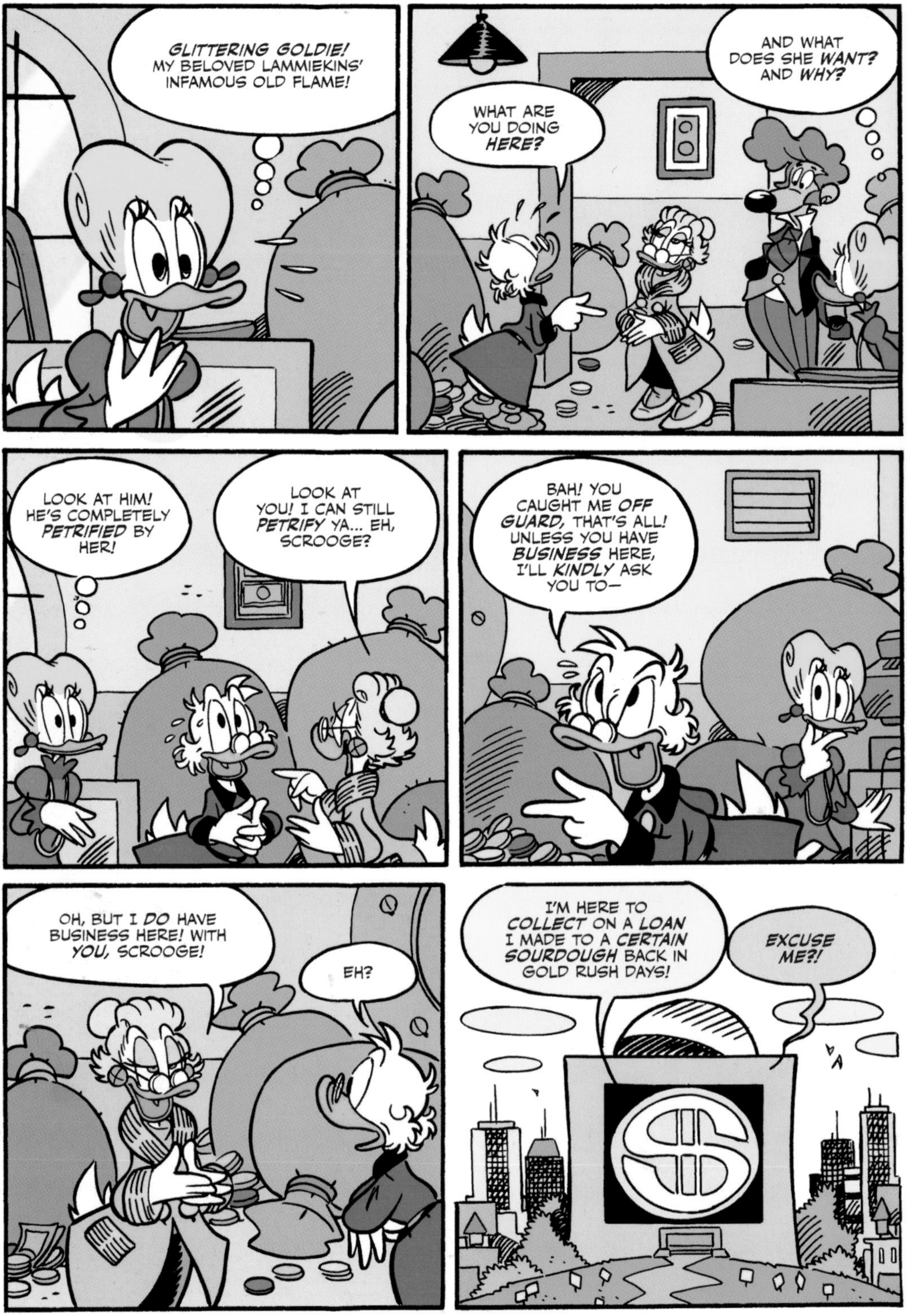
GLITTERING GOLDIE! MY BELOVED LAMMIEKINS' INFAMOUS OLD FLAME!
WHAT ARE YOU DOING HERE?
AND WHAT DOES SHE WANT? AND WHY?
LOOK AT HIM! HE'S COMPLETELY PETRIFIED BY HER!
LOOK AT YOU! I CAN STILL PETRIFY YA... EH, SCROOGE?
BAH! YOU CAUGHT ME OFF GUARD, THAT'S ALL! UNLESS YOU HAVE BUSINESS HERE, I'LL KINDLY ASK YOU TO—
OH, BUT I DO HAVE BUSINESS HERE! WITH YOU, SCROOGE!
EH?
I'M HERE TO COLLECT ON A LOAN I MADE TO A CERTAIN SOURDOUGH BACK IN GOLD RUSH DAYS!
EXCUSE ME?!

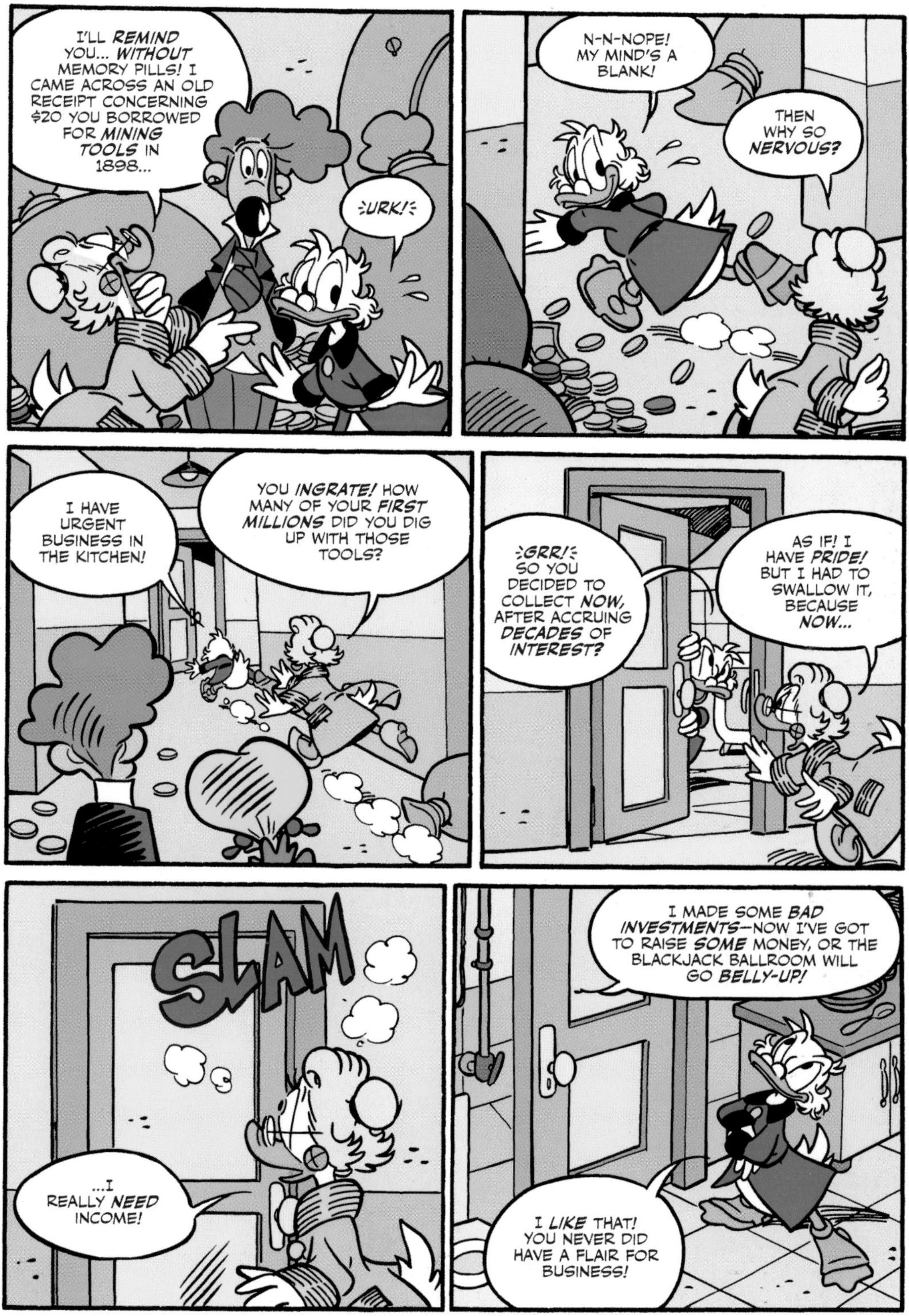
I'LL *REMIND* YOU... *WITHOUT* MEMORY PILLS! I CAME ACROSS AN OLD RECEIPT CONCERNING $20 YOU BORROWED FOR *MINING TOOLS* IN 1898...
URK!
N-N-NOPE! MY MIND'S A BLANK!
THEN WHY SO *NERVOUS?*
I HAVE URGENT BUSINESS IN THE KITCHEN!
YOU *INGRATE!* HOW MANY OF YOUR *FIRST MILLIONS* DID YOU DIG UP WITH THOSE TOOLS?
GRR! SO YOU DECIDED TO COLLECT *NOW,* AFTER ACCRUING *DECADES* OF *INTEREST?*
AS IF! I HAVE *PRIDE!* BUT I HAD TO SWALLOW IT, BECAUSE *NOW...*
SLAM
...I REALLY *NEED* INCOME!
I MADE SOME *BAD INVESTMENTS*—NOW I'VE GOT TO RAISE *SOME* MONEY, OR THE BLACKJACK BALLROOM WILL GO *BELLY-UP!*
I *LIKE* THAT! YOU NEVER DID HAVE A FLAIR FOR BUSINESS!

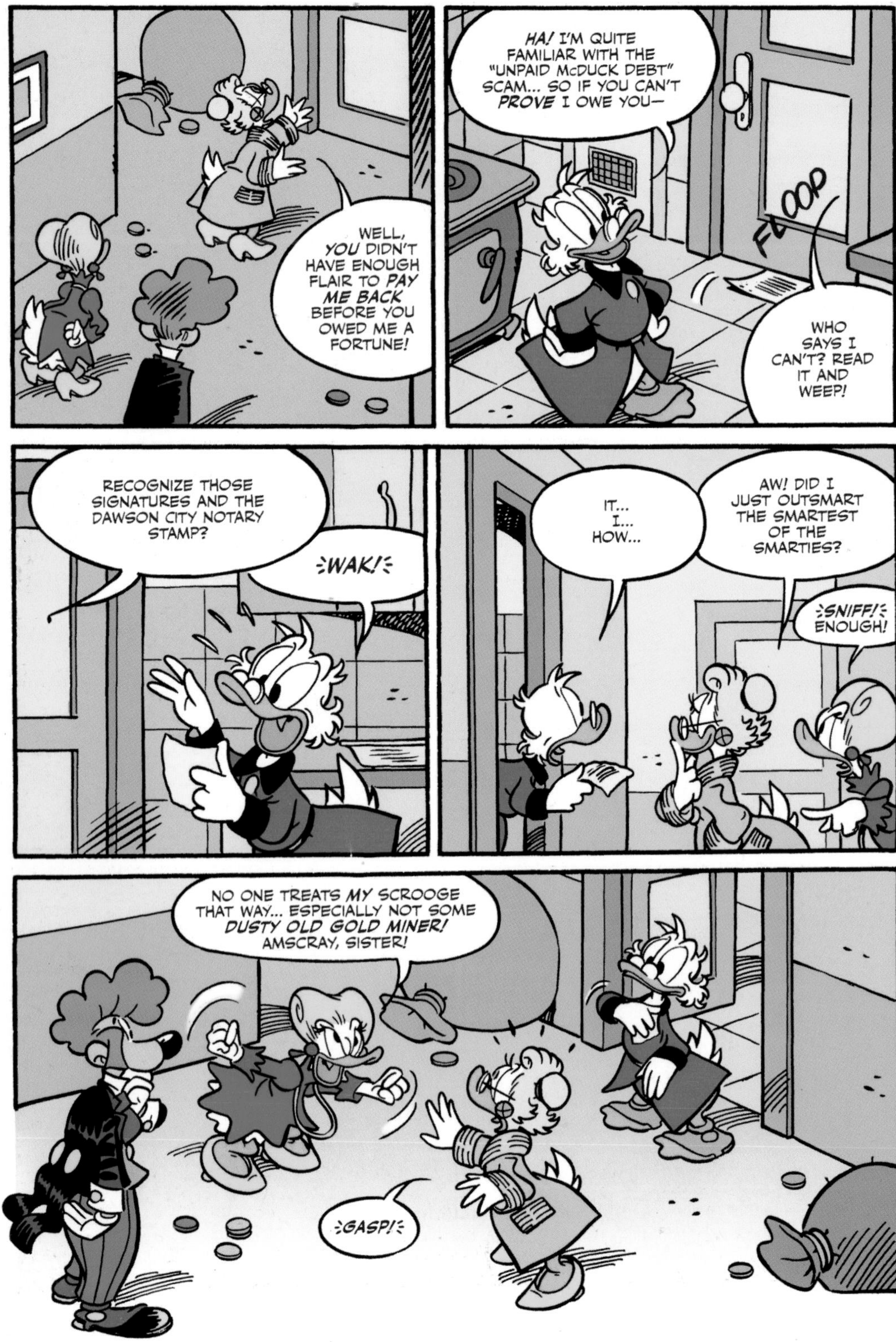
WELL, *YOU* DIDN'T HAVE ENOUGH FLAIR TO *PAY ME BACK* BEFORE YOU OWED ME A FORTUNE!
HA! I'M QUITE FAMILIAR WITH THE "UNPAID McDUCK DEBT" SCAM... SO IF YOU CAN'T *PROVE* I OWE YOU—
FLOOP
WHO SAYS I CAN'T? READ IT AND WEEP!
RECOGNIZE THOSE SIGNATURES AND THE DAWSON CITY NOTARY STAMP?
WAK!
IT... I... HOW...
AW! DID I JUST OUTSMART THE SMARTEST OF THE SMARTIES?
SNIFF! ENOUGH!
NO ONE TREATS *MY* SCROOGE THAT WAY... ESPECIALLY NOT SOME *DUSTY OLD GOLD MINER!* AMSCRAY, SISTER!
GASP!

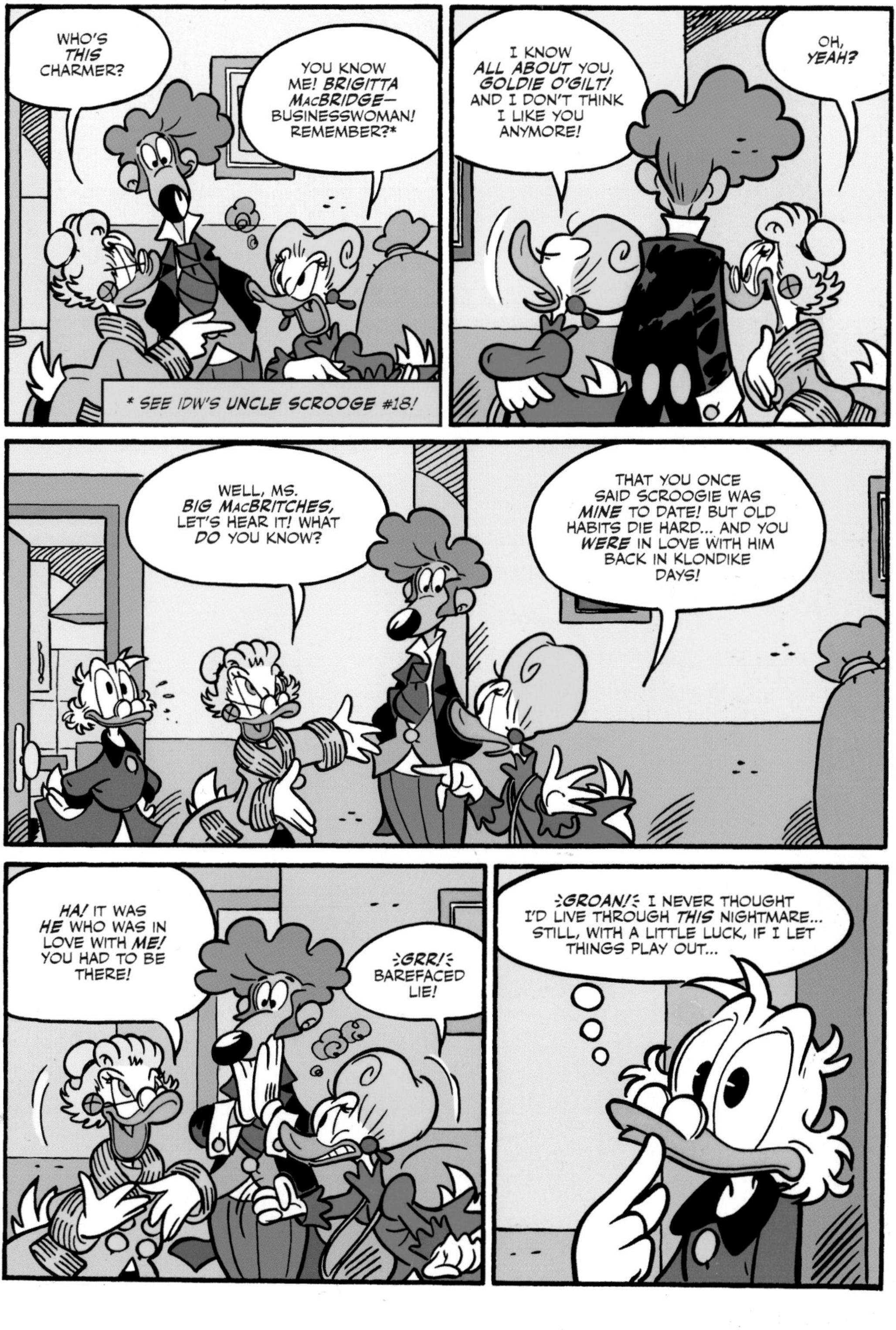

WHO'S *THIS* CHARMER?
YOU KNOW ME! ***BRIGITTA MacBRIDGE***— BUSINESSWOMAN! REMEMBER?*
* SEE IDW'S ***UNCLE SCROOGE #18!***
I KNOW ***ALL ABOUT*** YOU, ***GOLDIE O'GILT!*** AND I DON'T THINK I LIKE YOU ANYMORE!
OH, ***YEAH?***
WELL, MS. ***BIG MacBRITCHES,*** LET'S HEAR IT! WHAT *DO* YOU KNOW?
THAT YOU ONCE SAID SCROOGIE WAS ***MINE*** TO DATE! BUT OLD HABITS DIE HARD... AND YOU ***WERE*** IN LOVE WITH HIM BACK IN KLONDIKE DAYS!
HA! IT WAS ***HE*** WHO WAS IN LOVE WITH ***ME!*** YOU HAD TO BE THERE!
GRR! BAREFACED LIE!
GROAN! I NEVER THOUGHT I'D LIVE THROUGH ***THIS*** NIGHTMARE... STILL, WITH A LITTLE LUCK, IF I LET THINGS PLAY OUT...

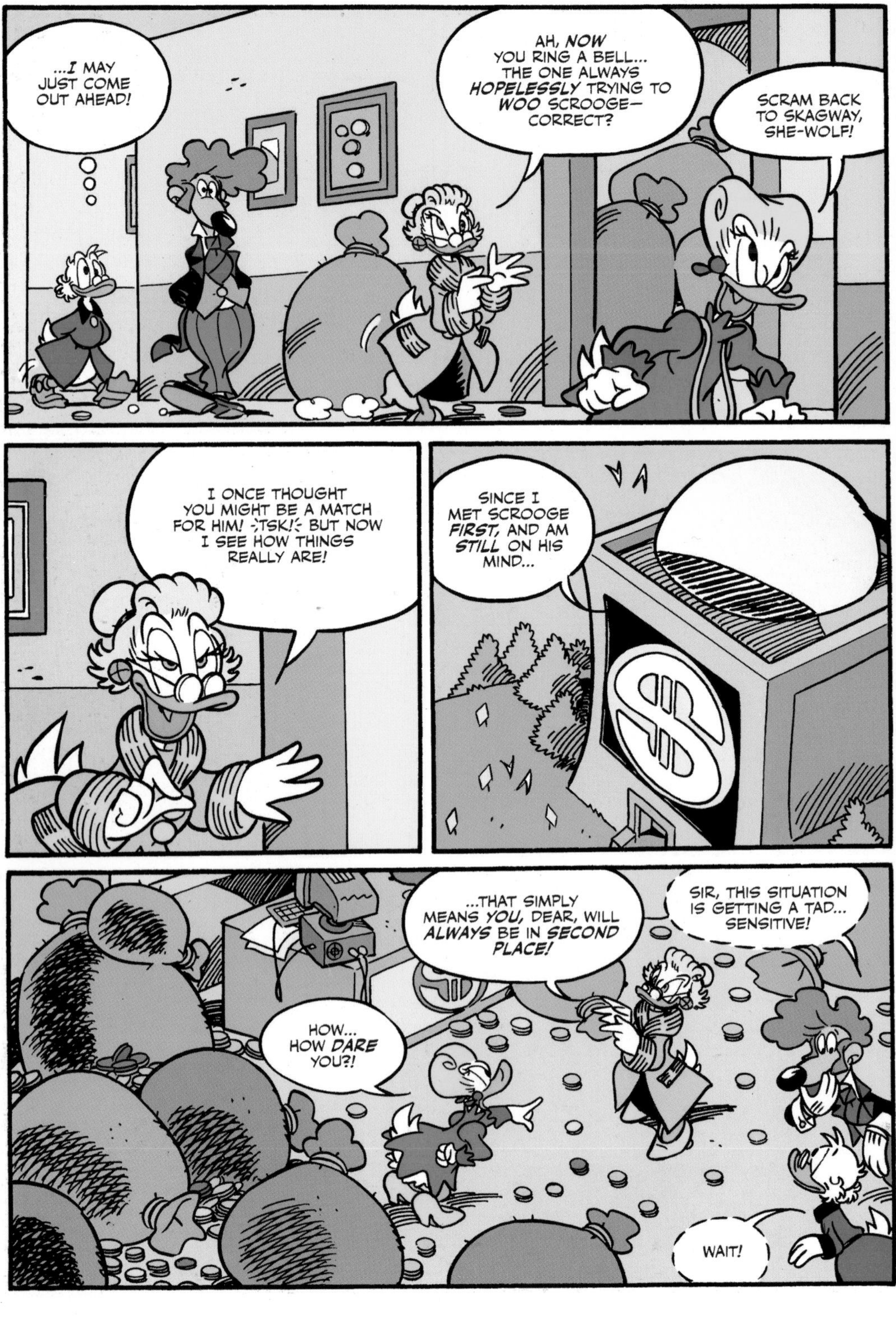
...I MAY JUST COME OUT AHEAD!
AH, NOW YOU RING A BELL... THE ONE ALWAYS HOPELESSLY TRYING TO WOO SCROOGE— CORRECT?
SCRAM BACK TO SKAGWAY, SHE-WOLF!
I ONCE THOUGHT YOU MIGHT BE A MATCH FOR HIM! -TSK!- BUT NOW I SEE HOW THINGS REALLY ARE!
SINCE I MET SCROOGE FIRST, AND AM STILL ON HIS MIND...
...THAT SIMPLY MEANS YOU, DEAR, WILL ALWAYS BE IN SECOND PLACE!
SIR, THIS SITUATION IS GETTING A TAD... SENSITIVE!
HOW... HOW DARE YOU?!
WAIT!

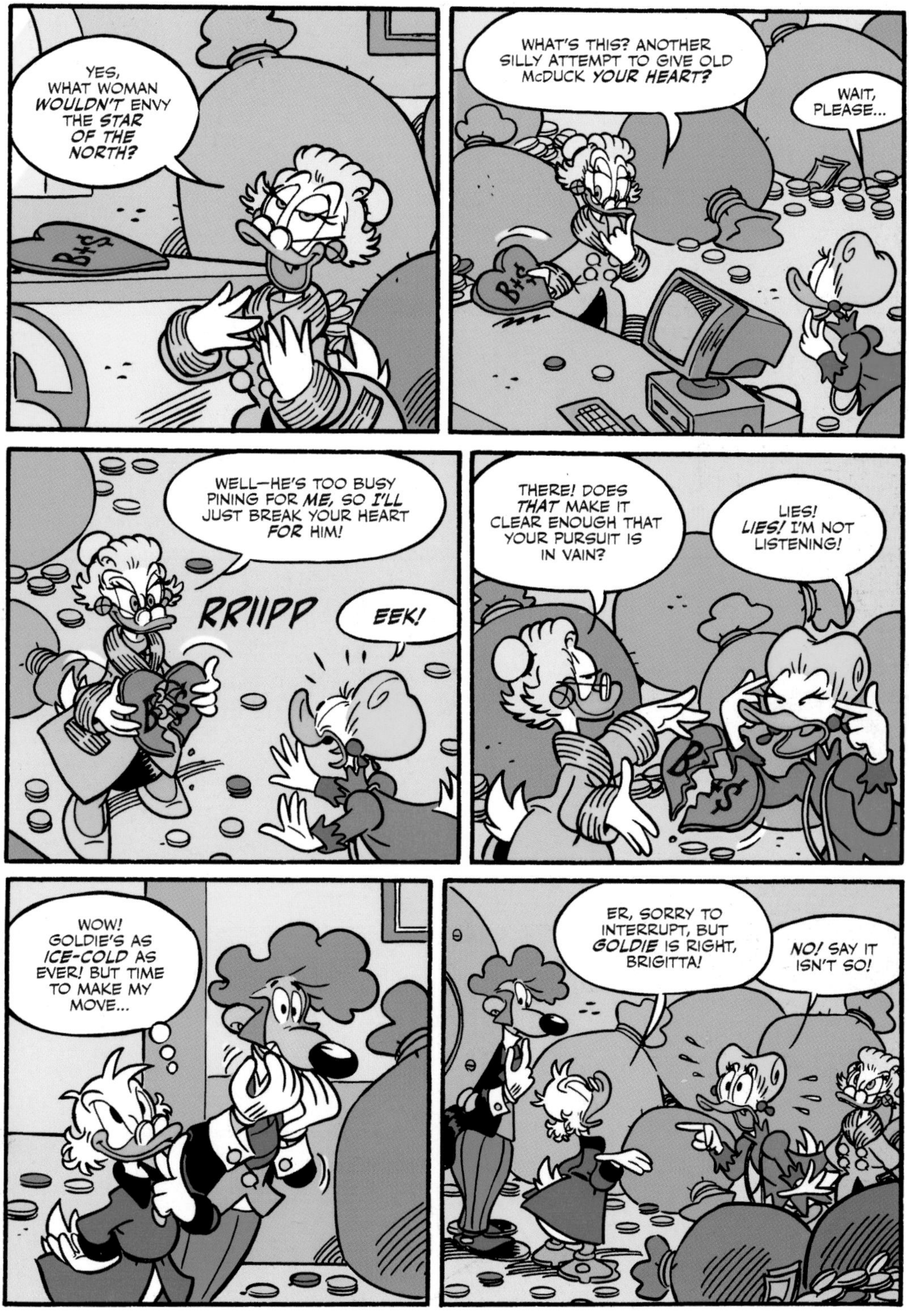
YES, WHAT WOMAN WOULDN'T ENVY THE STAR OF THE NORTH?
WHAT'S THIS? ANOTHER SILLY ATTEMPT TO GIVE OLD McDUCK YOUR HEART?
WAIT, PLEASE...
WELL—HE'S TOO BUSY PINING FOR ME, SO I'LL JUST BREAK YOUR HEART FOR HIM!
RRIIPP
EEK!
THERE! DOES THAT MAKE IT CLEAR ENOUGH THAT YOUR PURSUIT IS IN VAIN?
LIES! LIES! I'M NOT LISTENING!
WOW! GOLDIE'S AS ICE-COLD AS EVER! BUT TIME TO MAKE MY MOVE...
ER, SORRY TO INTERRUPT, BUT GOLDIE IS RIGHT, BRIGITTA!
NO! SAY IT ISN'T SO!

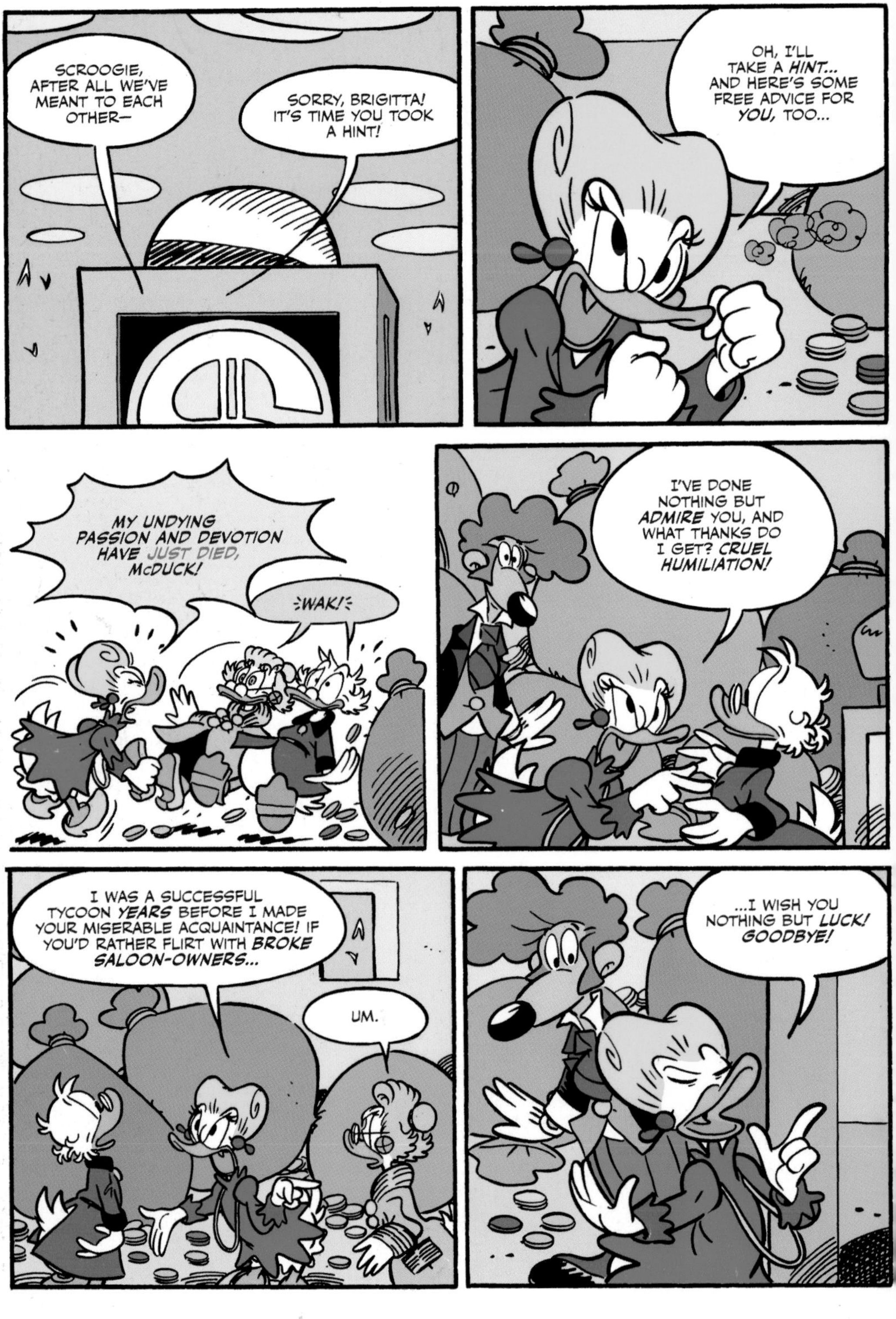
SCROOGIE, AFTER ALL WE'VE MEANT TO EACH OTHER—
SORRY, BRIGITTA! IT'S TIME YOU TOOK A HINT!
OH, I'LL TAKE A HINT... AND HERE'S SOME FREE ADVICE FOR YOU, TOO...
MY UNDYING PASSION AND DEVOTION HAVE JUST DIED, McDUCK!
WAK!
I'VE DONE NOTHING BUT ADMIRE YOU, AND WHAT THANKS DO I GET? CRUEL HUMILIATION!
I WAS A SUCCESSFUL TYCOON YEARS BEFORE I MADE YOUR MISERABLE ACQUAINTANCE! IF YOU'D RATHER FLIRT WITH BROKE SALOON-OWNERS...
UM.
...I WISH YOU NOTHING BUT LUCK! GOODBYE!

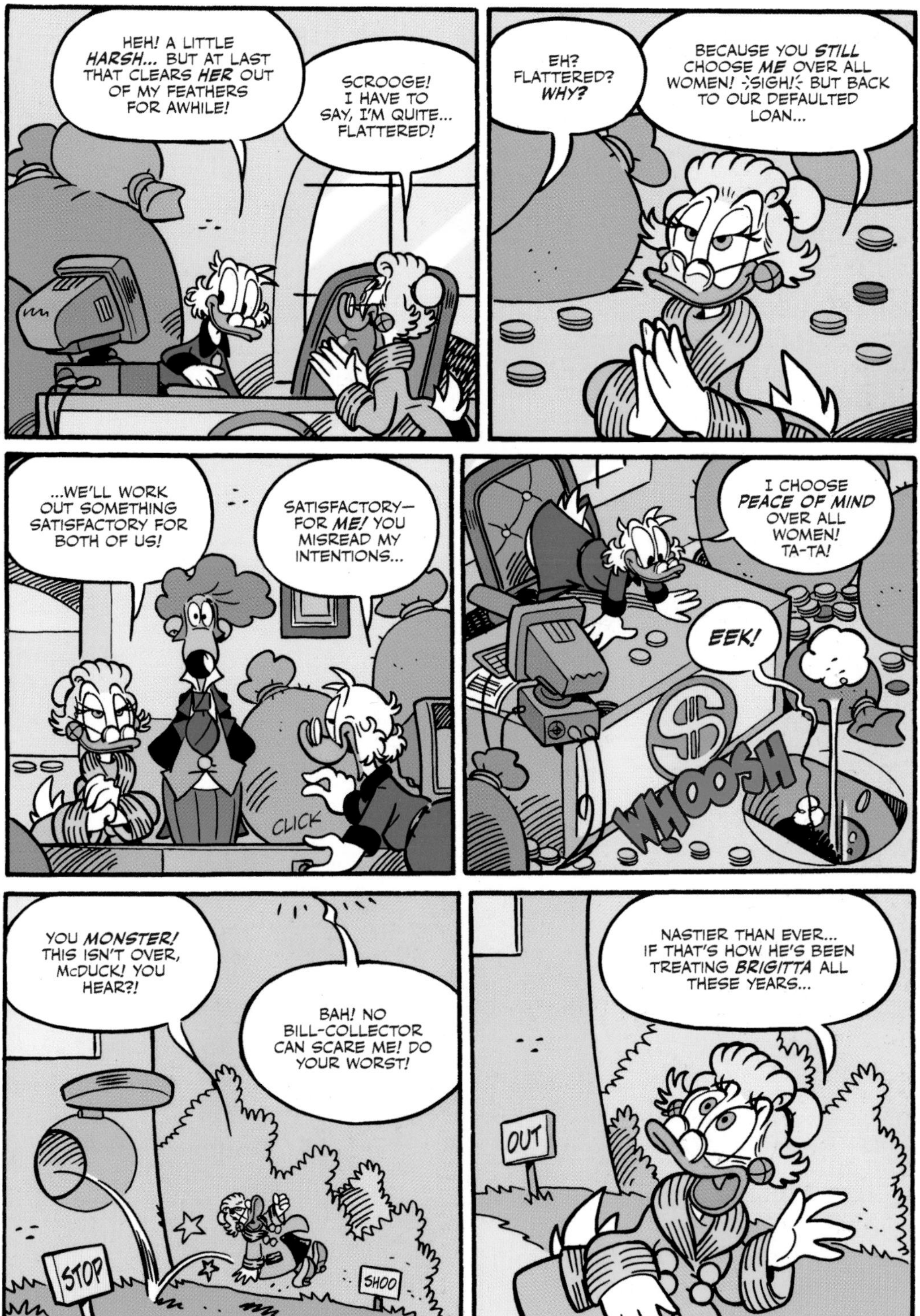

HEH! A LITTLE HARSH... BUT AT LAST THAT CLEARS HER OUT OF MY FEATHERS FOR AWHILE!
SCROOGE! I HAVE TO SAY, I'M QUITE... FLATTERED!
EH? FLATTERED? WHY?
BECAUSE YOU STILL CHOOSE ME OVER ALL WOMEN! -SIGH!- BUT BACK TO OUR DEFAULTED LOAN...
...WE'LL WORK OUT SOMETHING SATISFACTORY FOR BOTH OF US!
SATISFACTORY— FOR ME! YOU MISREAD MY INTENTIONS...
CLICK
I CHOOSE PEACE OF MIND OVER ALL WOMEN! TA-TA!
EEK!
WHOOSH
YOU MONSTER! THIS ISN'T OVER, McDUCK! YOU HEAR?!
BAH! NO BILL-COLLECTOR CAN SCARE ME! DO YOUR WORST!
STOP
SHOO
NASTIER THAN EVER... IF THAT'S HOW HE'S BEEN TREATING BRIGITTA ALL THESE YEARS...
OUT

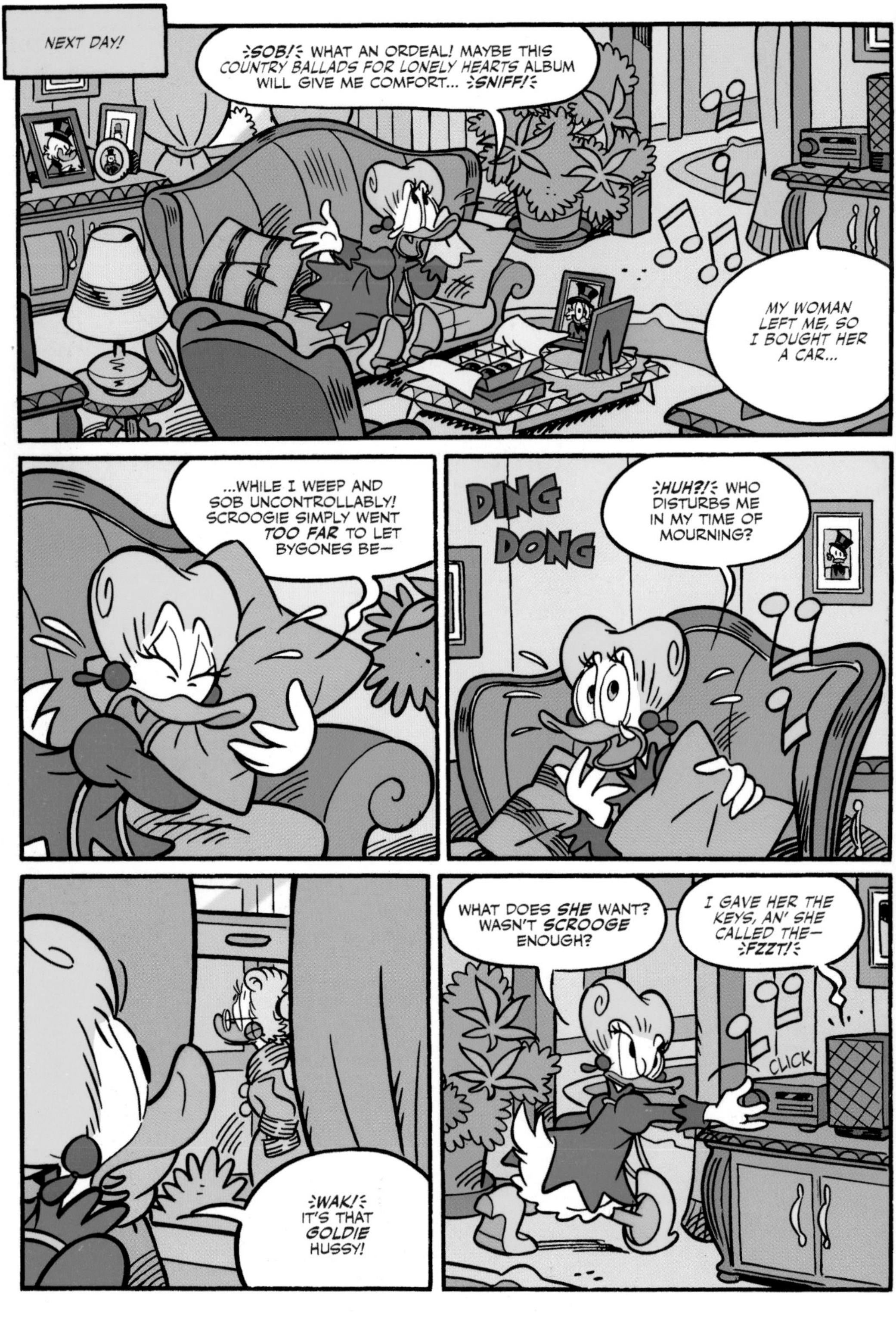
NEXT DAY!
SOB! WHAT AN ORDEAL! MAYBE THIS COUNTRY BALLADS FOR LONELY HEARTS ALBUM WILL GIVE ME COMFORT... *SNIFF!*
MY WOMAN LEFT ME, SO I BOUGHT HER A CAR...
...WHILE I WEEP AND SOB UNCONTROLLABLY! SCROOGIE SIMPLY WENT TOO FAR TO LET BYGONES BE—
DING DONG
HUH?! WHO DISTURBS ME IN MY TIME OF MOURNING?
WAK! IT'S THAT GOLDIE HUSSY!
WHAT DOES SHE WANT? WASN'T SCROOGE ENOUGH?
I GAVE HER THE KEYS, AN' SHE CALLED THE— *FZZT!*
CLICK

BRIGITTA! IT TOOK ME A WHILE TO LOOK YOU UP...

OH! HERE TO *RUB IT IN*, HUH? DON'T GET ME SORE, I TELL YA!

YOU HAVE EVERY RIGHT TO BE ANGRY... I'M HERE TO APOLOGIZE!

WHY SHOULD I BELIEVE *YOU?*

LOOK, I WAS AN ABSOLUTE *BRAT!* I ADMIT IT! I LOST MY HEAD BACK THERE... SCROOGE CAN HAVE THAT EFFECT...

HRMPH...

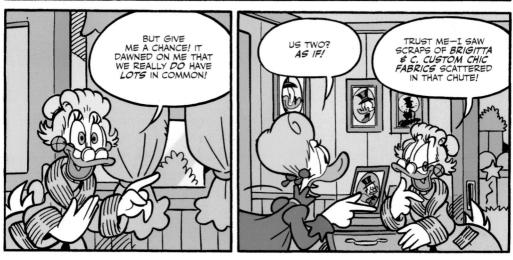

BUT GIVE ME A CHANCE! IT DAWNED ON ME THAT WE REALLY *DO* HAVE *LOTS* IN COMMON!

US TWO? *AS IF!*

TRUST ME—I SAW SCRAPS OF *BRIGITTA & C.* CUSTOM *CHIC FABRICS* SCATTERED IN THAT CHUTE!

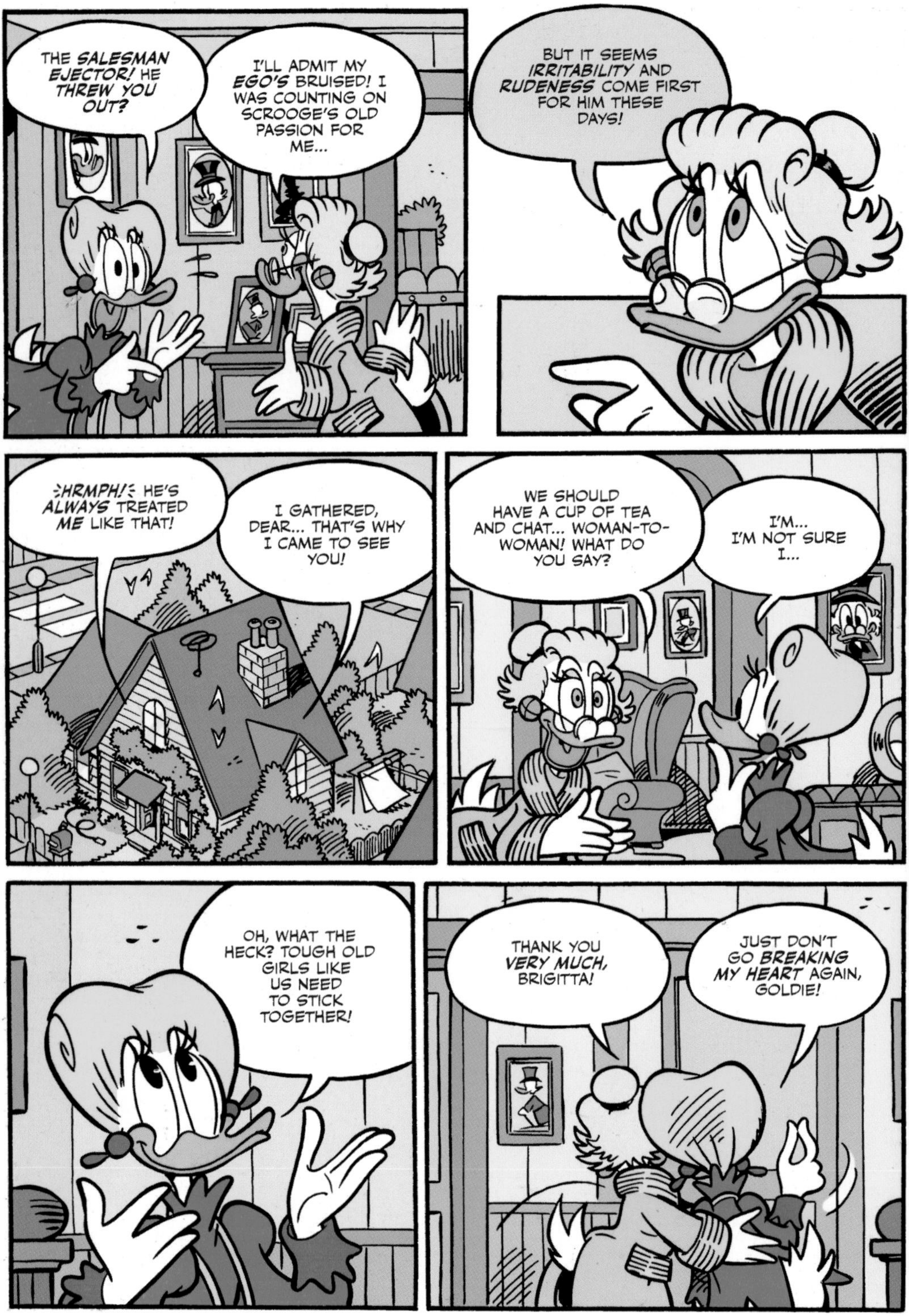
THE SALESMAN EJECTOR! HE THREW YOU OUT?
I'LL ADMIT MY EGO'S BRUISED! I WAS COUNTING ON SCROOGE'S OLD PASSION FOR ME...
BUT IT SEEMS IRRITABILITY AND RUDENESS COME FIRST FOR HIM THESE DAYS!
HRMPH! HE'S ALWAYS TREATED ME LIKE THAT!
I GATHERED, DEAR... THAT'S WHY I CAME TO SEE YOU!
WE SHOULD HAVE A CUP OF TEA AND CHAT... WOMAN-TO-WOMAN! WHAT DO YOU SAY?
I'M... I'M NOT SURE I...
OH, WHAT THE HECK? TOUGH OLD GIRLS LIKE US NEED TO STICK TOGETHER!
THANK YOU VERY MUCH, BRIGITTA!
JUST DON'T GO BREAKING MY HEART AGAIN, GOLDIE!

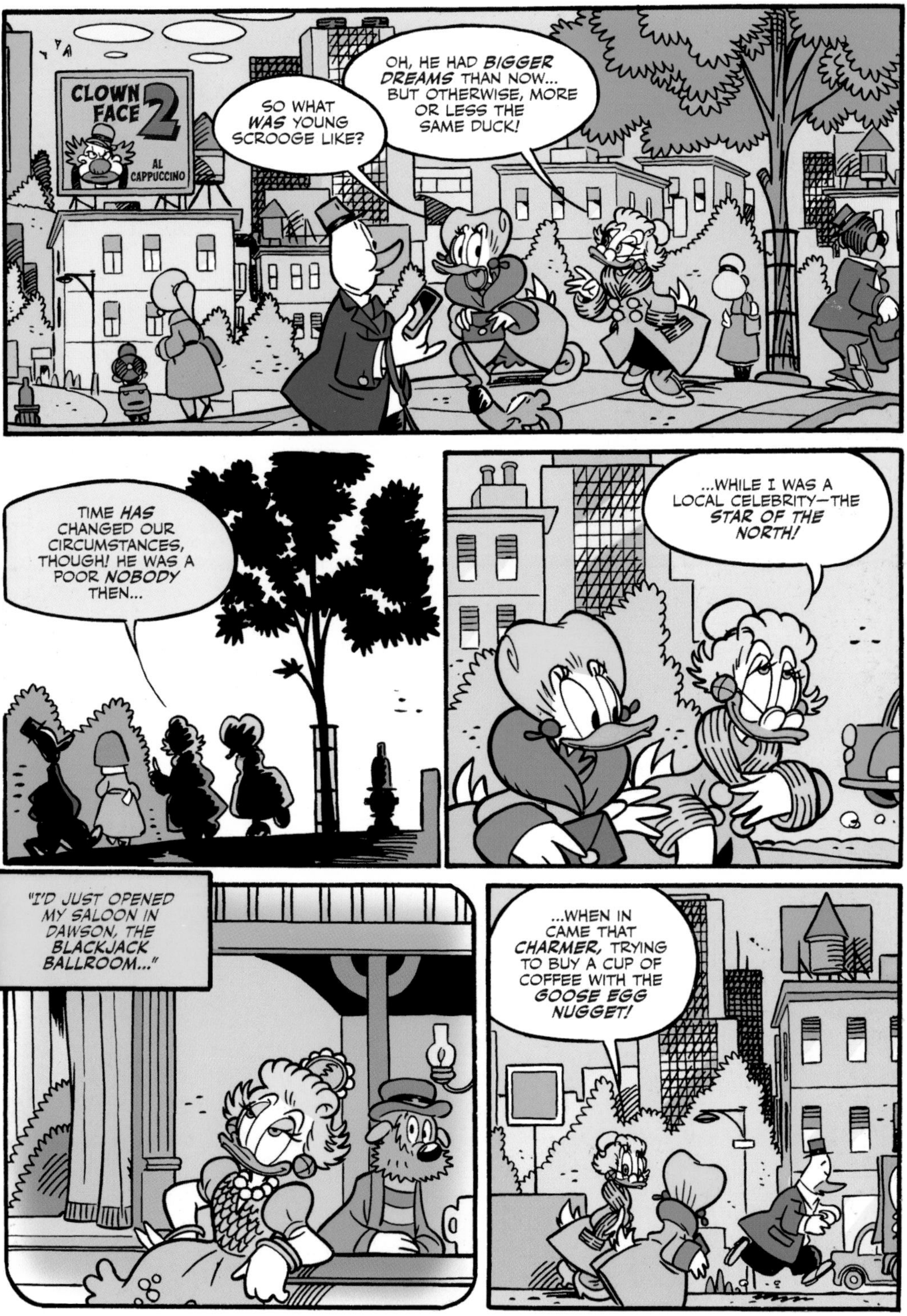
CLOWN FACE 2
AL CAPPUCCINO
SO WHAT *WAS* YOUNG SCROOGE LIKE?
OH, HE HAD *BIGGER DREAMS* THAN NOW... BUT OTHERWISE, MORE OR LESS THE SAME DUCK!
TIME *HAS* CHANGED OUR CIRCUMSTANCES, THOUGH! HE WAS A POOR *NOBODY* THEN...
...WHILE I WAS A LOCAL CELEBRITY—THE *STAR OF THE NORTH!*
"I'D JUST OPENED MY SALOON IN DAWSON, THE *BLACKJACK BALLROOM...*"
...WHEN IN CAME THAT *CHARMER,* TRYING TO BUY A CUP OF COFFEE WITH THE *GOOSE EGG NUGGET!*

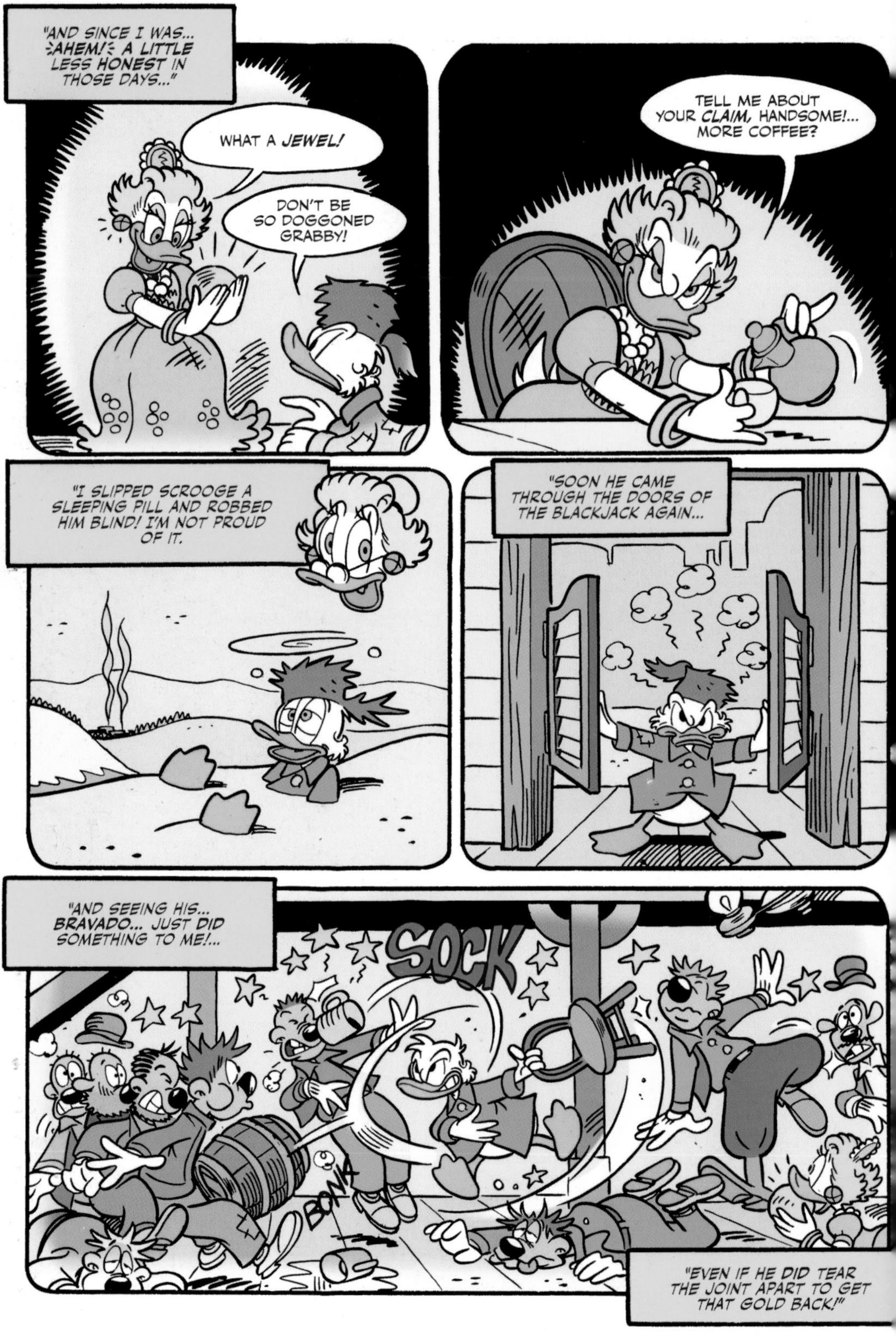
"AND SINCE I WAS... AHEM! A LITTLE LESS HONEST IN THOSE DAYS..."
WHAT A JEWEL!
DON'T BE SO DOGGONED GRABBY!
TELL ME ABOUT YOUR CLAIM, HANDSOME!... MORE COFFEE?
"I SLIPPED SCROOGE A SLEEPING PILL AND ROBBED HIM BLIND! I'M NOT PROUD OF IT.
"SOON HE CAME THROUGH THE DOORS OF THE BLACKJACK AGAIN...
"AND SEEING HIS... BRAVADO... JUST DID SOMETHING TO ME!...
SOCK
BONK
"EVEN IF HE DID TEAR THE JOINT APART TO GET THAT GOLD BACK!"

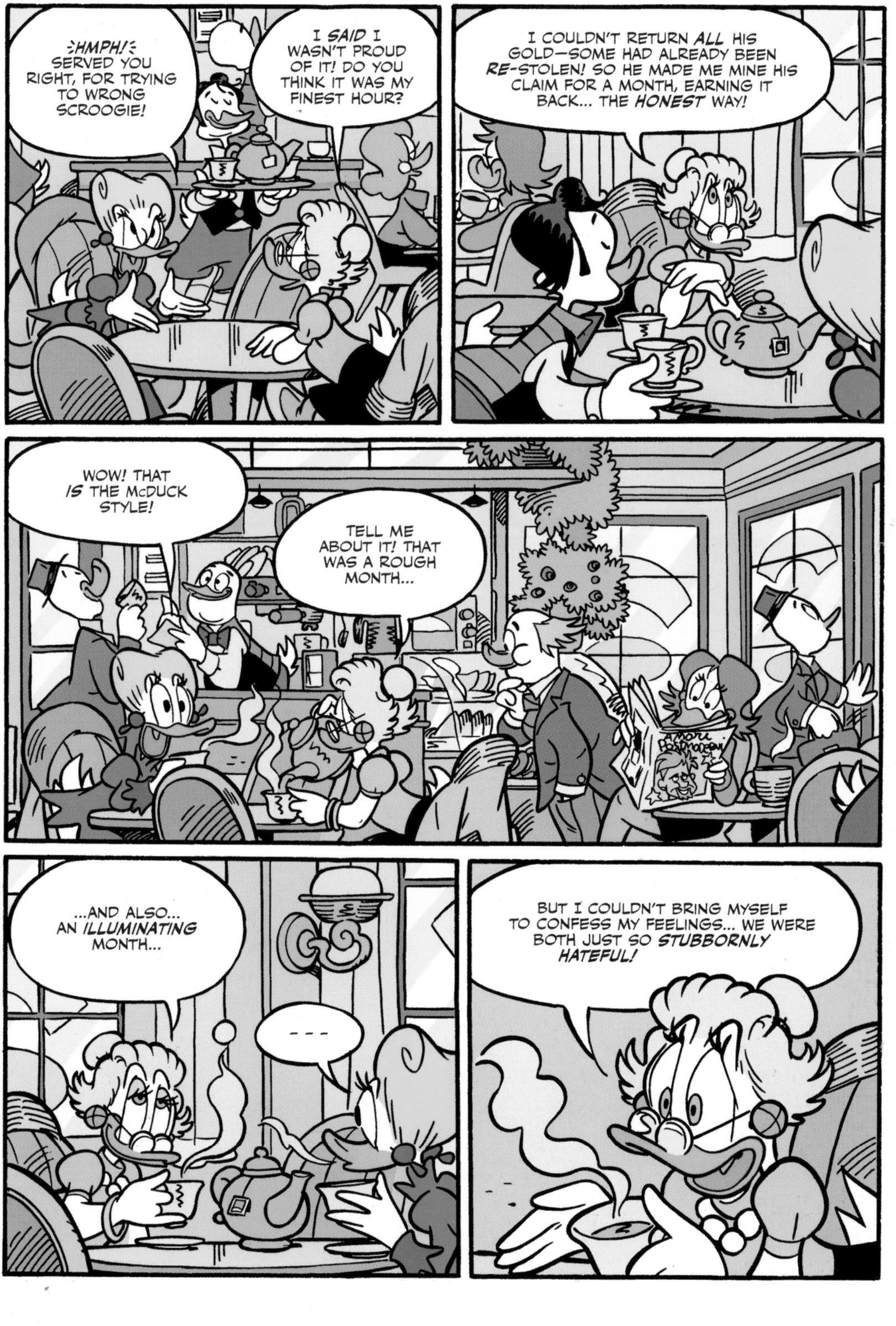
HMPH! SERVED YOU RIGHT, FOR TRYING TO WRONG SCROOGIE!
I SAID I WASN'T PROUD OF IT! DO YOU THINK IT WAS MY FINEST HOUR?
I COULDN'T RETURN ALL HIS GOLD—SOME HAD ALREADY BEEN RE-STOLEN! SO HE MADE ME MINE HIS CLAIM FOR A MONTH, EARNING IT BACK... THE HONEST WAY!
WOW! THAT IS THE McDUCK STYLE!
TELL ME ABOUT IT! THAT WAS A ROUGH MONTH...
...AND ALSO... AN ILLUMINATING MONTH...
- - -
BUT I COULDN'T BRING MYSELF TO CONFESS MY FEELINGS... WE WERE BOTH JUST SO STUBBORNLY HATEFUL!

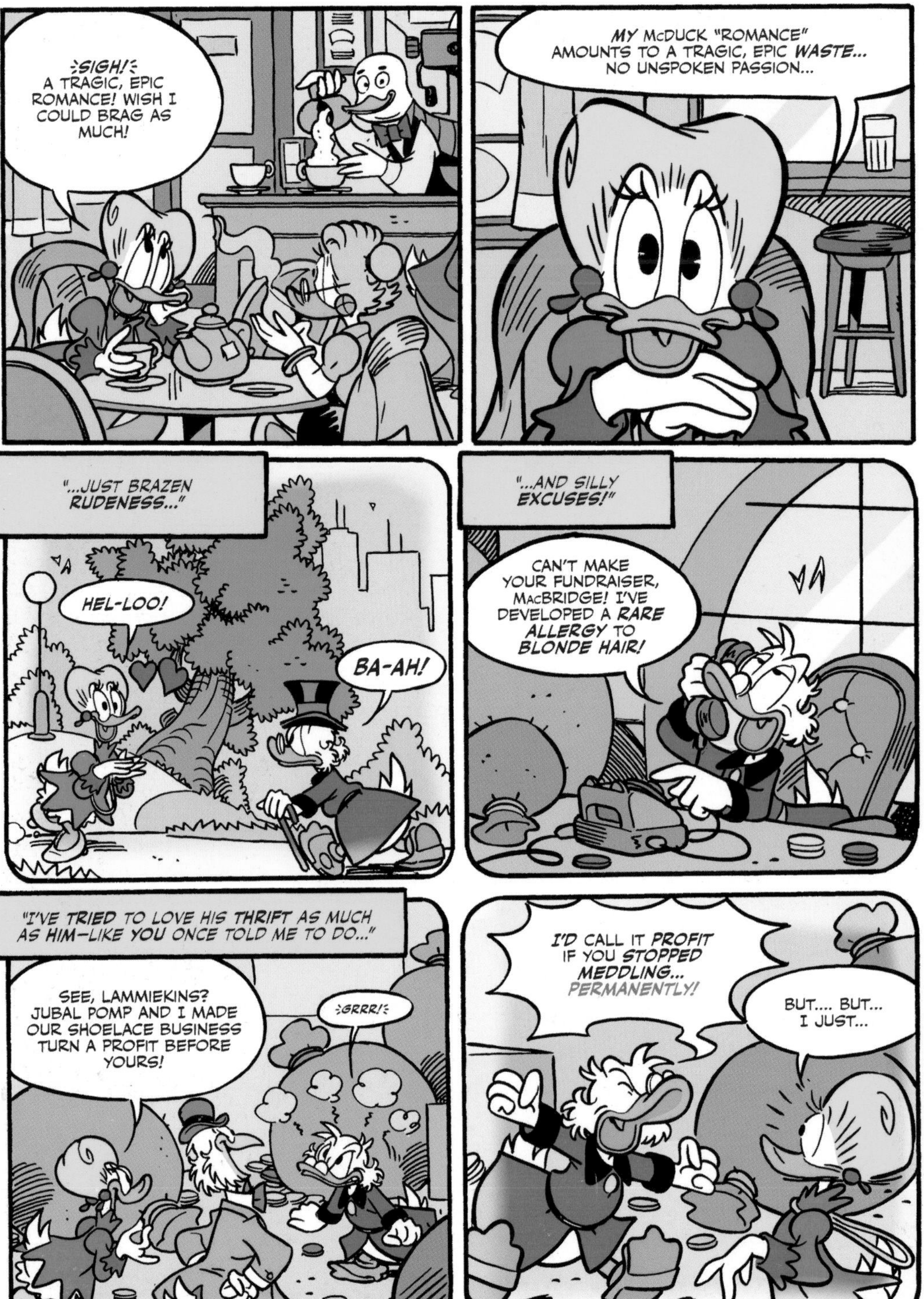
:SIGH!: A TRAGIC, EPIC ROMANCE! WISH I COULD BRAG AS MUCH!
MY McDUCK "ROMANCE" AMOUNTS TO A TRAGIC, EPIC WASTE... NO UNSPOKEN PASSION...
"...JUST BRAZEN RUDENESS..."
HEL-LOO!
BA-AH!
"...AND SILLY EXCUSES!"
CAN'T MAKE YOUR FUNDRAISER, MACBRIDGE! I'VE DEVELOPED A RARE ALLERGY TO BLONDE HAIR!
"I'VE TRIED TO LOVE HIS THRIFT AS MUCH AS HIM—LIKE YOU ONCE TOLD ME TO DO..."
SEE, LAMMIEKINS? JUBAL POMP AND I MADE OUR SHOELACE BUSINESS TURN A PROFIT BEFORE YOURS!
:GRRR!:
I'D CALL IT PROFIT IF YOU STOPPED MEDDLING... PERMANENTLY!
BUT.... BUT... I JUST...

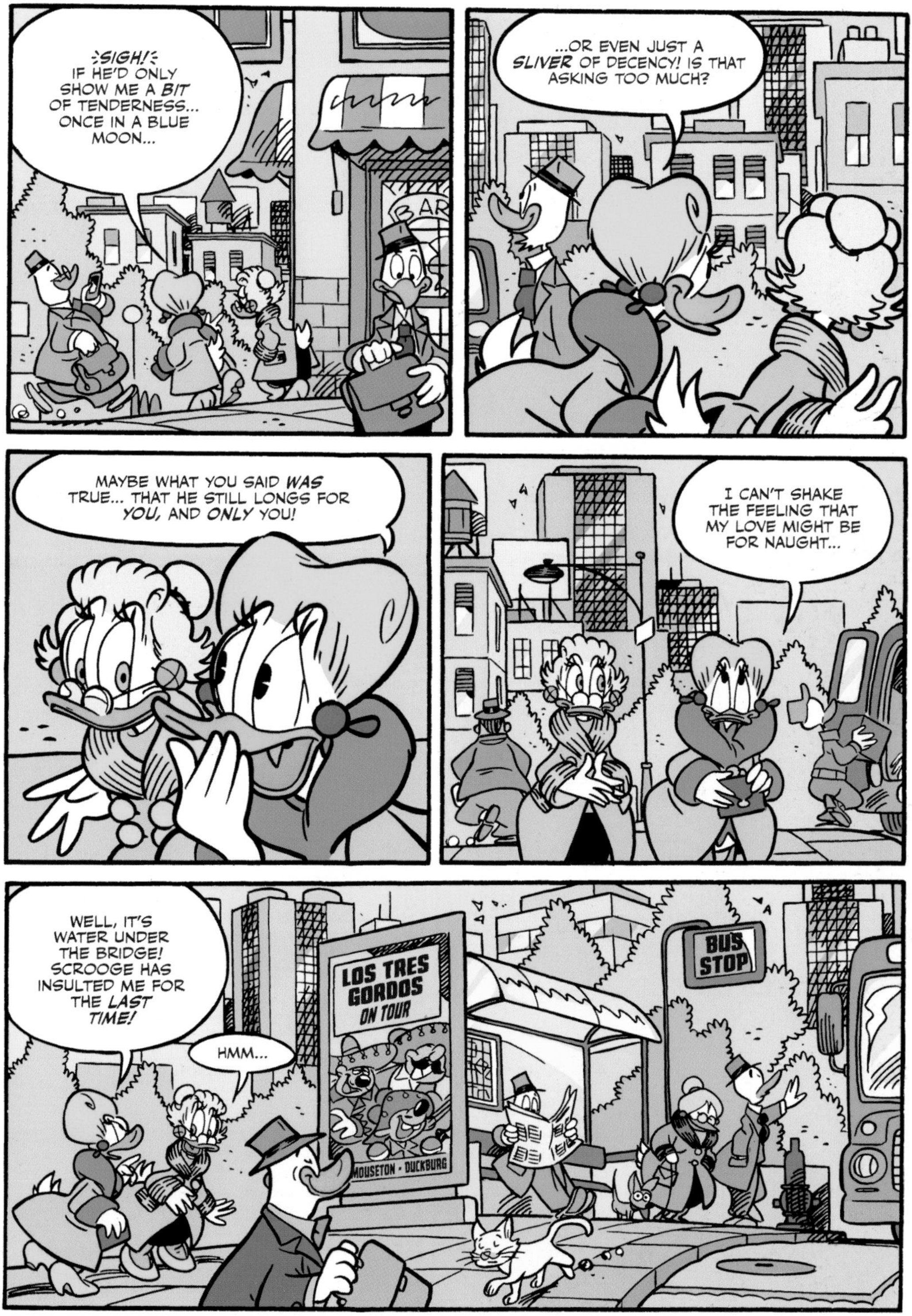

SIGH!
IF HE'D ONLY SHOW ME A BIT OF TENDERNESS... ONCE IN A BLUE MOON...
BAR
...OR EVEN JUST A SLIVER OF DECENCY! IS THAT ASKING TOO MUCH?
MAYBE WHAT YOU SAID WAS TRUE... THAT HE STILL LONGS FOR YOU, AND ONLY YOU!
I CAN'T SHAKE THE FEELING THAT MY LOVE MIGHT BE FOR NAUGHT...
WELL, IT'S WATER UNDER THE BRIDGE! SCROOGE HAS INSULTED ME FOR THE LAST TIME!
HMM...
LOS TRES GORDOS ON TOUR
MOUSETON • DUCKBURG
BUS STOP

FROM NOW ON, I REFOCUS... LIFE IS *STRICTLY BUSINESS!* AND IF I MEET A MAN *WORTHY* OF ME ALONG THE WAY—

MM-HMM...

KNOW WHAT I THINK, BRIGITTA?

NO... WHAT?

THAT'S GOING TOO FAR! YOU'VE MADE TYCOON HEADLINES FOR YEARS! YOU ALWAYS *WILL BE* A GENIUS BUSINESSWOMAN!

OH!

BUT... GET OVER IT, GIRL! YOU'LL *ALSO ALWAYS* BE SMITTEN WITH ONE MR. McDUCK!

NO, NO...!

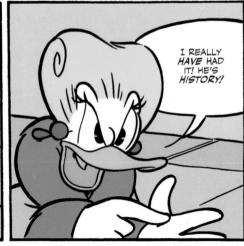

I REALLY *HAVE* HAD IT! HE'S *HISTORY!*

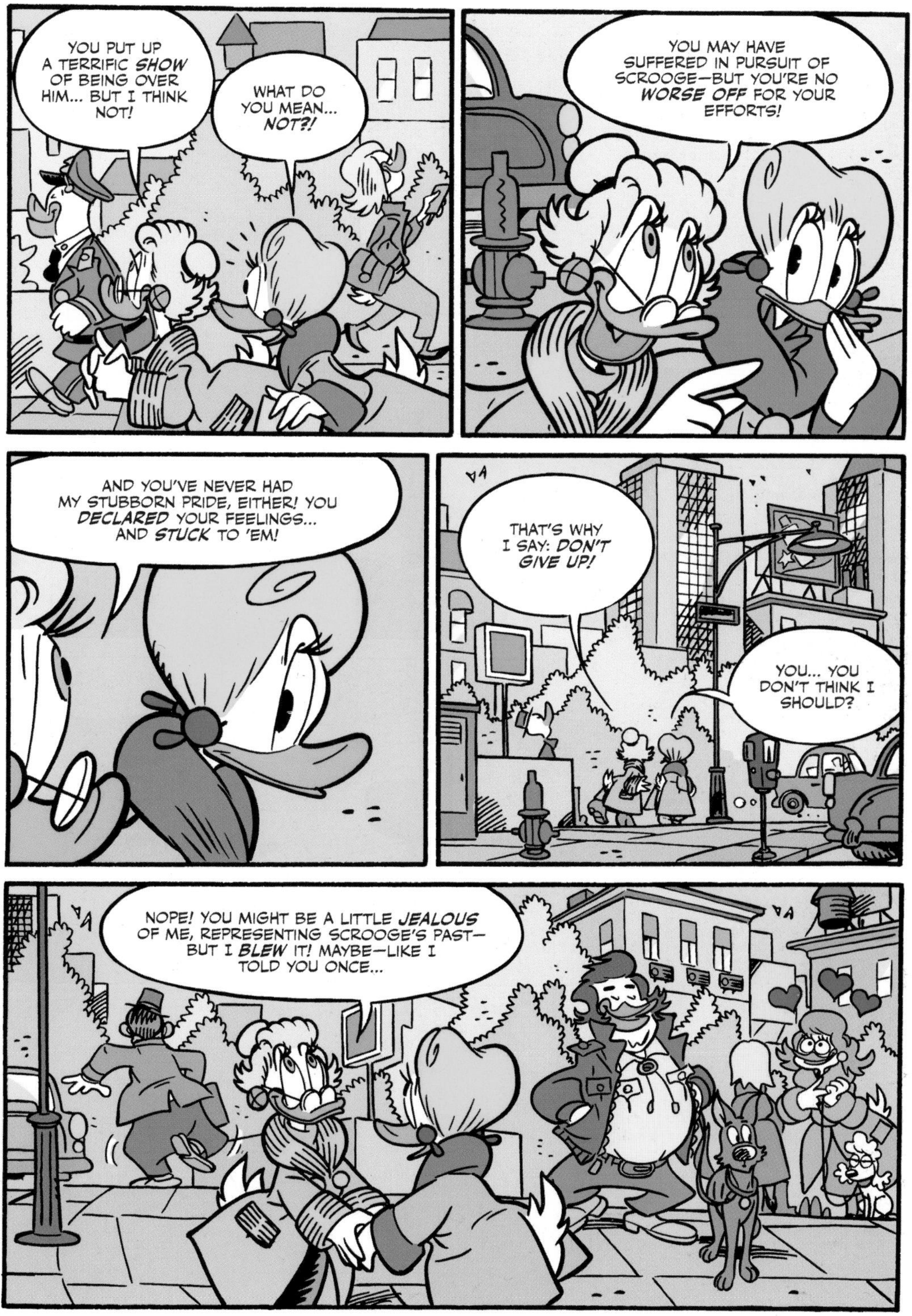
YOU PUT UP A TERRIFIC SHOW OF BEING OVER HIM... BUT I THINK NOT!
WHAT DO YOU MEAN... NOT?!
YOU MAY HAVE SUFFERED IN PURSUIT OF SCROOGE—BUT YOU'RE NO WORSE OFF FOR YOUR EFFORTS!
AND YOU'VE NEVER HAD MY STUBBORN PRIDE, EITHER! YOU DECLARED YOUR FEELINGS... AND STUCK TO 'EM!
THAT'S WHY I SAY: DON'T GIVE UP!
YOU... YOU DON'T THINK I SHOULD?
NOPE! YOU MIGHT BE A LITTLE JEALOUS OF ME, REPRESENTING SCROOGE'S PAST—BUT I BLEW IT! MAYBE—LIKE I TOLD YOU ONCE...

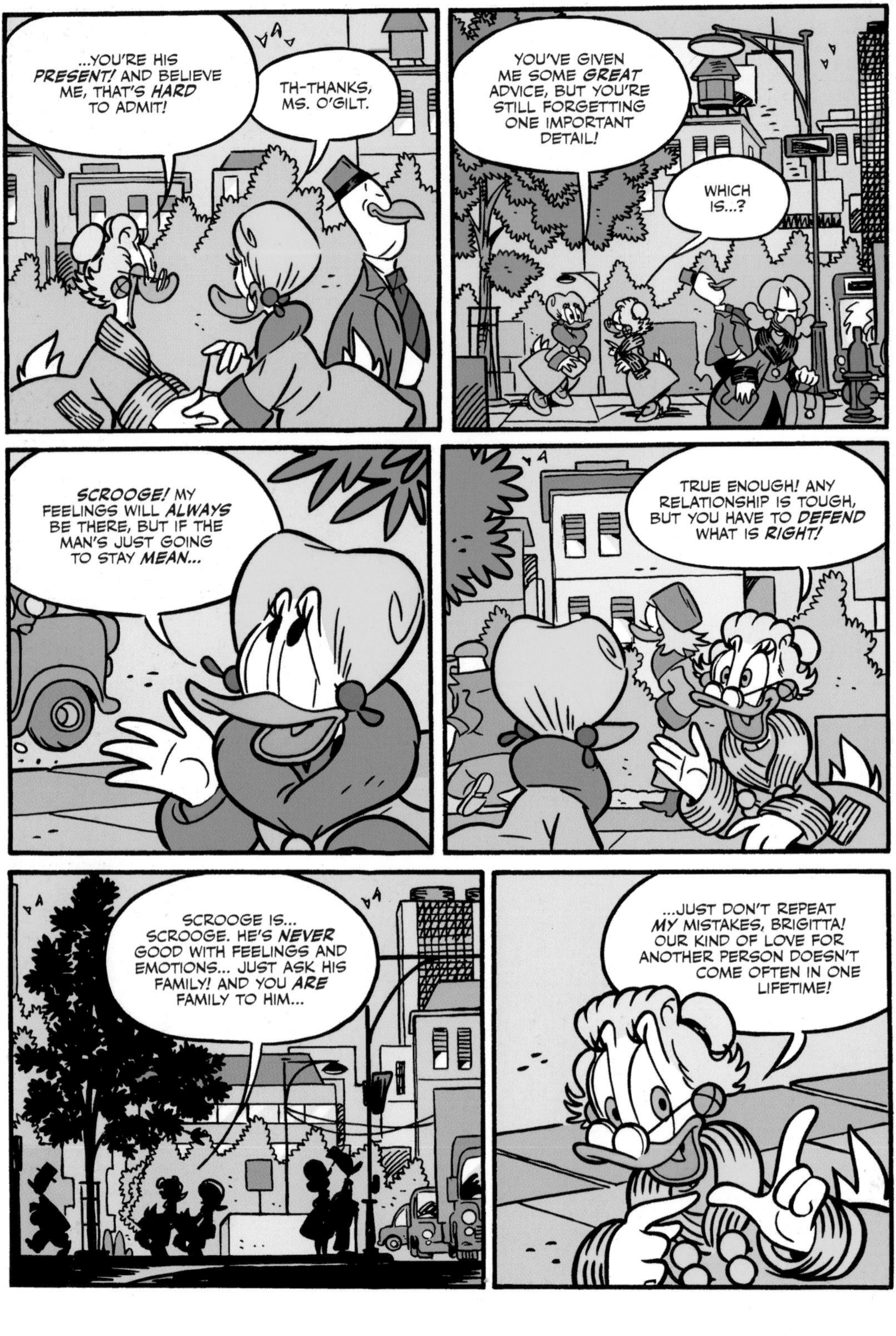
...YOU'RE HIS PRESENT! AND BELIEVE ME, THAT'S HARD TO ADMIT!
TH-THANKS, MS. O'GILT.
YOU'VE GIVEN ME SOME GREAT ADVICE, BUT YOU'RE STILL FORGETTING ONE IMPORTANT DETAIL!
WHICH IS...?
SCROOGE! MY FEELINGS WILL ALWAYS BE THERE, BUT IF THE MAN'S JUST GOING TO STAY MEAN...
TRUE ENOUGH! ANY RELATIONSHIP IS TOUGH, BUT YOU HAVE TO DEFEND WHAT IS RIGHT!
SCROOGE IS... SCROOGE. HE'S NEVER GOOD WITH FEELINGS AND EMOTIONS... JUST ASK HIS FAMILY! AND YOU ARE FAMILY TO HIM...
...JUST DON'T REPEAT MY MISTAKES, BRIGITTA! OUR KIND OF LOVE FOR ANOTHER PERSON DOESN'T COME OFTEN IN ONE LIFETIME!

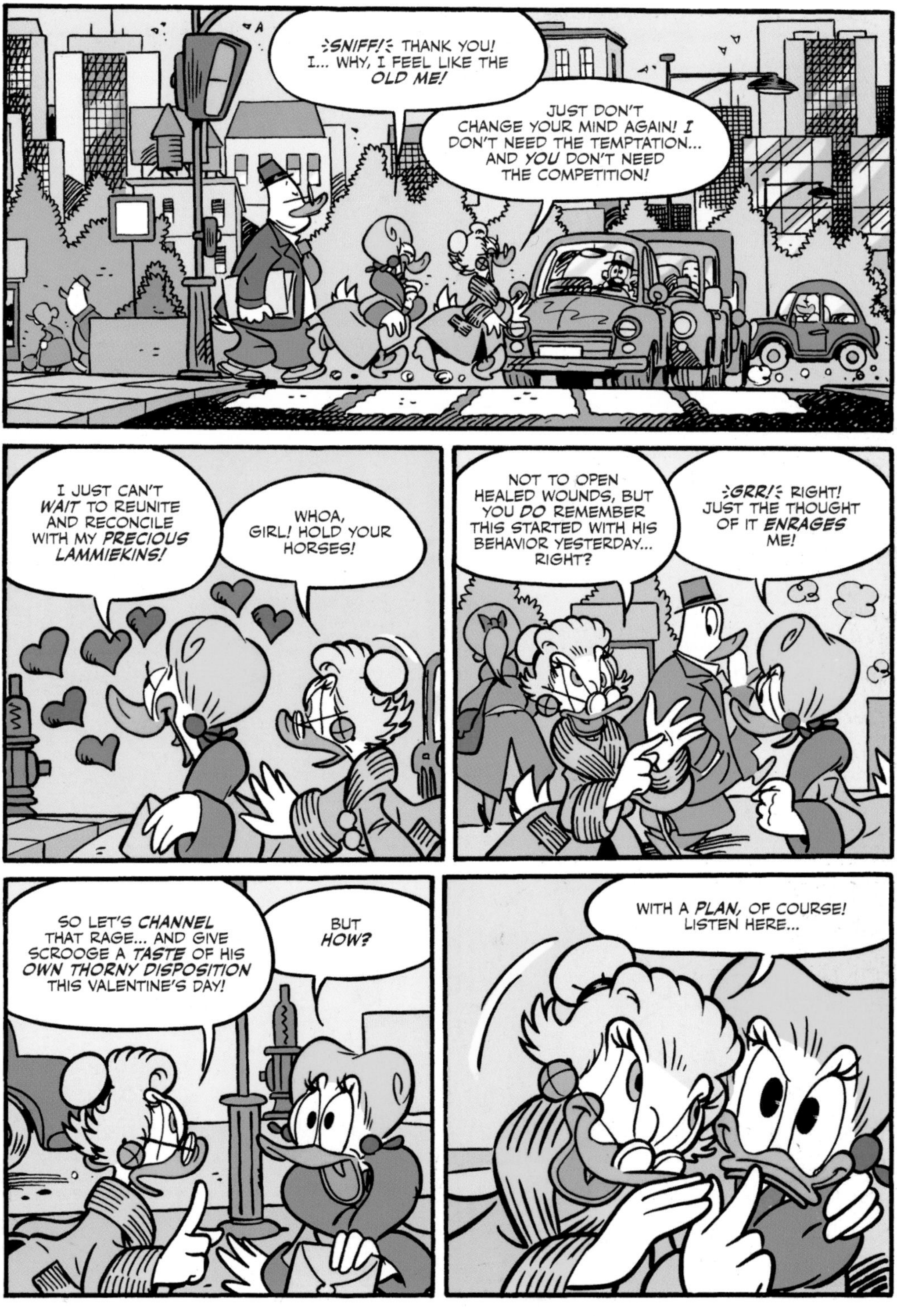
SNIFF! THANK YOU! I... WHY, I FEEL LIKE THE *OLD ME!*
JUST DON'T CHANGE YOUR MIND AGAIN! *I* DON'T NEED THE TEMPTATION... AND *YOU* DON'T NEED THE COMPETITION!
I JUST CAN'T *WAIT* TO REUNITE AND RECONCILE WITH MY *PRECIOUS LAMMIEKINS!*
WHOA, GIRL! HOLD YOUR HORSES!
NOT TO OPEN HEALED WOUNDS, BUT YOU *DO* REMEMBER THIS STARTED WITH HIS BEHAVIOR YESTERDAY... RIGHT?
GRR! RIGHT! JUST THE THOUGHT OF IT *ENRAGES* ME!
SO LET'S *CHANNEL* THAT RAGE... AND GIVE SCROOGE A *TASTE* OF HIS *OWN THORNY DISPOSITION* THIS VALENTINE'S DAY!
BUT *HOW?*
WITH A *PLAN,* OF COURSE! LISTEN HERE...

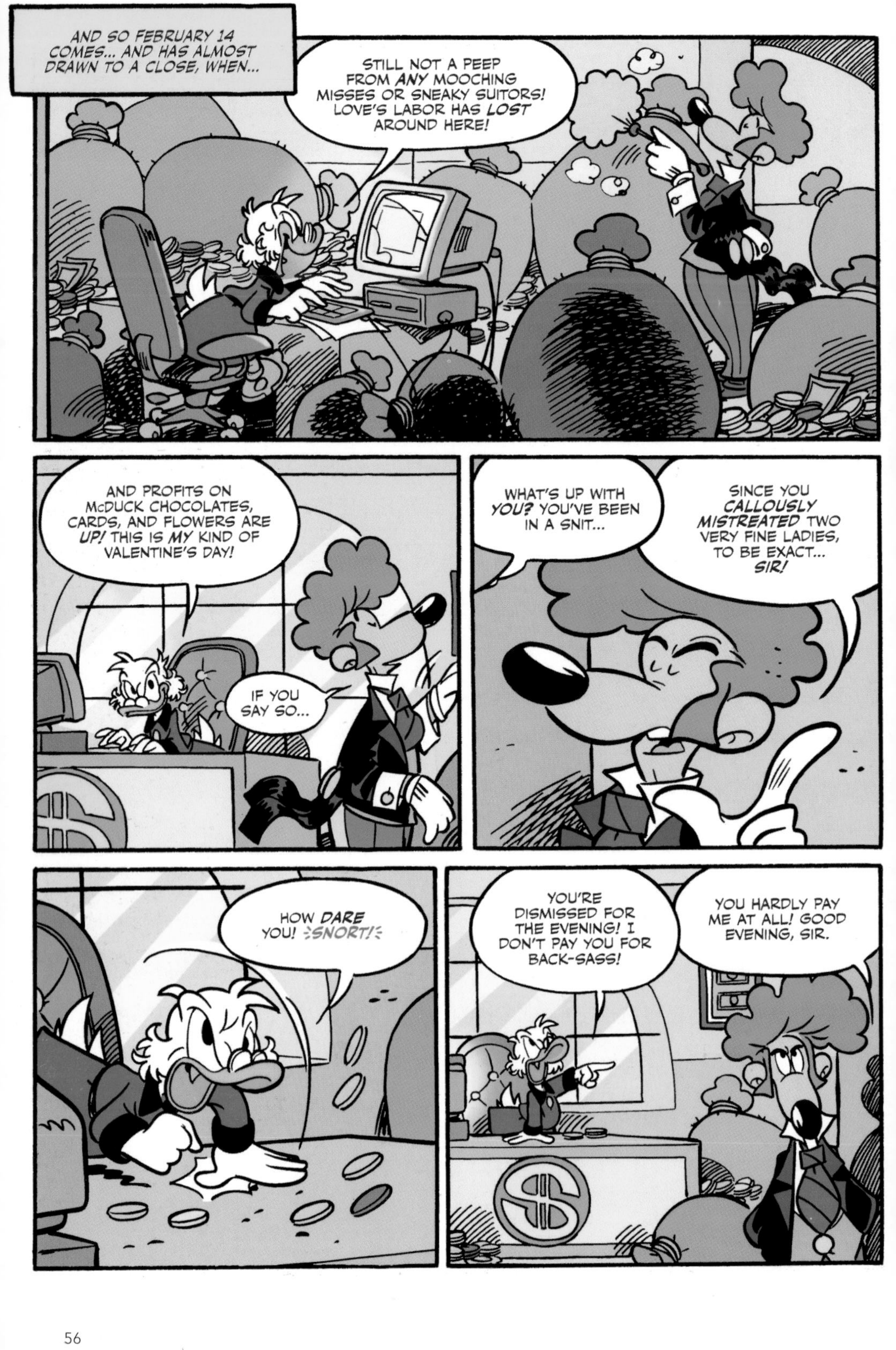
AND SO FEBRUARY 14 COMES... AND HAS ALMOST DRAWN TO A CLOSE, WHEN...
STILL NOT A PEEP FROM ANY MOOCHING MISSES OR SNEAKY SUITORS! LOVE'S LABOR HAS LOST AROUND HERE!
AND PROFITS ON McDUCK CHOCOLATES, CARDS, AND FLOWERS ARE UP! THIS IS MY KIND OF VALENTINE'S DAY!
IF YOU SAY SO...
WHAT'S UP WITH YOU? YOU'VE BEEN IN A SNIT...
SINCE YOU CALLOUSLY MISTREATED TWO VERY FINE LADIES, TO BE EXACT... SIR!
HOW DARE YOU! SNORT!
YOU'RE DISMISSED FOR THE EVENING! I DON'T PAY YOU FOR BACK-SASS!
YOU HARDLY PAY ME AT ALL! GOOD EVENING, SIR.

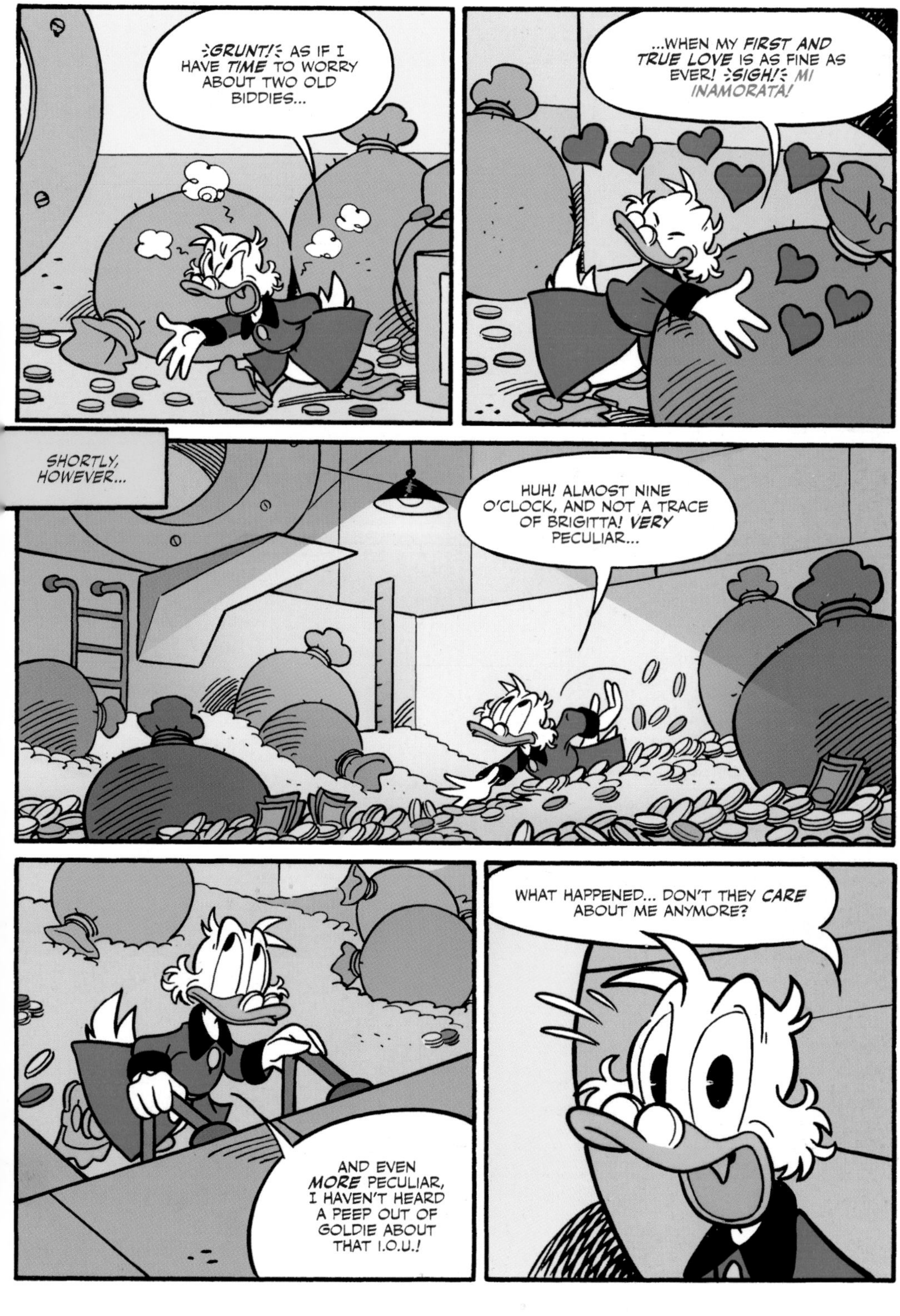

:GRUNT!: AS IF I HAVE TIME TO WORRY ABOUT TWO OLD BIDDIES...
...WHEN MY FIRST AND TRUE LOVE IS AS FINE AS EVER! :SIGH!: MI INAMORATA!
SHORTLY, HOWEVER...
HUH! ALMOST NINE O'CLOCK, AND NOT A TRACE OF BRIGITTA! VERY PECULIAR...
AND EVEN MORE PECULIAR, I HAVEN'T HEARD A PEEP OUT OF GOLDIE ABOUT THAT I.O.U.!
WHAT HAPPENED... DON'T THEY CARE ABOUT ME ANYMORE?

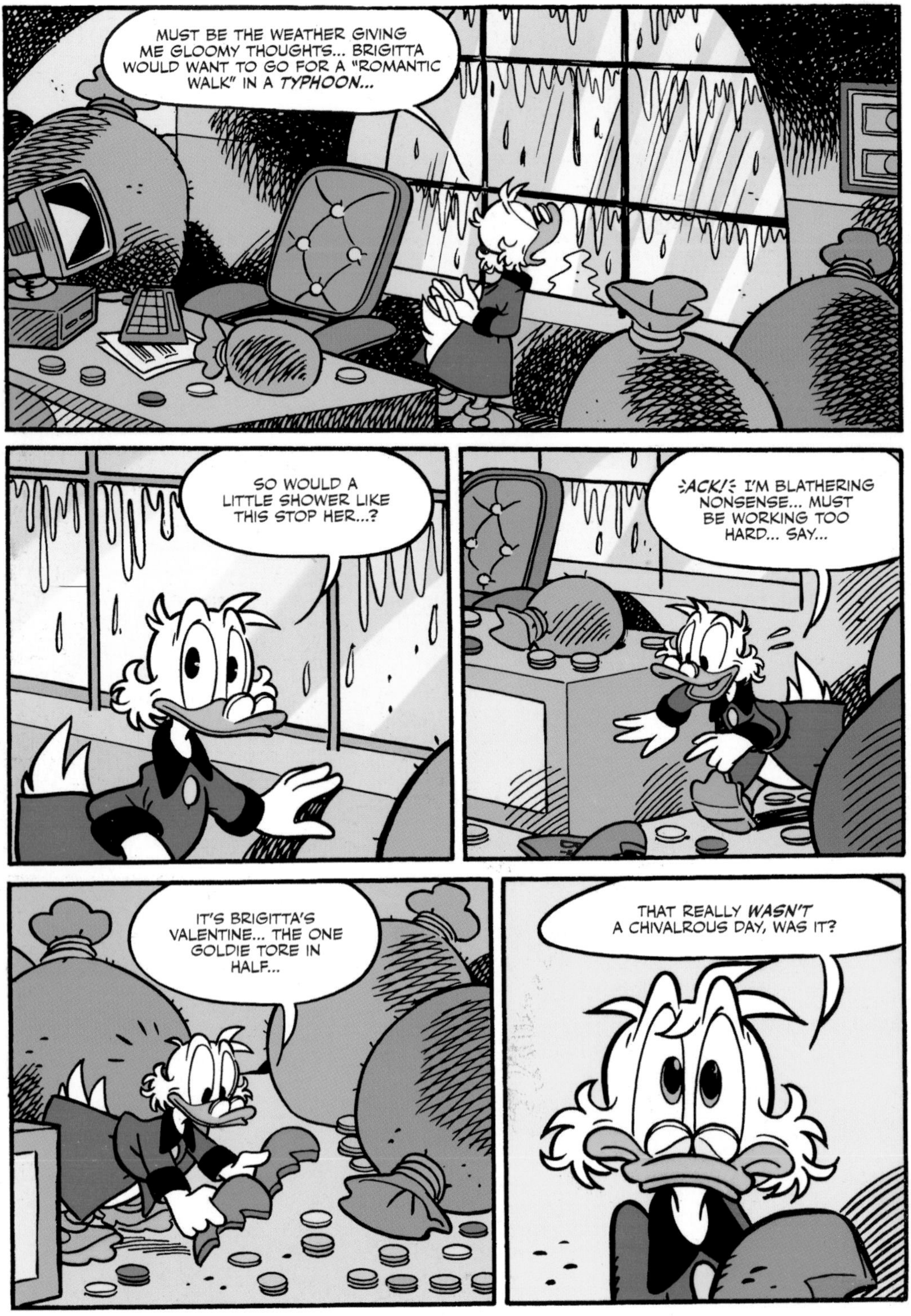
MUST BE THE WEATHER GIVING ME GLOOMY THOUGHTS... BRIGITTA WOULD WANT TO GO FOR A "ROMANTIC WALK" IN A *TYPHOON*...
SO WOULD A LITTLE SHOWER LIKE THIS STOP HER...?
ACK! I'M BLATHERING NONSENSE... MUST BE WORKING TOO HARD... SAY...
IT'S BRIGITTA'S VALENTINE... THE ONE GOLDIE TORE IN HALF...
THAT REALLY *WASN'T* A CHIVALROUS DAY, WAS IT?

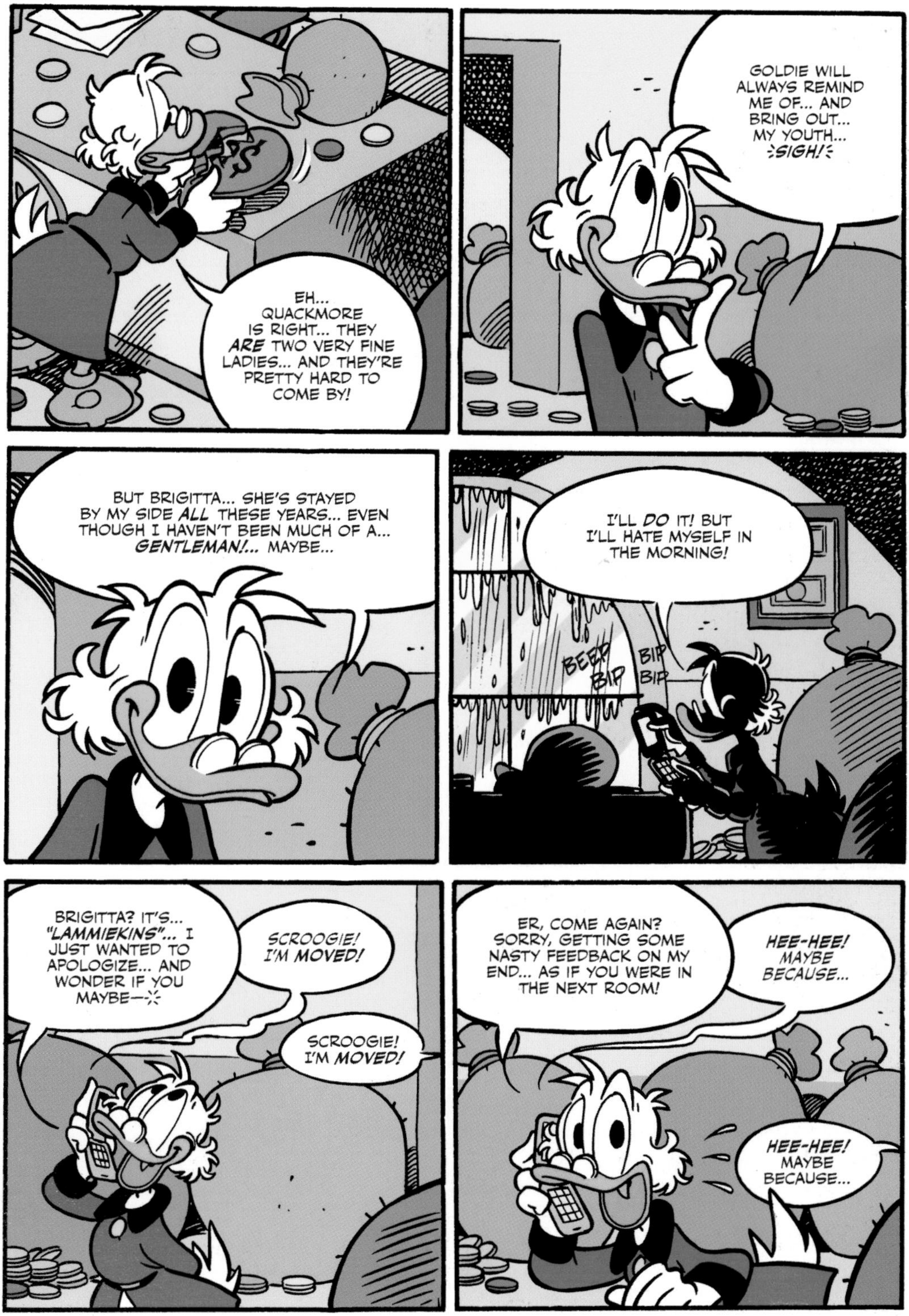

EH... QUACKMORE IS RIGHT... THEY ARE TWO VERY FINE LADIES... AND THEY'RE PRETTY HARD TO COME BY!
GOLDIE WILL ALWAYS REMIND ME OF... AND BRING OUT... MY YOUTH... SIGH!
BUT BRIGITTA... SHE'S STAYED BY MY SIDE ALL THESE YEARS... EVEN THOUGH I HAVEN'T BEEN MUCH OF A... GENTLEMAN!... MAYBE...
I'LL DO IT! BUT I'LL HATE MYSELF IN THE MORNING!
BEEP BIP
BIP BIP
BRIGITTA? IT'S... "LAMMIEKINS"... I JUST WANTED TO APOLOGIZE... AND WONDER IF YOU MAYBE—
SCROOGIE! I'M MOVED!
SCROOGIE! I'M MOVED!
ER, COME AGAIN? SORRY, GETTING SOME NASTY FEEDBACK ON MY END... AS IF YOU WERE IN THE NEXT ROOM!
HEE-HEE! MAYBE BECAUSE...
HEE-HEE! MAYBE BECAUSE...

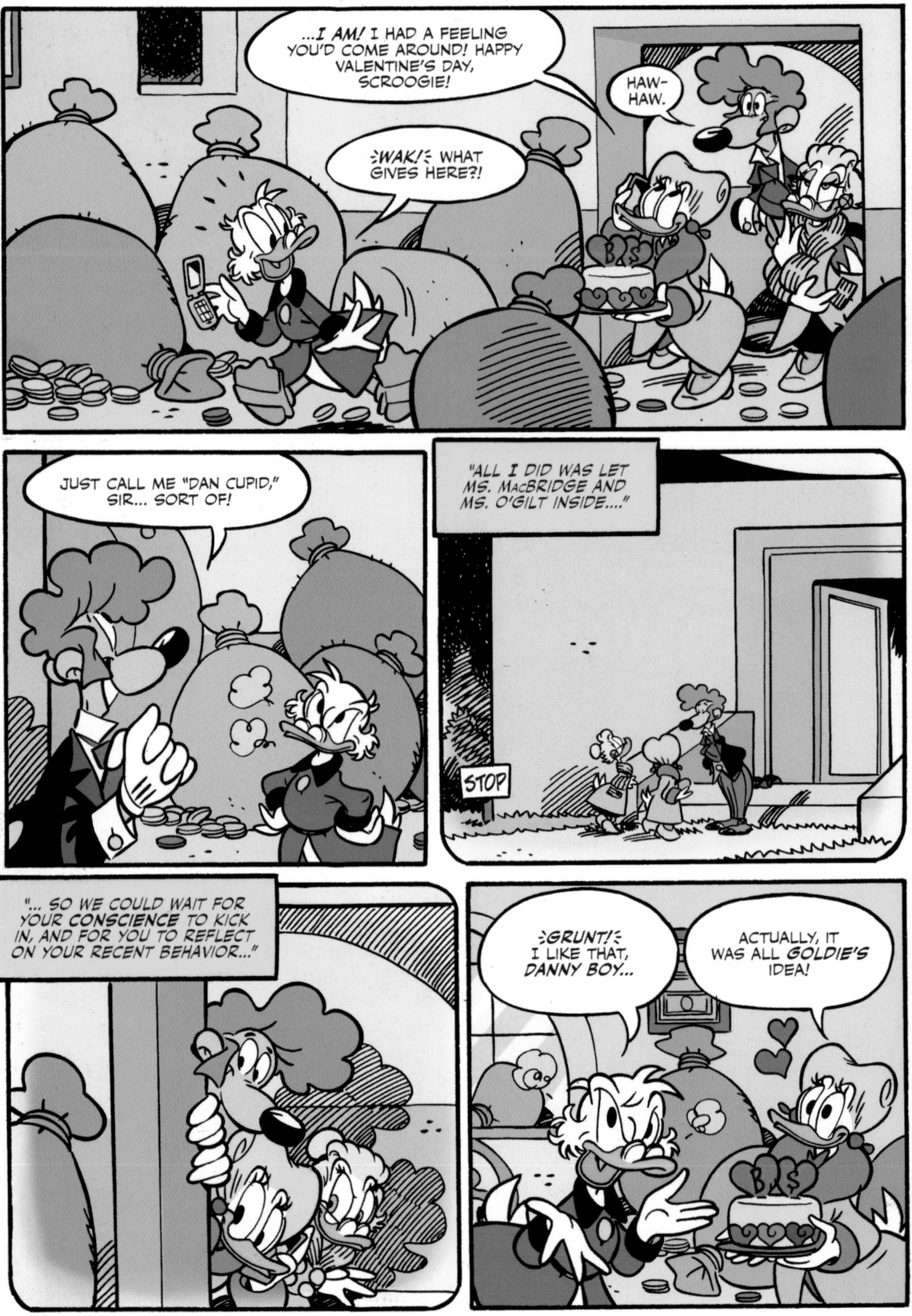
...I AM! I HAD A FEELING YOU'D COME AROUND! HAPPY VALENTINE'S DAY, SCROOGIE!
HAW-HAW.
WAK! WHAT GIVES HERE?!
JUST CALL ME "DAN CUPID," SIR... SORT OF!
"ALL I DID WAS LET MS. MACBRIDGE AND MS. O'GILT INSIDE...."
STOP
"... SO WE COULD WAIT FOR YOUR CONSCIENCE TO KICK IN, AND FOR YOU TO REFLECT ON YOUR RECENT BEHAVIOR..."
GRUNT! I LIKE THAT, DANNY BOY...
ACTUALLY, IT WAS ALL GOLDIE'S IDEA!

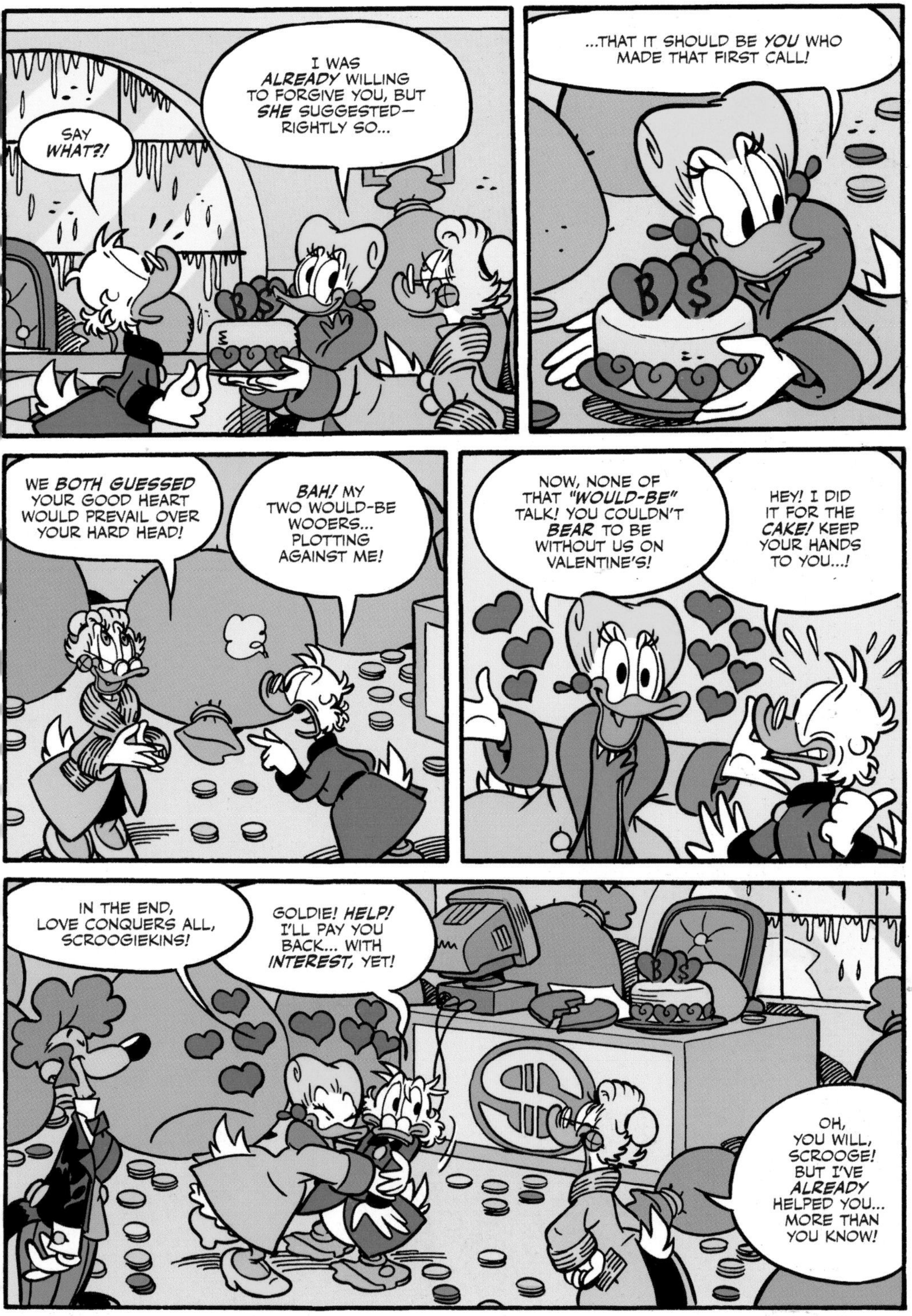
SAY WHAT?!
I WAS ALREADY WILLING TO FORGIVE YOU, BUT SHE SUGGESTED— RIGHTLY SO...
...THAT IT SHOULD BE YOU WHO MADE THAT FIRST CALL!
BS
WE BOTH GUESSED YOUR GOOD HEART WOULD PREVAIL OVER YOUR HARD HEAD!
BAH! MY TWO WOULD-BE WOOERS... PLOTTING AGAINST ME!
NOW, NONE OF THAT "WOULD-BE" TALK! YOU COULDN'T BEAR TO BE WITHOUT US ON VALENTINE'S!
HEY! I DID IT FOR THE CAKE! KEEP YOUR HANDS TO YOU...!
IN THE END, LOVE CONQUERS ALL, SCROOGIEKINS!
GOLDIE! HELP! I'LL PAY YOU BACK... WITH INTEREST, YET!
OH, YOU WILL, SCROOGE! BUT I'VE ALREADY HELPED YOU... MORE THAN YOU KNOW!

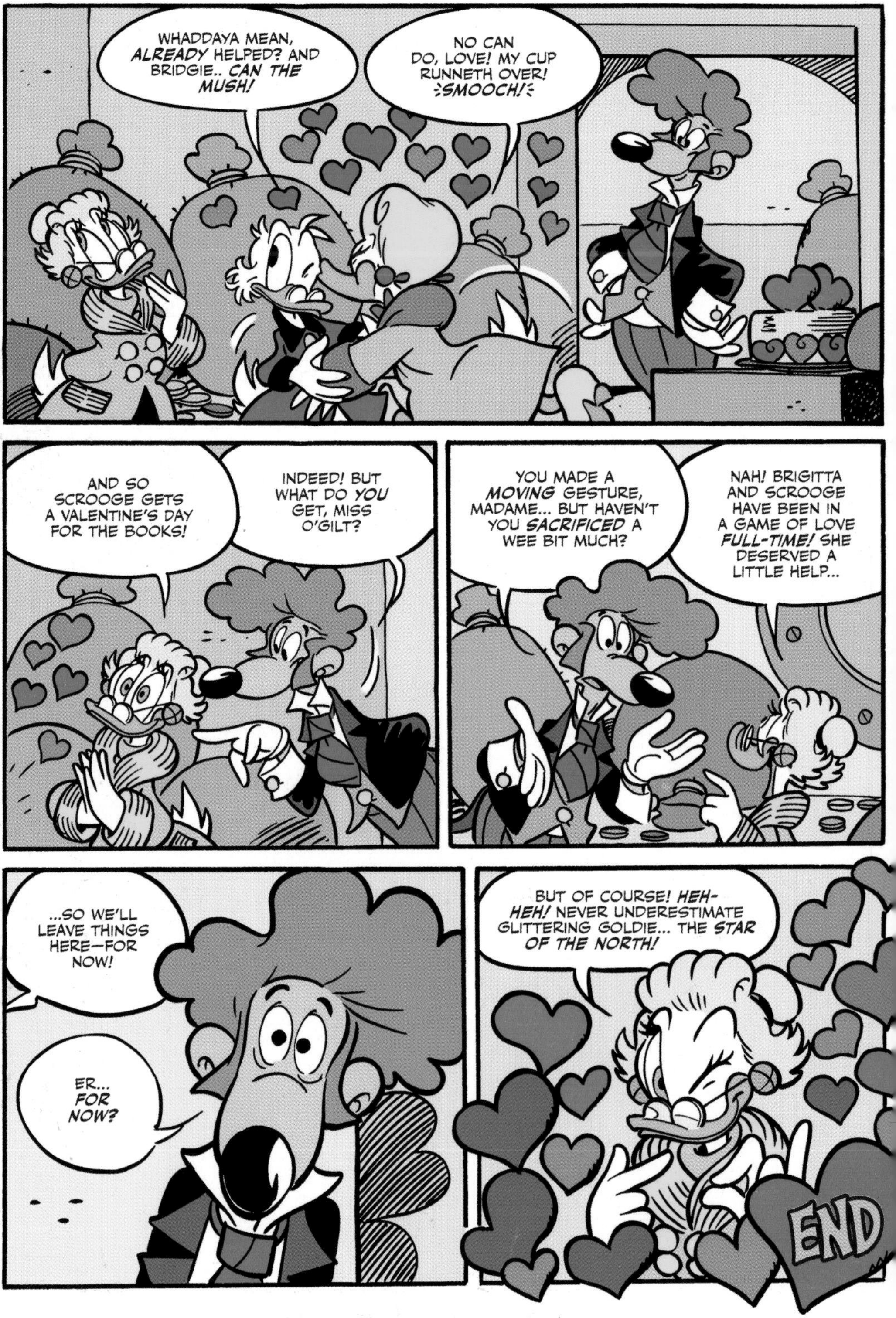
WHADDAYA MEAN, ALREADY HELPED? AND BRIDGIE.. CAN THE MUSH!
NO CAN DO, LOVE! MY CUP RUNNETH OVER! SMOOCH!
AND SO SCROOGE GETS A VALENTINE'S DAY FOR THE BOOKS!
INDEED! BUT WHAT DO YOU GET, MISS O'GILT?
YOU MADE A MOVING GESTURE, MADAME... BUT HAVEN'T YOU SACRIFICED A WEE BIT MUCH?
NAH! BRIGITTA AND SCROOGE HAVE BEEN IN A GAME OF LOVE FULL-TIME! SHE DESERVED A LITTLE HELP...
...SO WE'LL LEAVE THINGS HERE—FOR NOW!
ER... FOR NOW?
BUT OF COURSE! HEH-HEH! NEVER UNDERESTIMATE GLITTERING GOLDIE... THE STAR OF THE NORTH!
END

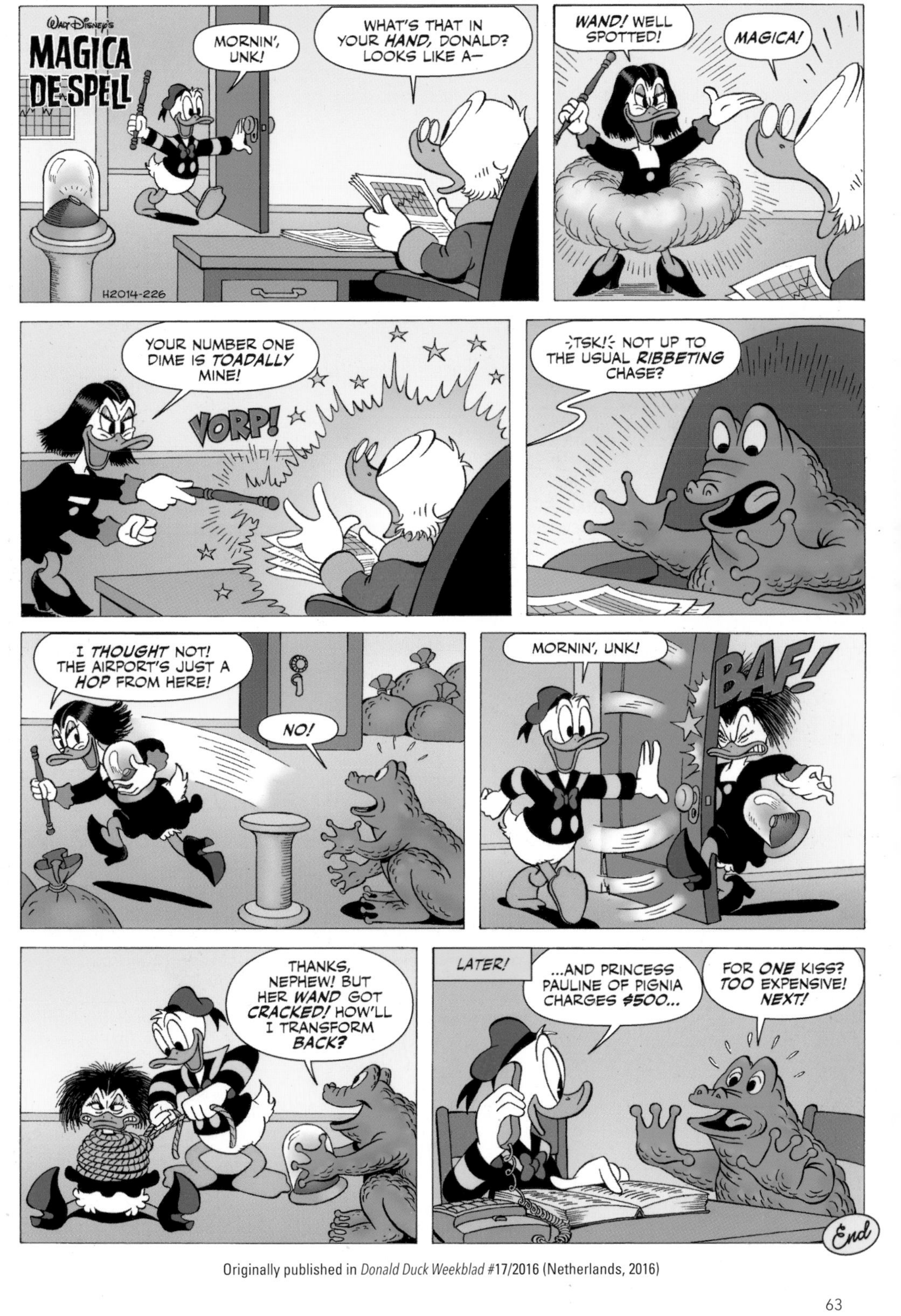

WALT DISNEY'S
MAGICA DE SPELL
H2014-226
MORNIN', UNK!
WHAT'S THAT IN YOUR HAND, DONALD? LOOKS LIKE A—
WAND! WELL SPOTTED!
MAGICA!
YOUR NUMBER ONE DIME IS TOADALLY MINE!
VORP!
TSK! NOT UP TO THE USUAL RIBBETING CHASE?
I THOUGHT NOT! THE AIRPORT'S JUST A HOP FROM HERE!
NO!
MORNIN', UNK!
BAF!
THANKS, NEPHEW! BUT HER WAND GOT CRACKED! HOW'LL I TRANSFORM BACK?
LATER!
...AND PRINCESS PAULINE OF PIGNIA CHARGES $500...
FOR ONE KISS? TOO EXPENSIVE! NEXT!
End

Originally published in *Donald Duck Weekblad* #17/2016 (Netherlands, 2016)

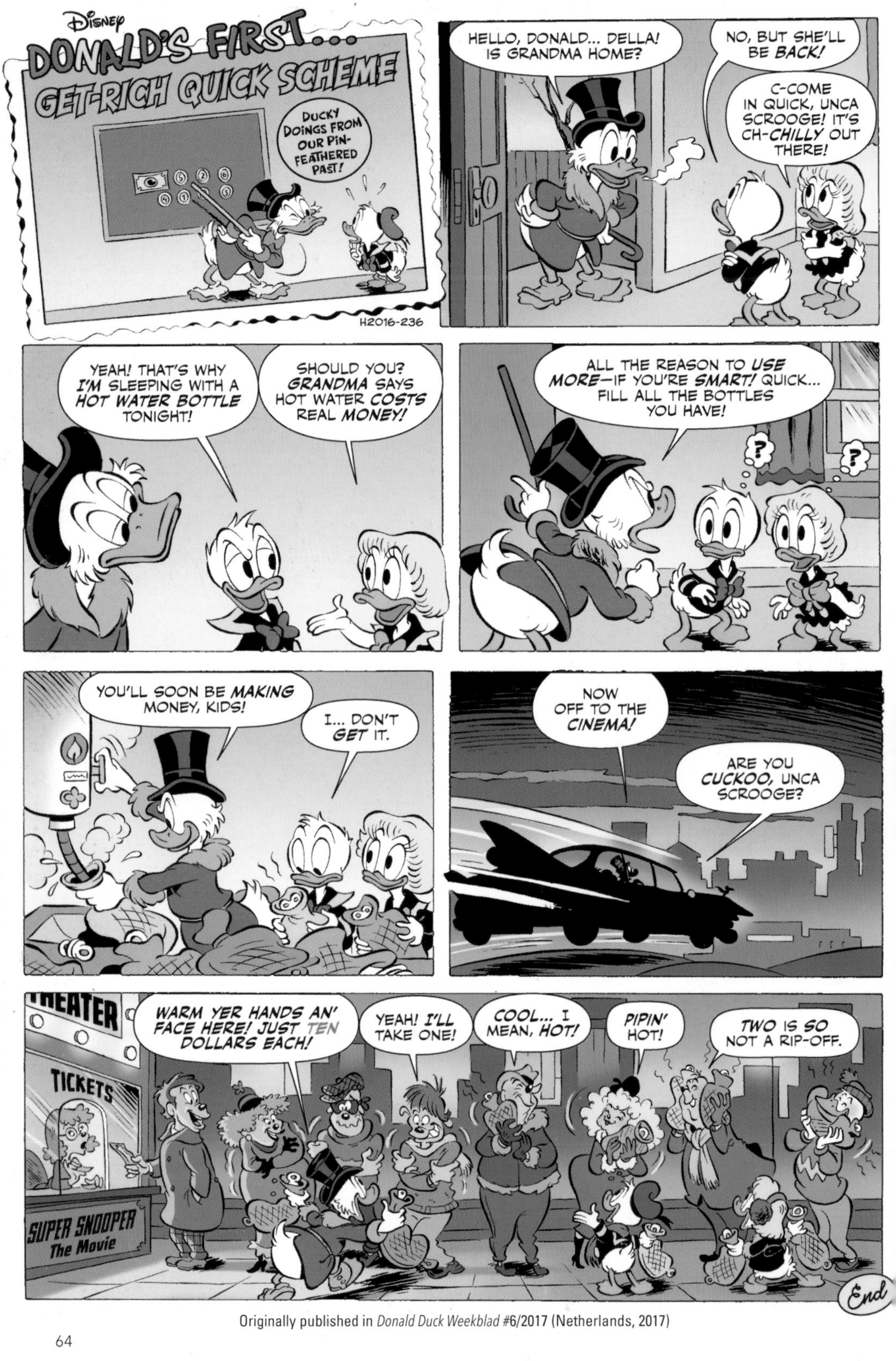
DISNEY
DONALD'S FIRST...
GET-RICH QUICK SCHEME
DUCKY DOINGS FROM OUR PIN-FEATHERED PAST!
H2016-236
HELLO, DONALD... DELLA! IS GRANDMA HOME?
NO, BUT SHE'LL BE BACK!
C-COME IN QUICK, UNCA SCROOGE! IT'S CH-CHILLY OUT THERE!
YEAH! THAT'S WHY I'M SLEEPING WITH A HOT WATER BOTTLE TONIGHT!
SHOULD YOU? GRANDMA SAYS HOT WATER COSTS REAL MONEY!
ALL THE REASON TO USE MORE—IF YOU'RE SMART! QUICK... FILL ALL THE BOTTLES YOU HAVE!
YOU'LL SOON BE MAKING MONEY, KIDS!
I... DON'T GET IT.
NOW OFF TO THE CINEMA!
ARE YOU CUCKOO, UNCA SCROOGE?
THEATER
TICKETS
SUPER SNOOPER The Movie
WARM YER HANDS AN' FACE HERE! JUST TEN DOLLARS EACH!
YEAH! I'LL TAKE ONE!
COOL... I MEAN, HOT!
PIPIN' HOT!
TWO IS SO NOT A RIP-OFF.
End

Originally published in *Donald Duck Weekblad* #6/2017 (Netherlands, 2017)

Walt Disney's Uncle $crooge in

MONEY IS THE ROOT OF UPHEAVAL!

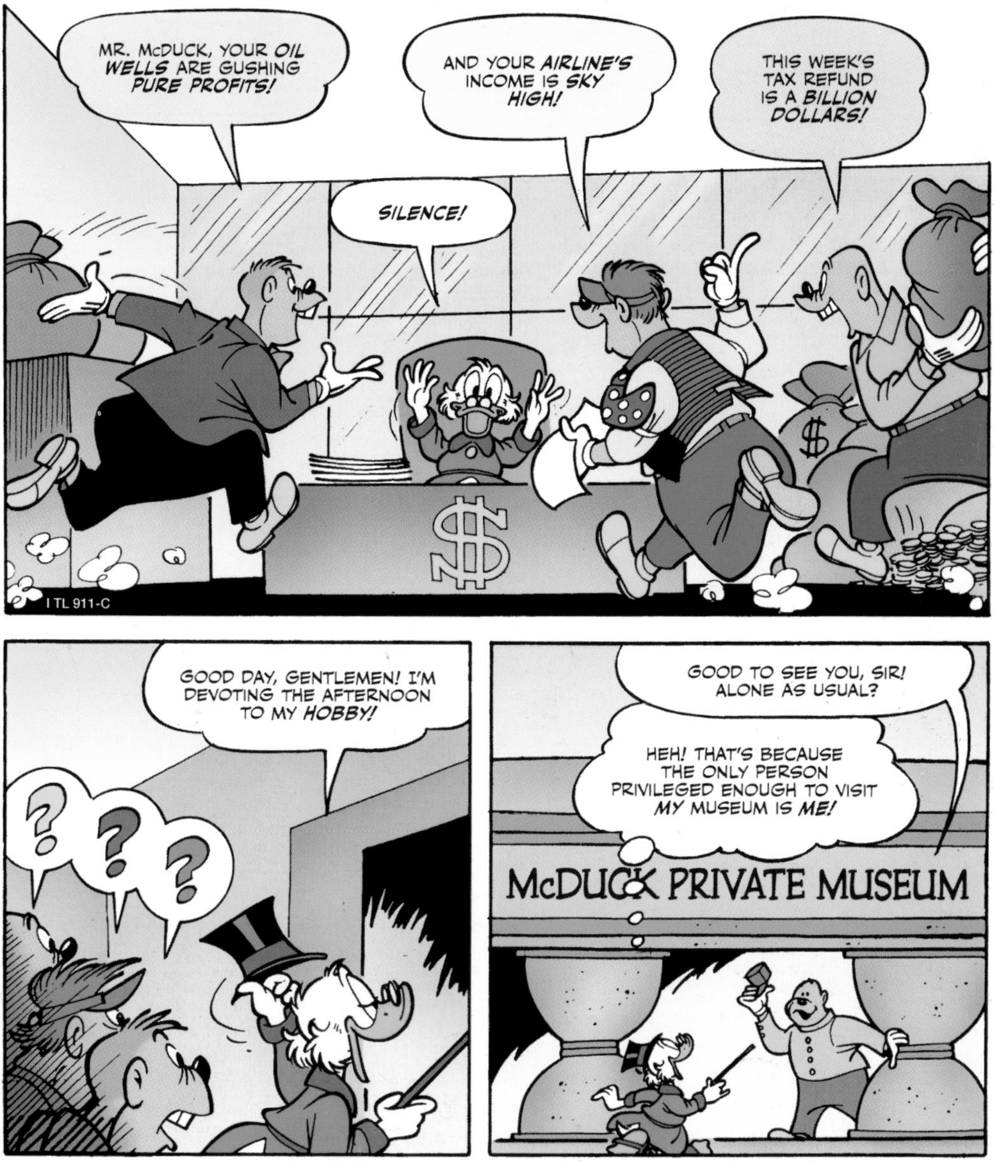

MR. McDUCK, YOUR *OIL WELLS* ARE GUSHING *PURE PROFITS!*
AND YOUR *AIRLINE'S* INCOME IS *SKY HIGH!*
THIS WEEK'S TAX REFUND IS A *BILLION DOLLARS!*
SILENCE!
I TL 911-C
GOOD DAY, GENTLEMEN! I'M DEVOTING THE AFTERNOON TO MY *HOBBY!*
?
?
?
GOOD TO SEE YOU, SIR! ALONE AS USUAL?
HEH! THAT'S BECAUSE THE ONLY PERSON PRIVILEGED ENOUGH TO VISIT *MY* MUSEUM IS *ME!*
McDUCK PRIVATE MUSEUM

Originally published in *Topolino* #911 (Italy, 1973)

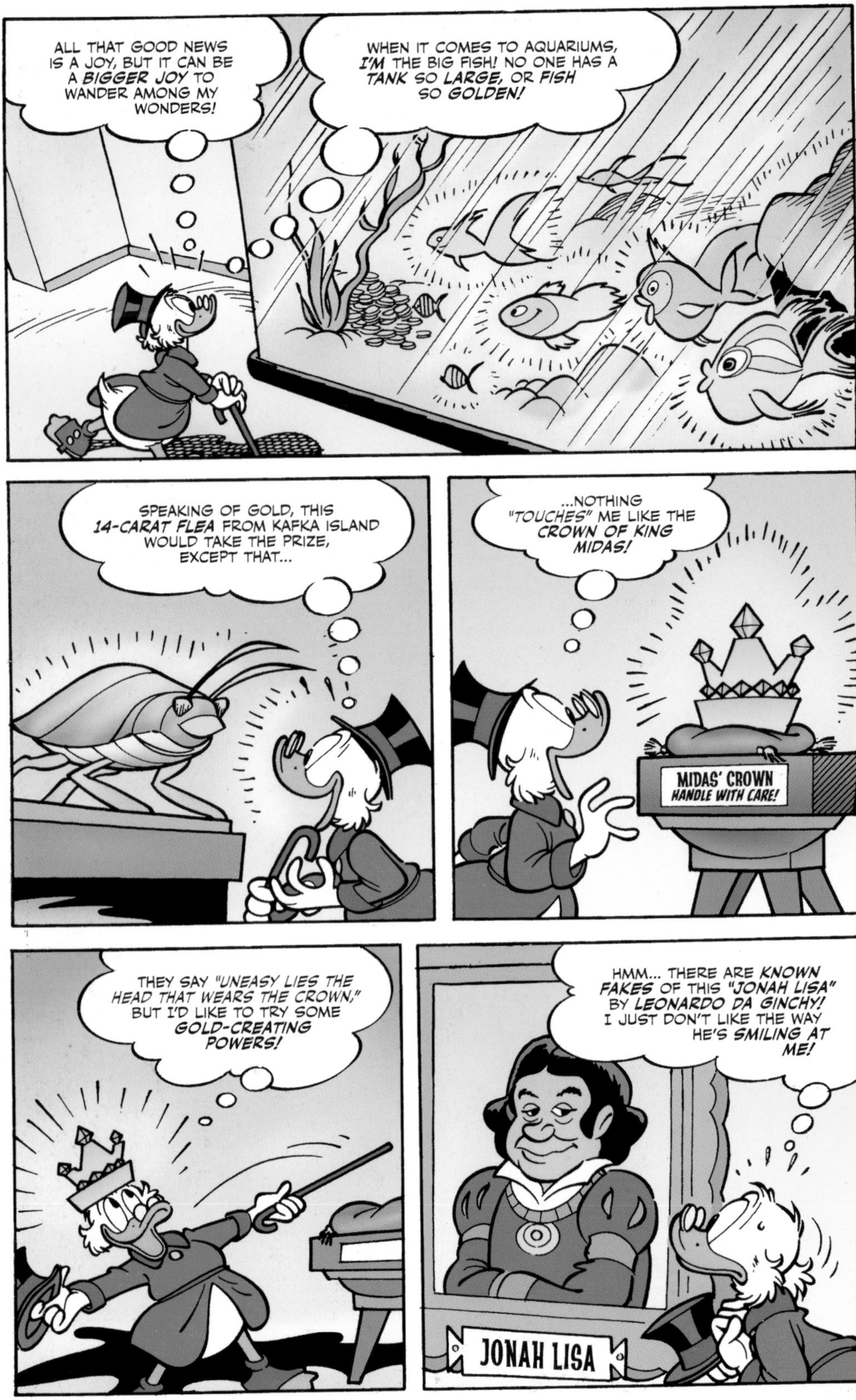
ALL THAT GOOD NEWS IS A JOY, BUT IT CAN BE A BIGGER JOY TO WANDER AMONG MY WONDERS!
WHEN IT COMES TO AQUARIUMS, I'M THE BIG FISH! NO ONE HAS A TANK SO LARGE, OR FISH SO GOLDEN!
SPEAKING OF GOLD, THIS 14-CARAT FLEA FROM KAFKA ISLAND WOULD TAKE THE PRIZE, EXCEPT THAT...
...NOTHING "TOUCHES" ME LIKE THE CROWN OF KING MIDAS!
MIDAS' CROWN
HANDLE WITH CARE!
THEY SAY "UNEASY LIES THE HEAD THAT WEARS THE CROWN," BUT I'D LIKE TO TRY SOME GOLD-CREATING POWERS!
HMM... THERE ARE KNOWN FAKES OF THIS "JONAH LISA" BY LEONARDO DA GINCHY! I JUST DON'T LIKE THE WAY HE'S SMILING AT ME!
JONAH LISA

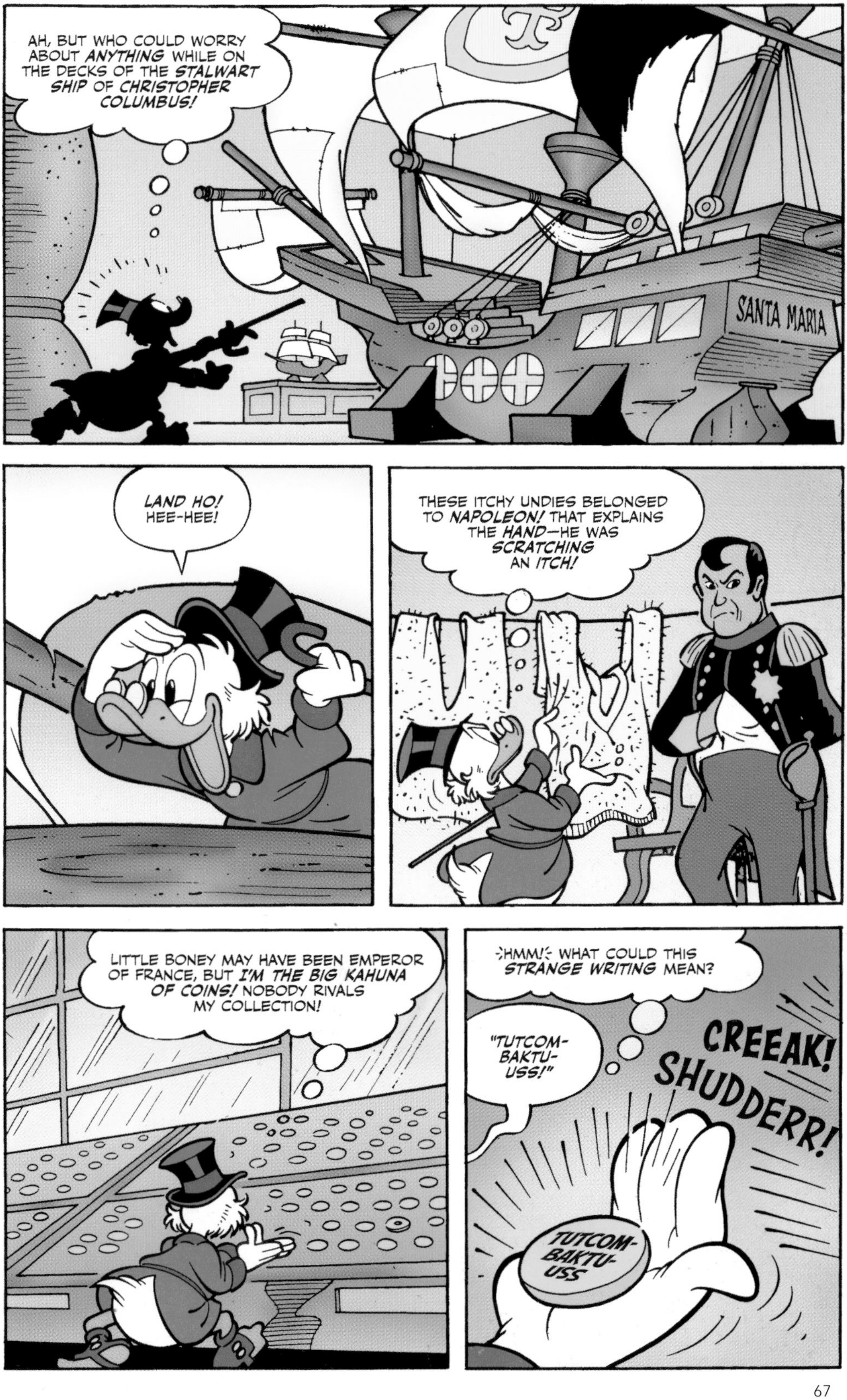
AH, BUT WHO COULD WORRY ABOUT ANYTHING WHILE ON THE DECKS OF THE STALWART SHIP OF CHRISTOPHER COLUMBUS!
SANTA MARIA
LAND HO! HEE-HEE!
THESE ITCHY UNDIES BELONGED TO NAPOLEON! THAT EXPLAINS THE HAND—HE WAS SCRATCHING AN ITCH!
LITTLE BONEY MAY HAVE BEEN EMPEROR OF FRANCE, BUT I'M THE BIG KAHUNA OF COINS! NOBODY RIVALS MY COLLECTION!
HMM! WHAT COULD THIS STRANGE WRITING MEAN?
"TUTCOM-BAKTU-USS!"
CREEAK!
SHUDDERR!
TUTCOM-BAKTU-USS

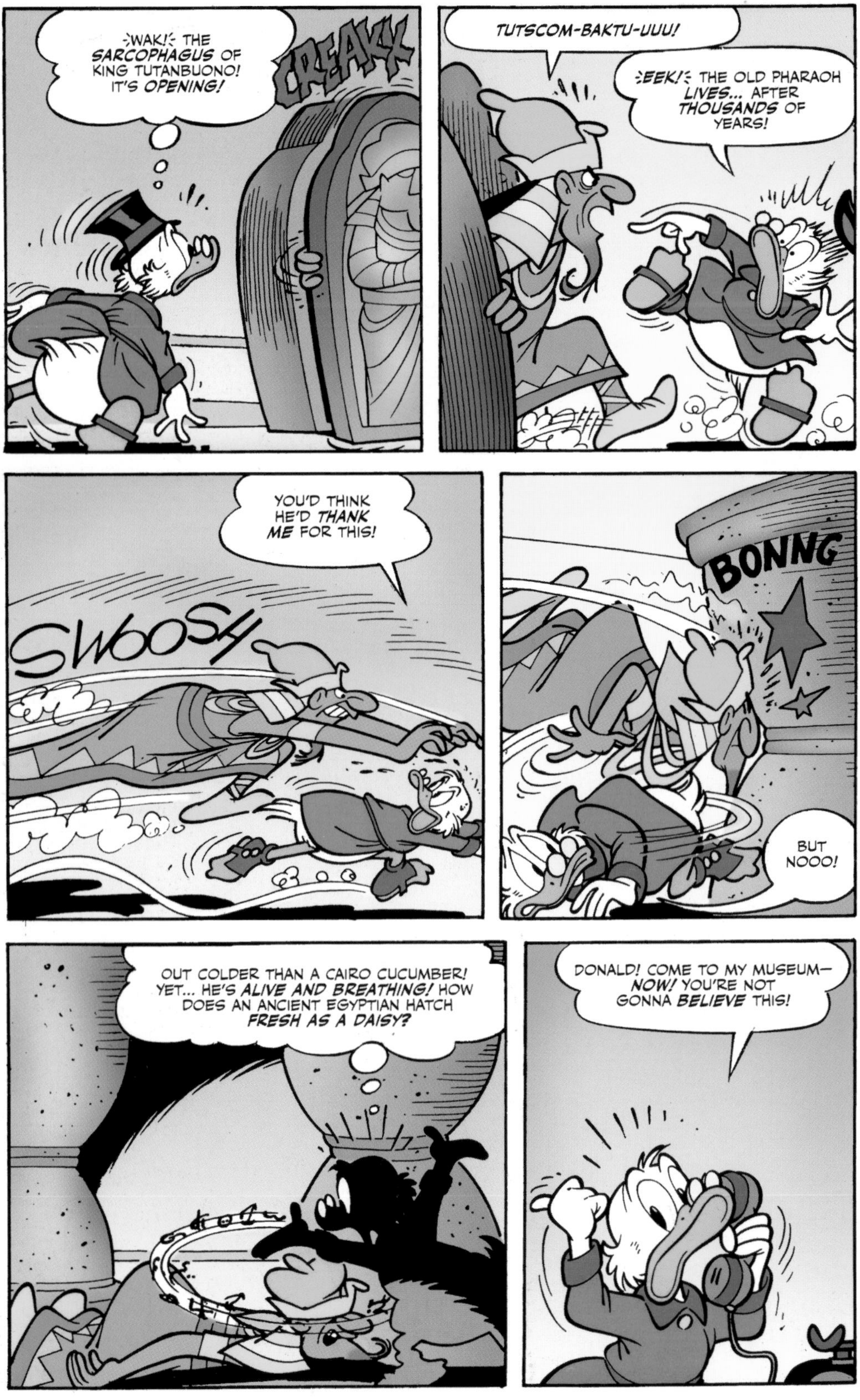

-WAK!- THE SARCOPHAGUS OF KING TUTANBUONO! IT'S OPENING!
CREAKK
TUTSCOM-BAKTU-UUU!
-EEK!- THE OLD PHARAOH LIVES... AFTER THOUSANDS OF YEARS!
YOU'D THINK HE'D THANK ME FOR THIS!
SWOOSH
BONNG
BUT NOOO!
OUT COLDER THAN A CAIRO CUCUMBER! YET... HE'S ALIVE AND BREATHING! HOW DOES AN ANCIENT EGYPTIAN HATCH FRESH AS A DAISY?
DONALD! COME TO MY MUSEUM— NOW! YOU'RE NOT GONNA BELIEVE THIS!

MINUTES LATER!

YOU'RE RIGHT! I *DON'T* BELIEVE IT!

BUT *HERE HE IS* IN THE FLESH! THE PHARAOH KING TUTANBUONO, REVIVED AFTER CENTURIES OF SLEEP!

THAT'S *ABSURD!*

WHEN I THINK "ABSURD," I THINK OF *GYRO GEARLOOSE!* HE CAN HELP!

THE GREAT INVENTOR IS CALLED...AND GOES TO WORK!

YOU'VE REVIVED TUT! NOW *MAKE HIM TALK!*

THESE *CEREBRO-COLANDERS* WILL GIVE YOU A *CRASH COURSE* IN ENGLISH—STRAIGHT FROM *OUR BRAINS!*

SOON, LESSON TIME IS OVER, AND TUT'S STORY *DRAINS OUT* LIKE WATER FROM FRESH-COOKED PASTA!

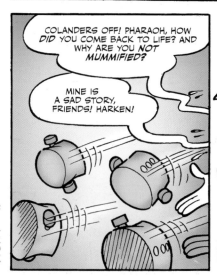

COLANDERS OFF! PHARAOH, HOW *DID* YOU COME BACK TO LIFE? AND WHY ARE YOU *NOT MUMMIFIED?*

MINE IS A SAD STORY, FRIENDS! HARKEN!

"WHILE STILL ANOTHER PYRAMID WAS BEING ERECTED IN MY HONOR, MEMBERS OF MY *ROYAL APOTHECARY* APPROACHED..."

DRINK OF THIS POTION, O PHARAOH, AND *LIFE* WILL BE YOURS FOR *ETERNITY!*

69

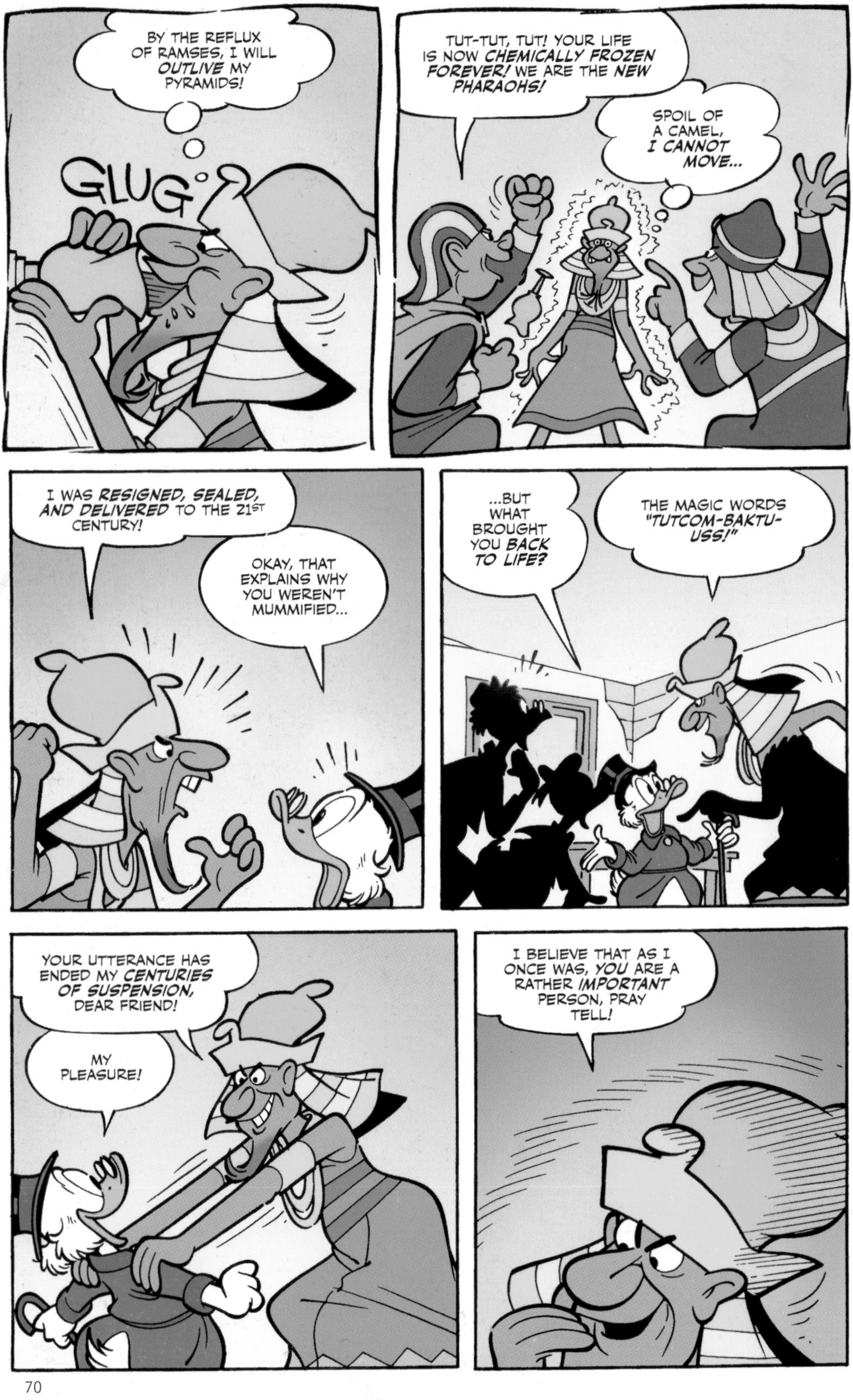
BY THE REFLUX OF RAMSES, I WILL OUTLIVE MY PYRAMIDS!
GLUG
TUT-TUT, TUT! YOUR LIFE IS NOW CHEMICALLY FROZEN FOREVER! WE ARE THE NEW PHARAOHS!
SPOIL OF A CAMEL, I CANNOT MOVE...
I WAS RESIGNED, SEALED, AND DELIVERED TO THE 21ST CENTURY!
OKAY, THAT EXPLAINS WHY YOU WEREN'T MUMMIFIED...
...BUT WHAT BROUGHT YOU BACK TO LIFE?
THE MAGIC WORDS "TUTCOM-BAKTU-USS!"
YOUR UTTERANCE HAS ENDED MY CENTURIES OF SUSPENSION, DEAR FRIEND!
MY PLEASURE!
I BELIEVE THAT AS I ONCE WAS, YOU ARE A RATHER IMPORTANT PERSON, PRAY TELL!

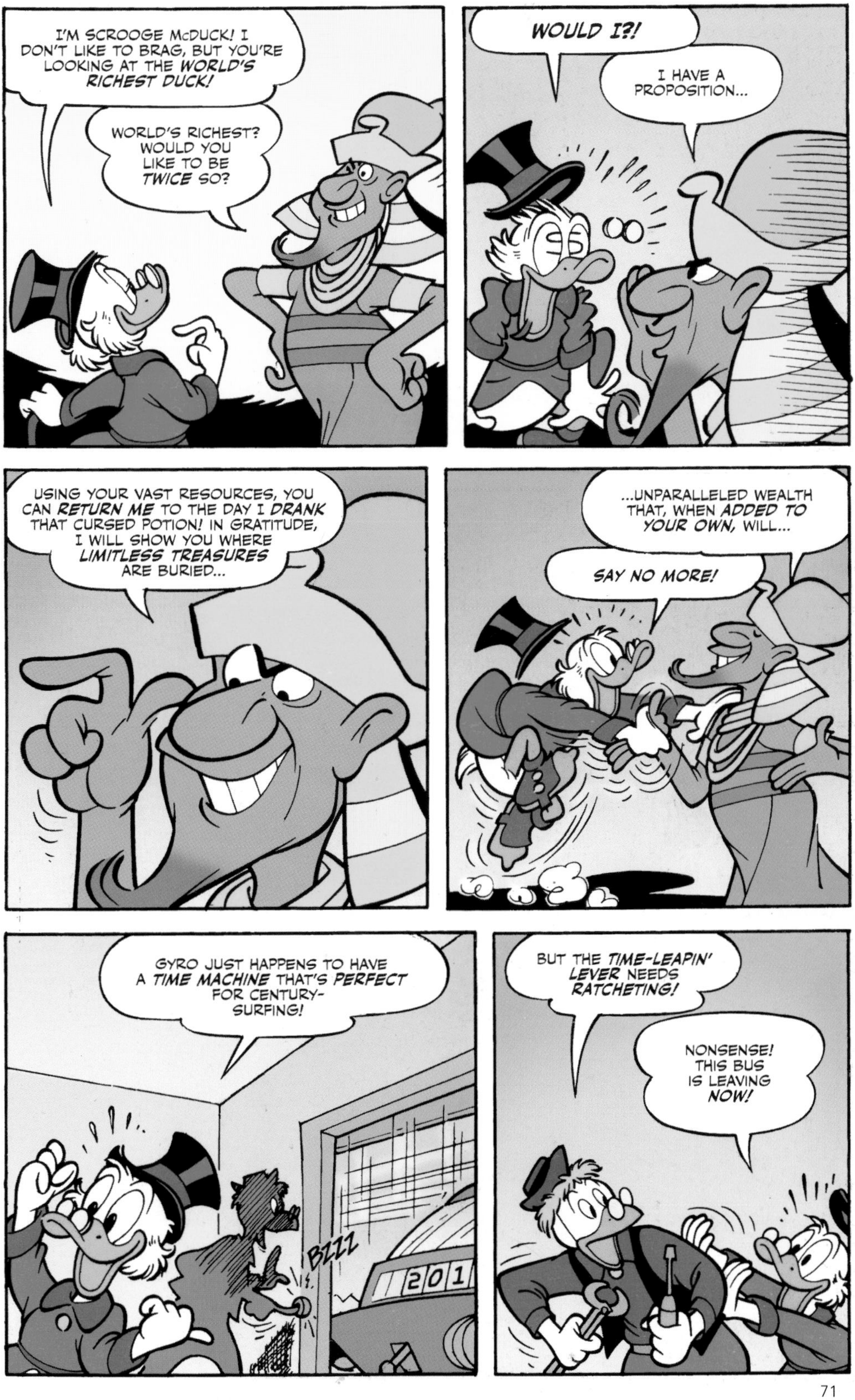
I'M SCROOGE McDUCK! I DON'T LIKE TO BRAG, BUT YOU'RE LOOKING AT THE WORLD'S RICHEST DUCK!
WORLD'S RICHEST? WOULD YOU LIKE TO BE TWICE SO?
WOULD I?!
I HAVE A PROPOSITION...
USING YOUR VAST RESOURCES, YOU CAN RETURN ME TO THE DAY I DRANK THAT CURSED POTION! IN GRATITUDE, I WILL SHOW YOU WHERE LIMITLESS TREASURES ARE BURIED...
...UNPARALLELED WEALTH THAT, WHEN ADDED TO YOUR OWN, WILL...
SAY NO MORE!
GYRO JUST HAPPENS TO HAVE A TIME MACHINE THAT'S PERFECT FOR CENTURY-SURFING!
BZZZ
201
BUT THE TIME-LEAPIN' LEVER NEEDS RATCHETING!
NONSENSE! THIS BUS IS LEAVING NOW!

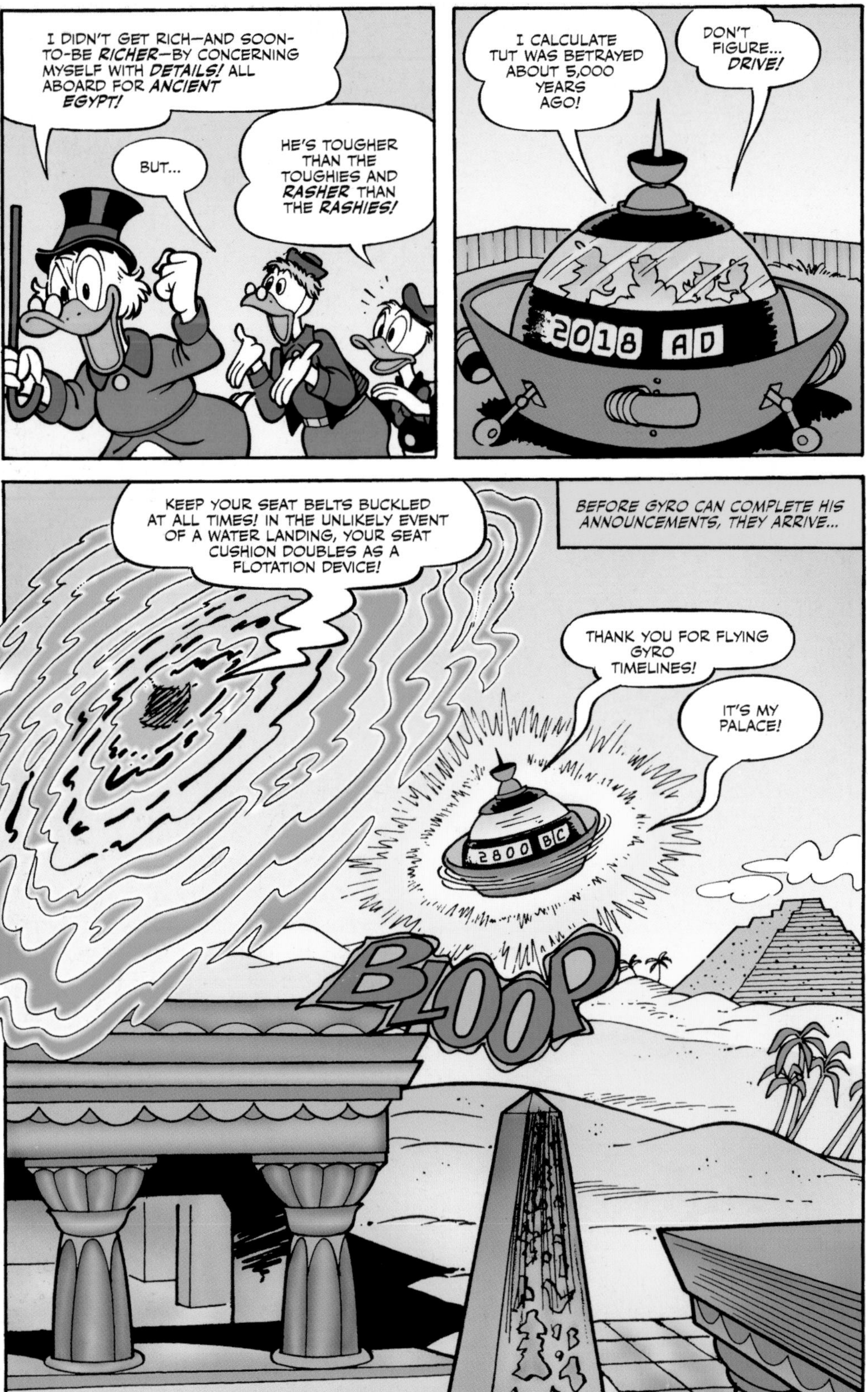
I DIDN'T GET RICH—AND SOON-TO-BE RICHER—BY CONCERNING MYSELF WITH DETAILS! ALL ABOARD FOR ANCIENT EGYPT!
BUT...
HE'S TOUGHER THAN THE TOUGHIES AND RASHER THAN THE RASHIES!
I CALCULATE TUT WAS BETRAYED ABOUT 5,000 YEARS AGO!
DON'T FIGURE... DRIVE!
2018 AD
KEEP YOUR SEAT BELTS BUCKLED AT ALL TIMES! IN THE UNLIKELY EVENT OF A WATER LANDING, YOUR SEAT CUSHION DOUBLES AS A FLOTATION DEVICE!
BEFORE GYRO CAN COMPLETE HIS ANNOUNCEMENTS, THEY ARRIVE...
THANK YOU FOR FLYING GYRO TIMELINES!
IT'S MY PALACE!
2800 BC
BLOOP

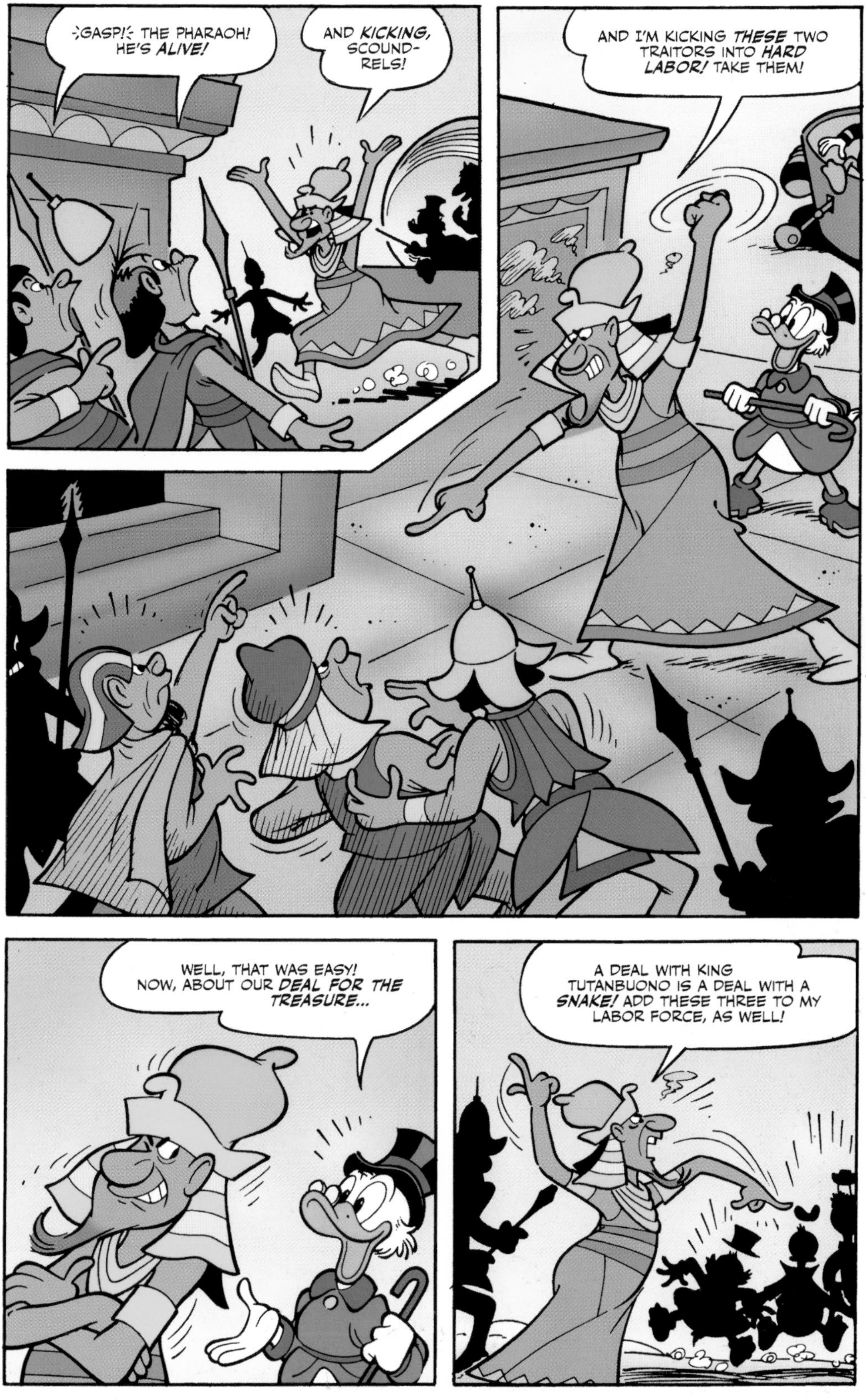
GASP! THE PHARAOH! HE'S ALIVE!
AND KICKING, SCOUNDRELS!
AND I'M KICKING THESE TWO TRAITORS INTO HARD LABOR! TAKE THEM!
WELL, THAT WAS EASY! NOW, ABOUT OUR DEAL FOR THE TREASURE...
A DEAL WITH KING TUTANBUONO IS A DEAL WITH A SNAKE! ADD THESE THREE TO MY LABOR FORCE, AS WELL!

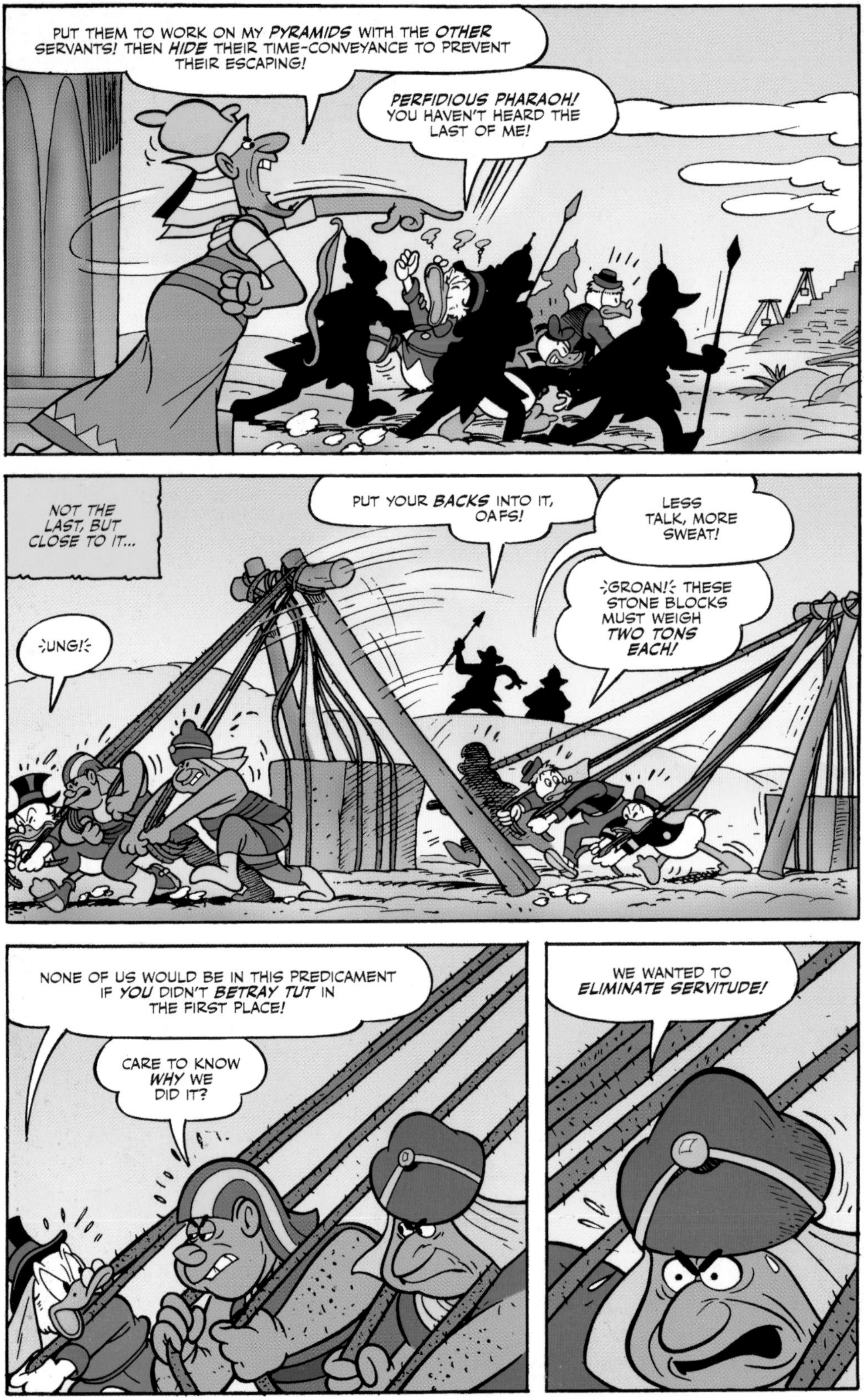
PUT THEM TO WORK ON MY PYRAMIDS WITH THE OTHER SERVANTS! THEN HIDE THEIR TIME-CONVEYANCE TO PREVENT THEIR ESCAPING!
PERFIDIOUS PHARAOH! YOU HAVEN'T HEARD THE LAST OF ME!
NOT THE LAST, BUT CLOSE TO IT...
PUT YOUR BACKS INTO IT, OAFS!
LESS TALK, MORE SWEAT!
UNG!
GROAN! THESE STONE BLOCKS MUST WEIGH TWO TONS EACH!
NONE OF US WOULD BE IN THIS PREDICAMENT IF YOU DIDN'T BETRAY TUT IN THE FIRST PLACE!
CARE TO KNOW WHY WE DID IT?
WE WANTED TO ELIMINATE SERVITUDE!

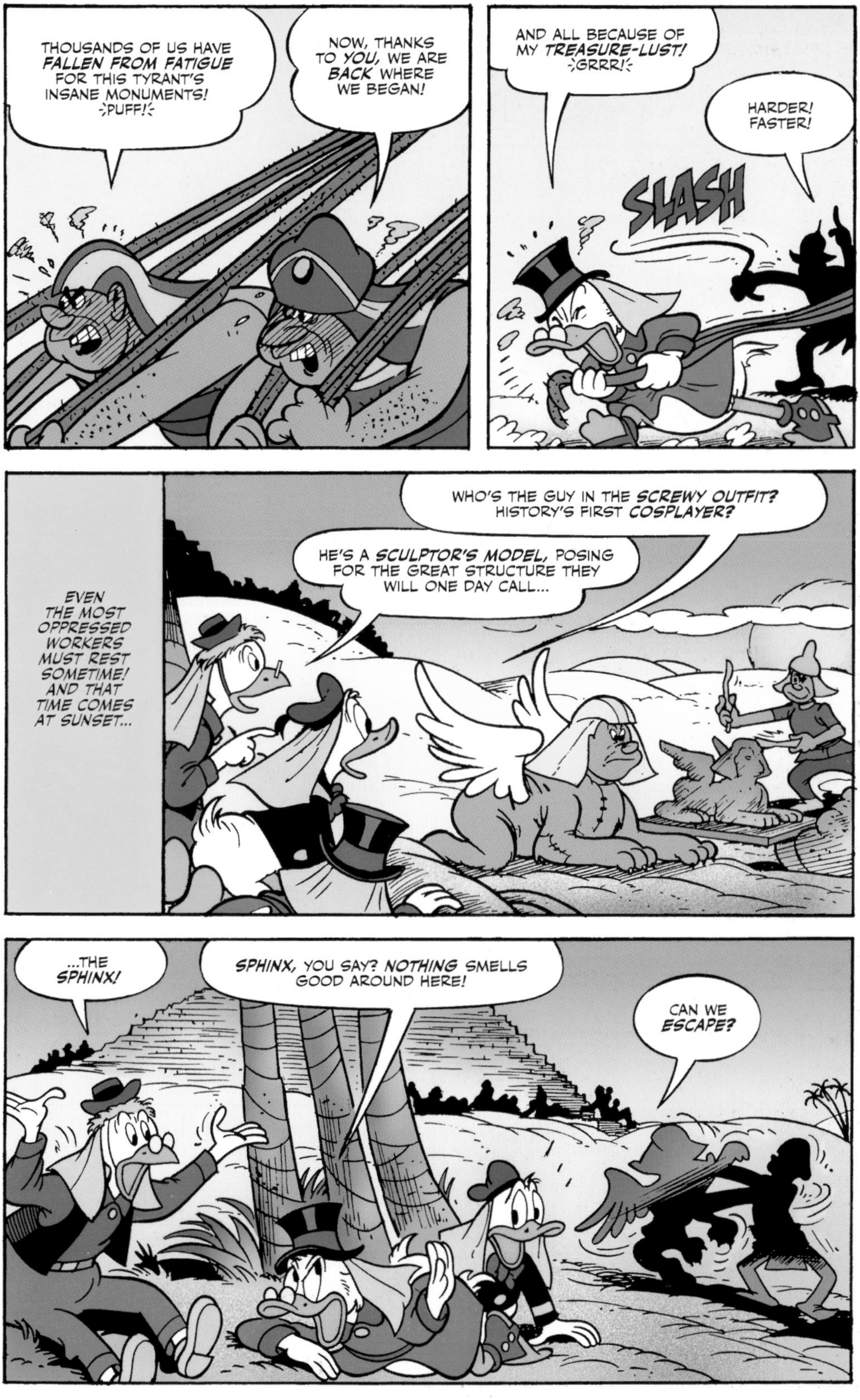
THOUSANDS OF US HAVE *FALLEN FROM FATIGUE* FOR THIS TYRANT'S INSANE MONUMENTS! PUFF!
NOW, THANKS TO *YOU,* WE ARE *BACK* WHERE WE BEGAN!
AND ALL BECAUSE OF MY *TREASURE-LUST!* GRRR!
HARDER! FASTER!
SLASH
EVEN THE MOST OPPRESSED WORKERS MUST REST SOMETIME! AND THAT TIME COMES AT SUNSET...
WHO'S THE GUY IN THE *SCREWY OUTFIT?* HISTORY'S FIRST *COSPLAYER?*
HE'S A *SCULPTOR'S MODEL,* POSING FOR THE GREAT STRUCTURE THEY WILL ONE DAY CALL...
...THE *SPHINX!*
SPHINX, YOU SAY? *NOTHING* SMELLS GOOD AROUND HERE!
CAN WE *ESCAPE?*

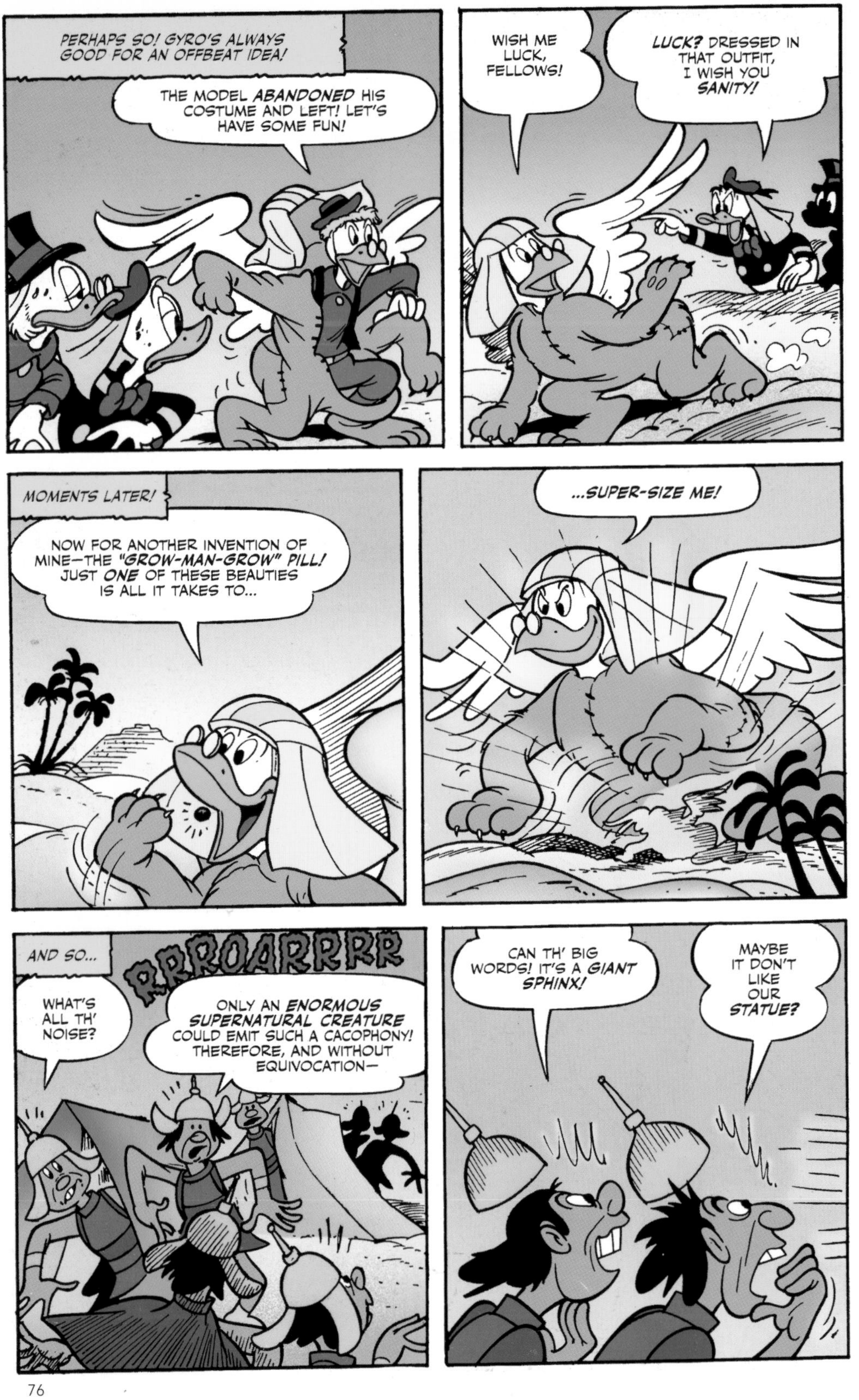
PERHAPS SO! GYRO'S ALWAYS GOOD FOR AN OFFBEAT IDEA!
THE MODEL *ABANDONED* HIS COSTUME AND LEFT! LET'S HAVE SOME FUN!
WISH ME LUCK, FELLOWS!
LUCK? DRESSED IN THAT OUTFIT, I WISH YOU *SANITY!*
MOMENTS LATER!
NOW FOR ANOTHER INVENTION OF MINE—THE *"GROW-MAN-GROW" PILL!* JUST *ONE* OF THESE BEAUTIES IS ALL IT TAKES TO...
...SUPER-SIZE ME!
AND SO...
RRROARRRR
WHAT'S ALL TH' NOISE?
ONLY AN *ENORMOUS SUPERNATURAL CREATURE* COULD EMIT SUCH A CACOPHONY! THEREFORE, AND WITHOUT EQUIVOCATION—
CAN TH' BIG WORDS! IT'S A *GIANT SPHINX!*
MAYBE IT DON'T LIKE OUR *STATUE?*

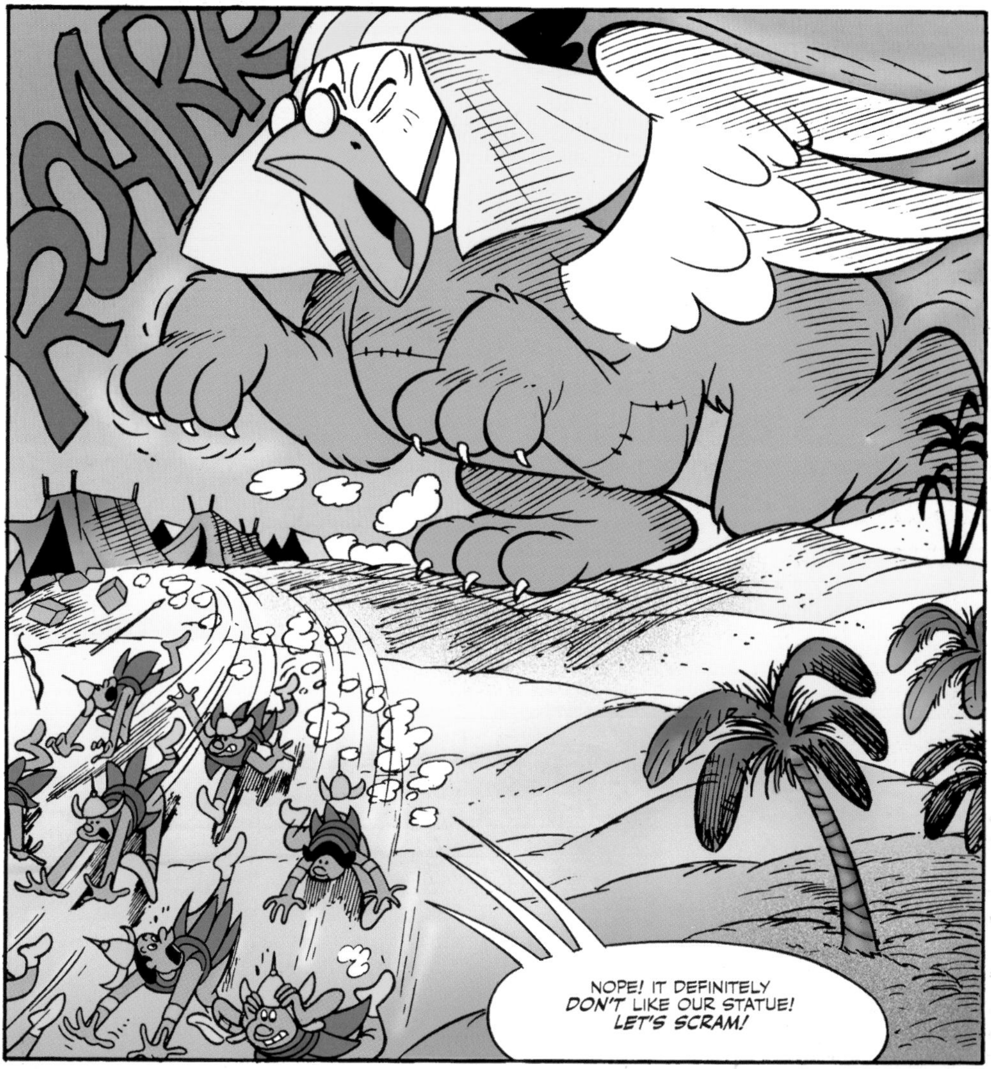
ROARR
NOPE! IT DEFINITELY DON'T LIKE OUR STATUE! LET'S SCRAM!

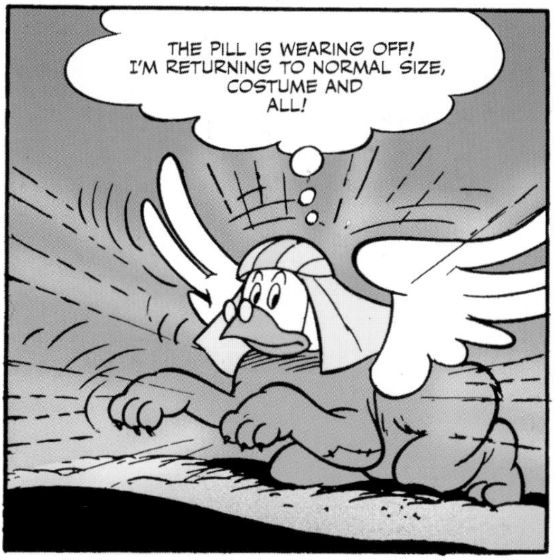
THE PILL IS WEARING OFF! I'M RETURNING TO NORMAL SIZE, COSTUME AND ALL!

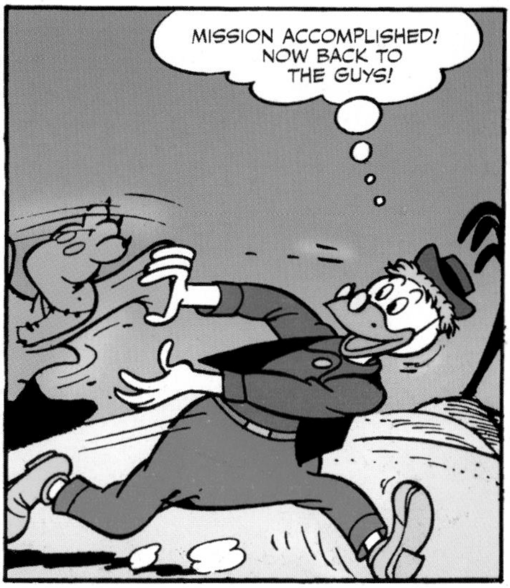
MISSION ACCOMPLISHED! NOW BACK TO THE GUYS!

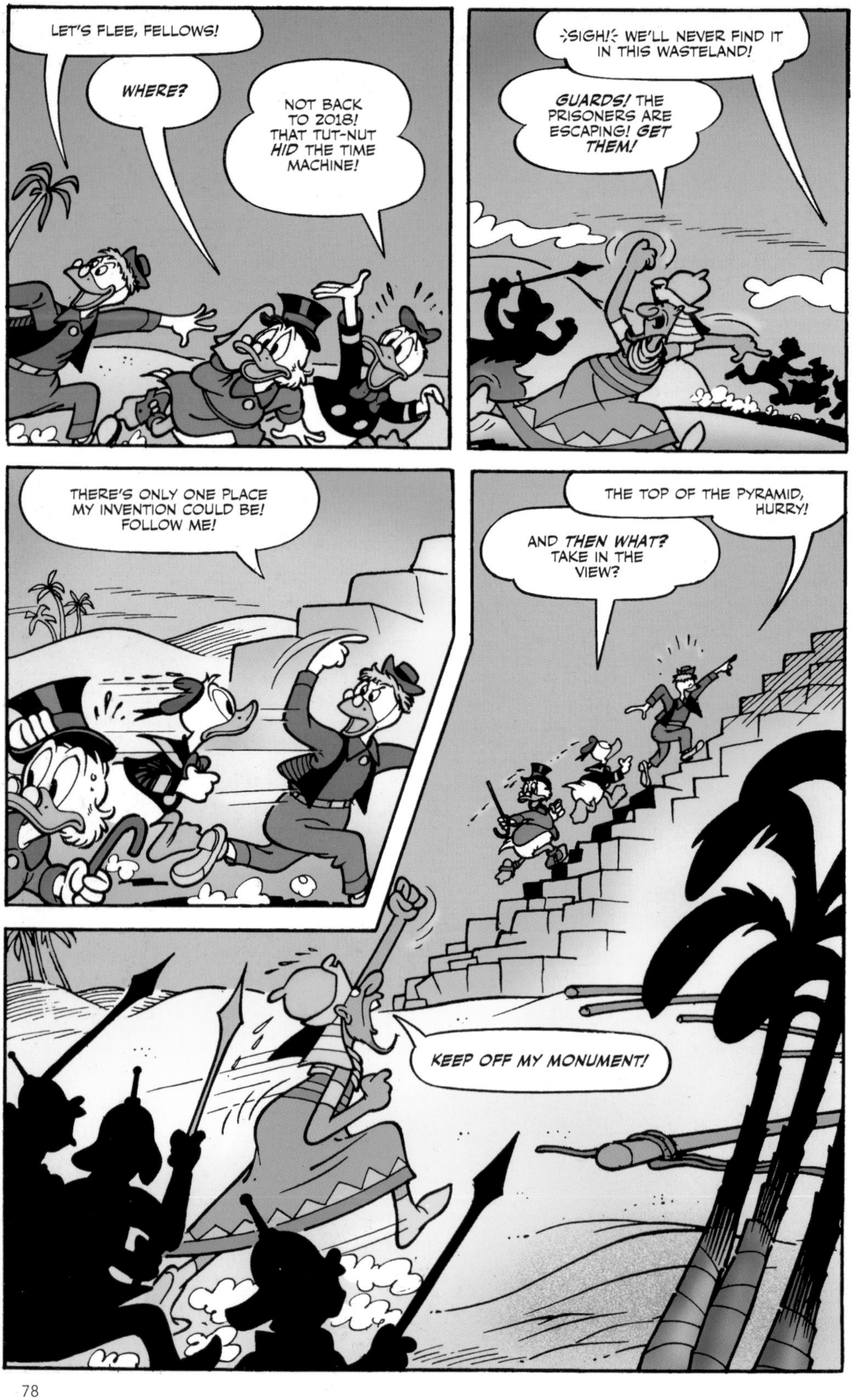
LET'S FLEE, FELLOWS!
WHERE?
NOT BACK TO 2018! THAT TUT-NUT HID THE TIME MACHINE!
-SIGH!- WE'LL NEVER FIND IT IN THIS WASTELAND!
GUARDS! THE PRISONERS ARE ESCAPING! GET THEM!
THERE'S ONLY ONE PLACE MY INVENTION COULD BE! FOLLOW ME!
THE TOP OF THE PYRAMID, HURRY!
AND THEN WHAT? TAKE IN THE VIEW?
KEEP OFF MY MONUMENT!

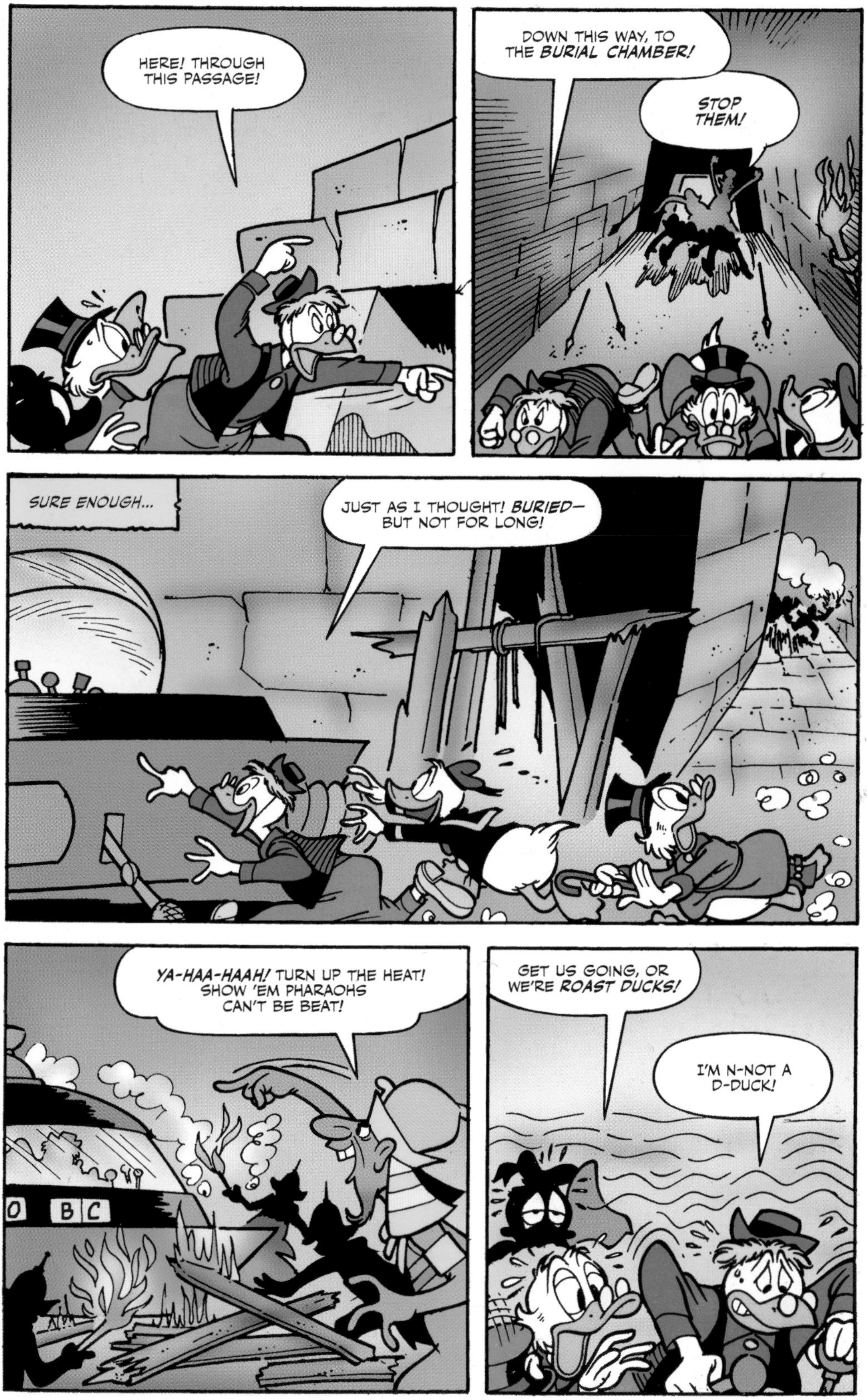
HERE! THROUGH THIS PASSAGE!
DOWN THIS WAY, TO THE BURIAL CHAMBER!
STOP THEM!
SURE ENOUGH...
JUST AS I THOUGHT! BURIED— BUT NOT FOR LONG!
YA-HAA-HAAH! TURN UP THE HEAT! SHOW 'EM PHARAOHS CAN'T BE BEAT!
O BC
GET US GOING, OR WE'RE ROAST DUCKS!
I'M N-NOT A D-DUCK!

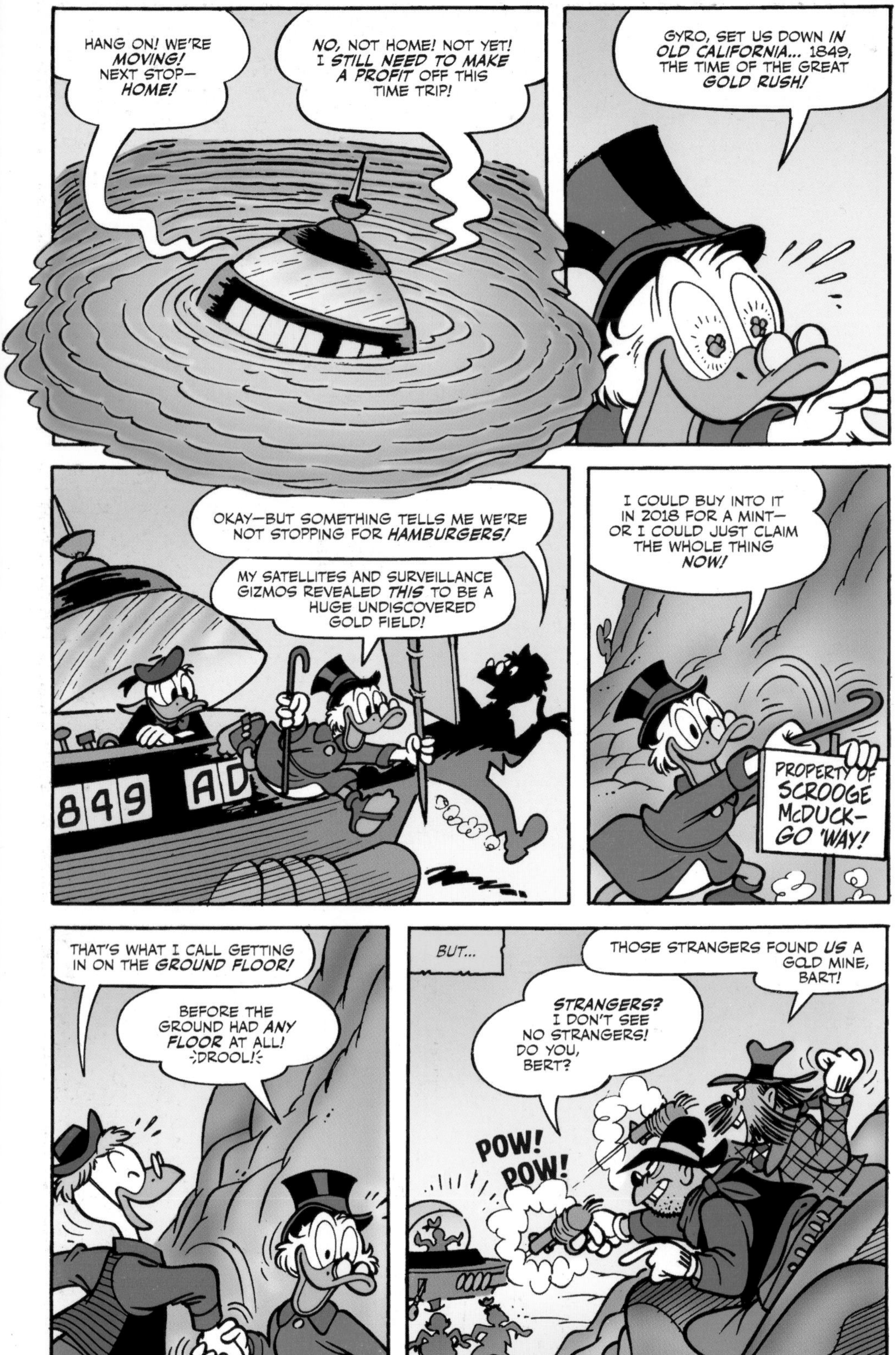
HANG ON! WE'RE MOVING! NEXT STOP— HOME!
NO, NOT HOME! NOT YET! I STILL NEED TO MAKE A PROFIT OFF THIS TIME TRIP!
GYRO, SET US DOWN IN OLD CALIFORNIA... 1849, THE TIME OF THE GREAT GOLD RUSH!
OKAY—BUT SOMETHING TELLS ME WE'RE NOT STOPPING FOR HAMBURGERS!
MY SATELLITES AND SURVEILLANCE GIZMOS REVEALED THIS TO BE A HUGE UNDISCOVERED GOLD FIELD!
849 AD
I COULD BUY INTO IT IN 2018 FOR A MINT— OR I COULD JUST CLAIM THE WHOLE THING NOW!
PROPERTY OF SCROOGE McDUCK— GO 'WAY!
THAT'S WHAT I CALL GETTING IN ON THE GROUND FLOOR!
BEFORE THE GROUND HAD ANY FLOOR AT ALL! DROOL!
BUT...
THOSE STRANGERS FOUND US A GOLD MINE, BART!
STRANGERS? I DON'T SEE NO STRANGERS! DO YOU, BERT?
POW! POW!

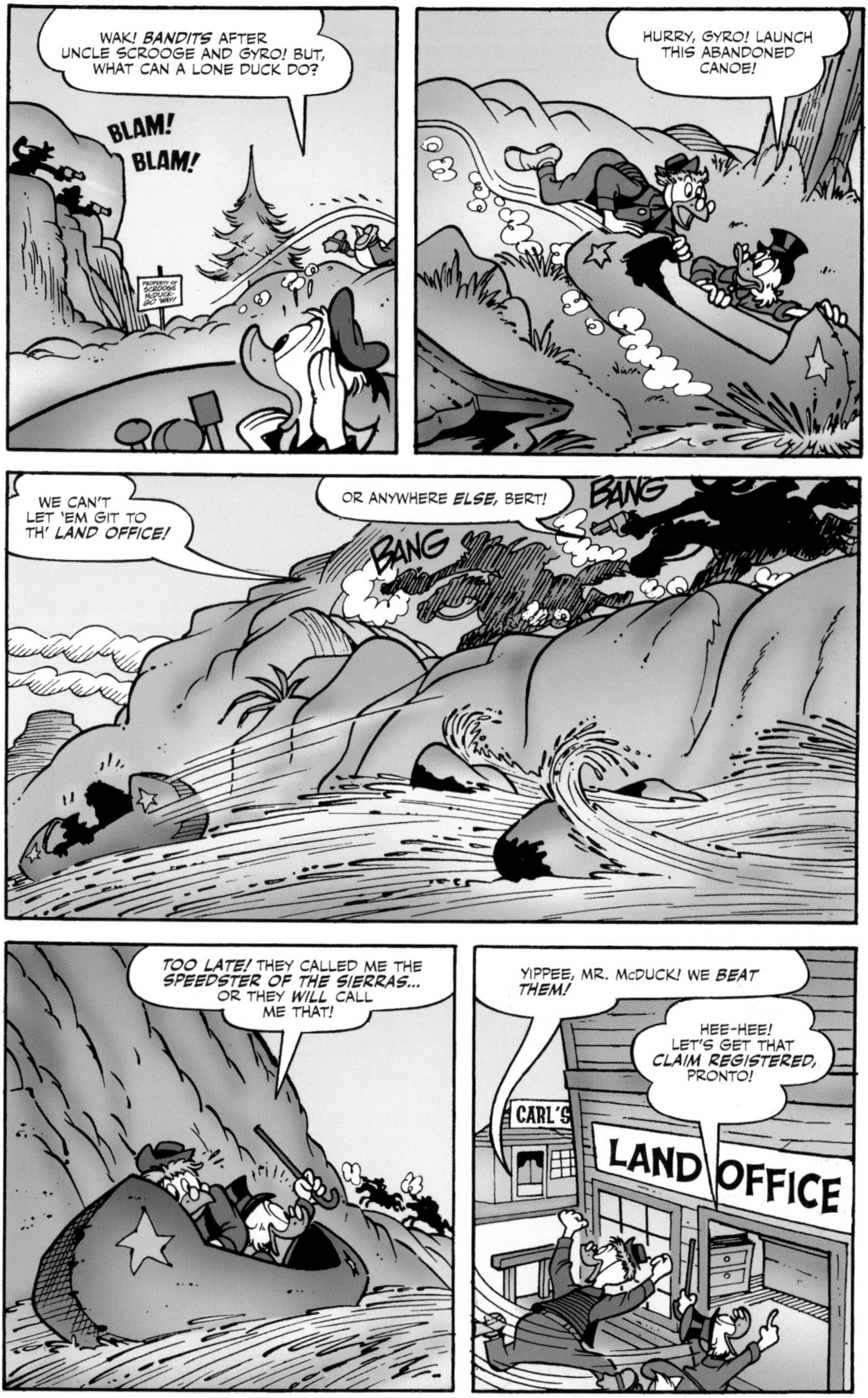
WAK! BANDITS AFTER UNCLE SCROOGE AND GYRO! BUT, WHAT CAN A LONE DUCK DO?
BLAM!
BLAM!
PROPERTY OF SCROOGE McDUCK- GO 'WAY!
HURRY, GYRO! LAUNCH THIS ABANDONED CANOE!
WE CAN'T LET 'EM GIT TO TH' LAND OFFICE!
OR ANYWHERE ELSE, BERT!
BANG
BANG
TOO LATE! THEY CALLED ME THE SPEEDSTER OF THE SIERRAS... OR THEY WILL CALL ME THAT!
YIPPEE, MR. McDUCK! WE BEAT THEM!
HEE-HEE! LET'S GET THAT CLAIM REGISTERED, PRONTO!
CARL'S
LAND OFFICE

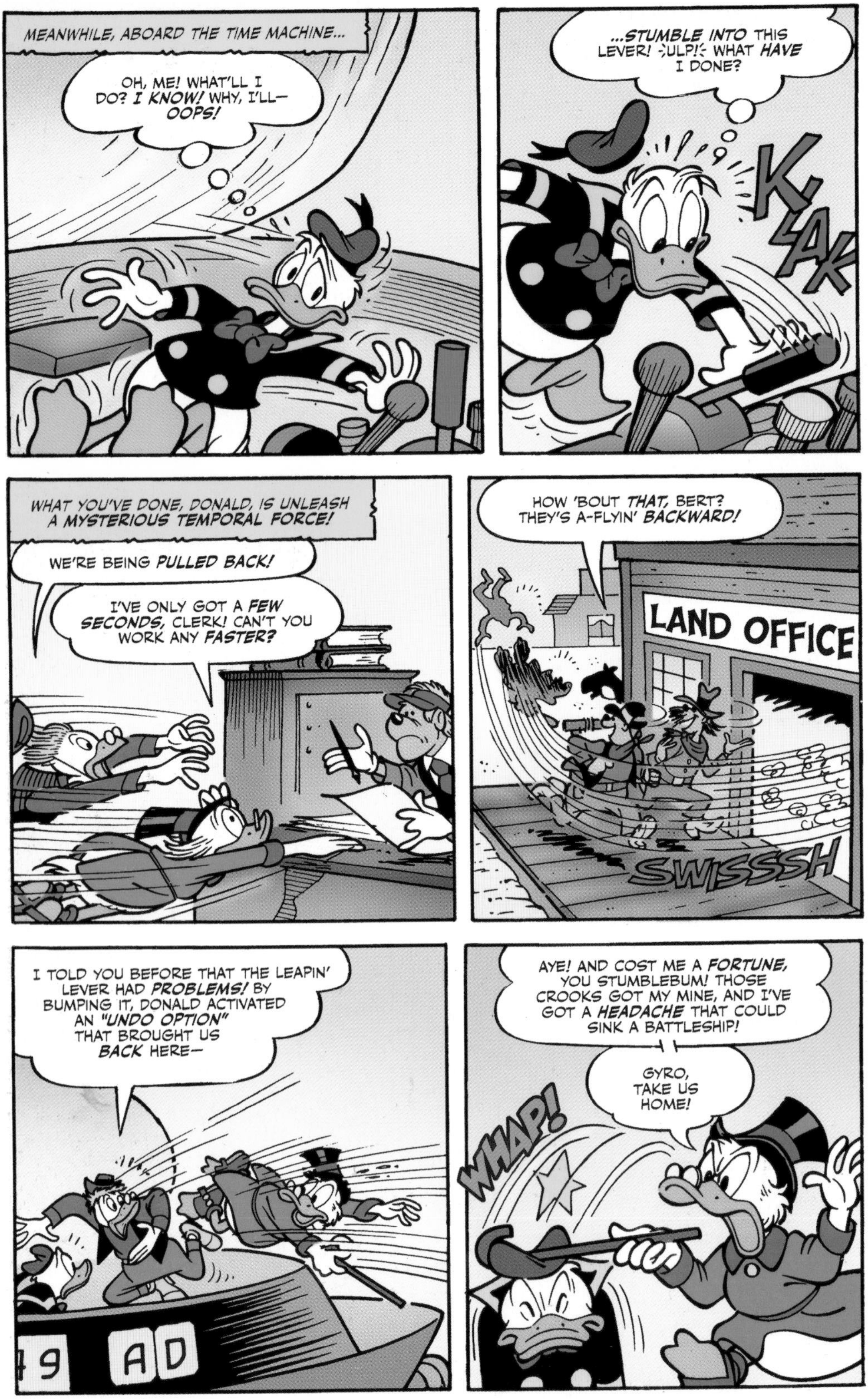
MEANWHILE, ABOARD THE TIME MACHINE...
OH, ME! WHAT'LL I DO? I KNOW! WHY, I'LL— OOPS!
...STUMBLE INTO THIS LEVER! -ULP!- WHAT HAVE I DONE?
KLAK
WHAT YOU'VE DONE, DONALD, IS UNLEASH A MYSTERIOUS TEMPORAL FORCE!
WE'RE BEING PULLED BACK!
I'VE ONLY GOT A FEW SECONDS, CLERK! CAN'T YOU WORK ANY FASTER?
HOW 'BOUT THAT, BERT? THEY'S A-FLYIN' BACKWARD!
LAND OFFICE
SWISSSH
I TOLD YOU BEFORE THAT THE LEAPIN' LEVER HAD PROBLEMS! BY BUMPING IT, DONALD ACTIVATED AN "UNDO OPTION" THAT BROUGHT US BACK HERE—
49 AD
AYE! AND COST ME A FORTUNE, YOU STUMBLEBUM! THOSE CROOKS GOT MY MINE, AND I'VE GOT A HEADACHE THAT COULD SINK A BATTLESHIP!
GYRO, TAKE US HOME!
WHAP!

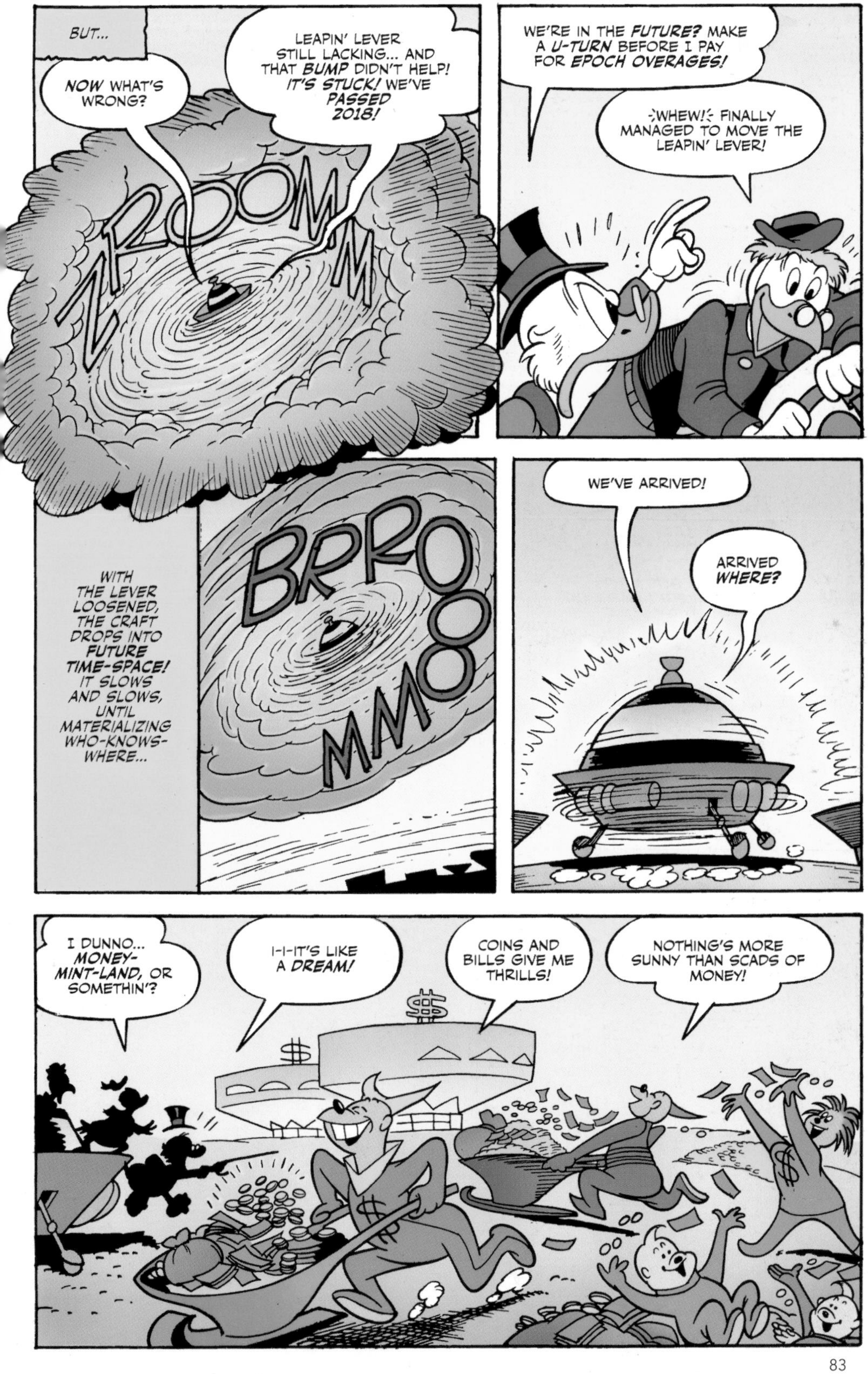
BUT...
NOW WHAT'S WRONG?
LEAPIN' LEVER STILL LACKING... AND THAT BUMP DIDN'T HELP! IT'S STUCK! WE'VE PASSED 2018!
ZROOOMM
WE'RE IN THE FUTURE? MAKE A U-TURN BEFORE I PAY FOR EPOCH OVERAGES!
WHEW! FINALLY MANAGED TO MOVE THE LEAPIN' LEVER!
WITH THE LEVER LOOSENED, THE CRAFT DROPS INTO FUTURE TIME-SPACE! IT SLOWS AND SLOWS, UNTIL MATERIALIZING WHO-KNOWS-WHERE...
BRROOOMM
WE'VE ARRIVED!
ARRIVED WHERE?
I DUNNO... MONEY-MINT-LAND, OR SOMETHIN'?
I-I-IT'S LIKE A DREAM!
COINS AND BILLS GIVE ME THRILLS!
NOTHING'S MORE SUNNY THAN SCADS OF MONEY!

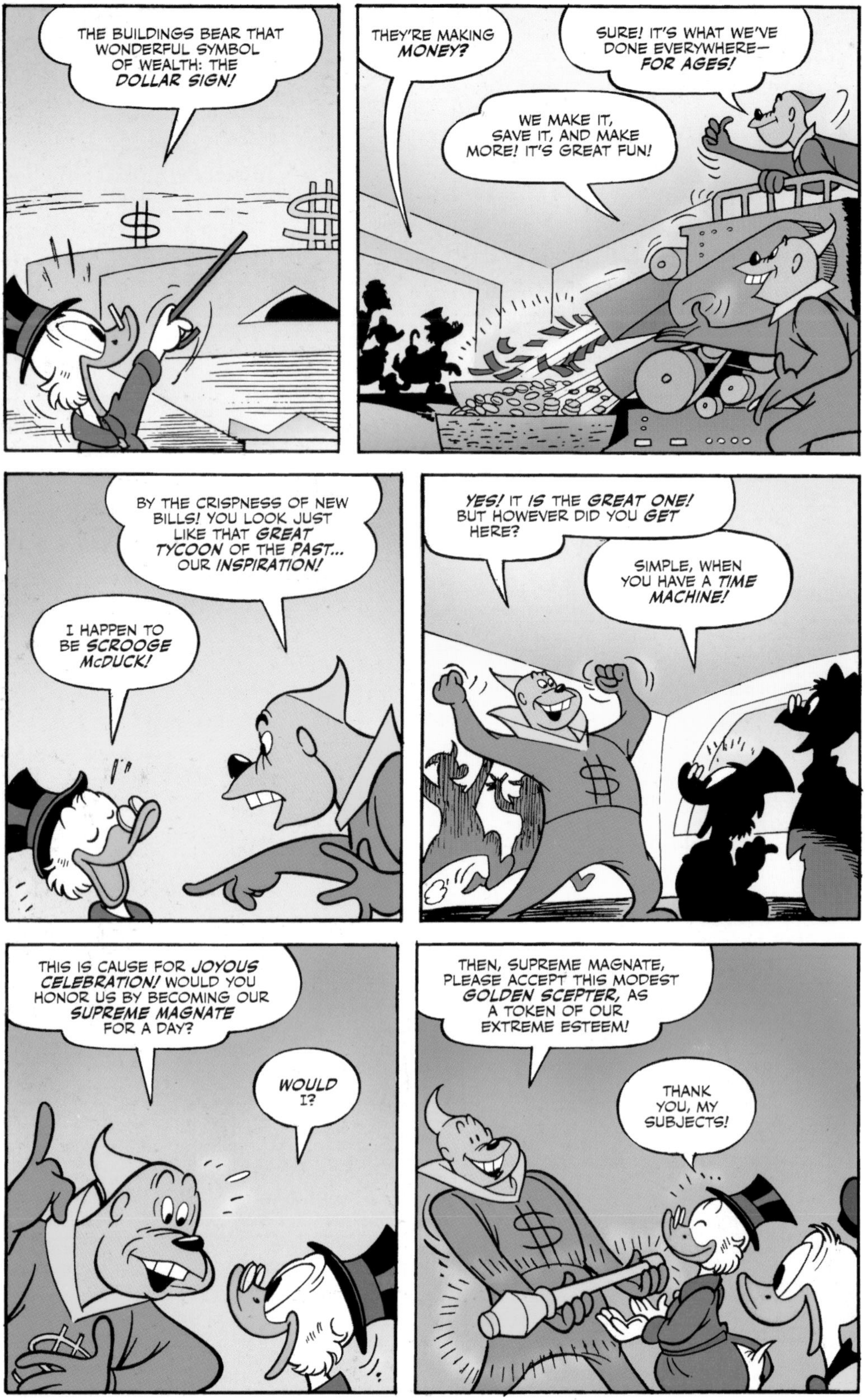
THE BUILDINGS BEAR THAT WONDERFUL SYMBOL OF WEALTH: THE DOLLAR SIGN!
THEY'RE MAKING MONEY?
SURE! IT'S WHAT WE'VE DONE EVERYWHERE— FOR AGES!
WE MAKE IT, SAVE IT, AND MAKE MORE! IT'S GREAT FUN!
BY THE CRISPNESS OF NEW BILLS! YOU LOOK JUST LIKE THAT GREAT TYCOON OF THE PAST... OUR INSPIRATION!
I HAPPEN TO BE SCROOGE McDUCK!
YES! IT IS THE GREAT ONE! BUT HOWEVER DID YOU GET HERE?
SIMPLE, WHEN YOU HAVE A TIME MACHINE!
THIS IS CAUSE FOR JOYOUS CELEBRATION! WOULD YOU HONOR US BY BECOMING OUR SUPREME MAGNATE FOR A DAY?
WOULD I?
THEN, SUPREME MAGNATE, PLEASE ACCEPT THIS MODEST GOLDEN SCEPTER, AS A TOKEN OF OUR EXTREME ESTEEM!
THANK YOU, MY SUBJECTS!

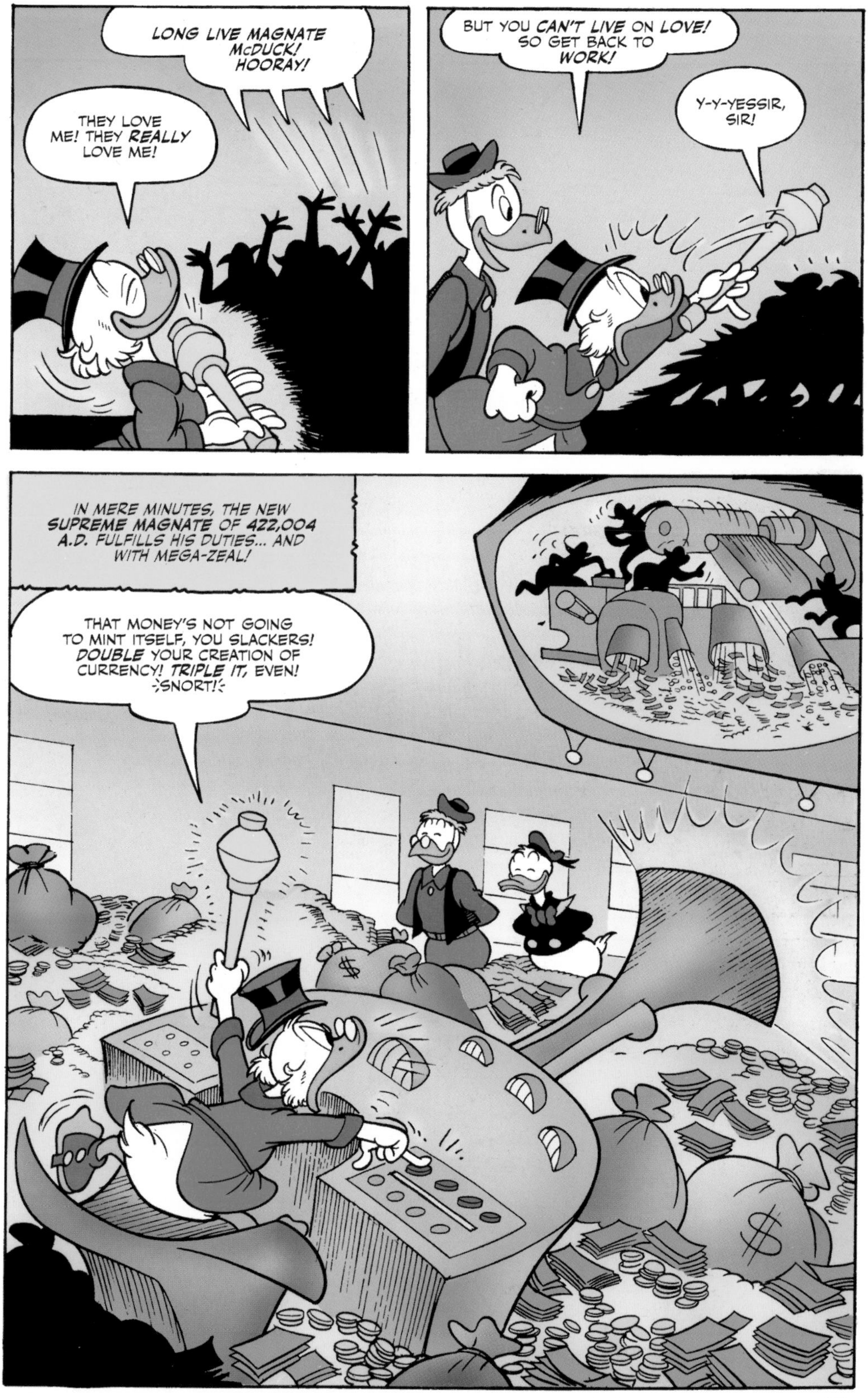

LONG LIVE MAGNATE McDUCK! HOORAY!
THEY LOVE ME! THEY REALLY LOVE ME!
BUT YOU CAN'T LIVE ON LOVE! SO GET BACK TO WORK!
Y-Y-YESSIR, SIR!
IN MERE MINUTES, THE NEW SUPREME MAGNATE OF 422,004 A.D. FULFILLS HIS DUTIES... AND WITH MEGA-ZEAL!
THAT MONEY'S NOT GOING TO MINT ITSELF, YOU SLACKERS! DOUBLE YOUR CREATION OF CURRENCY! TRIPLE IT, EVEN! SNORT!

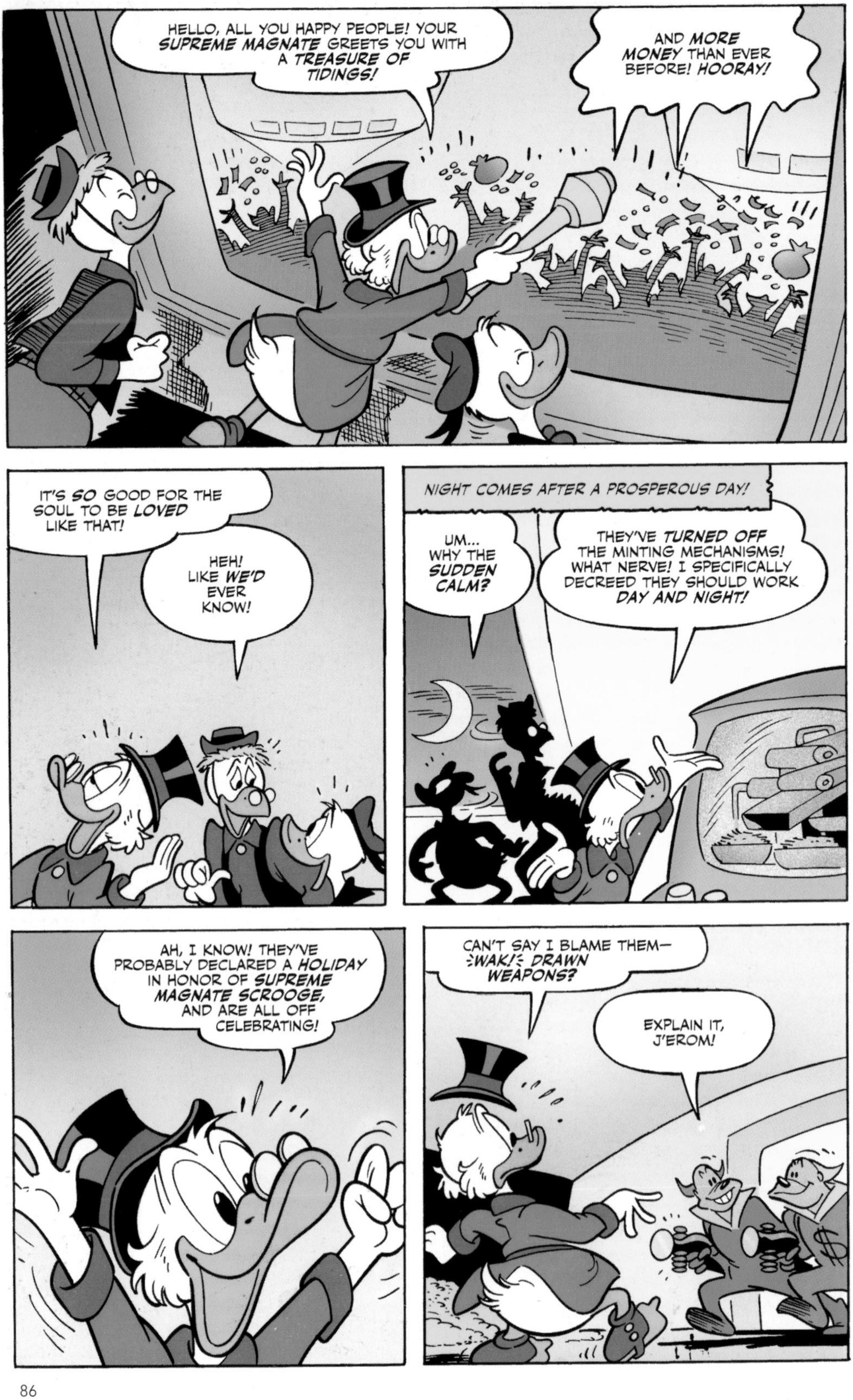

HELLO, ALL YOU HAPPY PEOPLE! YOUR SUPREME MAGNATE GREETS YOU WITH A TREASURE OF TIDINGS!
AND MORE MONEY THAN EVER BEFORE! HOORAY!
IT'S SO GOOD FOR THE SOUL TO BE LOVED LIKE THAT!
HEH! LIKE WE'D EVER KNOW!
NIGHT COMES AFTER A PROSPEROUS DAY!
UM... WHY THE SUDDEN CALM?
THEY'VE TURNED OFF THE MINTING MECHANISMS! WHAT NERVE! I SPECIFICALLY DECREED THEY SHOULD WORK DAY AND NIGHT!
AH, I KNOW! THEY'VE PROBABLY DECLARED A HOLIDAY IN HONOR OF SUPREME MAGNATE SCROOGE, AND ARE ALL OFF CELEBRATING!
CAN'T SAY I BLAME THEM— WAK! DRAWN WEAPONS?
EXPLAIN IT, J'EROM!

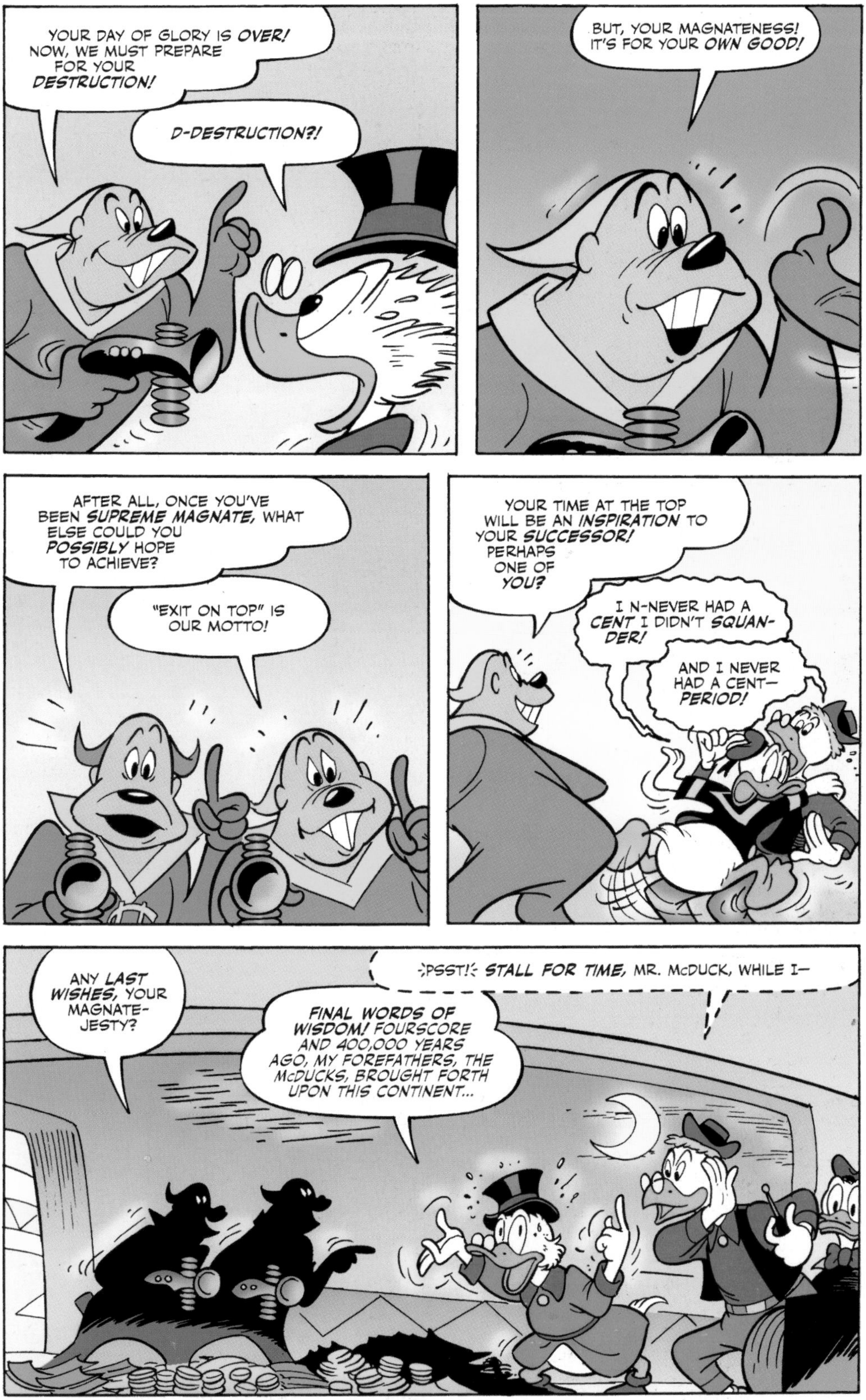
YOUR DAY OF GLORY IS OVER! NOW, WE MUST PREPARE FOR YOUR DESTRUCTION!
D-DESTRUCTION?!
BUT, YOUR MAGNATENESS! IT'S FOR YOUR OWN GOOD!
AFTER ALL, ONCE YOU'VE BEEN SUPREME MAGNATE, WHAT ELSE COULD YOU POSSIBLY HOPE TO ACHIEVE?
"EXIT ON TOP" IS OUR MOTTO!
YOUR TIME AT THE TOP WILL BE AN INSPIRATION TO YOUR SUCCESSOR! PERHAPS ONE OF YOU?
I N-NEVER HAD A CENT I DIDN'T SQUANDER!
AND I NEVER HAD A CENT—PERIOD!
ANY LAST WISHES, YOUR MAGNATE-JESTY?
-PSST!- STALL FOR TIME, MR. McDUCK, WHILE I—
FINAL WORDS OF WISDOM! FOURSCORE AND 400,000 YEARS AGO, MY FOREFATHERS, THE McDUCKS, BROUGHT FORTH UPON THIS CONTINENT...

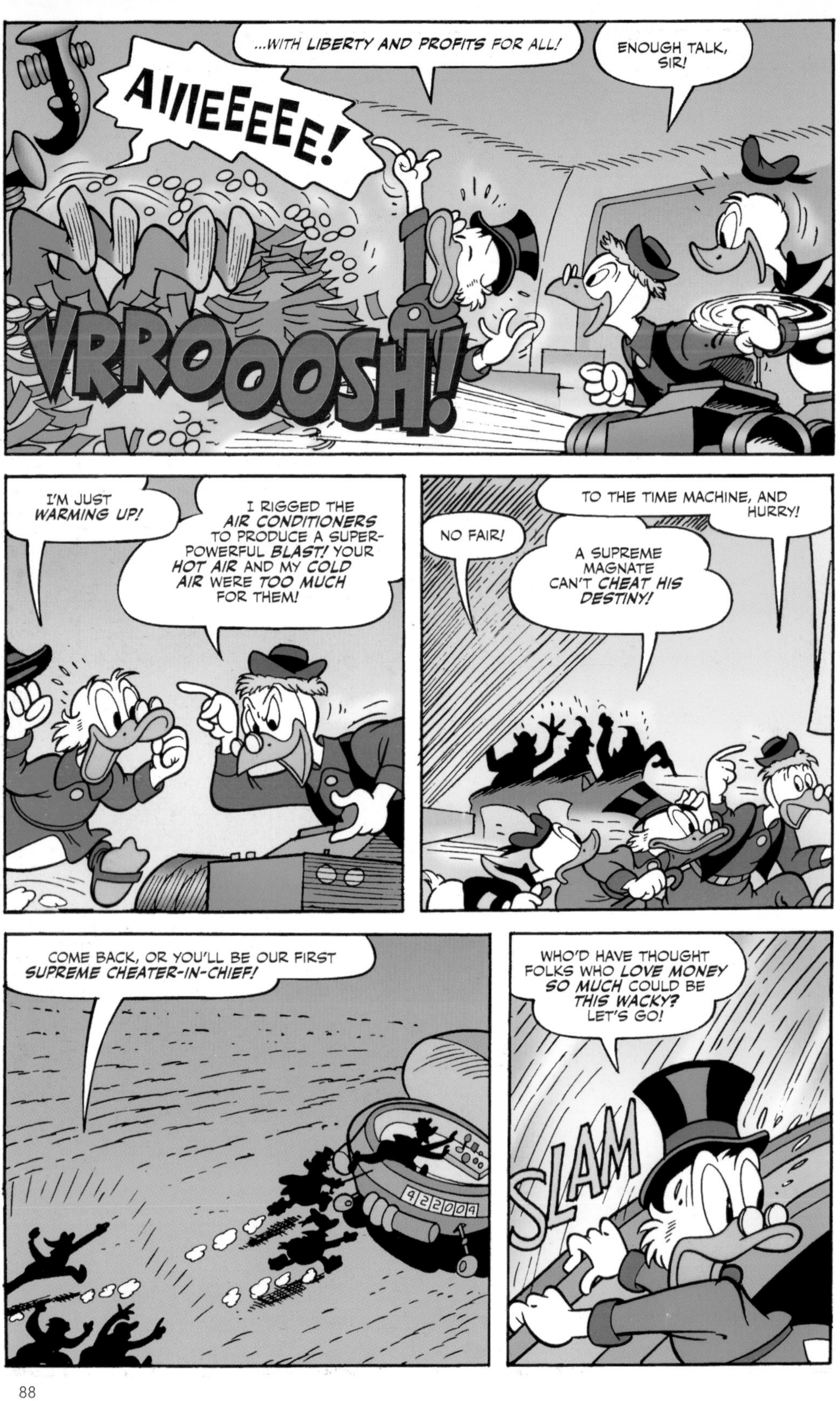
...WITH LIBERTY AND PROFITS FOR ALL!
AIIIEEEEE!
ENOUGH TALK, SIR!
VRROOOSH!
I'M JUST WARMING UP!
I RIGGED THE AIR CONDITIONERS TO PRODUCE A SUPER-POWERFUL BLAST! YOUR HOT AIR AND MY COLD AIR WERE TOO MUCH FOR THEM!
TO THE TIME MACHINE, AND HURRY!
NO FAIR!
A SUPREME MAGNATE CAN'T CHEAT HIS DESTINY!
COME BACK, OR YOU'LL BE OUR FIRST SUPREME CHEATER-IN-CHIEF!
4220004
WHO'D HAVE THOUGHT FOLKS WHO LOVE MONEY SO MUCH COULD BE THIS WACKY? LET'S GO!
SLAM

THE LEAPIN' LEVER'S LOUSED-UP AGAIN!

YOU MEAN WE'RE *STUCK?* IN THE SIGHTS OF THAT *CANNON?*

READY! AIM!

422004 AD

WELL, I'LL BE BANK-RUPTED... THEY *VANISHED!*

AFTER *SO MUCH COST* TO MOBILIZE THE CANNON, TOO! ⸴SOB! SOB!⸴

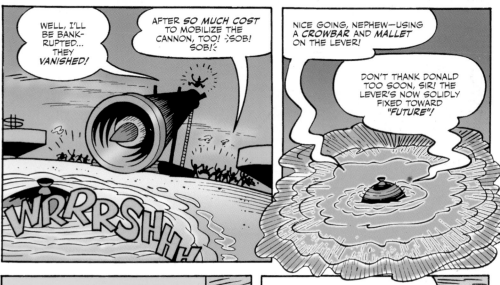

NICE GOING, NEPHEW—USING A *CROWBAR* AND *MALLET* ON THE LEVER!

DON'T THANK DONALD TOO SOON, SIR! THE LEVER'S NOW SOLIDLY FIXED TOWARD *"FUTURE"!*

WRRRSHH!

BY THE TIME GYRO UNDOES DONALD'S (ADMITTEDLY LIFE-SAVING) DAMAGE...

WE'VE STOPPED, BUT *DOUBLED THE DURATION* OF OUR PREVIOUS TRIP—FROM 422,004 TO *844,008 A.D.!*

THE *SUN!* IT'S WEAK! RECEDING! *GROWING DIM!*

⸴BRRR!⸴ PREPARE FOR A *COLD LANDING!*

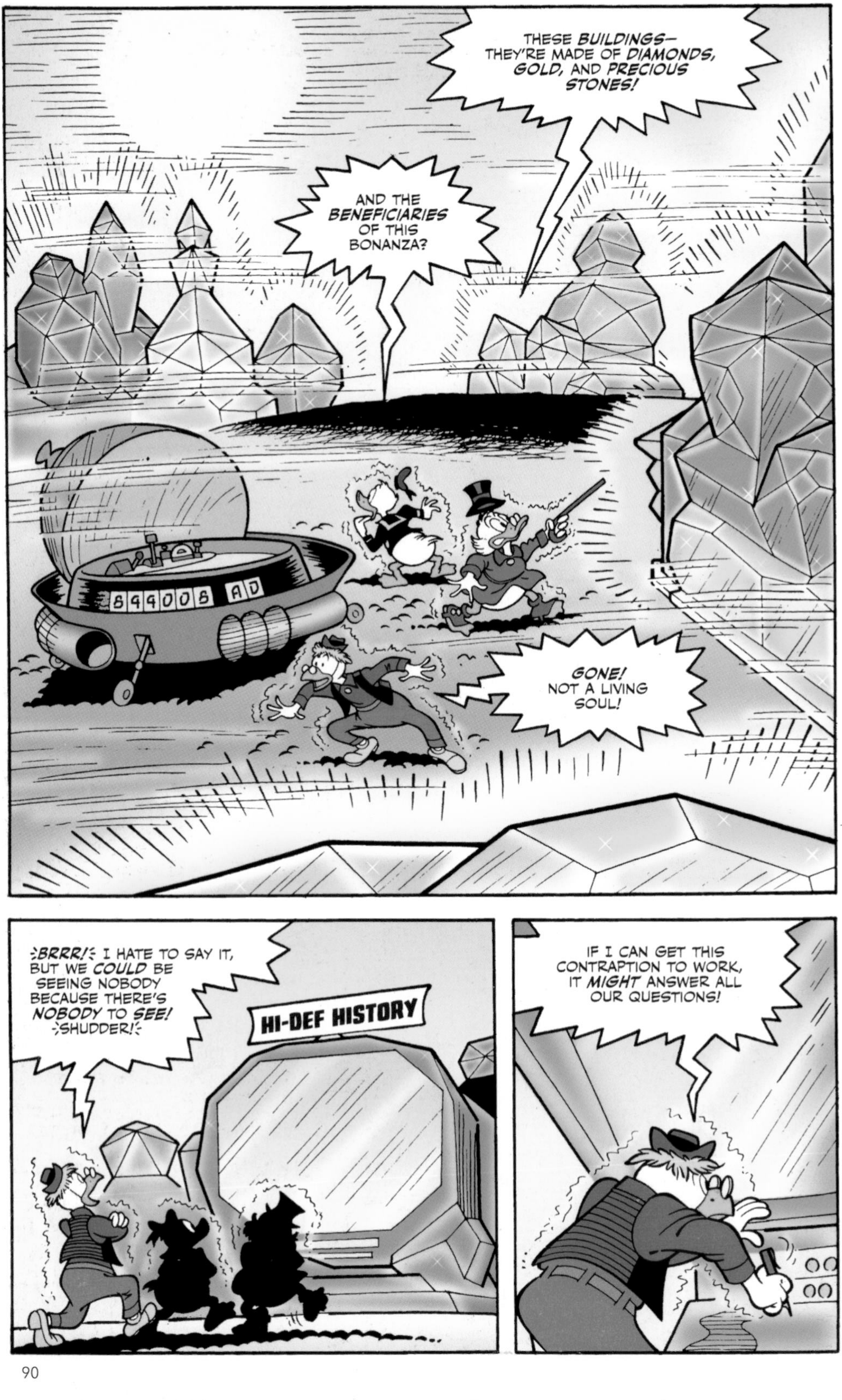
THESE BUILDINGS— THEY'RE MADE OF DIAMONDS, GOLD, AND PRECIOUS STONES!
AND THE BENEFICIARIES OF THIS BONANZA?
GONE! NOT A LIVING SOUL!
BRRR! I HATE TO SAY IT, BUT WE COULD BE SEEING NOBODY BECAUSE THERE'S NOBODY TO SEE! SHUDDER!
HI-DEF HISTORY
IF I CAN GET THIS CONTRAPTION TO WORK, IT MIGHT ANSWER ALL OUR QUESTIONS!

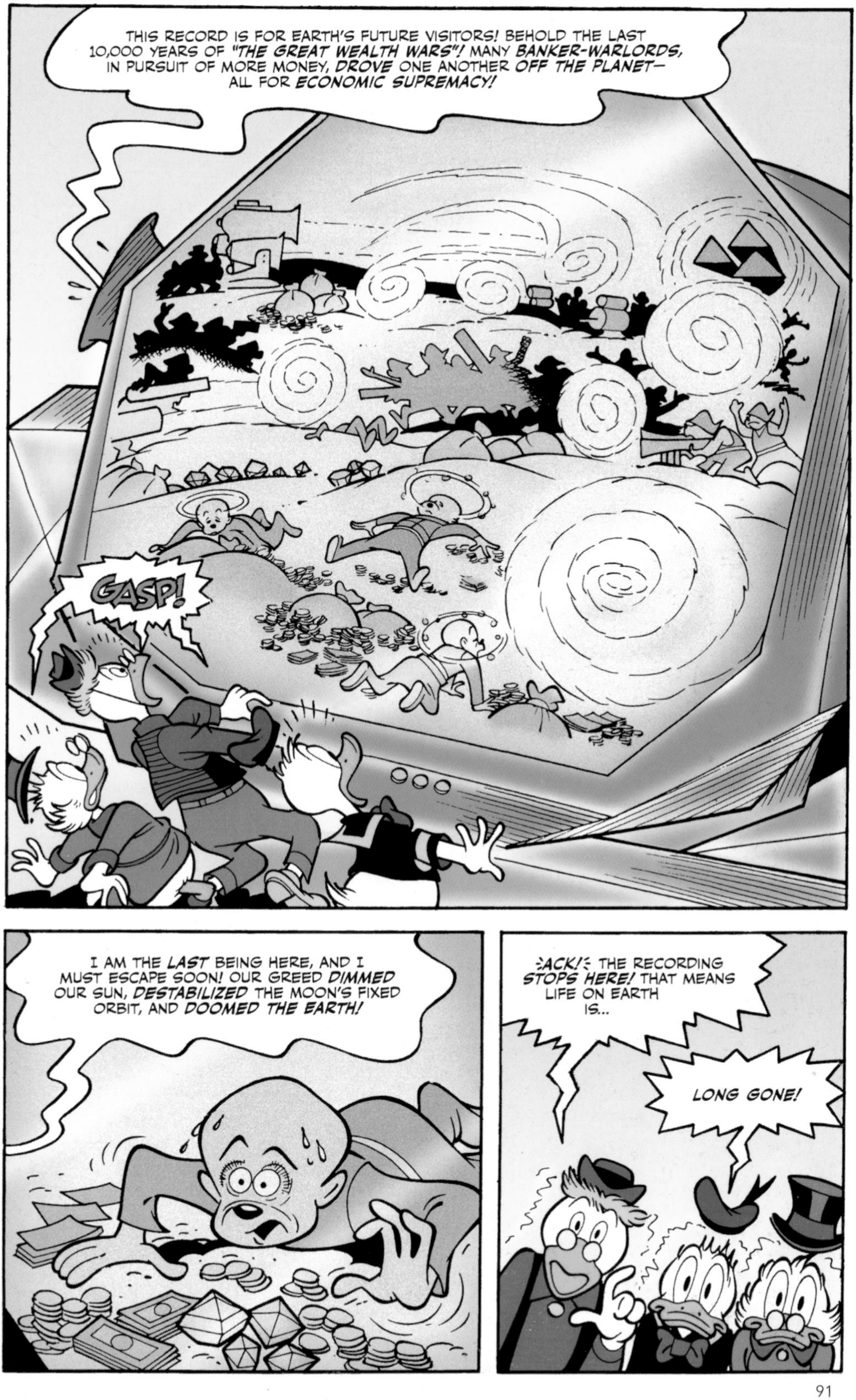
THIS RECORD IS FOR EARTH'S FUTURE VISITORS! BEHOLD THE LAST 10,000 YEARS OF "THE GREAT WEALTH WARS"! MANY BANKER-WARLORDS, IN PURSUIT OF MORE MONEY, DROVE ONE ANOTHER OFF THE PLANET— ALL FOR ECONOMIC SUPREMACY!
GASP!
I AM THE LAST BEING HERE, AND I MUST ESCAPE SOON! OUR GREED DIMMED OUR SUN, DESTABILIZED THE MOON'S FIXED ORBIT, AND DOOMED THE EARTH!
ACK! THE RECORDING STOPS HERE! THAT MEANS LIFE ON EARTH IS...
LONG GONE!

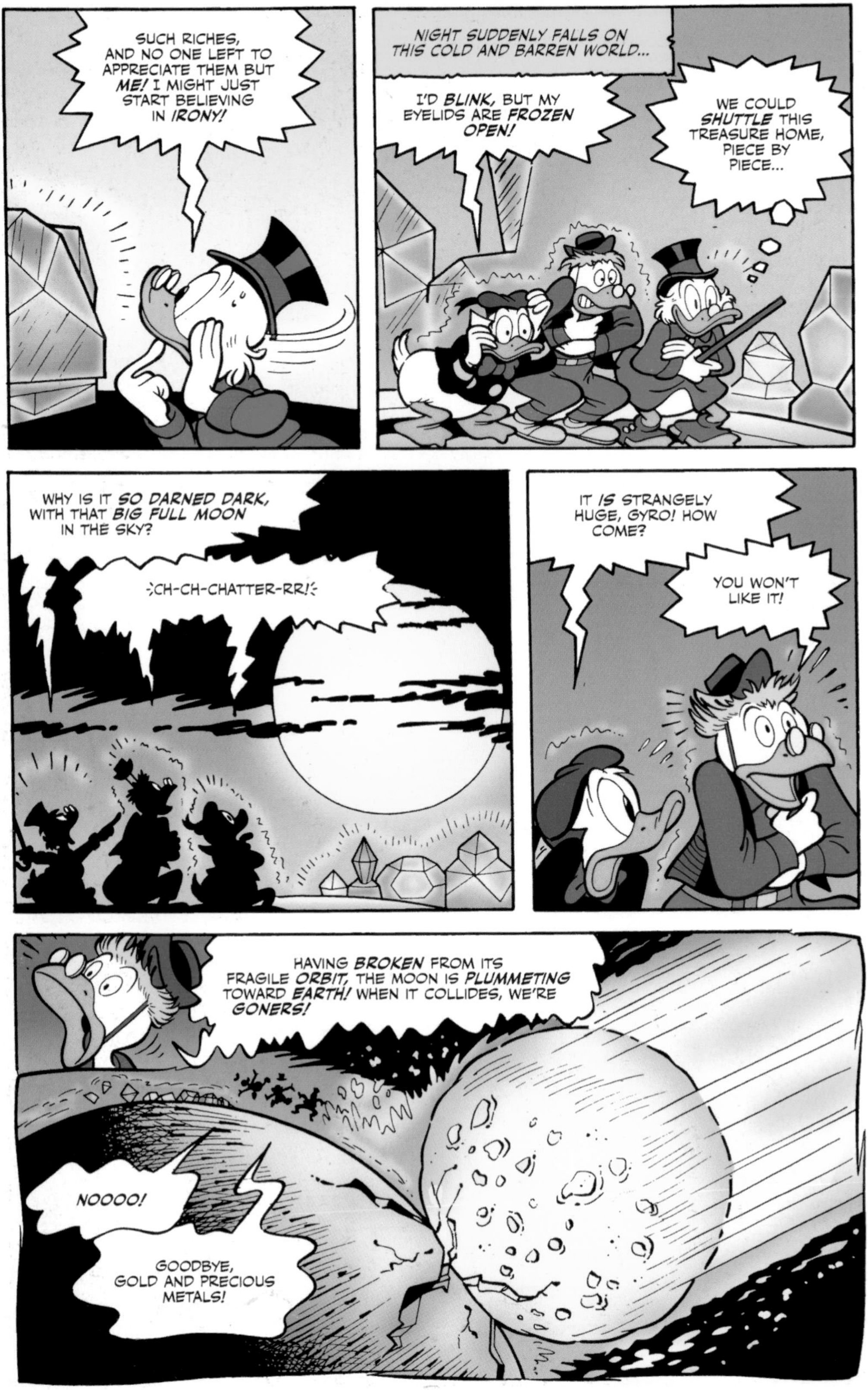
SUCH RICHES, AND NO ONE LEFT TO APPRECIATE THEM BUT ME! I MIGHT JUST START BELIEVING IN IRONY!
NIGHT SUDDENLY FALLS ON THIS COLD AND BARREN WORLD...
I'D BLINK, BUT MY EYELIDS ARE FROZEN OPEN!
WE COULD SHUTTLE THIS TREASURE HOME, PIECE BY PIECE...
WHY IS IT SO DARNED DARK, WITH THAT BIG FULL MOON IN THE SKY?
CH-CH-CHATTER-RR!
IT IS STRANGELY HUGE, GYRO! HOW COME?
YOU WON'T LIKE IT!
HAVING BROKEN FROM ITS FRAGILE ORBIT, THE MOON IS PLUMMETING TOWARD EARTH! WHEN IT COLLIDES, WE'RE GONERS!
NOOOO!
GOODBYE, GOLD AND PRECIOUS METALS!

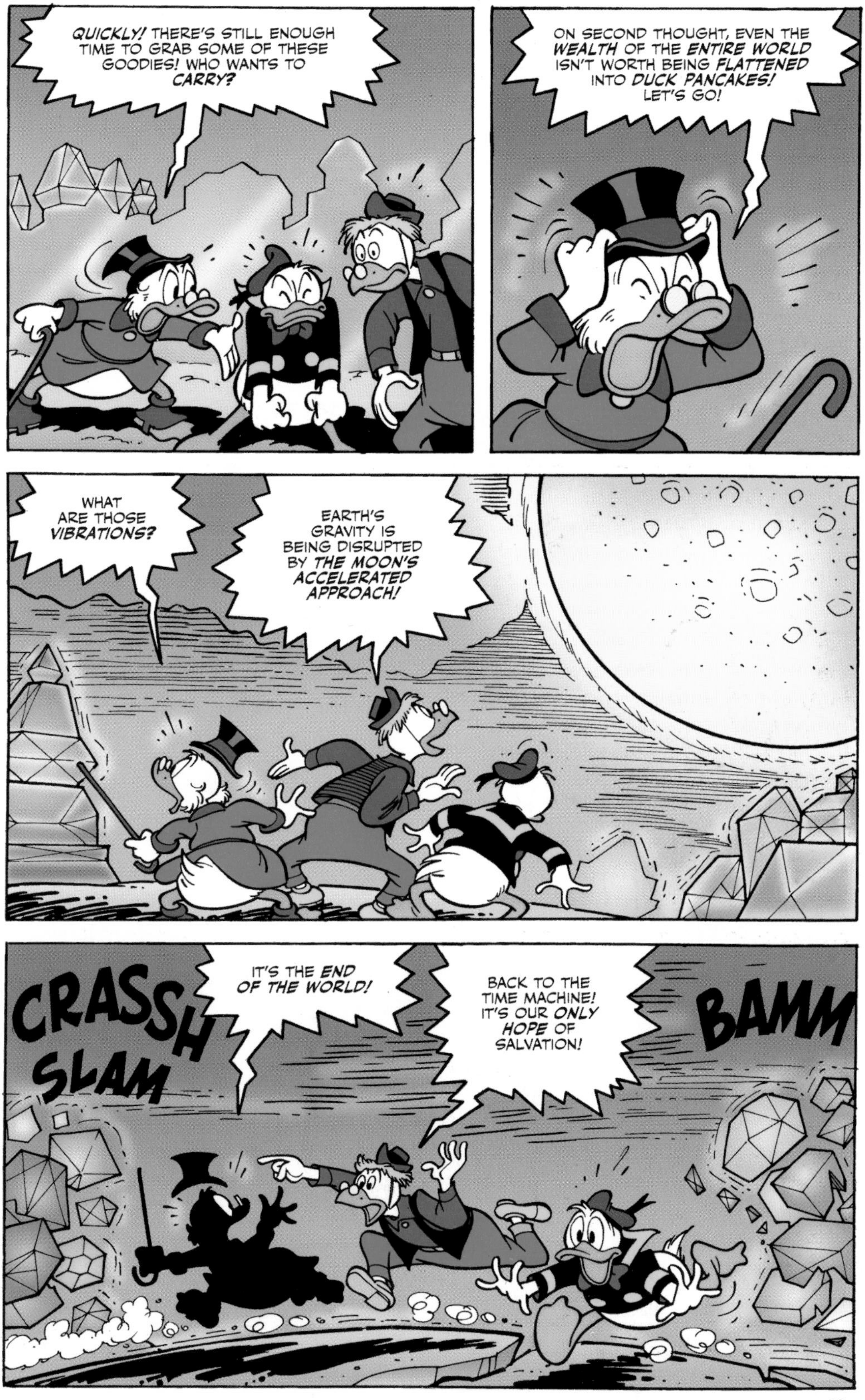
QUICKLY! THERE'S STILL ENOUGH TIME TO GRAB SOME OF THESE GOODIES! WHO WANTS TO CARRY?
ON SECOND THOUGHT, EVEN THE WEALTH OF THE ENTIRE WORLD ISN'T WORTH BEING FLATTENED INTO DUCK PANCAKES! LET'S GO!
WHAT ARE THOSE VIBRATIONS?
EARTH'S GRAVITY IS BEING DISRUPTED BY THE MOON'S ACCELERATED APPROACH!
CRASSH
SLAM
IT'S THE END OF THE WORLD!
BACK TO THE TIME MACHINE! IT'S OUR ONLY HOPE OF SALVATION!
BAMM

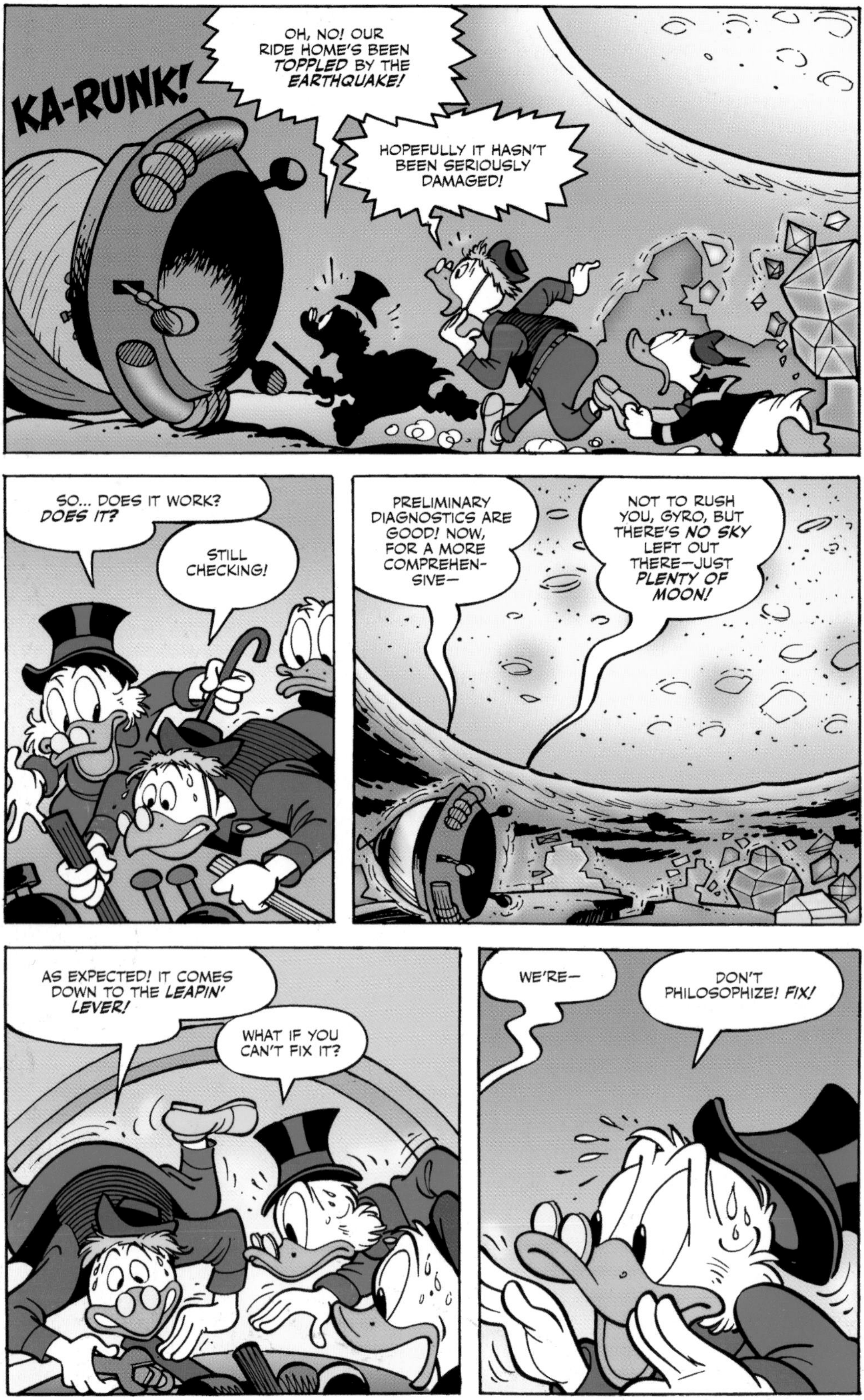
KA-RUNK!
OH, NO! OUR RIDE HOME'S BEEN *TOPPLED* BY THE *EARTHQUAKE!*
HOPEFULLY IT HASN'T BEEN SERIOUSLY DAMAGED!
SO... DOES IT WORK? *DOES IT?*
STILL CHECKING!
PRELIMINARY DIAGNOSTICS ARE GOOD! NOW, FOR A MORE COMPREHEN-SIVE—
NOT TO RUSH YOU, GYRO, BUT THERE'S *NO SKY* LEFT OUT THERE—JUST *PLENTY OF MOON!*
AS EXPECTED! IT COMES DOWN TO THE *LEAPIN' LEVER!*
WHAT IF YOU CAN'T FIX IT?
WE'RE—
DON'T PHILOSOPHIZE! *FIX!*

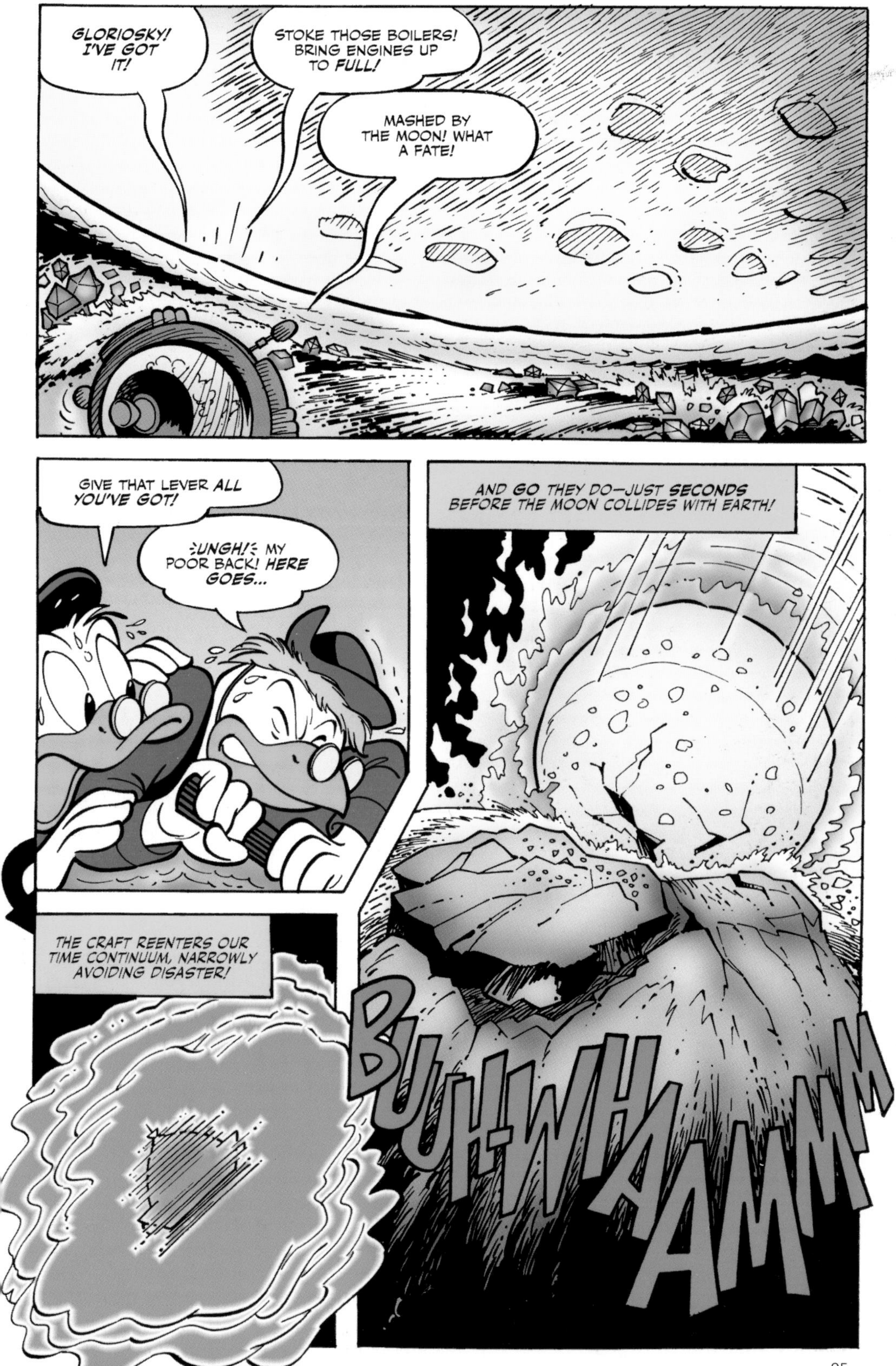
GLORIOSKY! I'VE GOT IT!
STOKE THOSE BOILERS! BRING ENGINES UP TO FULL!
MASHED BY THE MOON! WHAT A FATE!
GIVE THAT LEVER ALL YOU'VE GOT!
UNGH! MY POOR BACK! HERE GOES...
AND GO THEY DO—JUST SECONDS BEFORE THE MOON COLLIDES WITH EARTH!
THE CRAFT REENTERS OUR TIME CONTINUUM, NARROWLY AVOIDING DISASTER!
BUH-WHAAMMM

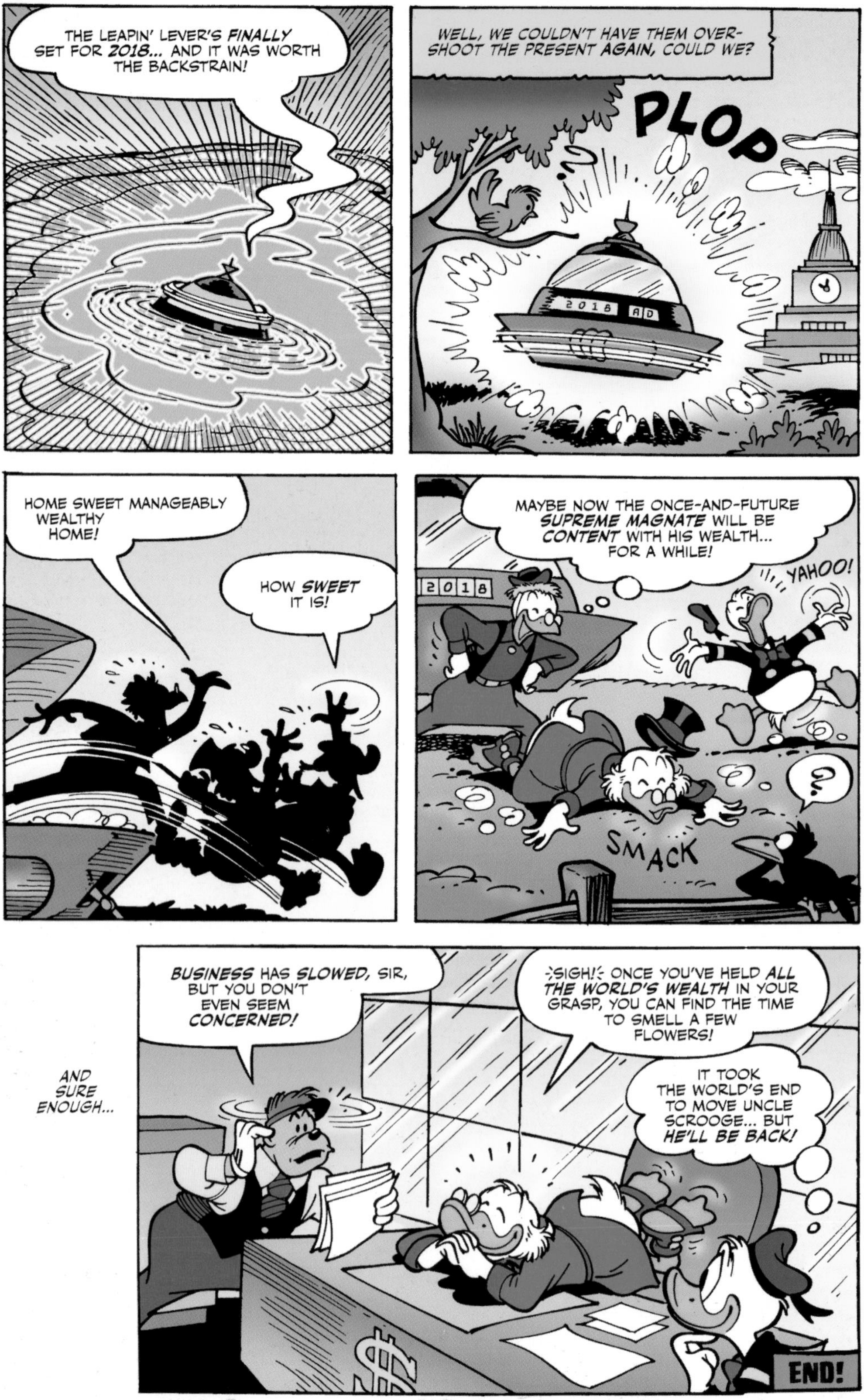
THE LEAPIN' LEVER'S FINALLY SET FOR 2018... AND IT WAS WORTH THE BACKSTRAIN!
WELL, WE COULDN'T HAVE THEM OVERSHOOT THE PRESENT AGAIN, COULD WE?
PLOP
2018 AD
HOME SWEET MANAGEABLY WEALTHY HOME!
HOW SWEET IT IS!
MAYBE NOW THE ONCE-AND-FUTURE SUPREME MAGNATE WILL BE CONTENT WITH HIS WEALTH... FOR A WHILE!
2018
YAHOO!
SMACK
AND SURE ENOUGH...
BUSINESS HAS SLOWED, SIR, BUT YOU DON'T EVEN SEEM CONCERNED!
-SIGH!- ONCE YOU'VE HELD ALL THE WORLD'S WEALTH IN YOUR GRASP, YOU CAN FIND THE TIME TO SMELL A FEW FLOWERS!
IT TOOK THE WORLD'S END TO MOVE UNCLE SCROOGE... BUT HE'LL BE BACK!
END!

COVER GALLERY

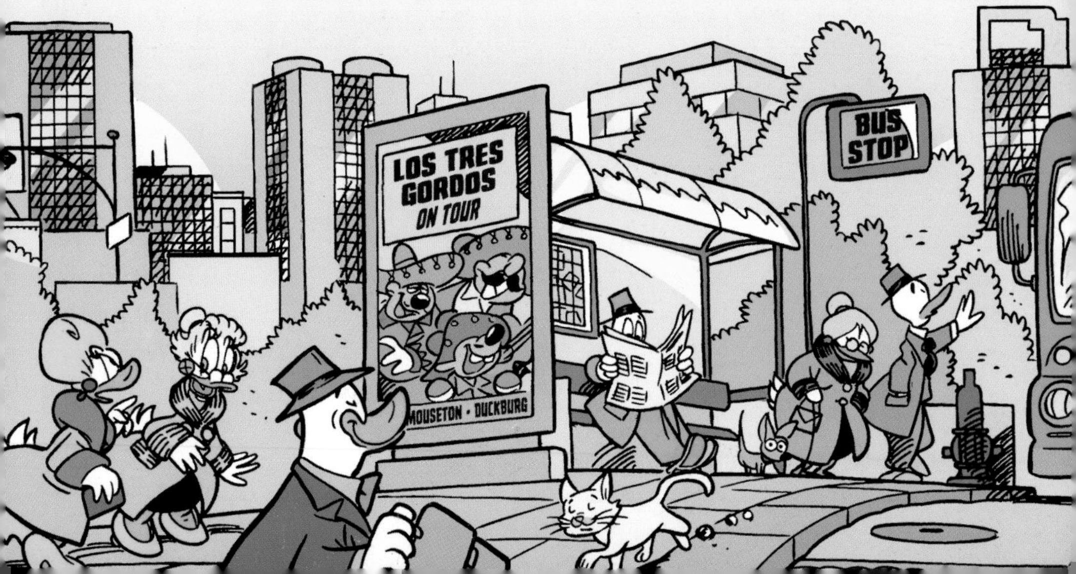
LOS TRES GORDOS
ON TOUR
MOUSETON • DUCKBURG
BUS STOP

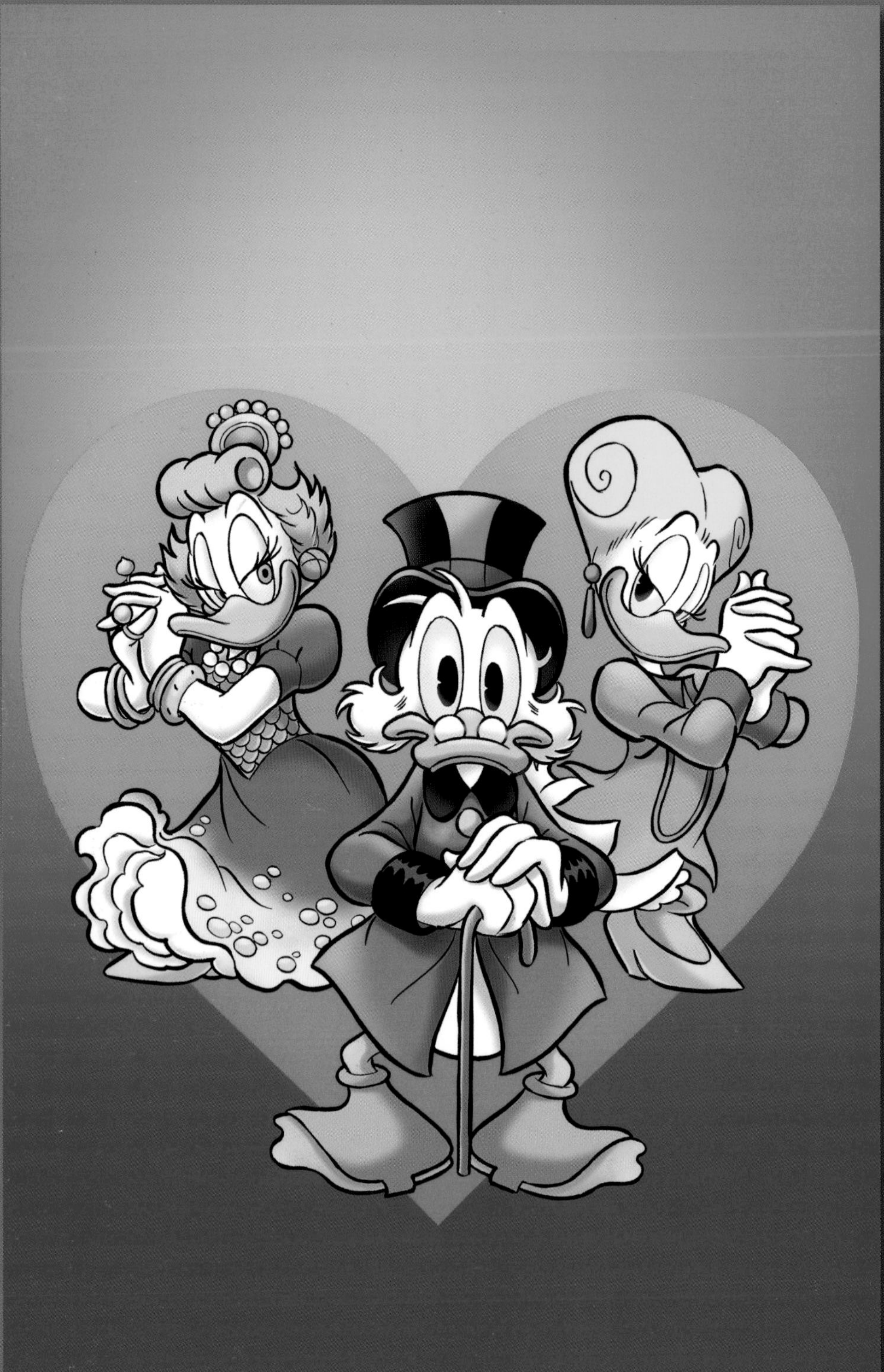

ART BY **ANDREA FRECCERO,** COLORS BY **MARCO COLLETTI**

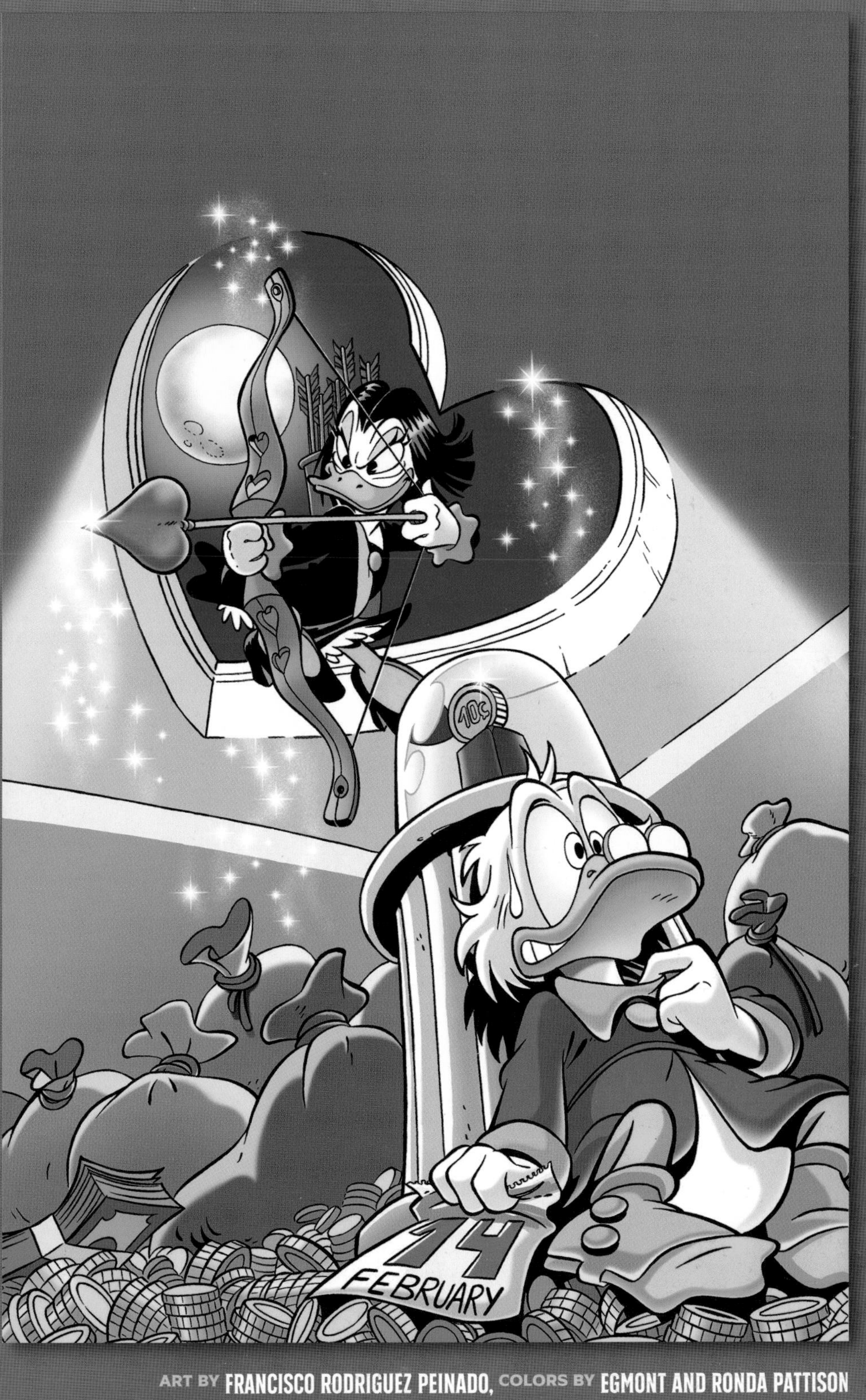
10¢
14
FEBRUARY

ART BY FRANCISCO RODRIGUEZ PEINADO, COLORS BY EGMONT AND RONDA PATTISON

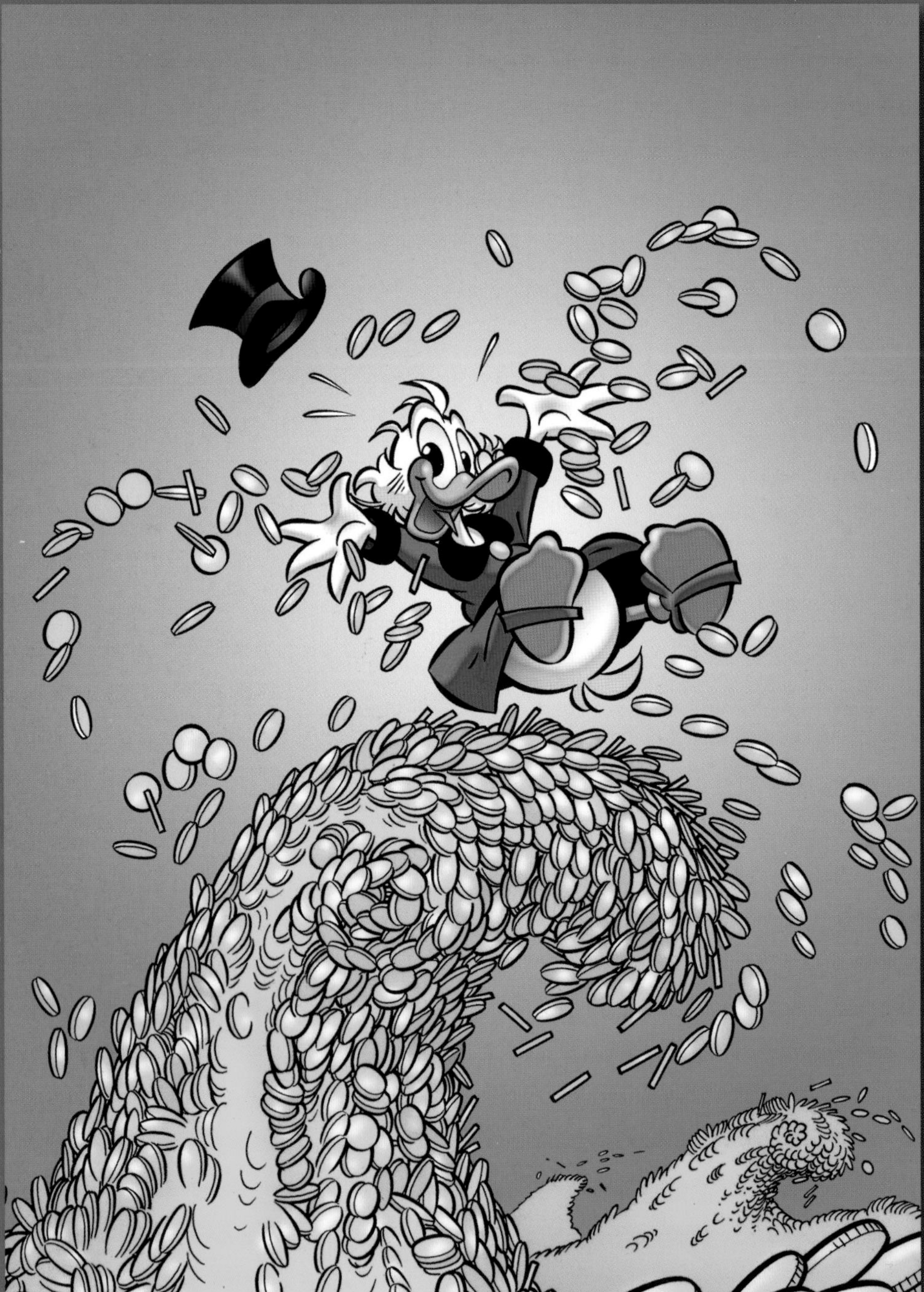

ART BY ANDREA FRECCERO, COLORS BY MAX MONTEDURO

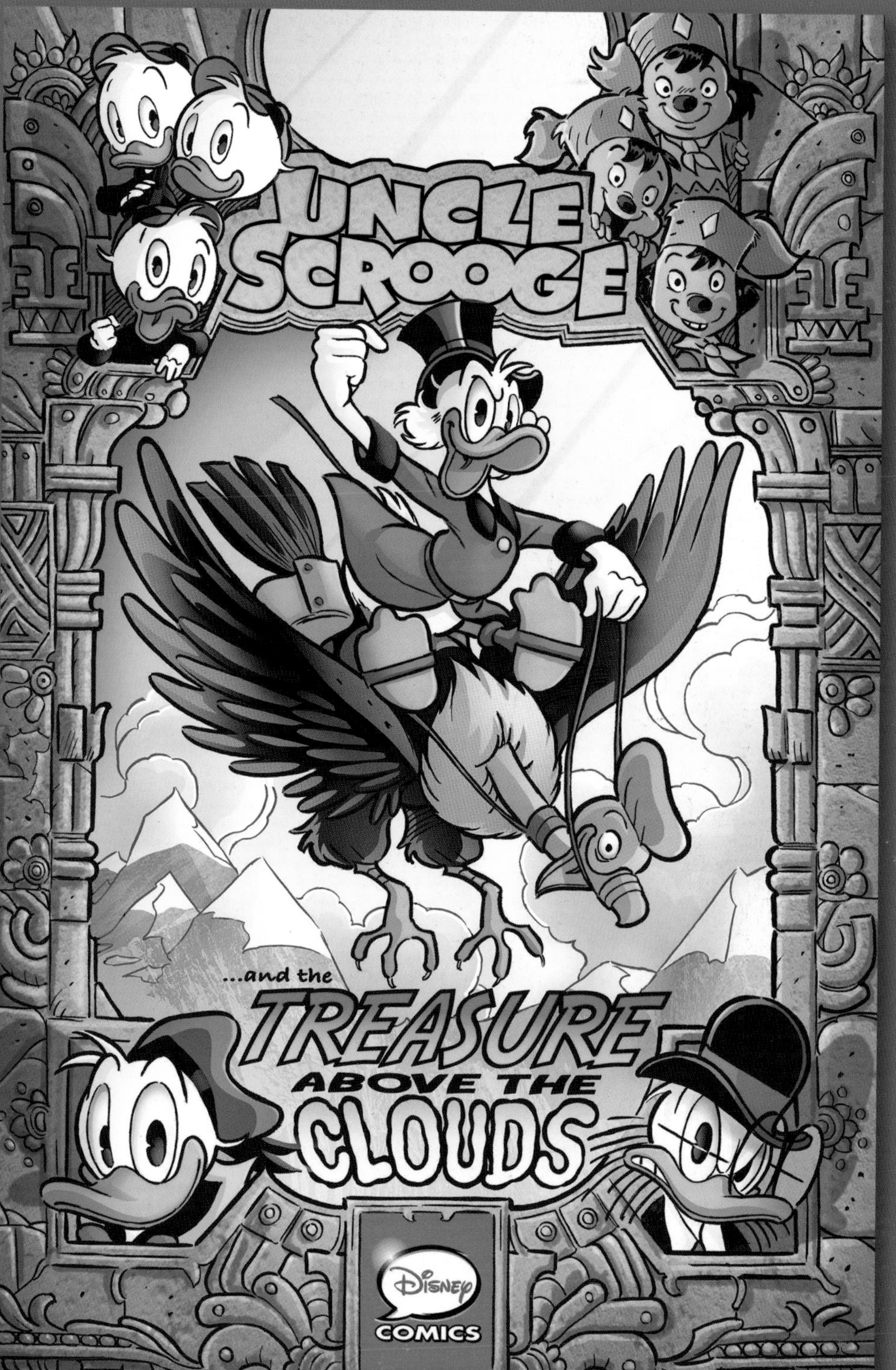
UNCLE SCROOGE
...and the
TREASURE
ABOVE THE
CLOUDS
DISNEY
COMICS

PENCILS BY JONATHAN GRAY AND ANDREA FRECCERO, INKS BY ANDREA FRECCERO
COLORS BY FABIO LO MONACO FOR FELM ART STUDIO

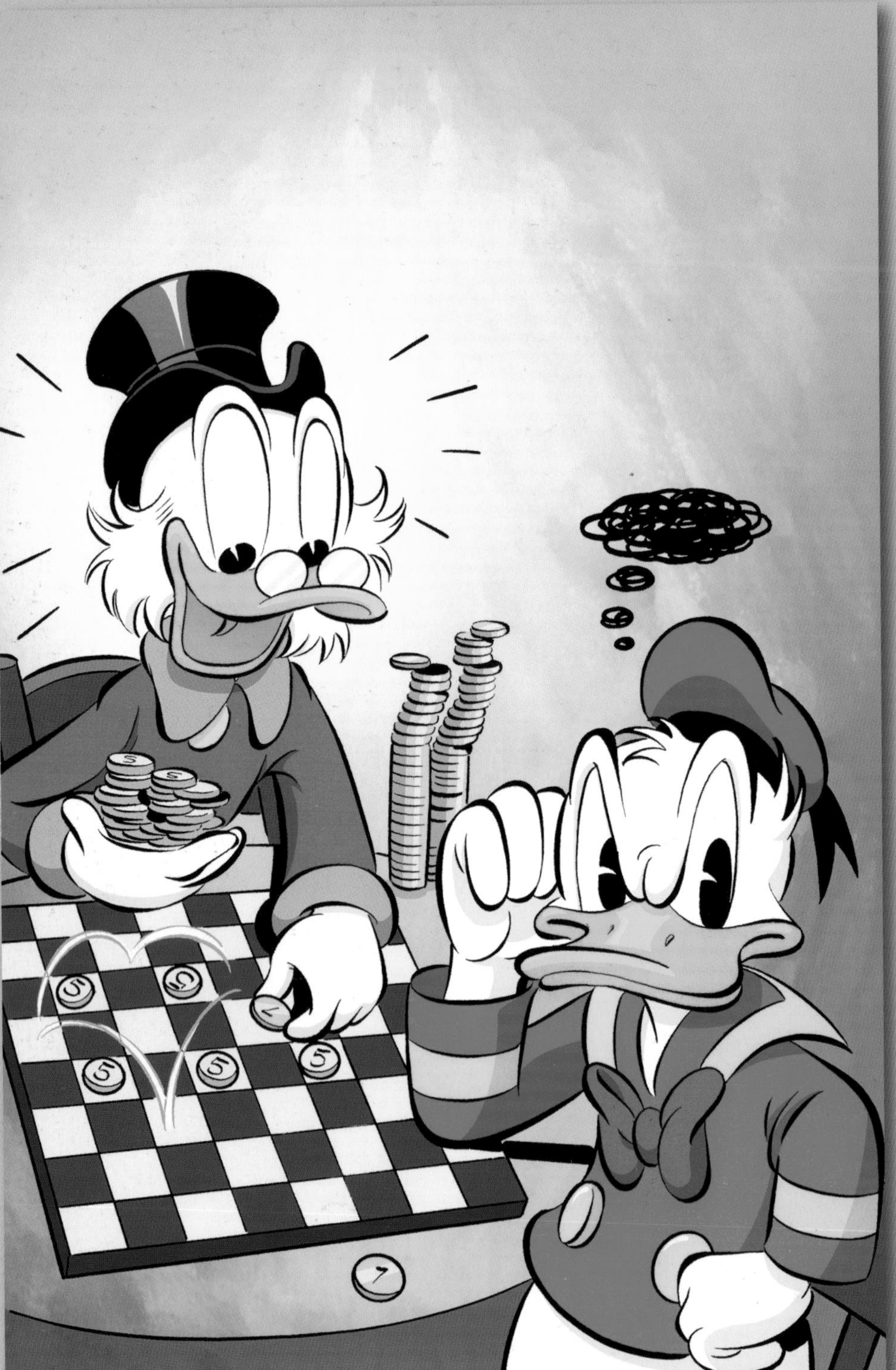

ART BY MICHAEL NADORP, COLORS BY FABIO LO MONACO FOR FELM ART STUDIO

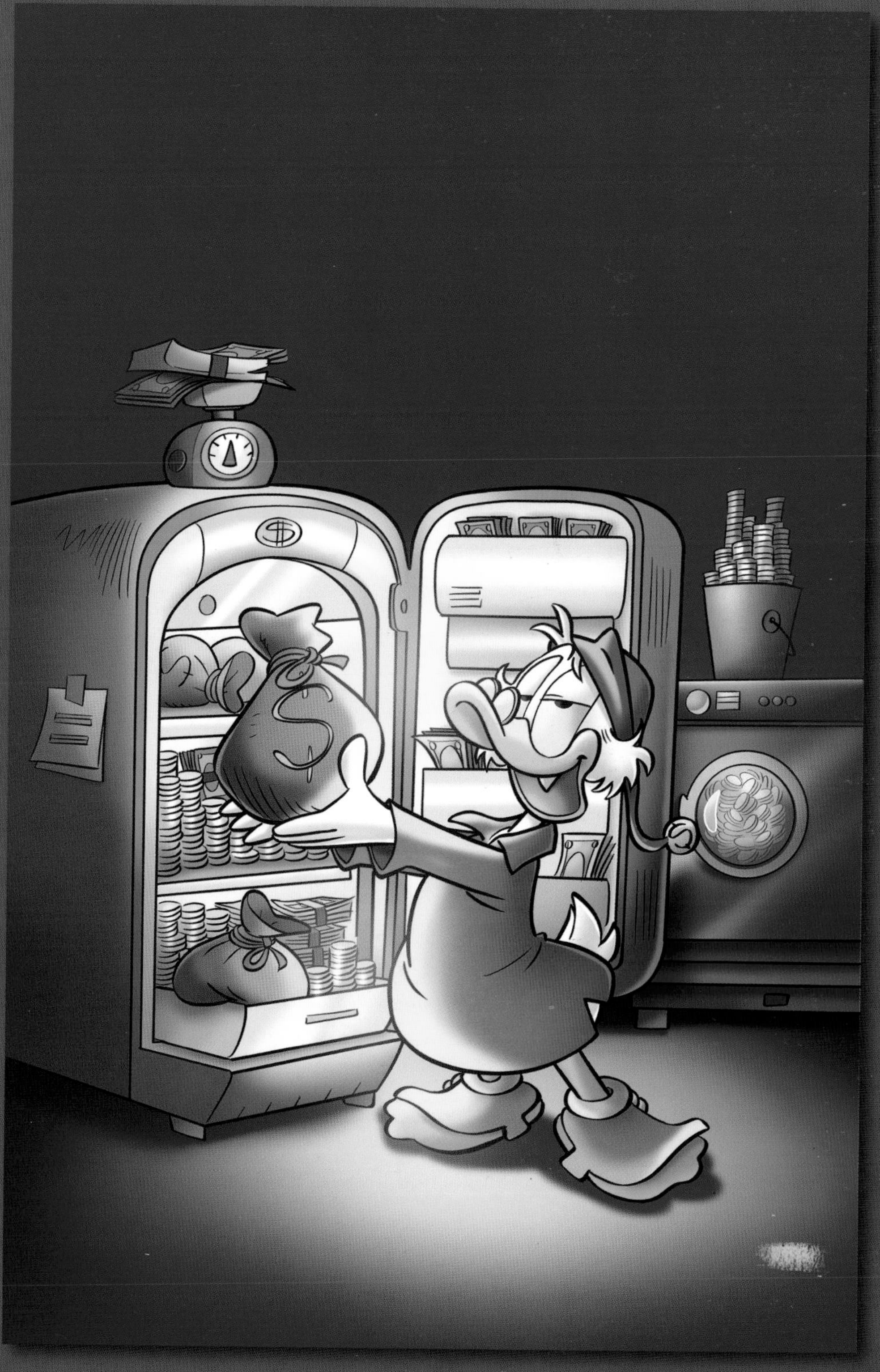

ART BY MARCO GERVASIO, COLORS BY MARCO COLLETTI

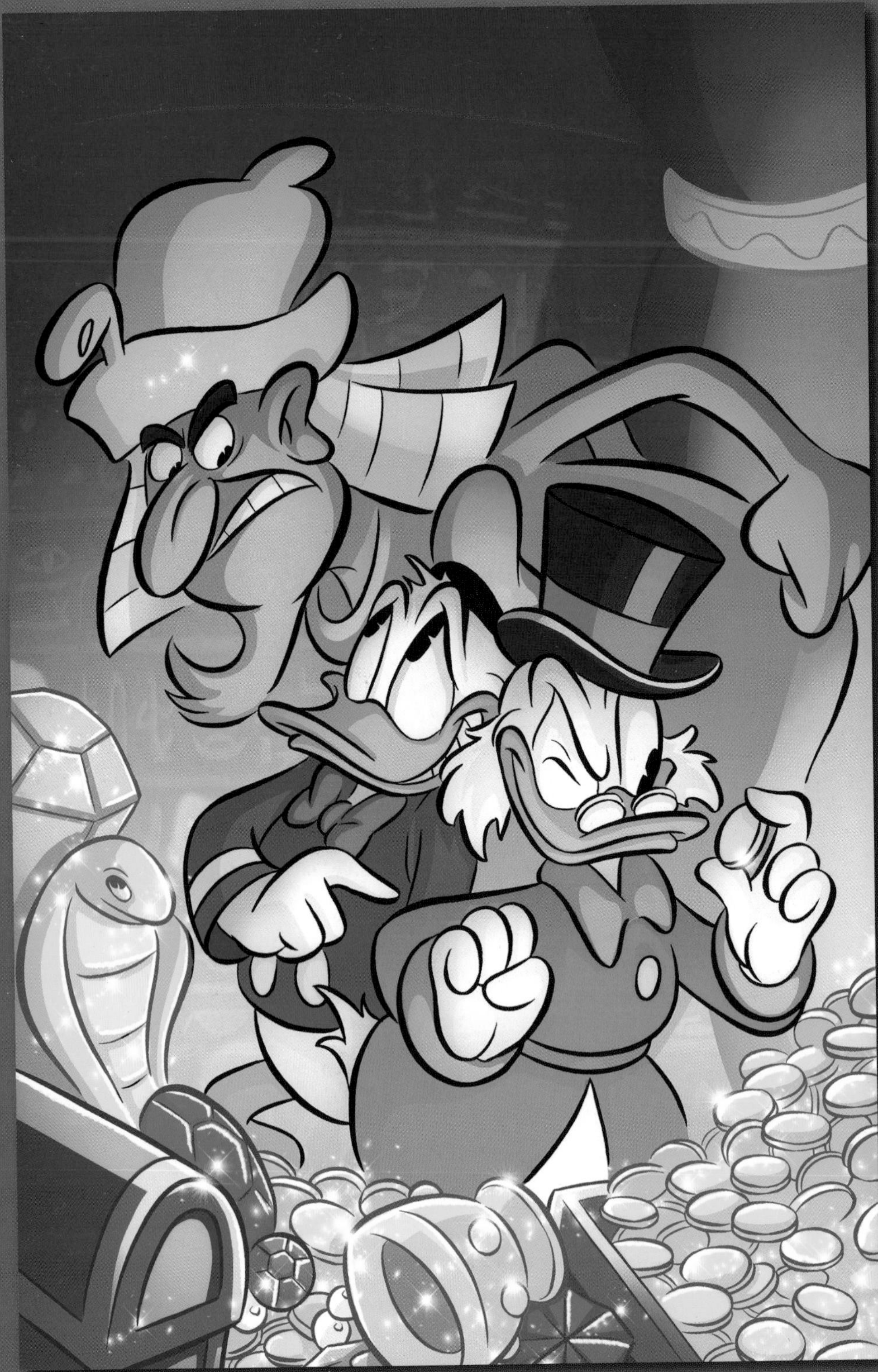

PENCILS BY DAVE ALVAREZ AND JOHN LOTER, INKS BY ULRICH SCHROEDER
COLORS BY FABIO LO MONACO FOR FELM ART STUDIO

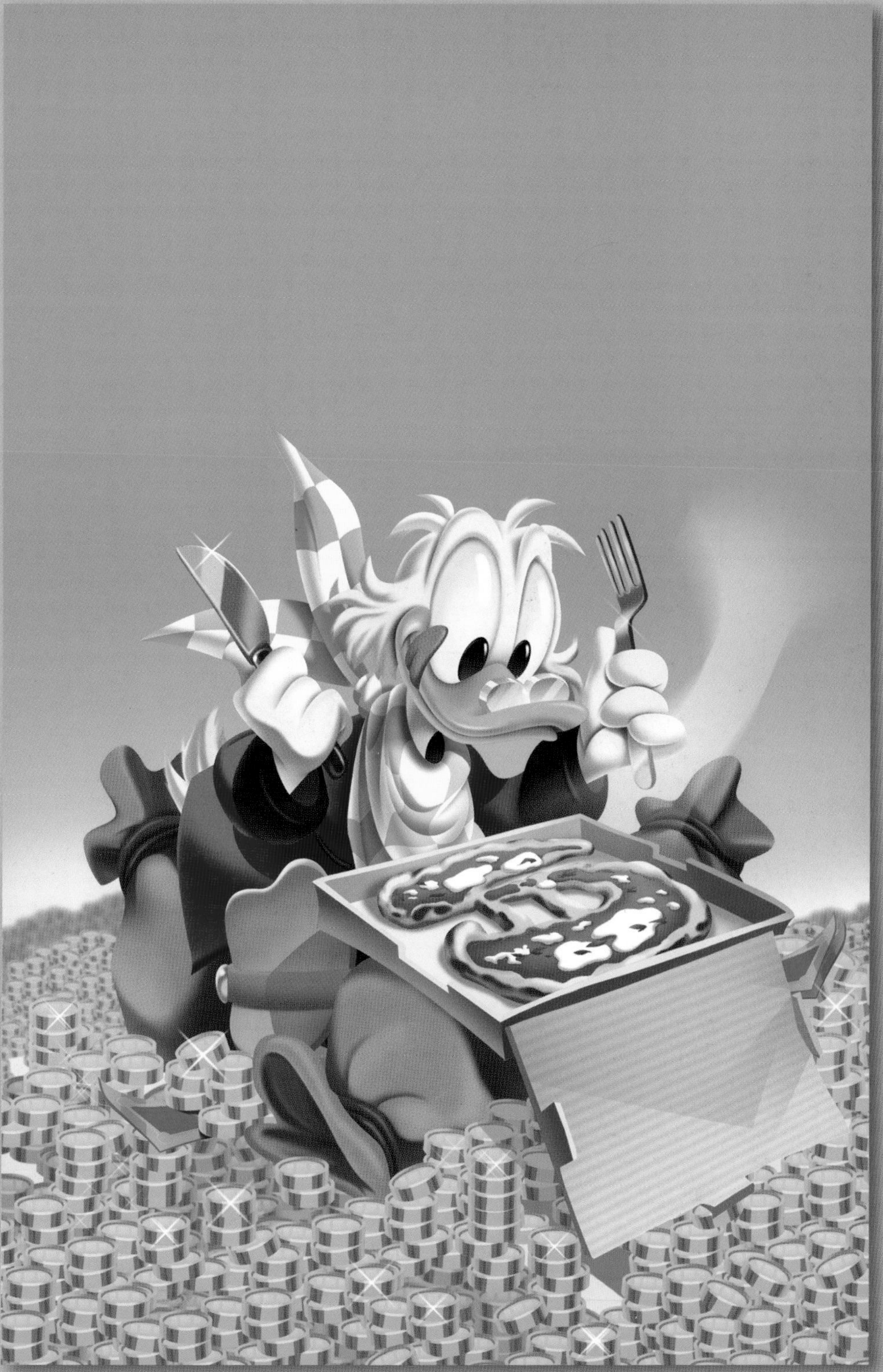

ART BY ROBERTA MIGHELI, COLORS BY GIUSEPPE FONTANA

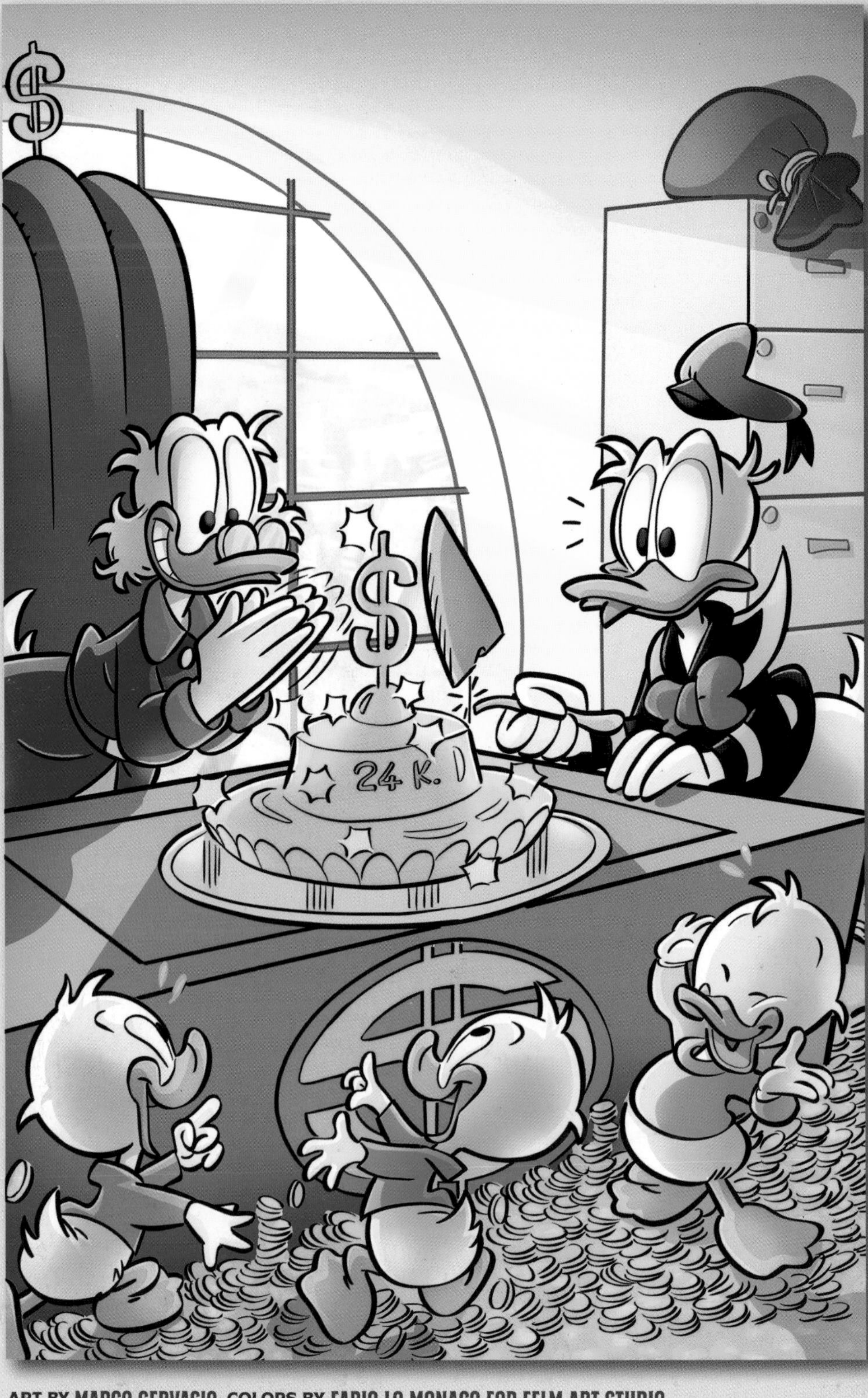
24 K.

ART BY MARCO GERVASIO, COLORS BY FABIO LO MONACO FOR FELM ART STUDIO

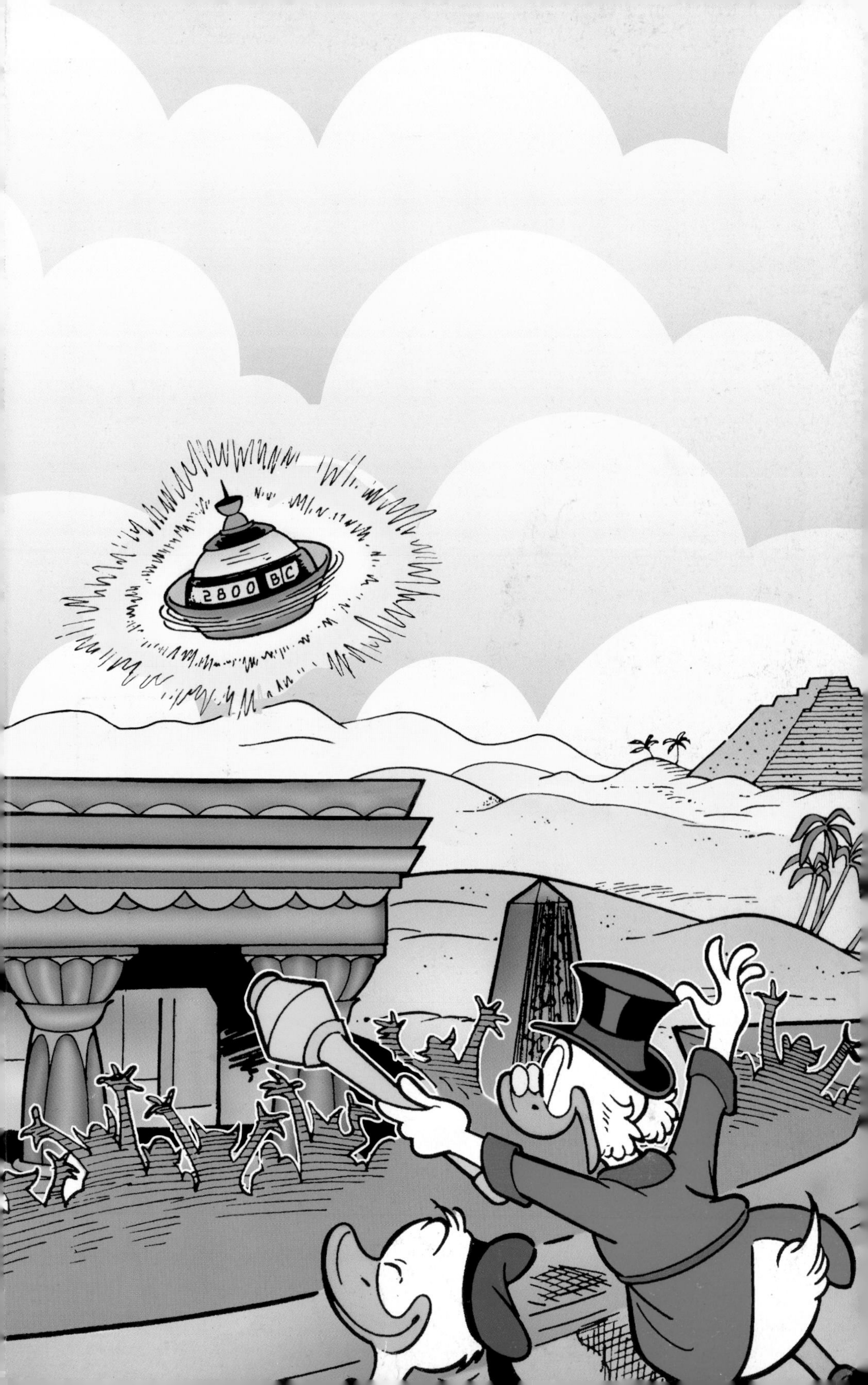
2800 BC

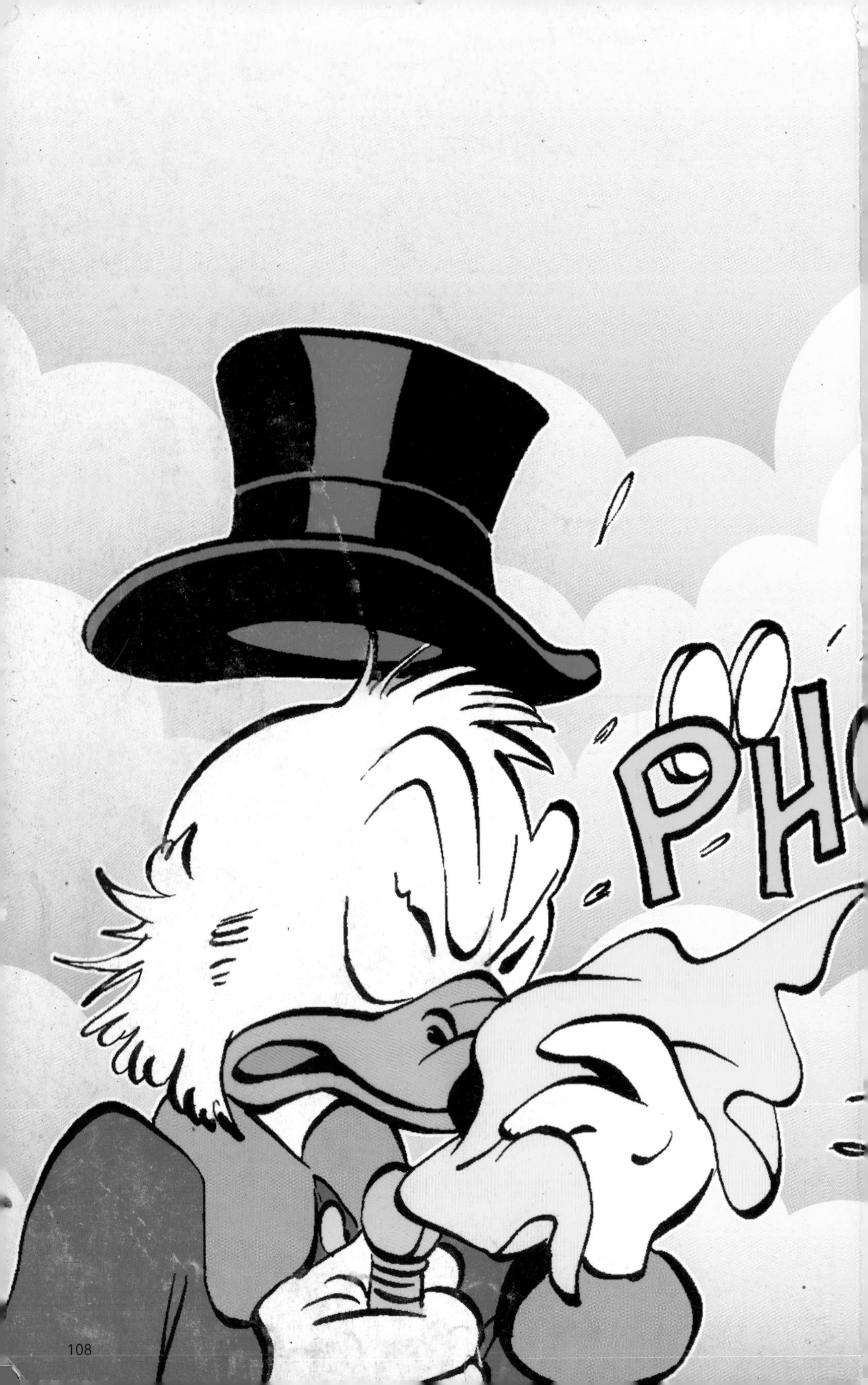
PH